THE SPIES OF WARSAW

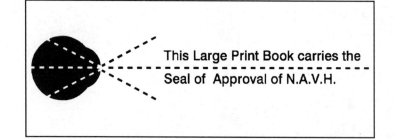

This Large Print Book carries the Seal of Approval of N.A.V.H.

THE SPIES OF WARSAW

A NOVEL

ALAN FURST

THORNDIKE PRESS
A part of Gale, Cengage Learning

Detroit • New York • San Francisco • New Haven, Conn • Waterville, Maine • London

GALE
CENGAGE Learning™

LIBRARY OF CONGRESS CATALOGING-IN-PUBLICATION DATA

Furst, Alan.
   The spies of Warsaw / by Alan Furst.
      p. cm.
   ISBN-13: 978-1-4104-0803-7 (hardcover : alk. paper)
   ISBN-10: 1-4104-0803-5 (hardcover : alk. paper)
   1. Military attach's — Fiction. 2. French — Poland — Warsaw
— Fiction. 3. Warsaw (Poland) — Fiction. 4. Poland — History —
1918–1945 — Fiction. 5. Large type books. I. Title.
PS3556.U76S75 2008
813'.54—dc22
                                                            2008016685

Published in 2008 in arrangement with Random House, Inc.

Printed in the United States of America
1 2 3 4 5 6 7 12 11 10 09 08

As looking at a portrait suggests the impression of the subject's destiny to the observer, so the map of France tells our own fortune. The body of the country has in its centre a citadel, a forbidding mass of age-old mountains, flanked by the tablelands of Provence, Limousin, and Burgundy; and, all around, vast slopes, for the most part difficult of access to anyone attacking them from the outside and split by the gorges of the Saône, the Rhône, and the Garonne, barred by the walls of the Jura Alps and the Pyrenees or else plunging in the distance into the English Channel, the Atlantic, or the Mediterranean; but in the Northeast, there is a terrible breach between the essential basins of the Seine and the Loire and German territory. The Rhine, which nature meant for the Gauls to have as their boundary and their protection, has hardly touched France before it leaves her and lays her open to attack.

— CAPTAIN CHARLES DE GAULLE
The Army of the Future, 1934

■ ■ ■ ■

Hotel Europejski

■ ■ ■ ■

In the dying light of an autumn day in 1937, a certain Herr Edvard Uhl, a secret agent, descended from a first-class railway carriage in the city of Warsaw. Above the city, the sky was at war; the last of the sun struck blood-red embers off massed black cloud, while the clear horizon to the west was the color of blue ice. Herr Uhl suppressed a shiver; *the sharp air of the evening,* he told himself. But this was Poland, the border of the Russian steppe, and what had reached him was well beyond the chill of an October twilight.

A taxi waited on Jerozolimskie street, in front of the station. The driver, an old man with a seamed face, sat patiently, knotted hands at rest on the steering wheel. "Hotel Europejski," Uhl told the driver. He wanted to add, *and be quick about it,* but the words would have been in German, and it was not so good to speak German in this city. Germany had absorbed the western part of

Poland in 1795 — Russia ruled the east, Austria-Hungary the southwest corner — for a hundred and twenty-three years, a period the Poles called "the Partition," a time of national conspiracy and defeated insurrection, leaving ample bad blood on all sides. With the rebirth of Poland in 1918, the new borders left a million Germans in Poland and two million Poles in Germany, which guaranteed that the bad blood would stay bad. So, for a German visiting Warsaw, a current of silent hostility, closed faces, small slights: *we don't want you here.*

Nonetheless, Edvard Uhl had looked forward to this trip for weeks. In his late forties, he combed what remained of his hair in strands across his scalp and cultivated a heavy dark mustache, meant to deflect attention from a prominent bulbous nose, the bulb divided at the tip. A feature one saw in Poland, often enough. So, an ordinary-looking man, who led a rather ordinary life, a more-than-decent life, in the small city of Breslau: a wife and three children, a good job — as a senior engineer at an ironworks and foundry, a subcontractor to the giant Rheinmetall firm in Düsseldorf — a few friends, memberships in a church and a singing society. Oh, maybe the political situation — that wretched Hitler and his wretched Nazis strutting about — could have been better, but one abided, lived quietly, kept one's opinions to oneself; it wasn't so difficult. And the paycheck came every week. What more could a man want?

Instinctively, his hand made sure of the leather satchel on the seat by his side. A tiny stab of regret touched his heart. *Foolish, Edvard, truly it is.* For the satchel, a gift from his first contact at the French embassy in Warsaw, had a false bottom, beneath which lay a sheaf of engineering diagrams. Well, he thought, one did what one had to do, so life went. No, one did what one had to do in order to do what one *wanted* to do — so life *really* went. He wasn't supposed to be in Warsaw; he was supposed, by his family and his employer, to be in Gleiwitz — just on the German side of the frontier dividing German Lower Silesia from Polish Upper Silesia — where his firm employed a large metal shop for the work that exceeded their capacity in Breslau. With the Reich rearming, they could not keep up with the orders that flowed from the *Wehrmacht*. The Gleiwitz works functioned well enough, but that wasn't what Uhl told his bosses. "A bunch of lazy idiots down there," he said, with a grim shake of the head, and found it necessary to take the train down to Gleiwitz once a month to straighten things out.

And he did go to Gleiwitz — that pest from Breslau, back again! — but he didn't stay there. When he was done bothering the local management he took the train up to Warsaw where, in a manner of speaking, one very particular thing got straightened out. For Uhl, a blissful night of lovemaking, followed by a brief meeting at dawn, a secret meeting, then back to Breslau, back to Frau Uhl and his more-than-decent life. Refreshed. Reborn. Too much, that word? No. Just right.

Uhl glanced at his watch. *Drive faster, you peasant! This is an automobile, not a plow.* The taxi crawled along Nowy Swiat, the grand avenue of Warsaw, deserted at this hour — the Poles went home for dinner at four. As the taxi passed a church, the driver slowed for a moment, then lifted his cap. It was not especially reverent, Uhl thought, simply something the man did every time he passed a church.

At last, the imposing Hotel Europejski, with its giant of a doorman in visored cap and uniform worthy of a Napoleonic marshal. Uhl handed the driver his fare — he kept a reserve of Polish zloty in his desk at the office — and added a small, proper gratuity, then said *"Dankeschön."* It didn't matter now, he was where he wanted to be. In the room, he hung up his suit, shirt, and tie, laid out fresh socks and underwear on the bed, and went into the bathroom to have a thorough wash. He had just enough time; the Countess Sczelenska would arrive in thirty minutes. Or, rather, that was the time set for the rendezvous; she would of course be late, would make him wait for her, let him think, let him anticipate, let him steam.

And was she a countess? A real Polish countess? Probably not, he thought. But so she called herself, and she was, to him, *like* a countess: imperious, haughty, and demanding. Oh how this provoked him, as the evening lengthened and they drank champagne, as her mood slid, subtly, from courteous disdain to sly submission, then on to breathless urgency. It was the same always, their private melodrama, with an ending that never changed. Uhl the stallion — despite the image in the mirrored armoire, a middle-aged gentleman with thin legs and potbelly and pale chest home to a few wisps of hair — demonstrably excited as he knelt on the hotel carpet, while the countess, looking down at him over her shoulder, eyebrows raised in mock surprise, deigned to let him roll her silk underpants down her great, saucy, fat bottom. *Noblesse oblige.* You may have your little pleasure, she seemed to say, if you are so inspired by what the noble Sczelenska bloodline has wrought. Uhl would embrace her middle and honor the noble heritage with tender kisses. In time very effective, such honor, and she would raise him up, eager for what came next.

He'd met her a year and a half earlier, in Breslau, at a *Weinstube* where the office employees of the foundry would stop for a little something after work. The *Weinstube* had a small terrace in back, three tables and a vine, and there she sat, alone at one of the tables on the deserted terrace: morose and preoccupied. He'd sat at the next table, found her attractive — not young, not old, on the buxom side, with brassy hair pinned up high and an appealing face — and said good evening. And why so glum, on such a pleasant night?

She'd come down from Warsaw, she explained, to see her sister, a family crisis, a catastrophe. The family had owned, for several generations, a small but profitable lumber mill in the forest along the eastern border. But they had suffered financial reverses, and then the storage sheds had been burned down by a Ukrainian nationalist gang, and they'd had to borrow money from a Jewish speculator. But the problems wouldn't stop, they could not repay the loans, and now that dreadful man had gone to court and taken the mill. Just like them, wasn't it.

After a few minutes, Uhl moved to her table. Well, that was life for you, he'd said. Fate turned evil, often for those who least deserved it. But, don't feel so bad, luck had gone wrong, but it could go right, it always did, given time. Ah but he was *sympathique,* she'd said, an aristocratic reflex to use the French word in the midst of her fluent German. They went on for a while, back and forth. Perhaps some day, she'd said, if he should find himself in Warsaw, he might telephone; there was the loveliest café near her apartment. Perhaps he would, yes, business took him to Warsaw now and again; he guessed he might be there soon. Now, would she permit him to order another glass of wine? Later, she took his hand beneath the table and he was, by the time they parted, on fire.

Ten days later, from a public telephone at the Breslau railway station, he'd called her. He planned to be in Warsaw next week, at the Europejski, would she care to join him for dinner? Why yes, yes she would. Her tone of voice, on the other end of the line, told him all he needed to know, and by the following Wednesday — those idiots in Gleiwitz had done it again! — he was on his way to Warsaw. At dinner, champagne and langoustines, he suggested that they go on to a nightclub after dessert, but first he wanted to visit the room, to change his tie.

And so, after the cream cake, up they went.

For two subsequent, monthly, visits, all was paradise, but, it turned out, she was the unluckiest of countesses. In his room at the hotel, brassy hair tumbled on the pillow, she told him of her latest misfortune. Now it was her landlord, a hulking beast who leered at her, made *chk-chk* noises with his mouth when she climbed the stairs, who'd told her that she had to leave, his latest girlfriend to be installed in her place. Unless . . . Her misty eyes told him the rest.

Never! Where Uhl had just been, this swine would not go! He stroked her shoulder, damp from recent exertions, and said, "Now, now, my dearest, calm yourself." She would just have to find another apartment. Well, in fact she'd already done that, found one even nicer than the one she had now, and very private, owned by a man in Cracow, so nobody would be watching her if, for example, her sweet Edvard wanted to come for a visit. But the rent was two hundred zloty more than she paid now. And she didn't have it.

A hundred reichsmark, he thought. "Perhaps I can help," he said. And he could, but not for long. Two months, maybe three — beyond that, there really weren't any corners he could cut. He tried to save a little, but almost all of his salary went to support his family. Still, he couldn't get the "hulking beast" out of his mind. *Chk-chk.*

The blow fell a month later, the man in Cracow had to raise the rent. What would she do? What was she to do? She would have to stay with relatives or be out in the street. Now Uhl had no answers. But the countess did. She had a cousin who was seeing a Frenchman, an army officer who worked at the French embassy, a cheerful, generous fellow who, she said, sometimes hired "industrial experts." Was her sweet Edvard not an engineer? Perhaps he ought to meet this man and see what he had to offer. Otherwise, the only hope for the poor countess was to go and stay with her aunt.

And where was the aunt?

Chicago.

Now Uhl wasn't stupid. Or, as he put it to himself, not *that* stupid. He had a strong suspicion about what was going on. But — and here he surprised himself — he didn't care.

17

The fish saw the worm and wondered if maybe there might just be a hook in there, but, what a delicious worm! Look at it, the most succulent and tasty worm he'd ever seen; never would there be such a worm again, not in this ocean. So . . .

He first telephoned — to, apparently, a private apartment, because a maid answered in Polish, then switched to German. And, twenty minutes later, Uhl called again and a meeting was arranged. In an hour. At a bar in the Praga district, the workers' quarter across the Vistula from the elegant part of Warsaw. And the Frenchman was, as promised, as cheerful as could be. Likely Alsatian, from the way he spoke German, he was short and tubby, with a soft face that glowed with self-esteem and a certain tilt to the chin and tension in the upper lip that suggested an imminent sneer, while a dapper little mustache did nothing to soften the effect. He was, of course, not in uniform, but wore an expensive sweater and a blue blazer with brass buttons down the front.

"Henri," he called himself and, yes, he did sometimes employ "industrial experts." His job called for him to stay abreast of developments in particular areas of German industry, and he would pay well for drawings or schematics, any specifications relating to,

18

say, armament or armour. How well? Oh, perhaps five hundred reichsmark a month, for the right papers. Or, if Uhl preferred, a thousand zloty, or two hundred American dollars — some of his experts liked having dollars. The money to be paid in cash or deposited in any bank account, in any name, that Uhl might suggest.

The word *spy* was never used, and Henri was very casual about the whole business. Very common, such transactions, his German counterparts did the same thing; everybody wanted to know what was what, on the other side of the border. And, he should add, nobody got caught, as long as they were discreet. What was done privately stayed private. These days, he said, in such chaotic times, smart people understood that their first loyalty was to themselves and their families. The world of governments and shifty diplomats could go to hell, if it wished, but Uhl was obviously a man who was shrewd enough to take care of his own future. And, if he ever found the arrangement uncomfortable, well, that was that. So, think it over, there's no hurry, get back in touch, or just forget you ever met me.

And the countess? Was she, perhaps, also an, umm, "expert"?

From Henri, a sophisticated laugh. "My

dear fellow! Please! That sort of thing, well, maybe in the movies."

So, at least the worm wasn't in on it.

Back at the Europejski — a visit to the new apartment lay still in the future — the countess exceeded herself. Led him to a delight or two that Uhl knew about but had never experienced; her turn to kneel on the carpet. Rapture. Another glass of champagne and further novelty. In time he fell back on the pillow and gazed up at the ceiling, elated and sore. And brave as a lion. He *was* a shrewd fellow — a single exchange with Henri, and that thousand zloty would see the countess through her difficulties for the next few months. But life never went quite as planned, did it, because Henri, not nearly so cheerful as the first time they'd met, insisted, really did insist, that the arrangement continue.

And then, in August, instead of Henri, a tall Frenchman called André, quiet and reserved, and much less pleased with himself, and the work he did, than Henri. Wounded, Uhl guessed, in the Great War, he leaned on a fine ebony stick, with a silver wolf's head for a grip.

At the Hotel Europejski, in the early evening of an autumn day, Herr Edvard Uhl finished

with his bath and dressed, in order to un-
dress, in what he hoped would be a little
while. The room-service waiter had delivered
a bottle of champagne in a silver bucket, one
small lamp was lit, the drapes were drawn.
Uhl moved one of them aside, enough to see
out the window, down to the entry of the
hotel, where taxis pulled up to the curb and
the giant doorman swept the doors open
with a genteel bow as the passengers
emerged. Fine folks indeed, an army officer
and his lavish girlfriend, a gentleman in top
hat and tails, a merry fellow with a beard and
a monocle. Uhl liked this life very well, this
Warsaw life, his dream world away from the
brown soot and lumpy potatoes of Breslau.
He would pay for that with a meeting in the
morning; then, home again.

Ah, here she was.

The Milanowek Tennis Club had been
founded late one June night in 1937. Something of a lark, at that moment. "Let's have a
tennis club! Why not? The *Milanowek* Tennis
Club — isn't it fabulous?" The village of Milanowek was a garden in a pine forest, twenty
miles from Warsaw, famous for its resin-
scented air — "mahogany air," the joke
went, because it was expensive to live there
and breathe it — famous for its glorious

manor houses surrounded by English lawns, Greek statues, pools, and tennis courts. Famous as well for its residents, the so-called "heart of the Polish nation," every sort of nobility in the *Alamanach de Gotha,* every sort of wealthy Jewish merchant. If one's driver happened to be unavailable, a narrow-gauge railway ran out from the city, stopping first at the village of Podkowa. Podkowa was the Polish word for horseshoe, which led the unknowing to visions of a tiny ancient village, where a peasant blacksmith labored at his forge, but they would soon enough learn that Podkowa had been designed, at the turn of the century, by the English architect Arthur Howard, with houses situated in the pattern of a horseshoe and a common garden at the center.

The manor house — owned by Prince Kaz, formally Kazimierz, and Princess Toni, Antowina — had three tennis courts, for the noble Brosowicz couple, with family connections to various branches of the Radziwills and Poniatowskis, didn't have *one* of anything. This taste for variety, long a tradition on both sides of the family, included manor houses — their other country estate had six miles of property but lay far from Warsaw — as well as apartments in Paris and London and vacation homes — the chalet in Saint

Moritz, the palazzo in Venice — and extended to servants, secretaries, horses, dogs, and lovers. But for Prince Kaz and Princess Toni, the best thing in the world was to have, wherever they happened to be at the moment, lots of friends. The annual production of Christmas cards went on for days.

At the Milanowek house, their friends came to play tennis. The entire nation was passionate for the game; in Poland, only a single golf course was to be found but, following the re-emergence of the country, there were tennis courts everywhere. And so they decided, late that June night, to make it official. "It's the Milanowek Tennis Club now," they would tell their friends, who were honored to be included. "Come and play whenever you like; if we're not here, Janusz will let you in." *What a good idea,* the friends thought. They scheduled their matches by telephone and stopped by at all hours of the day and early evening: the baron of this and the marchioness of that, the nice Jewish dentist and his clever wife, a general of the army and a captain of industry, a socialist member of the Sejm, the Polish parliament, the royalist Minister of Posts and Telegraph, various elegant young people who didn't do much of anything, and the newly arrived French military attaché, the dashing Colonel Mercier.

In fact a lieutenant colonel, and wounded in two wars, he didn't dash very well. He did the best he could, usually playing doubles, but still, a passing shot down the line would often elude him — if it didn't go out, the tennis gods punishing his opponent for taking advantage of the colonel's limping stride.

That Thursday afternoon in October, the vast sky above the steppe dark and threatening, Colonel Mercier was partnered by Princess Toni herself, in her late thirties as perfect and pretty as a doll, an effect heightened by rouged cheeks and the same straw-colored hair as Prince Kaz. They did look, people said, like brother and sister. And, you know, sometimes in these noble families . . . No, it wasn't true, but the similarity was striking.

"Good try, Jean-François," she called out, as the ball bounced away, brushing her hair off her forehead and turning her racquet over a few times as she awaited service.

Across the net, a woman called Claudine, the wife of a Belgian diplomat, prepared to serve. Here one could see that the doubles teams were fairly constituted, for Claudine had only her right arm; the other — her tennis shirt sleeve pinned up below her shoulder — had been lost to a German shell in the Great War, when she'd served as a nurse.

Standing at the back line, she held ball and racquet in one hand, tossed the ball up, re-gripped her racquet, and managed a fairly brisk serve. Princess Toni returned cross-court, with perfect form but low velocity, and Dr. Goldszteyn, the Jewish dentist, sent it back toward the colonel, just close enough — he never, when they played together, hit balls that Mercier couldn't reach. Mercier drove a low shot to center court; Claudine returned backhand, a high lob. "Oh damn," Princess Toni said through clenched teeth, running backward. Her sweeping forehand sent the ball sailing over the fence on the far side of the court. "Sorry," she said to Mercier.

"We'll get it back," Mercier said. He spoke French, the language of the Polish aristocracy, and thus the Milanowek Tennis Club.

"Forty–fifteen," Claudine called out, as a passing servant tossed the ball back over the fence. Serving to Mercier, her first try ticked the net, the second was in. Mercier hit a sharp forehand, Dr. Goldszteyn swept it back, Princess Toni retrieved, Claudine ran to the net and tried a soft lob. Too high, and Mercier reached up and hit an overhand winner — that went into the net. "Game to us," Claudine called out.

"My service," Princess Toni answered, a

challenge in her voice: *we'll see who takes this set.* They almost did, winning the next game, but eventually going down six–four. Walking off the court, Princess Toni rested a hand on Mercier's forearm; he could smell perfume mixed with sweat. "No matter," she said. "You're a good partner for me, Jean-François."

What? No, she meant tennis. Didn't she? At forty-six, Mercier had been a widower for three years, and was considered more than eligible by the smart set in the city. But, he thought, not the princess. "We'll play again soon," he said, the response courteous and properly amicable.

He managed almost always to hit the right note with these people because he was, technically, one of them — Jean-François Mercier de Boutillon, though the nobiliary particule *de* had been dropped by his democratically inclined grandfather, and the name of his ancestral demesne had disappeared along with it, except on official papers. But participation in the rites and rituals of this world was not at all something he cared about — membership in the tennis club, and other social activities, were requirements of his profession; otherwise he wouldn't have bothered. A military attaché was supposed to hear things and know things, so he made it his business to be around people who occasionally said things worth knowing. *Not very often,* he thought. *But in truth* — he had to admit — *often enough.*

In the house, he paused to pick up his white canvas bag, then headed down the hallway. The old boards creaked with every step, the scent of beeswax polish perfumed the air — nothing in the world smelled quite like a perfectly cleaned house. Past the drawing room, the billiard room, a small study lined with books, was one of the downstairs bathrooms made available to the tennis club members. *How they live.* On a travertine shelf by the sink, fresh lilies in a Japanese vase, fragrant soap in a gold-laced dish. A grid of heated copper towel bars held thick Turkish towels, the color of fresh cream, while the shower curtain was decorated with a surrealist half-head and squiggles — where on God's green earth did they find such a thing?

He peeled off his tennis outfit, then opened the bag, took out a blue shirt, flannel trousers, and fresh linen, made a neat pile on a small antique table, stowed his tennis clothes in the bag, worked the *chevalière,* the gold signet ring of the nobility, off his ring finger and set it atop his clothes, and stepped into the shower.

Ahhh.

An oversized showerhead poured forth a broad, powerful spray of hot water. Where he lived — the longtime French military attaché apartment in Warsaw — there was only a bathtub and a diabolical gas water heater, which provided a tepid bath at best and might someday finish the job that his German and Russian enemies had failed to complete. What medal did they have for that? he wondered. The *Croix de Bain,* awarded posthumously.

Very quietly, so that someone passing by in the hall would not hear him, he began to sing.

Turning slowly in the shower, Mercier was tall — a little over six feet, with just the faintest suggestion of a slouch, an apology for height — and lean; well muscled in the legs and shoulders and well scarred all over. On the outside of his right knee, a patch of red, welted skin — some shrapnel still in there, they told him — and sometimes, on damp, cold days, he walked with a stick. On the left side of his chest, a three-inch white furrow; on the back of his left calf, a burn scar; running along the inside of his right wrist, a poorly sutured tear made by barbed wire; and, on his back, just below his left shoulder blade, the puckered wound of a sniper's bullet. From the last, he should not have recovered, but he had, which left him better off than most of the class of 1912 at the Saint-Cyr military academy, who rested beneath white crosses in the fields of northeast France.

Well, he was done with war. He doubted he could face that again, he'd simply seen too much of it. With some effort, he forced his mind away from such thoughts, which, he believed, visited him more often than he should allow, and this sort of determination was easily read in his face. Not unhandsome, he had heavy, dark hair parted on the left, which lay too thick, too high, across the right side of his head. He had fair skin, pale, and refined features, all of which made him seem younger than he was, though these proportions, classic in the French aristocrat, were somehow contradicted by very deep, very thoughtful, gray-green eyes. Nonetheless, he was what he was, with the relaxed confidence of the breed and, when he smiled, a touch of the insouciant view of the world common to the southern half of France.

They'd been there a long, long time, the Mercier de Boutillons, in a lost corner of the Drôme, just above Provence, with the title of *chevalier* — knight — originally bestowed in the twelfth century, which had given them the village of Boutillon and its surrounding countryside, and the right to die in France's wars. Which they had done, again and again, as far back as the Knight Templars of Jerusalem — Mercier was also a thirty-sixth-generation Knight of Malta and Rhodes — and as recently as the 1914 war, which had claimed his brother, at the Marne, and an uncle, wounded, and drowned in a shellhole, at the second battle of Verdun.

In a muted baritone, Mercier sang an old French ballad, which had haunted him for years. A dumb thing, but it had a catchy melody, sad and sweet. Poor *petite* Jeanette, how she adored her departed lover, how she remembered him, *"encore et encore."* Jeanette may have remembered, Mercier didn't, so he sang the chorus and hummed the rest, turning slowly in the streaming water.

When he heard the bathroom door open, and close, he stopped. Through the heavy cotton of the shower curtain he could see a silhouette, which divested itself of shirt and shorts. Then, slowly, drew the curtain aside, its rings scraping along the metal bar. Standing there, in a cloud of steam, a lavender-colored cake of soap in one hand, was the Princess Antowina Brosowicz.

Without clothes, she seemed small but, again like a doll, perfectly proportioned. With an impish smile, she reached a hand toward him and, using her fingernail, drew a line down the wet hair plastered to his chest. "That's nice," she said. "I can draw a picture on you." Then, after a moment, "Are you going to invite me in, Jean-François?"

"Of course." His laugh was not quite a nervous laugh, but close. "You surprised me."

She entered the shower, closed the curtain, stepped toward him so that the tips of her breasts just barely touched his chest, stood on her toes, and kissed him lightly on the lips. "I meant to," she said. Then she handed him the lavender soap. *Only a princess,* he thought, *would join a man in the shower but disdain the use of the guest soap.*

She turned once around beneath the spray, raised her face to the water, and finger-combed her hair back. Then she leaned on the tile wall with both hands and said, "Would you be kind enough to wash my back?"

"With pleasure," he said.

"What was that you were singing?"

"An old French song. It stays with me, I don't know why."

31

"Oh, reasons," she said, who knew why anything happened.

"Do you sing in the shower?"

She turned her head so that he could see that she was smiling. "Perhaps in a little while, I will."

The skin of her back was still lightly tanned from the summer sun, then, below the curved line of her bathing suit, very white. He worked up a creamy lather, put the soap in a dish on the wall, and slid his hands up and down, sideways, round and round.

"Mmm," she said. Then, "Don't neglect my front, dear."

He re-soaped his hands and reached around her. As the water drummed down on them, the white part of her, warm and slippery, gradually turned a rosy pink. And, in time, she did sing, or something like it, and, even though they were there for quite some time, the hot water never ran out.

17 October, 5:15 A.M. Crossing the Vistula in a crowded trolley car, Mercier leaned on a steel pole at the rear. He wore a battered hat, the front of the brim low on his forehead, and a grimy overcoat, purchased from a used-clothing pushcart in the poor Jewish district. He carried a cheap briefcase be-

neath his arm and looked, he thought, like some lost soul sentenced to live in a Russian novel. The workers packed inside the trolley, facing a long day in the Praga factories, were grim-faced and silent, staring out the windows at the gray dawn and the gray river below the railway bridge.

At the third stop in Praga, Mercier stepped down from the rear platform, just past the Wedel candy factory, the smell of burned sugar strong in the raw morning air. He walked the length of the factory, crossed to a street of brick tenements, then on to a row of workshops, machinery rattling and whining inside the clapboard sheds. At one of them, the high doors had been rolled apart, and he could see dark shapes shoveling coal into open furnaces, the fires flaring yellow and orange.

He turned down an alley to a nameless little bar, open at dawn, crowded with workers who needed a shot or two in order to get themselves into the factories. Here too it was silent. The men at the bar drank off their shots, left a few groszy by their empty glasses, and walked out. At a table on the opposite wall, Edvard Uhl, the engineer from Breslau, sat stolidly with a coffee and a Polish newspaper, folded on the table by his cup and saucer.

Mercier sat across from him and said good morning. He spoke German, badly and slowly, but he could manage. As the language of France's traditional enemy, German had been a compulsory course at Saint-Cyr.

Uhl looked up at him and nodded.

"All goes well with you," Mercier said. It wasn't precisely a question.

"Best I can expect." *Poor me.* He didn't much like the business they did together. He was, Mercier could see it in his face, reluctant, and frightened. Maybe life had gone better with Mercier's predecessor, "Henri," Emile Bruner, now a full colonel and Mercier's superior at the General Staff, but he doubted it. "Considering what I must do," Uhl added.

Mercier shrugged. What did he care? For him, best to be cold and formal at agent meetings — they had a commercial arrangement; friendship was not required. "What have you brought?"

"We're retooling for the *Ausf B*." He meant the B version of the *Panzerkampfwagen 1,* the *Wehrmacht*'s battle tank. "I have the first diagrams for the new turret."

"What's different?"

"It's a new design, from the Krupp works; the turret will now be made to rotate, three hundred and sixty degrees, a hand traverse operated by the gunner."

"And the armour?"

"The same. Thirteen millimeters on the sides, eight millimeters on the top of the turret, six millimeters on the top and bottom of the hull. But now the plates are to be face-hardened — that means carbon cementation, very expensive but the strength is greatly increased."

"From stopping rifle and machine-gun fire to stopping antitank weapons."

"So it would seem."

Mercier thought for a moment. The *Panzerkampfwagen 1A* had not done well in Spain, where it had been used by Franco's forces against the Soviet T-26. Armed only with a pair of 7.92-millimeter machine guns in the turret, it was effective against infantry but could not defeat an armoured enemy tank. Now, with the 1B, they were preparing for a different kind of combat. Finally he said, "All right, we'll have a look at it. And next time we'd like to see the face-hardening process you're using, the formula."

"Next time," Uhl said. "Well, I'm not sure I'll be able . . ."

Mercier cut him off. "Fifteen November. If there's an emergency, a real emergency, you have a telephone number."

"What would happen if I just couldn't be here?"

"We will reschedule." Mercier paused. "But it's not at all easy for us, if we have to do that."

"Yes, but there's always the possibility . . ."

"You will manage, Herr Uhl. We know you are resourceful, there are always problems in this sort of work; we expect you to deal with them."

Uhl started to speak, but Mercier raised his hand. Then he opened his briefcase and withdrew a folded Polish newspaper and a slip of paper, typewritten and then copied on a roneo duplicator: a receipt form, with date, amount, and Uhl's name typed on the appropriate lines, and a line for signature at the bottom. "Do you need a pen?" Mercier said.

Uhl reached into an inside pocket, withdrew a fountain pen, then signed his name at the bottom of the receipt. Mercier put the slip of paper in his briefcase and slid the newspaper toward Uhl. "A thousand zloty," he said. He peeled up a corner of Uhl's newspaper, revealing the edges of engineering diagrams.

Uhl took Mercier's folded newspaper, secured it tightly beneath his arm, then rose to leave.

"Fifteen November," Mercier said. "We'll

meet here, at the same time."

A very subdued Herr Uhl nodded in agreement, mumbled a goodby, and left the bar.

Mercier looked at his watch — the rules said he had to give Uhl a twenty-minute head start. A pair of workers, in gray oil-stained jackets and trousers, entered the bar and ordered vodka and beer. One of them glanced over at Mercier, then looked away. Which meant nothing, Mercier thought. Officer A met Agent B in a country foreign to both, neutral ground, it wasn't even against the law. So they'd told him, anyhow, when he'd taken the six-week course for new military attachés at the *Ecole Supérieure de Guerre,* part of the Invalides complex in Paris.

With a one-week section on the management of espionage — thus the folded newspapers. And the cold exterior. This was no pretense for Mercier; he didn't like Uhl, who betrayed his country for selfish reasons. In fact, he didn't like any of it. "Witness the ingenuity of Monsieur D," said the elfin captain from the *Deuxième Bureau* who taught the course. "During the war, with a complex set of figures to be conveyed to his case officer, Monsieur D shaved a patch of hair on his dog's back, wrote the numbers on the dog's skin in indelible pen, waited for the dog's coat to grow out, then easily crossed the frontier." Yes, very clever, like Messieurs A, B, and C. Mercier could only imagine himself shaving his Braques Ariégeoises, his beloved pointers, Achille and Céleste. He could imagine their eyes: *why are you doing this to me?*

Stay. Good boy, good girl. Remember the ingenious Monsieur D.

In Mercier's desk drawer, at his office on the second floor of the embassy, was a letter resigning his commission. Written at a bad moment, in the difficult early days of a new job, but not thrown away. He couldn't imagine actually sending it, but the three-year appointment felt like a lifetime, and he might be reappointed. Perhaps he would try, the next time he was at the General Staff headquarters in Paris, to request a transfer, to field command. His first request, using the prescribed channels, had been denied, but he would try again, he decided, this time in person. It might work, though, if it didn't, he couldn't ask again. That was the unofficial rule, set in stone: two attempts, no more.

Riding the trolley back to central Warsaw, he wondered where he'd gone wrong, why he'd been reassigned, six months earlier, from a staff position in the Army of the Levant, headquartered in Beirut, to the embassy in Warsaw. The reason, he suspected, had most of all to do with Bruner, who wanted to move up, wanted to be at the center of power in Paris. This he'd managed to do, but they had to replace him, and replace him with someone that the Polish General Staff would find an appealing substitute.

And for Mercier, it should have been a plum, a career victory. An appointment in Warsaw, to any French officer or diplomat, was considered an honor, for Poland and France had a special relationship, a long, steady history of political friendship. In the time of the French kings, the French and Polish royal families had intermarried, French had become, and remained, the polite language of the Polish aristocracy, and the Poles, especially Polish intellectuals, had been passionate for the ideals of the Enlightenment and the Revolution of 1789. Napoleon had supported the Polish quest to re-establish itself as a free nation, and French governments had, since the eighteenth century, welcomed Polish exiles and supported their struggle against partition.

Thus, in the summer of 1920, after fighting broke out in the Ukraine between Polish army units and Ukrainian partisan bands, and the Red Army had attacked Polish forces around Kiev, it was France that came to Poland's aid, in what had come to be known as the Russo-Polish War. In July, France sent a military mission to Poland, commanded by no less than one of the heroes of the Great War, General Maxime Weygand. The mission staff included Mercier's fellow officer, more colleague than friend, Captain Charles de Gaulle — they had graduated from Saint-Cyr together with the class of 1912 — and Mercier as well. Both had returned from German prison camps in 1918, after unsuccessful attempts to escape. Both had been decorated for service in the Great War. Now both went to Poland, in July of 1920, to serve as instructors to the Polish army officer corps.

But, in mid-August, when the Red Army, having broken through Polish defense lines in the Ukraine, reached the outskirts of Warsaw, Mercier had become involved in the fighting. The Russians were poised for conquest, foreign diplomats had fled Warsaw, the Red Army was just a few miles east of the Vistula, and the Red Army was unstoppable. Captain Mercier was ordered to join a Polish cavalry squadron as an observer but had then, after the deaths of several officers and with the aid of an interpreter, taken command of the squadron. And so took part in the now-famous flank attack led by Marshal Pilsudski, cutting across the Red Army line of advance in what was later called "the Miracle of the Vistula."

At five in the afternoon, on the thirteenth of August, 1920, the final assault on Warsaw began in the town of Radzymin, fifteen miles east of the city. As Pilsudski's counterattack was set in motion, the 207th Uhlan Regiment, with Mercier leading his squadron, was ordered to take the Radzymin railway station. A local fourteen-year-old was hauled up to sit behind a Uhlan's saddle and guide them to the station. It was almost eight o'-clock, but the summer evening light was just beginning to darken, and, when Mercier saw the station at the foot of a long, narrow street, he raised his revolver, waved it forward, and spurred his horse. The Uhlans shouted as they charged, people in the apartments above the street leaned out their windows and cheered, and the thunder of hooves galloping over cobblestones echoed off the sides of the buildings.

As they rode down the street, the Uhlans began to fire at the station, and rifle rounds snapped past Mercier's head. The answering Russian fire blew spurts of brick dust off building walls, glass showered onto the cobblestones, a horse went down, and the rider to Mercier's left cried out, dropped his rifle, tumbled sideways, and was dragged by a stirrup until another rider grabbed the horse's bridle.

They poured out of the street at full gallop and then, at a call from Mercier's interpreter, split left and right, as drivers ran from the Radzymin taxis, and passengers dropped their baggage and dove full length, huddling by the curb for protection. Only a small unit, a platoon or so, of Russian troops protected the station, and they were quickly overcome, one of them, an officer with a red star on his cap, speared with a Uhlan's lance.

For a few minutes, all was quiet. Mercier's horse, flanks heaving, whickered as Mercier trotted him a little way up the track, just to see what he could see. Where was the Red Army? Somewhere in Radzymin, for now the first artillery shell landed in the square surrounding the station, a loud explosion, a column of black dirt blown into the air, a plane tree split in half. Mercier hauled his horse around and galloped back toward the station house. He saw the rest of the squadron leaving the square, headed for the cover of an adjoining street.

The next thing he knew, he was on the ground, vision blurred, ears ringing, blood running from his knee, the horse galloping off with the rest of the squadron. For a time, he lay there; then a Uhlan and a shopkeeper ran through the shell bursts and carried him into a drygoods store. They set him down carefully on the counter, tore long strips of upholstery fabric from a bolt — cotton toile with lords and ladies, he would remember it as long as he lived — and managed to stop the bleeding.

The following morning found him in a horse-drawn cart with other wounded Uhlans, heading back toward Warsaw on a road lined with Poles of every sort, who raised their caps as the wagon rolled past. Back in the city, he learned that Pilsudski's daring gamble had been successful, the Red Army, in confusion, was in full flight back toward the Ukraine: thus, "the Miracle of the Vistula." Though, in certain sectors of the Polish leadership, it was not considered a miracle at all. The Polish army had beaten the Russians, outmaneuvered them, and outfought them. In crisis, they'd been strong — strong enough to overcome a great power, and, therefore, strong enough to stand alone in Europe.

A few months later, Captain Mercier and Captain de Gaulle were awarded Polish military honors, the Cross of *Virtuti Militari*.

After that, the two careers did, for a time,

continue to run parallel, as they served with French colonial forces in the Lebanon, fighting bandit groups, known as the Dandaches, in the Bekaa valley. Divergence came in the 1930s when de Gaulle, by then the most prestigious intellectual in France's military — known, because of his books and monographs, as the "pen officer" of the French army — won assignment to teach at the *École Supérieure de Guerre*. He was, by then, well known in the military, and oft-quoted. For a number of memorable statements, particularly a line delivered during the Great War when, under sudden machine-gun fire, his fellow officers had thrown themselves to the ground, and de Gaulle called out, "Come, gentlemen, behave yourselves."

For Mercier there was no such notoriety, but he had continued, quite content, with a series of General Staff assignments in the Lebanon. Until, as a French officer decorated by both France and Poland, he'd been ordered, a perfect and appealing substitute for Colonel Emile Bruner, to serve as military attaché in Warsaw.

At the central Warsaw tram stop, Mercier got off the trolley. The gray dawn had now given way to a gray morning, with a damp, cold wind, and Mercier's knee hurt like hell. But

44

in truth, he told himself, not unamused, the ache was in both knees, so not so much the condition of the wounded warrior as that of a tall man who, the previous evening, had been making love with a short woman in the shower.

Mercier went first to his apartment, changed quickly into uniform, then walked back to the embassy, a handsome building on Nowy Swiat, a few doors from the British embassy, on a tree-lined square with a statue. In his office, he typed out a brief report of his contact with Uhl. Very terse: the date and time and location, the delivery of diagrams for the production of the new — 1B — version of the Panzer tank, the payment made, establishment of the next meeting.

Should he include the fact that Uhl was wriggling? No, nothing had really happened; surely they didn't care, in Paris, to be bothered with such trivia. He had a long, careful look at the diagrams to make sure they were as described — there was potential here for real disaster; it had happened more than once, they'd told him; plans for a public lavatory or a design for a mechanical can opener — then gave the report, the diagrams, and the signed receipt to one of the embassy clerks for transmission back to the General

Staff in Paris, with a copy of the report to the ambassador's office and another for the safe that held his office files.

Next he took a taxi — he had an embassy car and driver available to him, but he didn't want to bother — out to the neighborhood of the Citadel, where the Polish General Staff had its offices, to a small café where he was to meet with his Polish counterpart, Colonel Anton Vyborg. He was first to arrive. They came to this café not precisely for secrecy, rather for privacy — it was more comfortable to speak openly away from their respective offices. That was one reason, there was another.

As soon as Mercier was seated at their usual table, the proprietor produced a large platter of *ponczkis,* a kind of small jelly doughnut, dusted with granulated sugar, light and fluffy, to which Mercier was gravely addicted. The proprietor, chubby and smiling, in a well-spattered apron, produced also a silver carafe of coffee. It required all of Mercier's aristocratic courtesy and diplomatic reserve to leave the warm, damnably fragrant *ponczkis* on the platter.

Vyborg, thank heaven, was precisely on time, and together they set upon the pastries. There was something of the Baltic knight in Colonel Vyborg. In his forties, he was tall and well-built and thin-lipped, with webbed lines at the corners of eyes made to squint into blizzards, and stiff, colorless hair cut short in the cavalry officer fashion. He wore high leather boots, supple and dark, well rubbed with saddle soap — Mercier always caught a whiff of it in Vyborg's presence, mixed with the smell of the little cigars he smoked.

Vyborg was a senior officer in the intelligence service, the Oddzial II — the *Deuxième Bureau,* named in the French tradition — of the Polish Army General Staff, known as the *Dwojka,* which meant "the two." Vyborg worked in Section IIb, where they dealt with Austria, Germany, and France; Section IIa occupied itself with the country's primary enemies — thus the *a* — Russia, Lithuania, Byelorussia, and the Ukraine. Did Vyborg's section run agents on French territory? Likely they did. Did France do the same thing? Mercier thought so, but was kept ignorant of such operations, at any rate officially ignorant, but it was more than probable that the French SR, the *Service des Renseignements,* the clandestine service of the *Deuxième Bureau,* did precisely that. Know your enemies, know your friends, avoid surprise at all costs. But the discovery of such operations, when they came to light, was always an unhappy moment. Allies were, for reasons of the heart more than the brain, supposed to trust each other. And when they demonstrably didn't, it was as though the state of the human condition had slipped a notch.

"Have the last one," Vyborg said, refilling Mercier's coffee cup.

"For you, Anton."

"No, I must insist."

Gracefully, Mercier acceded to diplomacy.

Breakfast over, Vyborg lit one of his miniature cigars, and Mercier a Mewa — a Seagull — one of the better Polish cigarettes.

"So," Vyborg said, "the Renault people will be here the day after tomorrow." A delegation of executives and engineers was scheduled to visit Warsaw, a step in the process of selling Renault tanks to the Polish army.

"Yes," Mercier said, "we are ready for them. They're bringing a senator."

"You'll be at the dinner?"

From Mercier, a rather grim smile: *no escape.*

Their eyes met, they had in common a distaste for the obligatory social engagements required for their work. "It will be very boring," Vyborg said. "In case you were concerned."

"I was counting on it."

"You'll be accompanied?"

Mercier nodded. With no wife or fiancée, he would be with the deputy director of protocol at the embassy, who served as table partner to Mercier, and one other bachelor diplomat, when the need arose. "You've met Madame Dupin?"

"I've had the pleasure," Vyborg said.

"Where is it?"

"We sent a note to your office," Vyborg said, one eyebrow arched. *Don't you read your mail?* "A private dining room at the Europejski," Vyborg said. "They're going to watch a field maneuver earlier in the day, so they're sure to be exhausted, which will make the evening even more amusing. Then we're going on to a nightclub — the Adria, of course — for dancing until dawn."

"I can't wait," Mercier said.

"It's obligatory. When the purchasing delegation went to Renault in Paris, they were taken to some naughty cancan place — they're still talking about it — so . . ."

"Will you buy anything?"

"We shouldn't, but there's always a possibility. They want to sell us the R Thirty-five, which was demonstrated when the delegation visited the factory. This visit is supposed to close the deal."

"The R Thirty-five isn't so bad." Mercier,

officially loyal to the national industries, had to say that and Vyborg knew it. "For infantry support."

Vyborg shrugged. "A thirty-seven-millimeter cannon, one machine gun. And they only go twelve miles an hour, with a range of eighty miles. The armour's thick enough, but you don't get much machine for the money. Truthfully, if it wasn't French, we wouldn't bother, but this is up to Smigly-Rydz's office." He meant the inspector general of the Polish army. "And they may have to bow to political pressure, so, potentially, our tank crews will die for the cancan."

"What do you have now? The last figure I heard was two hundred."

"That's about right, unfortunately. The Russians have two thousand, best we know, and the same for the Germans. The Ursus factory is working on the Seven TP, our own model, under license from Vickers, but Ursus has to make farm tractors as well, and we need those. In the end, it's always the same problem: money. You've been out to the Ursus factory?"

"I was. At the end of the summer."

"Maybe that's the answer, maybe not. It really depends on how much time we have until the next war starts."

Mercier finished his coffee, then refilled

both their cups. "Hitler loves his tanks," he said.

"Yes, we heard that story. 'These are wonderful! Make more of them!' An infantry soldier in the war, he knows what the British did at Cambrai, a hundred tanks, all at once. The Germans broke and ran."

"Not like them."

"No, but they did that day."

For a moment, they were both in the past.

"Who else is coming to the dinner?" Mercier said.

"Well, they have a senator, so we'll have somebody from the Sejm. Then a few people from the French community: the ubiquitous Monsieur Travas, the Pathé agency manager, is coming, with some gorgeous girlfriend, no doubt, and we've asked your ambassador, of course, but he's declined. We may get the chargé d'affaires."

"Who's the senator?"

"Bernand? Bertrand? Something like that. I have it back at the office. One of the Popular Front politicians. Somebody from Beck's office will talk with him, though we doubt he'll have anything new to say."

Josef Beck was the Polish foreign minister, and Vyborg now referred to the issue that stood between him and Mercier, between France and Poland. Treaties aside, would

51

France come to Poland's aid if Poland were attacked?

"Likely he won't," Mercier said.

"We think not," Vyborg agreed. "But we must try."

France's political condition — strikes, communist pressure, a right wing divided into fascists and conservatives, failure to aid the Spanish Republic — continued to deteriorate. The most absurd views were held sacred, and there was too much deal-making, though all of this was seen by a tolerant world as a kind of amiable chaos — a British politician had said that a map of French political opinion would look like Einstein's hair. But, to Mercier, it wasn't so amusing. "You know what I think, Anton. If the worst happens, and it starts again, you must be prepared to stand alone. A map of Europe tells the story. It's that, or alliance with Russia — which we favor but Poland will never do — or alliance with Germany, which we certainly don't favor, and you won't do that either."

"I know," Vyborg said. "We all know." He paused, then brightened. "But, nevertheless, we'll see you at the Renault dinner."

"And then at the Adria."

"You will ask my wife to dance?"

"I shall. And you, Madame Dupin."

"Naturally," Vyborg said. "More coffee?"

At eleven, Mercier was back at the embassy for the daily political meeting. The ambassador presided, touched on political events of the last twenty-four hours, and looked ahead to the Renault visit — special care here, don't bother there. Then LeBeau, the chargé d'affaires and first officer, reported on unrest, potential anti-Jewish demonstrations in Danzig, and a border incident in Silesia. Then the ambassador moved on to the topic of electricity consumption at the embassy. How difficult was it, really, to turn off the lights when not in use?

Mercier had a bowl of soup for lunch at a nearby restaurant; half a bowl — Polish chicken soup was rich and powerful, laden with heavy, twisted noodles — because the *ponczkis* had finished his appetite for the day. He did paperwork in his office until two-thirty, then returned to his apartment, changed from uniform back into civilian clothes — gray flannel trousers, dark wool jacket, subdued striped tie — and set out for his third café of the day. This time on Marszalkowska avenue, a lively and elegant street with trees, awnings, nightclubs, and smart shops.

At midafternoon, the Café Cleo was a perfect sanctuary: marble tables, black-and-white tiled floor, a bow window looking out on the avenue, where a less-favored world hurried by. The small room was almost full; the customers chattered away, read the papers, played chess, drank foamy cups of hot chocolate with whipped cream; their dogs, mostly beagles, lay attentive under the tables, waiting for cake crumbs. In a corner at the back, Hana Musser, spectacles pushed down on her pert nose, worked at a crossword puzzle, lost in concentration, tapping her teeth with a pencil.

Mercier liked Hana Musser, a half-Czech, half-German woman of uncertain age, who, two years earlier, had fled the fulminous Nazi politics of the Sudetenland and settled in Warsaw, where she worked at whatever she could but found the economic life of the city more than difficult. She had fine skin and fine features, a mass of brass-colored hair drawn back in a clip, and wore a bulky, home-knit cardigan sweater of a dreadful pea-green shade. How Colonel Bruner had discovered her — to play the part of Countess Sczelenska — Mercier did not know, but he had his suspicions. Was she a prostitute? Never a true professional, he guessed, but perhaps a woman who, from time to time, might meet a man at a café, with some kind of gift to follow an afternoon spent in a hotel room. And, if the man had money, the affair might continue.

As Mercier seated himself, she looked up, took her spectacles off, smiled at him, and said, "Good afternoon," in German.

"And to you," Mercier said. "All goes well?"

"Quite well, thank you. And yourself?"

"Not so bad," Mercier said. A waiter appeared, Mercier ordered coffee. "May I get you something?"

"Another chocolate, please."

When the waiter left, Mercier said, "We've made our usual deposit."

"Yes, I know, thank you, as always."

"How do you find your friend, these days?"

"Much as usual. Herr Uhl is a very straightforward fellow. His journeys to Warsaw are the high points of his life. Otherwise, he labors away, the good family man."

"And you, Hana?"

From Hana, a half smile and a certain sparkle in her eyes — she always flirted with him, he never minded. "The Countess Sczelenska never changes. She can be difficult, at times, but is captive to her heart's desires."

She laughed and said, "I rather like her, actually."

The waiter appeared with coffee and hot chocolate; someone, probably the waiter himself, had added a particularly generous gobbet of whipped cream atop the chocolate. Hana pressed her hands together and said, "Oh my!" How not to reward such a waiter? She spooned up almost all of the cream, then stirred in the rest.

"We are appreciative," Mercier said, "of what you do for us."

"Yes?" She liked the compliment. "I suppose there are legions of us."

"No, countess, there's only you."

"Oh I bet," she said, teasing him. "Anyhow, I think I was born to be a spy. Wouldn't you agree?"

"Born? I couldn't say. Perhaps more the times one lives in. Circumstance. There's a French saying, *'Où le Dieu a vous semé, il faut savoir fleurir.'* Let's see, 'Wherever God has planted you, you must know how to flower,' " he said in German.

"That's good," she said.

"I've never forgotten it."

She paused, then said, "If you knew what came before, you'd see that being a countess is much of an improvement. Have you ever been hungry, André? Really hungry?"

"During the war, sometimes."

"But dinner was coming, sooner or later."

He nodded.

"So," she said. "Anyhow, I wanted to say, if Herr Uhl should — well, if he goes away, or whatever happens to such people, perhaps I could continue. Perhaps you would want something — something different."

"We might," he said. "One never knows the future."

"No," she said. "Probably it's better that way."

"Speaking of the future, your next meeting with Herr Uhl will take place on the fifteenth of November. He doesn't say anything about me, does he?"

"No, never. He comes to Warsaw on business."

Would she tell him if he did?

"In a week or two he will telephone," she said. "From the Breslau railway station. That much he does tell me."

"A different kind of secret," Mercier said.

"Yes," she said. "The secret of a love affair." Again the smile, and her eyes meeting his.

18 October, 4:20 P.M. On the 2:10 train from Warsaw, the first-class compartment was full, but Herr Edvard Uhl had been

57

early and taken the seat by the window. The gray afternoon had at last produced a slow rain over the October countryside, where narrow sandy roads led away into the forest.

As the train clattered across central Poland, Uhl was not at ease. He stared at the droplets sliding across the window, or at the brown fields beyond, but his mind was too much occupied by going home, going back to Breslau, to work and family. The unease was not unlike that of a schoolboy's Sunday night; the weekend teased you with freedom, then the looming Monday morning took it away. The woman in the seat across from him occupied herself with the consumption of an apple. She'd spread a newspaper over her lap, cut slices with a paring knife, then chewed them, slowly, deliberately, and Uhl couldn't wait for her to be done with the thing. The man sitting next to her was German, he thought, with a long, gloomy Scandinavian face, and wore a black leather coat, much favored by the Gestapo. But that, Uhl told himself, was just nerves. The man stared out into space, in a kind of traveler's trance, and, if he looked at Uhl, Uhl never caught him at it.

The train stopped at Lodz, then at Kalisz, where it stood a long time in the station, the locomotive's beat steady and slow. On the

58

platform, the stationmaster stood by the first-class carriage and smoked a cigarette until, at last, he drew a pocket watch from his vest and waited as the second hand swept around the dial. Then, as he started to raise his flag, two businessmen, both with briefcases, came trotting along the platform and climbed aboard just as the stationmaster signaled to the engineer, and, with a jerk, the train began to move. The two businessmen, one of them wiping the rain from his eyeglasses with a handkerchief, came down the corridor and peered through the window into Uhl's compartment. There was no room for them. They took a moment, satisfying themselves that the compartment was full, then went off to find seats elsewhere.

Uhl didn't like them. *Calm down,* he told himself, *think pleasant thoughts.* His night with Countess Sczelenska. In detail. He'd woken in the darkness and begun to touch her until, sleepily, with a soft, compliant sigh, she started to make love to him. *Make love.* Was she in love with him? No, it was an "arrangement." But she did seem to enjoy it, every sign he knew about said she did, and, as for himself, it was better than anything else in his life. What if they ran away together? This happened only in the movies, at least in his experience, but people surely did it, just not the people he knew. And then, if you ran away, you had to run away *to* someplace. What place would that be?

Some years earlier, he had encountered an old school friend in Breslau, who'd left Germany in the early 1930s and gone off to South Africa, where he'd become, evidently, quite prosperous as the proprietor of a commercial laundry. "It's a fine country," his friend had said. "The people, the Dutch and the English, are friendly." But, he thought, would a countess, even a pretend countess, want to go to such a place? He doubted it. He tried to imagine her there, in some little bungalow with a picket fence, cooking dinner. Baking a cake.

Uhl looked at his watch. Was the train slow today? He returned to his reverie, soothing himself with daydreams of some sweet moment in the future, happy and carefree in a far-off land. The man in the black coat suddenly stood up — he was tall, with military posture — unclicked the latch on the compartment door, and turned left down the corridor. Left? The first-class WC was to the right — Uhl knew this; he'd used it often on his trips between Breslau and Warsaw. So then, why left? That led only to the second-class carriages, why would he go there? Was there another WC down that way which, for

some eccentric personal reason, he preferred? Uhl didn't know. He could, of
course, go and find out for himself, but that
would mean following the man down the
corridor. This he didn't care to do. Why not?
He didn't care to, period.

So he waited. The train slowed for the
town of Krotoszyn, chugged past the small
outdoor station. A group of passengers,
stolid country people, sat on a bench, surrounded by boxes and suitcases. Waiting for
some other train, a local train, to take them
somewhere else. Outside Krotoszyn, a cluster of small shacks came to the edge of the
railway. Uhl saw a dog in a window, watching the train go by, and somebody had left
shirts on a wash line; now they were wet.
Where was the man in the black coat? Were
the two businessmen his friends? Had he
gone to visit them? Impulsively, Uhl stood
up. "Excuse me," he said, as the other passengers drew their feet in so he could pass.
Outside the door, he saw that the corridor
was empty. He turned left, the sound of the
wheels on the track deepened as the train
crossed a railroad bridge over a river, then,
on the other side, returned to its usual pitch.
The carriage swayed, they were picking up
speed now, as Uhl walked along the corridor. He was tempted to look in at each com-

partment, to see where the businessmen were, to see if the man in the black coat had joined them, but he couldn't bring himself to do it. It didn't feel right, to Uhl, to do something like that. He was now certain that when he got off this train he would be arrested, beaten until he confessed, and, then, hanged.

There was no WC at the end of the carriage. Only a door that would open to the metal plate above the coupling, then another door, and a second-class carriage. Above the seats, arranged in rows divided by an aisle, a haze of smoke. In the first seat, a man and a woman were asleep; the woman's mouth was wide open, which made her face seem worried and tense. As Uhl turned, he discovered that the first-class conductor had come down the corridor behind him. Gesturing with his thumb, back and forth above his shoulder, he said something in Polish. Then, when he saw that Uhl didn't understand, he said in German, "It's back there, sir. What you're looking for."

"How long until we reach Leszno?"

The conductor looked at his watch. "About an hour, not much more."

Uhl returned to the compartment. At Leszno, after Polish border guards checked the first-class passports, the train would continue to Glogau, where the passengers had to get off for German frontier *kontrol;* then he would change trains, for a local that went south to Breslau. Back in his compartment, Uhl kept looking at his watch. Diagonally across from him, an empty seat. The man in the black coat had not returned. Had the train stopped? No. He was simply somewhere else.

It was almost six when they reached the Polish border at Leszno. Uhl decided to get off the train and wait for the next one, but the conductor had stationed himself to block the door. Broad and stocky, feet spread wide, he stood like an official wall. "You must wait for the passport officers, sir," he said. He wasn't polite. Did he think Uhl wanted to run away? No, he knew that Uhl wanted to run away. Six days a week he worked on this train, what hadn't he seen? Fugitives, certainly, who'd lost their nerve and couldn't face the authorities.

"Of course," Uhl said, returning to his compartment.

What a fool he was! He was an ordinary man, not cut out for a life like this. He'd been born to put on his carpet slippers after dinner, to sit in his easy chair, read his newspaper, and listen to music on the radio. In the compartment, the other passengers were restive. They didn't speak but shifted about, cleared their throats, touched their faces. And there they sat, as twenty minutes crawled by. Then, at last, at the end of the car, the sound of boots on the steel platform, a little joke, a laugh. The two officers entered the compartment, took each passport in turn, glanced at the owner, found the proper page, and stamped it: *Odjazd Polska — 18 Pazdziernik 1937.*

Well, that wasn't so bad. The passengers relaxed. The woman across from Uhl searched in her purse, found a hard candy, unwrapped it, and popped it in her mouth — so much for the Polish frontier! Then she noticed that Uhl was watching her. "Would you care for a candy?" she said.

"No, thank you."

"Sometimes, the motion of the train . . ." she said. There was sympathy in her eyes.

Did he look ill? What did she see, in his face? He turned away and stared out the window. The train had left the lights of Leszno; outside it was dark, outside it was Germany. Now what Uhl saw in the window was his own reflection, but if he pressed his forehead against the cold glass he could just make out a forest, a one-street village, a black car, shiny in the rain, waiting at the lowered bar of a railway crossing. What if, he wondered, the next time he went to Warsaw, he simply didn't show up for André's meeting? What would they do? Would they betray him? Or just let him go? The former, he thought. He was trapped, and they would not set him free; the world didn't work that way, not their world. His mind was working like a machine gone wild; fantasies of escape, fantasies of capture, a dozen alibis, all of them absurd, the possibility that he was afraid of shadows, that none of it was real.

"Glo-gau!"

The conductor's voice was loud in the corridor. Then, from further away, "Glogau!"

The train rumbled through the outlying districts of the city, then slowed for the bridge that crossed the river Oder, a long span of arches, the current churning white as it curled around the stone block. An ancient border, no matter where the diplomats drew their lines, "east of the Oder" meant Slavic Europe, the other Europe.

"All out for Glogau."

The passport *kontrol* was set up at the door to the station, beneath a large swastika flag. Uhl counted five men, one of them seated at a small table, another with an Alsatian shepherd on a braided leash. Three were in uniform, their holstered sidearms worn high, and two were civilians, standing so they could see a sheaf of papers on the table. A list.

Uhl's heart was pounding as he stepped down onto the platform. *You have nothing to fear,* he told himself. If they searched him they would find only a thousand zloty. So what? Everyone carried money. *But they have a list.* What if his name was on it? A few months earlier he'd seen it happen, right here, at Glogau station. A heavy man, with a red face, led quietly away, a guiding hand above his elbow. Now he saw the two businessmen; they were ahead of him on the line that led to the passport *kontrol.* One of them looked over his shoulder, then said something, something private, to his friend. *Yes, he's just back there, behind us.* And then Uhl discovered the man in the black leather coat. He was *not* on the line, he was sitting on a bench by the wall of the station, hands in pockets, legs crossed, very much at ease. Because he did not have to go through passport *kontrol,* because he was *one of them,* a Gestapo man, who'd followed him down from Warsaw, making sure he didn't get off the train. And now his job was done, work over for the day. Tomorrow, a new assignment. Uhl felt beads of sweat break out at his hairline, took off his hat, and wiped them away. *Run.* "Ach," he said, to the man behind him in the line, "I have forgotten my valise."

He left the line and walked back toward the train, his briefcase clamped tightly beneath his arm. At the door to the train, where second-class passengers were gathering, waiting in a crowd to join the line, the conductor was smoking a cigarette. "Excuse me," Uhl said, "but I have forgotten my suitcase."

No you haven't. The conductor's face showed perfectly what he knew: there was no suitcase. And Uhl saw it. *So now my life ends,* he thought. Then, quietly, he said, "Please."

The conductor shifted his eyes, looking over Uhl's shoulder toward the SS troopers, the civilians, the flag, the dog, the list. His expression changed, and then he stepped aside, just enough to let Uhl pass. When he spoke, his voice was barely audible. "Ahh, fuck these people." Uhl took a tentative step toward the iron stair that led up to the carriage. The conductor, still watching the Germans and their table, said, "Not yet." Uhl felt a drop of sweat break free of his hatband and work its way down his forehead; he wanted to wipe it away but his arm wouldn't move.

"Now," the conductor said.

19 October, 3:30 P.M. The weekly intelligence meeting was held in the conference room of the chancery — the political section of the embassy — secured from public areas, away from the seekers of travel documents, replacements for lost passports, commercial licenses, and all other business that brought the civilian world to the building. The code clerks were in the basement — which they didn't like, claiming the dampness was hard on their equipment — along with the mailroom that handled sealed embassy pouches, while Mercier's office was on the top floor.

The meeting was chaired by Jourdain, the second secretary and political officer — which meant he too scurried about the city to dark corners for secret contacts — and Mercier's best friend at the embassy. Sandy-haired and sunny, in his mid-thirties, Jourdain was a third-generation diplomat — his father due to become ambassador to Singapore — with three young children in private academies in Warsaw. Across the table from Mercier was the air attaché, at one end the naval attaché, at the other, Jourdain's secretary, who took shorthand notes, which Jourdain would turn into a report for the Quai d'Orsay, the foreign ministry in Paris.

"Not much new," the air attaché said. He was in his fifties, corpulent and sour-faced. "The production of the Pezetelkis is going full steam ahead." Pezetelki was the nickname, taken from initials, of the PZT-24F, Poland's best fighter plane, four years earlier the most advanced pursuit monoplane in Europe. "But the air force won't get near them; that hasn't changed either. For export only."

"The same orders?" Jourdain said.

"Yes. Turkey, Greece, and Yugoslavia."

"They'll regret that, one of these days," the naval attaché said.

The air attaché shrugged. "They're trying to balance the budget, the country's damn close to broke. So they sell what people will buy."

"I guess they know best," said Jourdain, who clearly didn't believe that at all.

"Otherwise, very little new." The air attaché studied his notes. "They had an accident, last Wednesday, over Okecie field. One of their P-Sevens clipped the tail of another. Both pilots safe, both planes badly banged up, one a loss — he parachuted — the other landed." Again he shrugged. "So we can say" — the air attaché looked toward the secretary — "that their numbers are reduced by one, anyhow."

"Just note," Jourdain said to the secretary, "that we should repeat the fact that the relation of the Polish air force to the *Luftwaffe* remains twenty-five to one in favor of the Germans." Then he turned to the naval attaché and said, "Jean-Paul?"

As the naval attaché lit a cigarette and shuffled through his papers, there were two sharp knocks at the door, which opened to reveal one of the women who worked the embassy switchboard. "Colonel Mercier? May I speak with you for a moment?"

"Excuse me," Mercier said. He went out into the corridor and closed the door behind him. The operator, a middle-aged Frenchwoman, was, like many who worked at the embassy, the widow of an officer killed in the 1914 war. "A Monsieur Uhl has telephoned your apartment," she said. "He left a number with your maid. I hope it's correct, sir, she was very nervous."

"Poor Wlada," Mercier said. *Now what?* The operator handed him a slip of paper, and Mercier went up the stairs to his office. Looking in his drawer, he found a list of German telephone exchanges, dialed the switchboard, and asked for a foreign operator. When she came on the line he gave her the number. "Can you put it through right away?" he said, his Polish slow but correct.

"I can, sir, it's quiet this afternoon."

As Mercier waited, he stared out his window onto the square in front of the embassy. Beneath the bare branches of a chestnut tree, a man with a wagon was selling a sausage on a roll to a father with a small child. Far away, a telephone rang once. "Hello? Hello?" Uhl's voice was tense and high.

"Yes, I'm here. Herr Uhl?"

"Hello? André?"

"Yes. What's wrong?"

"I'm at the railway station." Mercier could hear a train. "I had a problem yesterday, on the way back. In Glogau."

"What problem?"

"I was being watched, on the train."

"How do you know?"

"I — ah, I sensed it. Two businessmen, and a Gestapo man."

"Did they question you? Search you?" Mercier had to make himself relax the grip of his hand on the phone.

"Oh no. I eluded them."

"Really. How did you do that?"

"At the border *kontrol,* in Glogau station, I left the line and went back into the Warsaw train, climbed down between carriages, and *crawled.* Along the track. At the end of the train there is Glogau bridge, but I found a

71

stairway that led down to the bank of the river. I walked back toward the city and took a taxi to the next station on the line, where I got on the local train to Breslau."

"Good work," Mercier said.

"What?"

"I said, *good work*."

"It was very close. They almost had me, in the station."

"Perhaps they did. Tell me, Herr Uhl, what happened this morning?"

"This morning? I went to the office."

"Did someone question you? Were you confronted?"

"No. All was normal."

"Then you're in the clear. Did the people on the train say anything to you?"

"No. But they looked at me. They behaved, in a furtive manner."

"I would doubt that German surveillance operatives would be furtive, Herr Uhl. Perhaps your imagination . . . misled you."

"Well, maybe. But maybe not. In any event, I think I shouldn't continue our meetings."

"Oh, let's not be scared off so easily. Believe me, if the Gestapo had any reason to suspect you, you wouldn't be talking to me on the telephone. By the way, you mentioned a Gestapo man. How did you know that? I presume he was in uniform."

"He wasn't. He wore a leather coat. It was the way he looked."

Mercier laughed. "The way he looked?"

"Well . . ."

"Your work is important, Herr Uhl, and we don't lose people who help us; we can't afford that. Would you like me to do some checking? To see if you're being watched?"

After a silence, Uhl said, "You're able to do that?"

"We are a resourceful service," Mercier said. "We're able to do all sorts of things. Why don't I ask some people to see what's going on; then I'll send you a postal card, if everything is normal."

"And what if it isn't?"

"I'll find a way to let you know. What time do you leave your office?"

"At six, generally."

"Every night?"

"Yes, almost every night."

"Then we'll know how to find you. For the moment, I expect to see you in November. You recall the information I requested."

"Yes."

"Just remember, it's in our interest to keep you safe, and it's in your interest to continue your work."

After a time, Uhl said, "Very well, we'll see.

If everything is — as it was. . . ."

"You did very well, Herr Uhl. If nothing else, you erred on the side of caution, and we admire that. Clearly, you have a gift for this sort of business."

Uhl didn't answer.

"On the fifteenth," Mercier said, "we can talk it over, if you like. We want you safe and sound, do keep that in mind. And, after all, you do have other interests that bring you to Warsaw — would you simply remain in Germany?"

"No, but —"

"Then it's settled. I'll be waiting for you. Or, if there's a problem, I'll make sure you know about it."

"All right," Uhl said. He wasn't happy but he would, Mercier thought, hold up. For a while, anyhow.

Mercier said goodby, hung up the phone, and wrote himself a note: *Send Uhl a post-card.* "All going well here, hope to see you soon, Aunt Frieda." There was no possibility of finding out if Uhl was under Gestapo surveillance — maybe the *Deuxième Bureau* had spies inside the German security apparatus, but Uhl was not important enough for such an effort. The lie had been recommended at his training class and it had evidently worked the way they'd said it would. From the telephone call, Mercier sensed that Uhl had frightened himself.

He returned to the conference room, where the meeting continued, in a fog of cigarette smoke. "Everything all right?" Jourdain said, concern in his voice.

"A problem with an agent," Mercier said.

"Not going to lose him, are we?"

"I don't think so. I suspect he saw phantoms."

"They like what he's bringing, at *deux bis*," Jourdain said. He referred to the *Deuxième Bureau* by its Paris address, 2 bis, rue de Tourville.

Mercier nodded. Perhaps they liked it at the General Staff as well — they never said, simply took what there was, then asked for more. Nevertheless, you didn't want to lose agents, you'd find yourself transferred to some fever-ridden island in a distant ocean — *far-flung* barely described the remote outposts of the French colonial empire.

"I'm just finishing up," the naval attaché said. "Baltic maneuvers off the Gdynia coast. A destroyer squadron."

"They hit their targets?" Mercier said.

"Now and then. They almost hit the towing ship, but we all do that."

Mercier finished his paperwork at six, then

headed back to his apartment. He had the Renault dinner at eight-thirty, with Madame Dupin, the deputy director of protocol at the embassy. He sighed, inside, at the prospect of a long, boring, political dinner, where one said nothing much and could only hope it was the right nothing much. As for Madame Dupin, she was a noble soul, able to sparkle and chatter endlessly at social functions, an ability that some might find frivolous, until they joined the diplomatic service.

He appreciated her efforts, but the evening reminded him of what had been — of Annemarie, his wife, who'd died three years earlier. He recalled how, as they'd dressed for the evening, they would banter about the awful people they would meet, would have to *entertain*. That made it easier, theatre for husband and wife, shared misery and the instinct to find it some way, somehow, amusing.

The apartment provided for the military attaché was on the second floor of 22, aleja Ujazdowska — Ujazdowska avenue — the Champs-Elysées of Warsaw, though not so broad, a street of elegant five-story buildings, exteriors lavishly wrought with every sort of decorative stonework, set well back behind trees and shrubbery, which was fronted by ornamental iron palings that ran the length of the block. The French embassy had for a long time been on Ujazdowska but had moved, two years earlier, to Nowy Swiat. Still, it was only a fifteen-minute walk from his apartment, just enough to clear the fog of work from his mind.

The apartment came with a maid, Wlada, thin and nervous, who lived in the maid's room, a cook, heavy and silent, who came every day but Sunday, and a driver, Marek, a tough old bird who'd served as a sergeant in Pilsudski's Polish Legion and drove Mercier around in what he persisted in calling the "Biook," in fact a 1936 S41 Buick sedan. The choice of the French and several other embassies, it was a heavily sprung eight-cylinder bear of an automobile, with a bulbous trunk, that negotiated Polish roads as long as you kept at least two spare tires with you, though nobody went anywhere in the spring and autumn rains — Poland's seasonal barrier against German expansion.

Entering the apartment, Mercier glanced at the mail on the foyer table, then headed for his dressing room. This took time. The place was enormous; ten vast rooms with high ceilings, plaster medallions at every corner, and, thanks to the inordinately wealthy wife of a previous tenant, sumptuously furnished. Better to have private means if you were a diplomat of higher rank, the salary didn't begin to pay for the necessary show. Thus the heavy floor-to-ceiling drapes at the windows, couches covered in damask, ebony drum tables, exotic oriental lamps with creamy silk shades, and a silver service to sink a small ship. In the apartment, Mercier felt forever a temporary guest. The rough, weary, mostly ancient furnishings of his country house in central France — dog hair everywhere, how did they still have coats? — the only style that felt, to him, comfortable.

In the dressing room, Wlada had laid out his best uniform, perfectly cleaned and ironed, and his kepi, visored military hat, which she'd ruthlessly brushed. The damn thing was expensive, but there was, in such matters, no interfering with Wlada. The more she thought it important, the harder she punished it. Opening the bottom drawer of his dresser, he brought out a square of blue felt with cardboard backing, which bore his service decorations, pinned in neat rows. There were a lot of them; twenty-eight years in the military brought medals. For the Renault crowd, much the best to go top class, so Mercier unpinned his *Croix de Guerre* and *Virtuti Militari* and set them on the dresser. A bath? No, it could wait. He took off his work uniform, shoes, and socks, put on a wool bathrobe, walked into the adjoining bedroom, and stretched out on a settee by the window. *Twenty minutes, no more.* Outside, the avenue was quiet under the streetlamps, a horse-drawn cab went clopping past, a dog barked, a couple spoke in gentle voices as they walked by. *Peace.* Another nineteenth-century evening on the Ujazdowska.

As he often did, Mercier thought of Annemarie as he drifted off. He was lonely for her, three years gone with influenza — thought at first, and for too long, to be a winter grippe. Despite all the time he'd spent away from her, they'd been a close couple, given to the small, continual affections of married life. They'd had two daughters, both now in their early twenties, one married to an archaeologist and living in Cairo, the other working at a museum in Copenhagen: adventurers like their father and, alas, like him, terribly independent. It was what he'd wished for, and what he got — so life went. Every now and then, a newsy letter, but it had been a long time since he'd seen either one of them. They were attractive, not beautiful, and moderately celestial, floating just above the daily world, not unlike Annemarie. *Annemarie.* Now and then, with a late supper for two planned, after the girls left home, they would make love at this time — that seductive hour between afternoon and night, *l'heure bleu,* in the French tradition, named for its deepening shadow. Sometimes she would . . .

From the study, several rooms away, the rattling bell of the telephone. He heard Wlada scurrying across the chestnut parquet, a breathless *"Rezydencja panstwa Mercier,"* a few more words of Polish, then the footsteps headed his way. "Colonel?" she said. "Are you awake?"

"Yes?"

"It is Madame Dupeen."

"All right. I'm coming."

He tied the belt of his bathrobe as he journeyed toward the study. "Madame Dupin?"

"Good evening, Colonel Mercier. Forgive me, please, for calling so late."

"Of course, no problem."

"I'm afraid there is, I'm unwell. Something" — she paused; how to say it? — "something I ate."

"I am sorry. Do you need anything? I can send Marek to the pharmacy."

"That is very kind of you, but no, thank you. What it means is that I can't attend the dinner tonight."

"It's nothing to worry about, I can go alone."

"Oh no, that won't do at all. I've found a

substitute, a friend of mine. She lives with some Russian, a journalist, but he won't care. Anyhow, she's agreed to go, my dear friend. Otherwise, an empty place, an unbalanced table, it simply can't be done. Do you have something to write on?"

"A moment," he said, then found a tablet and a pen on the antique desk. "Yes?"

She gave him a name, Anna Szarbek, and an address. "Your driver will know where it is," she said.

"Just feel better, Madame Dupin, I'm sure we'll manage."

"You'll like my friend," she said. "She's terribly bright."

"I'm sure I will," he said.

Promptly at eight, he climbed into the back of the "Biook" and gave Marek the address. "Yes," Marek said, "I'll find it."

But it wasn't so easy. Mumbling curses to himself, Marek worked back and forth through tiny streets north of the central city. Mercier had a street map — in his desk at the office, naturally. He looked at his watch, trying to keep it below the back of the front seat, but Marek caught him at it and mumbled louder. Finally, at twenty minutes past eight, they found the building. Now they would be late — which might, for some, be

81

fashionable, but Mercier wasn't fashionable.

The building was two stories high, and the janitor, when it suited him, answered his knock at the street door and swung an ill-tempered hand toward the staircase. On the second floor, two doors, and a powerful fragrance of boiled cabbage. He knocked at the first door, waited thirty seconds, then, as he knocked at the second door, the first one opened.

"Good evening," Mercier said. "Madame Szarbek? I'm Madame Dupin's friend, Lieutenant Colonel Mercier."

"That's me. Sorry to have kept you. Please, come inside."

Mercier was immediately relieved — this was not to be an evening spent in his undependable Polish; her French was rapid and fluent, with the barest hitch of an accent at the edges, her voice slightly husky and rough. She was, he guessed, in her late thirties, and very striking: thick hair, the color called dirty blond, swept low across her forehead, then pinned up in back, and a face that suggested, somehow, sensuality — a slight downward curve of the nose, full-lipped mouth, pallid skin, sharp jawline, and deep green eyes, wary and restless, not quite the night animal, but close. For a formal evening, she wore a black silk dress with matching jacket, then, more her true style, added a dark red scarf wound around her throat, pendant earrings with green gemstones, and a cloud of strong perfume, more spice than sugar. For a moment she stared at him, her mouth set in a hesitant smile: *will this do?* Then said, "I'll be ready right away," led him into the apartment, and fled down the hall, calling out, "Please introduce yourselves."

On the sofa, a burly man with gray hair curling out of the vee of his open shirt rose from a nest of newspapers. "Good evening, general," he said with a grin and a meaty handshake. "I'm Maxim." From the grin, Mercier could tell that Maxim knew he wasn't a general, this was just his way of being lovable. They stood there for a moment, not comfortable, then Anna Szarbek came hurrying out of the hallway, now clutching a small evening purse. "Are we awfully late?" she said.

"No, we'll be fine," Mercier said.

Anna kissed Maxim on the cheek and said something private by his ear.

"Not too late, general," Maxim said, and winked at Mercier. *Some dish, hey? Don't get any ideas.*

He followed her down the stairs — she was a little wobbly in very high heels, sliding one

83

hand along the banister — and out onto the sidewalk. As Marek held the door open for Anna, he gave Mercier a conspiratorial lift of the eyebrows. "We're going to the Europejski," Mercier said, glancing at his watch.

That gesture was all Marek needed to see — the Buick took off with a squeal of the tires and went hurtling down the narrow street. Anna settled herself in the corner of the backseat, bent over to peer into her purse, brought out a slim tortoiseshell cigarette case, and offered it to Mercier. On the lid, a laughing Bacchus and two pink nymphs were wearing only a grapevine. "Do you smoke?" she said.

"I do, but not right now."

She took out a cigarette, and Mercier lit it for her with a steel lighter. This she needed — took a deep draw, exhaled two long plumes of smoke from her nose, and sat back in the seat. "Marie didn't tell me much," she said, referring to Madame Dupin.

"It's very kind of you, to do this on short notice."

"For Saint Marie, anything. She does favors for everybody, so . . ."

"It's a dinner given by the Polish General Staff for a delegation from the Renault company; they've come in from Paris. Then, after that, a nightclub."

"A nightclub?"

"Yes, the Adria."

"Very fancy. I've never been there."

Mercier's expression said that it was what it was. "A floor show, likely dancing."

Her nod was grim, but determined — she would handle anything that came her way. "So, you're at the embassy."

"I am. The military attaché."

"Yes, that's what Marie said." She knew what military attachés did — at least some secret intelligence work — but apparently took it for an inevitable part of life in foreign service.

"A lot of paperwork is what it amounts to. Sometimes attendance at field maneuvers. And, as you would imagine, endless meetings." She didn't comment, so he said, "Have you always lived here, in Warsaw?" Marek was driving fast, the Buick's big engine a heavy purr. They came up close to a trolley and swung boldly around it, skidding on the track.

"No, I've been based here for, oh, maybe a year and a half, and I spend a lot of time traveling, mostly down south, and up to Gdansk. I'm a lawyer with the League of Nations, so sometimes I'm in Geneva. Talk about endless meetings."

"Where's home, then?"

"I'm Parisian by birth, Polish by heritage."

"An émigré family."

"Yes, I grew up speaking Polish at home, French everywhere else."

"What do you do for the League?"

"Report on legal claims, mostly, a form of arbitration. When the League redrew the Silesian border in 1921, after the third uprising, tens of thousands of Poles and Germans were in a new country, and private citizens continued to submit claims to the League, seeking satisfaction they couldn't get from local courts. It's the same up in Danzig, declared by the League a Free City, but what you have is a German population governed by Poles. All this led to local disputes — land ownership, unfair administration, tax problems. We don't have legal standing, but we try to arbitrate, and sometimes the local courts are responsive. Anyhow it's a last resort, for Poles *and* Germans, even though Germany left the League when Hitler came to power. The League is, if nothing else, persistent: war doesn't work, try the courts."

"Try anything," Mercier said.

That caught her attention, and she looked at him. "Not the usual sentiment," she said, "from someone in uniform."

"You'd be surprised," Mercier said. "Once you've been in the middle of it . . ."

She turned away and stubbed out her cigarette in the ashtray on the arm of the backseat. "Well, now you'll be in it again. Spain is just the beginning, it'll spread from there."

"Inevitable, you believe?"

"From the people I talk to, yes. Eaten up with grievance, especially the Germans. Getting even is what they think about."

"You have a difficult job, Madame Szarbek."

"Anna, please. And it's mademoiselle, for a while anyhow. Is your job easier than mine?"

"No, not really."

At the Europejski, they were led up a marble stairway to a private dining room, all wood-paneled walls and polished floor. Beneath crystal chandeliers, a long table was set for thirty; the sheen of the damask tablecloth, the heavy silver, and the gold-rimmed china glowed in the light of a dozen candelabra. They were greeted at the door by an officer of the Polish General Staff and his splendidly bejeweled wife. "We are so very pleased you could join us," she said, her smile gracious and warm. The room hummed with conversation; officers in uniform, most of the other men in evening wear, most of the women in formal gowns. Anna, perhaps momentarily taken aback by all the glitter, took

Mercier's arm. He was instantly aware of the touch of her hand, resting lightly on his sleeve.

From some distant century, an ancient waiter in a swallowtail coat moved toward them, parchment face lit by a beatific smile, parchment hands holding a silver tray, which trembled slightly, bearing two glasses of champagne. Drinks in hand, they watched him shuffle back toward the kitchen. Anna started to say something, but another officer wife descended on them, leading a small fellow in a dark suit, one of the men from Renault. After the introductions, she swept away, in search of other strays.

"So, Monsieur Blanc," Mercier said, "a worthwhile visit, so far?"

"Yes, I would say it is; we are making our case. The R-Thirty-five tank is a magnificent machine."

"And what do you do for the Renault company?"

"I am one of the senior engineers — I concern myself mostly with treads."

From Anna, an appreciative, encouraging nod. *Treads!*

"Yes, that's me. And you, colonel?"

"I'm the military attaché, at the embassy."

"Ah, then you must support us — these

88

Poles can be stubborn. Don't you think, Madame Mercier?"

"Oh yes, indeed, terribly stubborn."

"Tell me, Major Kulski," Anna said, "do you favor the Renault machine?"

"Mmm, well . . ."

"Oh, perhaps you are unpersuaded."

"Mm. And how do you come to be here tonight, Pana Szarbek?"

"I'm accompanying Colonel Mercier. He's over there, by the pillar."

"Then you must live in the city."

"Yes, I do, major."

"I wondered. You see, when I'm done with the army for the day, I'm something of an artist; that's my real passion in life. So, allow me to say that you would make a superb model, for a life drawing. Truly, superb."

Mercier shook hands with Colonel Vyborg and said, "How goes the visit?"

"Not too badly. This afternoon I had a talk with Habich's assistant — you know Habich?"

"I've met him."

"The best armaments designer in Europe. Anyhow, his assistant believes that if we buy this worm of an R-Thirty-five, the engineers can do something to improve it."

"That's encouraging. Are they thinking about numbers?"

"No, not yet. We need to get our hands on one of them and Habich's people will tear it to pieces, then we'll see what can be done, and *then* we'll talk about numbers."

"So, you're with the League of Nations." The woman was in her seventies, Anna thought; her husband, with grand white cavalry mustaches, at least in his eighties. "Such a hopeful notion, my dear, really. A *league,* of *nations!* How far we've come, in this dreadful world. My husband here, the general, was the late-life son of a colonel in the Hussars. In 1852, that was. A great hero, my husband's father, he fought in the Battle of Leipzig and was decorated for bravery — we still have the medal."

"At Leipzig, really."

"That's right, my dear, with Napoleon."

"At last," Mercier said, appearing at Anna's side. "It's time for dinner. Are you hungry?"

"Yes. I had a little caviar."

"You seem to have found people to talk to, I kept an eye on you."

"All sorts of people. I met a major who asked me to pose for a life drawing."

"The hound. And will you?"

90

"Oh certainly, wouldn't miss it. I think I'll need a feather boa. Or maybe not."

From the table, a woman called out, "Colonel Mercier? You're over here."

"Thank you." Mercier drew back a gilded chair and Anna seated herself, brushing her dress forward as she sat. "Here's the menu," he said.

Anna hunted around in her evening bag and came up with a pair of gold-rimmed spectacles. "At last, I can see."

The grand menu — both hands required — was printed in spidery italic, with gold cord and tassel down the middle, and simply named the courses to be served. As he watched her reading, it occurred to Mercier that Anna's long, searching glances were precisely that — not personality, myopia. "There's sole meunière," he said. "I've had that here, and it's good. Then a roast. Abundant, the roast."

"Abundant is the word," she said. "Six courses."

"That's the Europejski. And you should at least taste the wines, the cellar is famous."

From Anna, a wry smile. *Champagne, three wines — imagine.*

"Yes," Mercier said, falling in with her mood, "all of it rich and elaborate. And be sure to leave room for the tangerine flan."

On Mercier's right, the *placement* card said *Madame de Michaux:* a formidable woman, with low-cut neckline and a circle of rubies at her heavy throat. Evidently, she'd also read his card. "Mercier de Boutillon," she mused. "And your home, where is that?"

"Down in the Drôme, about an hour from Montélimar."

"I believe there's an Albertine, Mercier de Boutillon, in Paris. Is that the same family?"

"My cousin. A friend of yours?"

"Well, we've met. My husband is on the Renault board of directors, also the opera. I believe that's how I know her. A very engaging woman, a collector of certain antiquities — is that so?"

"It is. *Objets,* in onyx. Mostly cameos, I believe."

"You must tell her we sat together, at a dinner in Warsaw. Amusing, no?"

"Certainly I will, the next time I'm in Paris."

"Do you come often, colonel?"

After the duck pâté, the consommé, and the sole, as plates were brought with great red slices of roasted beef, the rules of the formal dinner dictated a turn to the other partner. For Mercier, a welcome turn, Anna Szarbek seemed easy and comfortable after the determined Madame de Michaux — one of those upper-class women who, polite as could be, worked like a beaver at discovering one's personal life. Anna reported that the man on her left, Julien Travas, the manager of the Pathé newsreel agency in Warsaw, had been extremely entertaining. Something of an adventurer, he'd traveled, as a young man, from Shanghai to Siam by foot and oxcart, and told a good story.

Mercier and Anna worked their way through the roast, then the macédoine of vegetables, left the quivering tangerine flan on their plates, drank the coffee, and tasted the cognac. Then it was time for the nightclub. The Adria was not far from the Europejski, but one had to arrive in one's automobile. As they drove away from the hotel, Anna said, "Is this something you do often?"

"Now and then, it's part of the job."

"Good lord."

"Sip the wine, taste the food, find everyone fascinating — a good motto for diplomacy."

She shook her head. "I guess that's one way to save the world."

"Yes, one way," he said. "After the fish."

There were tables reserved for them at the Adria, and more place cards, which led to a lighthearted interval of confusion and commentary in the dark, smoky nightclub. Mercier found that Colonel Vyborg had had them seated at his own table, with the director of Renault's armaments division and a major in the purchasing section of the Polish General Staff, an owlish, balding fellow, and their wives.

After they were settled, Vyborg ordered champagne, three bottles of Veuve Clicquot, and, as the waiter opened the first, a blue spotlight pierced the darkness to reveal, on the small platform that served as a stage, Marko the Magician — so said a card on an easel — in top hat and tails, his face stark white with makeup. And his assistant, a girl in a very brief spangled costume, who opened her mouth, from which Marko began to extract, with immaculate white gloves, a series of red balls. Another, then another, each one producing horrified glances at the audience as she discovered yet one more red ball inside her. The major's wife, on Mercier's left, began to giggle, and Mercier guessed she'd more than sampled the dinner wines. The wife of the Renault director whispered, "Next time, darling, don't eat so many balls."

"How was your dinner?" Vyborg asked Anna.

"Very good."

"And the wine?"

"That too, very good."

Leaning across his wife, the Renault director said to the major, "What did you think of our presentation, in Paris? You were with the purchasing delegation, as I recall."

"Yes, I was," said the major. "A strong field trial, I thought. Of course, the ground *was* dry."

"Yes, one's always at the mercy of the weather."

"As are we," the major said. "Our infamous roads, you know."

"It's very difficult for us," the major's wife said. "In this country, we stay home in the bad seasons."

"That's changing, is it not?" the director said.

"True," Vyborg said. "We're paving some of the roads, but it's a long process."

"Better roads in Germany," the director said, a tease in his voice.

"So I'm told," the major said. "We hope we don't have to find that out for ourselves."

"It's something they've been making bets

on," Vyborg said, "our young tank captains and lieutenants. How many hours to Berlin."

"To be encouraged, I guess, that sort of spirit," said the major. "But much better if everyone stays on their side of the frontier."

"Quite a number of people think the Germans might not," the director said. "What then?"

On stage, Marko had finished with the red balls, but then, to his surprise, he discovered that his assistant had swallowed a canary, greedy girl. This produced a scattering of applause from the audience and a chirp from the canary. Marko, with a flourish, then wheeled a coffinlike box into the spotlight. The assistant's eyes widened: *oh no, not this.*

"I believe she's to be sawn in half," Mercier said.

"She does seem pretty frightened," Anna said. "Acting, I hope."

Vyborg's wife laughed. "A new assistant for every performance."

The director's wife said, "I've heard they do that with birds, sacrifice one for each trick."

"No, really?" Mercier said.

"It's true, I've heard the same thing," the major's wife said.

"As I was saying" — the director's voice

was quiet but firm — "what then? You'll need all the armoured forces you can deploy."

"Of course you're right, monsieur," the major said, "but our resources are limited. Germany's industry recovered from the war faster than ours, and they outnumber us in tanks by thirty to one."

Mercier recalled Jourdain's meeting at the embassy. "Twenty-five to one," he'd said, unless Mercier's memory was failing him, but he didn't think it was.

"We know Poland isn't a rich country," the director said, "but that's what banks are for."

The major's assent was a grim nod. Rather gently he said, "They do expect to be paid back."

"Of course. But I'll tell you something, they won't be so finicky about it if German divisions come across your border."

"They'll regret it if they do," Vyborg's wife said. "They may overwhelm us, at first, but in time they'll be sorry. And, while we're working on that here, they'll have the French army coming across their other border."

"That could," the director said, "take a few weeks, you know. In all fairness. Apologies to Colonel Mercier."

"You needn't," Mercier said. "It took us time to organize ourselves in 1914, and it will again." *No, we're not coming, we're going to sit on the Maginot Line.*

"I suspect Hitler knows that," the director said.

Marko's assistant had now climbed into the coffin, bare feet protruding from one end, head from the other. With a lethal-looking saw in hand, Marko bent over the box and, on the side away from the audience, began to cut. The blade was obviously set between two metal bands that circled the coffin, but the progress of the saw was loud and realistic. Suddenly, the girl squeaked with real terror. Had the trick gone wrong? From the audience, a chorus of gasps. The director's wife raised her hand to her mouth and said, "Good heavens!"

The magician returned to work, sawing away, while the assistant raised her head and peered over the edge of the coffin. Finally, Marko raised the saw, turned to the audience and then, the grand finale, separated the box. The audience applauded, and the magician wheeled the two halves of his assistant offstage.

"False feet," Vyborg said.

"Or a second assistant, curled up in the other half," Anna said.

"And you'll notice," said the director's wife, triumphantly, "not a speck of sawdust."

The magician was followed by a *chanteuse,* who sang romantic songs, then three bearded acrobats in saggy tights who turned somersaults through a fiery hoop. Each time they landed they shouted "Hup!" and the Adria's floor shook. Then a trio — saxophone, drums, and guitar — appeared and began to play dance music. Vyborg stood and offered a hand to his wife, the director and the major followed his example. Mercier was the last to stand. "Shall we?" he said to Anna, his voice tentative, it wasn't *really* obligatory.

If I must. "I think we should."

A slow foxtrot. Mercier, stiff and mechanical, had never advanced much beyond lessons taken as a ten-year-old, girls and boys in white gloves. Anna was not much better, but they managed, going round and round in their private square to the slow beat. Mercier, his arm circled lightly about her, found her back firm, then soft above the hips. And the way she moved, lithe and supple beneath the thin silk of her dress, more than interesting — his arm wanting, almost by itself, to tighten around her waist. As she danced, she smiled up at him, her perfume intense. Was the smile complicit? Knowing?

Inviting? He wanted it to be, and smiled back at her. Finally she said, returning to polite conversation, "That man from Renault is something of a bully."

"Titles and prerogatives aside, he's a merchant. Selling his wares."

"Still . . ." Anna said. The bridge of the song was slow. Anna's hand, slightly damp, tightened on his. "You'd think he'd be more, oh, subtle about it."

"Yes, but the major held his own," Mercier said. As they turned, a woman behind Anna took a dramatic step backward, bumping against her and forcing her forward, so that she and Mercier were pressed together. "Sorry," she said, "I'm not very good at this." After a moment, she moved away.

"Nor am I," he said.

She looked up at him; she did have lovely eyes, he thought, green eyes. "Oh well," she said, laughing, "something I never expected, this evening."

"Not so bad?" Mercier smiled hopefully.

"No," she said. "Not so bad."

The song ended, they returned to the table.

Driving back after midnight, Anna had another cigarette, and this time Mercier joined her. They were silent, having talked themselves out during the evening, simply sat and watched the streets go by, a few lights on in the darkened city. As the Buick rolled up to the street door, she said, "You needn't see me upstairs."

"You're sure?" he said, reaching for the door handle. He assumed that fiancé Maxim would be up and waiting.

"I am. Thank you, colonel. An evening to remember."

"It's for me to thank you, Mademoiselle Szarbek." *And me to remember.*

Marek opened the door. Anna left the car, then turned and waved goodby. When she was safely inside, they drove away.

23 October. In Glogau, a wet morning, a cold front had arrived with the dawn and strands of white mist rose from the river. In the center of the city, not far from the rail-road bridge, a toy shop occupied the street floor of the brick building at 35 Heimer-strasse, its windows crowded with trains and dolls and soldiers. A local institution, the toy shop, it had stood there for years, closing only briefly, when the Jewish owner abruptly left the city, then reopening in a day or two, the glass in the windows replaced by the new owner, and the shop again selling toys as it always had.

The former owner, having prospered and bought the building, had installed his family on the second floor, in a large apartment of eight rooms. After he left, the furniture had been sold, and the apartment had become an office. It was now the Glogau station of the SD, the *Sicherheitsdienst,* the intelligence service of the SS, originally part of the security section of the early National Socialist party, now grown up to stand beside the *Abwehr,* the military intelligence section of the General Staff. The Nazi party, having come to power in 1933, required a service more responsive to its particular political objectives, so the SD became an official department, concerning itself with foreign counterintelligence, while its brother Gestapo functioned as the state security police. The Glogau office, an outstation of the SD Breslau office, worked against Poland and was staffed by two secretaries, two filing clerks, three lieutenants, and a supervisor, an SS Sturmbannführer — major — named August Voss, known by his underlings as Frogface.

Why? What was so froglike about him? Really, not that much. He did have pouchy cheeks and slightly bulging eyes, which stared out at the world from behind thick eyeglasses, but there was more, a certain predatory fury in the set of his mouth, as though he were eager to snap up a bug but could find no bugs in the water that flowed past his rock. Well, he found one every now and again, but never enough and, if he didn't find more, he'd remain on this Glogau rock forever. In his youth, as an economics instructor in Dresden, he'd joined the ambitious young lawyers, engineers, and journalists in the fledgling Nazi party, which was determined, after a lost war, to raise the nation to supremacy in Europe. They joined the SS, the Black Order, pledged to secrecy, pledged to obedience, and to whatever violence and terror might be required to bring them to power. And, in time, it did.

For August Voss, that meant a position in the SD and, on a wet October morning in Glogau, news of a potential bug. His office door stood open, but his senior lieutenant, making sure of the knot in his sober tie — the SD, a secret organization, wore civilian clothing — knocked politely on the jamb.

"Yes?" Voss said. Born angry, August Voss, even a single word from his mouth threatened consequence.

"We are in receipt, sir, of a report from the Glogau police."

"Which says?"

The lieutenant glanced over the form,

making very sure he got it right. "Which says, that a woman from Glogau has observed suspicious behavior by a German citizen. On the Warsaw/Glogau Express."

"What did he do?"

"Acted in a suspicious manner, not described, and possibly evaded the passport *kontrol* at Glogau station."

Voss extended a hand and snapped his fingers. He read over the form and said, "It doesn't say how. Just that one minute he was on the line, and the next he disappeared."

"Yes, sir."

Voss read it again. The lieutenant stood silent. In the quiet office, with only the clacking of typewriters and the hiss of the steam radiators, the sound of Voss drumming his fingers on the metal desktop was sharp and loud. "Mm," he said. "The Gestapo has this?"

"No, sir. Only us."

"Why?"

"Because the police supervisor is persuaded that, for him, it's better so."

From Voss, a faint tightening at the corners of the mouth, which the people around him had learned to understand as a smile. "Very good." He paused, placed the report flat on his desk, and read it yet again. *Perhaps next he will roll around on it,* the lieutenant thought. "Let him know," Voss said, "that we appreciate his good sense."

"I will, sir."

"And get her in here, this Frau Schimmel. She knows more than what's written in this report."

"Yes, sir. This afternoon, sir?"

"Now."

"Yes, sir. A bulletin to the Glogau *kontrol* office?"

"No, not yet."

"Yes, sir."

"Dismissed, lieutenant."

"Thank you, sir."

The two lieutenants did not leave immediately; they first checked the registries — suspected communists, socialists, homosexuals, free-masons, and persons of interest — to make certain that Frau Schimmel's name did not appear there. Then they drove to the shabbier part of Glogau: sad old three-story tenements from the last century.

Frau Schimmel, when she heard the knock on the door, an official knock, was in house-dress and hairnet. A widow with grown children, she preserved her good dress by leaving it in the closet until it was time to go outside. She'd been in the midst of preparing breakfast for her dachshund — meat scraps, a dab of precious lard to improve the shine on the dog's coat — when she heard the knock. She dropped what she was doing and hurried from the kitchen, her heart beating hard. It beat harder still when she opened the door, to reveal two young men in hats and coats, because they looked exactly like what they were. "Yes?"

"Frau Berta Schimmel?"

"Yes, sir."

"Your identity papers, Frau Schimmel."

She went to her purse and, hands trembling, retrieved the card.

The lieutenant handed it back to her and said, "We are from the security services, Frau Schimmel, you will please accompany us to our office."

She now suspected this had to do with the report she'd made to the police, the police in the person of a fat, paternal sergeant at the Glogau police station, a report she'd been forced to make. Innocently enough, she'd mentioned the man on the train to a neighbor, who had first suggested, then insisted, in a delicately threatening way, that she inform the authorities. Well, now see what that had brought down on her head. The dog, at her ankles, whined for her breakfast. "Later, Schatzi," she said. "Be good, now." She knew these men were not going to stand there while she fed a dog. She threw her coat over her housedress and pulled the net off her hair — she looked frightful, she thought, but when men like these came to the door, one did what one was told.

A new Glogau, for Frau Schimmel, who'd lived there all her life, the wet streets seen from the backseat of a Grosser Mercedes automobile. She had to resist the urge to make conversation, wanting to persuade them that she was a good, decent citizen who obeyed every law, but she knew to keep her mouth shut. A few minutes later, the car rolled to a stop in front of the toy shop on Heimerstrasse. Then she was taken up to the second floor.

In the office, she perched on a chair by a secretary's desk, and there she waited. The secretary was the youngest daughter of a local seamstress, and Frau Schimmel, occasionally employed for needlework when the woman had too much to do, had met her more than once, but neither woman acknowledged the other. At last, she was led into another office, where one of the men who had arrested her — so she thought of it — sat behind a bare desk. He was almost immediately joined by a second man, a frightening man with heavy glasses, who drew a chair to a position just to one side and behind her, so that she couldn't quite see him.

Questions, and more questions. She did her best to answer, her voice breathless with anxiety. "Speak up, Frau Schimmel," said the man sitting behind her. First of all, who was she? Who had her husband been, what work had he done, and her children: where were they, what did they do? How long had she lived at her present address? And, before that, where? And before that? Next, what had she been doing in Warsaw? A visit to her sister, married to a German Pole, who she saw twice a year, the only times she traveled anywhere — her pension did not permit her more than that, and her sister helped with the money. So then, her Polish brother-in-law, what did he do? On and on it went.

Finally, after forty-five minutes, they took her through the train trip from Warsaw: the man who'd sat across from her, pale and fidgety. How he stood quickly and left the compartment, then how he'd tried to leave the train before the passport *kontrol* in Poland. There was something in his manner that made her uncomfortable; he was frightened, she thought, as though he had something to hide: looking around, watching the other passengers. Then, at Glogau station, she'd seen him join the line that led to the passport *kontrol,* and then, when she was almost at the desk, she turned around and couldn't see him anywhere, he'd vanished. A day later, she'd informed the authorities at the police station.

If she'd expected them to be grateful, she was sadly disappointed. The man at the desk had no reaction whatsoever, and the man she couldn't see was silent.

"Now tell us, Frau Schimmel, what did he look like, this nervous man on the Warsaw/Glogau Express?" She did her best — a rather ordinary man, she told them, his height and weight not unusual. They'd spoken briefly, she'd offered him a candy, and he'd declined politely, his German very much the local Silesian variety that everybody spoke. He had thinning hair, combed carefully over his head, a dark mustache, rather full, and a bulbous nose divided at the end. No, he wasn't poor, and not rich either, from the way he dressed, perhaps a teacher, or a businessman. Next they took her back over it again, not once but twice, her interrogator rephrasing the questions, but the man on the train was the same. They might, he said, bring her in again, and, should she recall further details, it was her duty to get in touch with them; did she understand that? She did.

Finally, they let her go. She had a few

groschen in her pocket, enough to take a tram back to her neighborhood. Safely home, she gave the dog her food, went to the kitchen cupboard, took down a bottle of potato schnapps, poured herself a little in a water glass, then a little more. Exhausted, she fell back on the couch, the dog clambering up to sit beside her — it had been a bad morning for both of them. "Poor Schatzi," she said. The dog looked up and gave a single wag of its tail. "Your mama is such a goose, little girl, she talked too much. But never again, never again." Another wag: *here I am.* "You're a good girl, Schatzi. What if I hadn't come home? What then?"

31 October. The last quarter of the waning moon, so it said on Mercier's lunar calendar. It was just after eight in the morning, at the apartment on Ujazdowska, and very lively. Marek had arrived an hour earlier and was now reading his morning paper and chattering with Wlada and the silent cook. Mostly they ignored him, busy making sandwiches — ham and butter on thick slabs of fresh white bread from the bakery — boiling eggs until they were hard, baking a small egg-and-butter cake with raisins, all of it to be wrapped in brown paper and packed into a wicker basket, with six bottles of dark beer

110

and a thermos of coffee.

Mercier was in the study, cleaning and oiling his service sidearm — a Le Français 9-millimeter Browning automatic, in looks not unlike the German Luger. When he was done, he loaded it carefully, then put the box of bullets in one pocket of his waxed Barbour field jacket and the pistol in the other. Did the flashlight work? Mercier switched it on, ran the beam up a silk drape, and decided to change the batteries. Next he retrieved a pair of lace-up boots from the dressing room, pulled them on over heavy wool socks, and laced them up tight. They felt good on his feet. He liked wearing them, and liked the Barbour as well, though he now wore such things rarely, since he no longer went hunting. He was invited now and then, to go after *rogacz,* the great stag of the Polish mountain forest, but always he declined, since he no longer wished to shoot anything.

He was also, but for a certain familiar tightness in the pit of the stomach, glad to get away from the city. He'd been busy, filing dispatches, writing reports, making contact with two of Bruner's . . . well, one had to call them *agents,* both of whom worked in the armament industries. He learned all he needed to know from Vyborg and others,

111

who were glad to keep him current. But it was traditional to talk to knowledgeable informants, and he suspected that Vyborg and the *Dwojka* knew exactly what he was doing and didn't much care, since their attachés in France no doubt operated the same way.

So, for the past week, he'd been pretty much a prisoner of the office, though one afternoon, under a weak autumn sun, he'd worked in a set of tennis out in Milanowek. The foursome had included Princess Toni, as it happened, this time as opponent, but after the match they'd found themselves a moment for conversation. Warm and amiable, as always, with not the slightest suggestion that there had been an interlude in the guest bathroom. A man of the world, a woman of the world, a brief, pleasant adventure, all memory courteously erased. "We're off to Paris next week, then Switzerland, but we'll be back in the spring." He said he envied her the Paris visit, say hello to the city for him. Of course she would.

In the study, Mercier opened his briefcase and took out a map, which he'd brought home from the office. A very technical map, in small scale, with elevations, streams, and local features, such as farmhouses, precisely rendered. With this, a military map, he had to be very careful. Produced by General

112

Staff cartographers in Paris, these maps were sent to Warsaw in the diplomatic pouch to replace those received earlier, though they rarely changed. He slid the map into an inside pocket of his jacket, put the flashlight where he wouldn't forget it, and walked into the kitchen. The cake had come out of the oven and was cooling on a rack, Marek looked up from his newspaper, laid it aside, and put on a heavy wool coat. "The Biook has a full tank, sir," he said.

"Thank you, Marek," Mercier said.

A few minutes later, with Marek carrying the wicker basket, they went downstairs, where Mercier climbed into the passenger seat of the car. He happened to glance up at the apartment and saw that Wlada was looking out the window, seeing them off. She knew where they were going, her face unsmiling and worried as she watched them drive away.

It took all day to drive the roads from Warsaw to Katowice, in Polish Silesia. Through Skierniewice, Koluszki, Radomsko, and Czestochowa, where the road ran past the monastery that held the Black Madonna, Poland's most sacred ikon. Under a gray sky, the market towns and villages seemed dark to Mercier, as did the deserted fields of the countryside. *Too much fighting,* he thought, *the whole country's a battlefield.* The land was the land, it grew in spring and died in autumn, but Mercier could not unlock it from its past. Marek, his strong, bald head thrust forward as he squinted at the road ahead of them, was silent, no doubt thinking about what he had to do that night.

This was Mercier's second visit to the Silesian border fortifications, but Marek had done it at least twice with Bruner. He drove fast when the road was smooth, swung past battered old sedans, an occasional horse-drawn cart, now and then a slow truck. Sometimes the pavement was broken, with deep potholes, and they had to move at a crawl for a long time — it was either that or stop and change tires. At noon, in the shadows of an oak forest, Marek pulled off into the weeds by the side of the road and they each had a sandwich and a bottle of beer. They slowed down at the end of the afternoon, often on dirt roads, but, by dusk, they came to the crossroads where a sign pointed east to Cracow. Marek headed southwest, under a darkening sky.

By eight in the evening they were somewhere — only Marek knew exactly where — on the northern edge of Katowice, virtually on the German frontier. The border had been redrawn here, again and again, and Poles and Germans lived side by side. A man would rise from his bed in Poland, then go into his kitchen for breakfast in Germany; the line ran through factories and down the center of villages. On the outskirts of Katowice, they drove past coal mines and iron foundries, the tall stacks pouring black smoke into the sky, the air heavy with dust and the smell of burning coal.

Marek drove north for a time, then turned onto a deeply rutted dirt road, swearing under his breath as the car rocked and bucked, and the wheels spun on mud beneath puddled water. The lights of Katowice fell away behind them, and the road was closed in by tall reeds. The Buick worked its way up a long, gentle slope, then a farmhouse, with dim lights in the windows, appeared, and Marek stopped the car. With the contented grunt of a job completed, he shifted into neutral and turned off the ignition. Two dogs came bounding toward the car, big mastiff types, barking and circling, then going silent when a man came out of the house, adjusting his suspenders over his shoulders. He said a sharp word to the dogs and they lay down, panting, on their bellies.

"You remember Jozef," Marek said.

Mercier did — Marek's relative, or maybe

his wife's. He shook hands with the man, who had a hand like a board covered with sandpaper.

"Good to see you again. Come inside."

They walked past a small pen with two sleeping pigs, then into the farmhouse, where a pair of women rose from the table, one of them adjusting an oil lamp to make the room brighter. "You'll have something to drink, gentlemen?" said the other.

"No, thanks," Marek said. "We can't stay long."

"You made good time," Jozef said. "The next patrol comes through at eleven-thirty-five."

"They're always prompt?" Mercier said.

"Like a clock," Jozef said.

"Dogs?"

"Sometimes. The last time I was out there I think they had them, but they don't bark unless they smell something."

Mercier looked at his watch. "We ought to get moving," he said.

"You'll pass Rheinhart's place, about fifteen minutes north of here. Better to swing wide around it. You understand?"

"Yes," Mercier said. "We'll be back in two hours. If we don't show up, you'll have to do something with the car."

"We'll take care of it," Jozef said.

"Just be careful," the younger woman said.

When the lights of the farmhouse disappeared behind a hill, the night was almost completely black, a thin slice of waning moon visible now and then between shifting cloud. A sharp wind blew steadily from the west and Mercier was cold for a time, but it was marshy ground here and hard going, so soon enough the effort warmed him up. He kept the flashlight off — the German border patrol wasn't due for some time, but you could never be sure. To Mercier, the night felt abandoned, cut off from the world, in deep silence but for the sigh of the wind and, once, the cry of a night-hunting bird.

They kept their distance from the Rheinhart farm, a German farm, then climbed a steep hill that led to the Polish wire. Mercier had been shown the Polish defenses from the other side, an official visit with an army captain as his guide. Not very deep: three lines of barbed wire — tangled eight-foot widths of it — a few camouflaged casemates, concrete pillboxes with firing slits. Death traps, he well knew, designed to hold up an enemy for a few precious minutes. Where the Polish wire ended at the hillside, they climbed to the other side, bearing left, onto German soil.

Mercier tapped Marek on the arm, Marek held his coat open, and Mercier used the cover to run the flashlight beam over his map, refreshing the memory work he'd done early that morning. The first German wire was two hundred yards or so to the west, and they headed directly for it. They slowed down, now, feeling their way, stopping every few minutes to freeze and concentrate on listening. Only the wind. Once, as they resumed walking, Marek thought he heard something and signaled for Mercier to stop. Mercier reached into his pocket, feeling for the grip of his pistol. And Marek, he saw, did the same thing. Voices? Footsteps? No, silence, then a grumble of distant thunder far to the east. After a minute they moved again, and found themselves at the German wire, a snarled mass of barbed concertina rolls fixed to rusted iron stakes driven into the earth. Mercier and Marek, using heavy wire cutters, worked their way through it, gingerly holding the strands apart for each other until they were on the other side. Thirty yards forward, a second line, which they negotiated as they had the first.

A few yards beyond the wire, Mercier stumbled — the ground suddenly sank beneath him and he almost fell, catching himself with one hand on the earth. Soft, loose soil. What the hell was this? By his side, Marek was probing at the ground with his foot and Mercier, resisting the urge to use the flashlight, got down on his knees and began feeling around in the dirt, then digging with a cupped hand. Crawling ahead, he dug again and this time, down a foot or so in the loose soil, his hand encountered a rough edge of concrete, aggregate; he could feel the pebbles in the hard cement. As he dug further, Marek came crawling up beside him and whispered by his ear, "What is it?"

Dragon's tooth, but Mercier couldn't say it in Polish. "Tank trap," he said.

"Covered over?"

"Yes, abandoned."

"Why?"

Mercier shook his head; no reason — or, rather, too many reasons.

They crawled forward, their knees sinking into the soft earth, until they reached solid ground, which made the tank trap much as all the others Mercier had encountered: a ditch with steep sides about twenty feet wide, with a row of sloped concrete bollards midway across. If a tank commander didn't see it, his tank would slip over the edge, tilted forward against the so-called dragon's teeth, unable to move. Not an unexpected feature in border fortifications, but the Germans had built this, then filled it in, the disturbed soil settling with rain and time.

And Mercier knew it was not on the map, which showed a third line of wire. This they found a few minutes later and cut their way through it. Just barely visible, about fifty yards ahead of them, was a watchtower, a silhouette faint against the night sky. Suddenly, from somewhere to the right of the tower, a light went on, its beam probing the darkness, sweeping past them, then returning. By then, they were both flat on the ground. From the direction of the light, a shout: *"Halt!"* Then, in German, "Stand up!"

Mercier and Marek looked at each other. In Marek's hands, a Radom automatic, aimed toward the voice, and the light, which now went out. *Stand up?* Mercier thought. *Surrender? A sheepish admission of who they were? Phone calls to the French embassy in Berlin?* As Marek watched, Mercier drew the pistol from his pocket and braced it in the crook of his elbow. The light went on again, moving as its bearer came toward them. It was Marek who fired first, but Mercier was only an instant behind him, aiming at the light, the pistol bucking twice in his hand. Then he rolled — fast — away from Marek, away from the location of the shots. Out in the darkness, the light went off, a voice said,

"*Ach,*" then swore, and a responding volley snapped the air above his head. Something stung the side of his face, and, when he tried to aim again, the afterimages of the muzzle flares, orange lights, floated before his eyes. He ran a hand over the skin below his temple and peered at it; no blood, just dirt.

Silence. Mercier counted sixty seconds, seventy, ninety. The light came back on, only for a second or two, aimed not at them but at the ground beneath it, then went off. Mercier thought he heard whispers, and the faint sounds of people moving about. Was it possible they were going to get away with this? Very cautiously, he began to slide backward and Marek, when he saw what Mercier was doing, did the same thing. Again they waited, three minutes, four. Then Mercier signaled to Marek: *move again.* Another ten yards, and they stopped once more.

One last minute, then they rose to their feet and, crouched over, went running back to Poland.

Mercier had planned to spend the night at a hotel in Katowice but never gave it a second thought. When they reached the farm, they climbed into the Buick and drove at speed, bumping and bouncing over the rutted surface, turning the lights on only when they reached the main road. Once they left Katowice and were back in the countryside, Marek said, "A close thing."

"Yes. We were lucky, I think."

"I wasn't going to let them take me, colonel."

Mercier nodded. He knew that Marek had been captured by the Russians when he'd fought in the Polish Legion, under Pilsudski. Ten hours only, but Marek never forgot what they did to him.

"There is one thing I want to ask you," Marek said. "Why did they cover up their tank trap?"

"Maybe they changed their minds. Maybe it wasn't where they wanted it. Maybe there's another one a few hundred yards north, who can say, but that's the likely explanation. Or, if you wanted to think another way, an army that's going to attack, with a tank force, will get rid of the static defenses between them and the enemy border. Because, then, they're in the way." Mercier's technical description barely suggested what he feared. This was nothing less than preparation for war; a classic, telltale sign of planned aggression. The journalists could wring their hands from morning edition to night — War is coming! War is coming! — but what he'd found in the darkness wasn't opinion, it was an abandoned tank trap, defense put aside, and what came next was offense, attack, houses burning in the night.

Marek didn't want to believe it. After a moment he said, "They are coming this way, colonel, that is what you think, isn't it. German tanks, moving onto Polish soil."

"God knows, I don't. Sometimes governments prepare to act, then change their minds. The wire was still up."

"You'll report it, colonel?"

"Yes, Marek, that's what I do."

They drove all night long, Mercier taking a turn at the wheel for a few hours. East of Koluszki, Marek driving again, a tire blew out and they had to stop and change it, the iron wrench freezing their hands. The sky was turning light as they drove into Warsaw, and when Mercier let himself into the apartment, Wlada heard him walking around and, frightened of a possible intruder, called out, "Colonel?"

"Yes, Wlada, it's me."

She opened the door of her room off the kitchen. "You are home early," she said. "Thank God."

"Yes," he said. "I am. Go back to sleep."

He left his automatic pistol on the desk, now it would have to be cleaned again. Then, as he took off his field clothing, he thought about the letter in the drawer of his desk at the embassy, a letter requesting transfer. That would have to be torn up.

The abandoned tank trap had worked on him — it wasn't much, as evidence, would mean nothing to the lords of the General Staff, but it had hit him a certain way and he could not let go of it. Then too, he thought, settling the Barbour on its hanger, he might, if he stayed in Warsaw, see Anna Szarbek again. See her alone, somewhere. An afternoon together. Surely he wanted to, maybe she did too.

From the other side of the apartment, Wlada called out to him. "Good night, colonel."

Yes, dear Wlada, I am home and safe. "Good night, Wlada. Sleep well."

ON RAVEN HILL

7 November, 1937. The Polish Foreign Ministry, housed in an elegant building on Saxon Square, held its autumn cocktail party in the ministry library, removing the long polished tables, setting up a bar — Polish vodka, French champagne, a tribute to the eternal alliance — in front of the tall draped window at the end of the room. A magnificent library. Ancient texts in leather-bound rows to the ceiling, some of the works, in medieval Latin, on the national specialties, mathematics and astronomy — Copernicus was there, among others — at which their scholars had traditionally excelled. Always a crowd at this party, the library's imposing gloom inducing serious, sometimes elevated, conversation between the guests. And the fresh herring in cream was exceptional. So transcendently good one might be mindful of the country's right of access to the Baltic, up at Danzig.

The French contingent gathered at the embassy and departed in a phalanx of Buicks, led by the ambassador and his wife, followed by LeBeau, the chargé d'affaires, then Jourdain, joining Mercier in his car, with a splendid Marek in his most sober and official blue suit. Last in line, the naval and air attachés.

In the library, a glittering crowd: medals galore, the uniforms of at least eight armies and six navies. Mercier studied the faces of the women in the room, more than one of them finding such attention not unwelcome, but Anna Szarbek was nowhere to be found. The Biddles were there — he the American ambassador, the couple highly visible at the heights of the Warsovian social set — as well as the formidable Hungarian, Colonel de Vezenyi, doyen of the city's military attachés, accompanied by his mistress, the stunning Polish film star known as Karenka. Mercier spent a few minutes with them, de Vezenyi infamous for his insight into the private lives of the diplomatic community. "And he was, I'm told, in the closet for two hours, trembling in his underwear."

Mercier next found himself in the company of the Rozens, Viktor and Malka, the former a minor bureaucrat in the commercial section of the Soviet embassy. Communists were rare in Poland; the internal security was famously relentless in hunting them down, so no workers' marches, no petitions crying out for justice in wherever it was that week. For a view of the world from that particular angle, Mercier had to chat with the Rozens, or other available comrades, whenever chance offered the opportunity. But he didn't mind; he liked the Rozens.

How not? They were almost unbearably charming. Viktor Rozen, half stooped from some childhood malady in Odessa, looked up at his fellow humans, giving the fools among them the impression that they were somehow above him. His wife was irresistibly warm and maternal, with a smile that lingered just at the edge of a laugh. What a pair! At these affairs, always side by side — he with a monk's fringe of gray hair, she much the taller and heavier of the two — twinkly-eyed Jewish intellectuals, always eager to hear about your life. GRU, people said, the Russian military intelligence service, not the thuggish NKVD, not the gentle Rozens. Was Malka Rozen the chief spy of the family, or was that Viktor? Among local diplomats, opinion was divided.

"Tell me, dear colonel, how has life been treating you?" Viktor Rozen said, his German softened by a Yiddish lilt.

"Very well, thank you. And yourselves?"

"Could be better, but I can't complain. But we were having a little dispute just now, Malka and I."

"You?"

Malka's smile grew broader. "Only a little one."

"Perhaps you can decide it for us. We were wondering whatever became of von Sosnowski."

"In prison in Germany, I believe," Mercier said. Von Sosnowski, the center of what became known as "the von Sosnowski affair," a handsome aristocratic Polish cavalry officer living in Berlin, had recruited four or five beautiful German women, all of noble heritage. First as mistresses, stupefied with love for him, and then as agents, to spy on their employer, the German General Staff, where they, impoverished by the Great War, served as clerks.

"He was," Viktor said. "He surely was in prison, for life, poor soul, but I've heard he's been let out."

"Of a German prison?" Malka said. "Never."

"But a little bird told me he'd been traded, for a German woman spying on the Poles, at the behest of the SD people — Heydrich, that crowd."

Slowly, Mercier shook his head. "No, not that I've heard, anyhow."

"You see?" Rozen said to Malka. "The colonel is a great friend of the local administration, surely they would have mentioned it. Too good not to mention, no?"

"They don't tell me all that much, Herr Rozen." The seeming ingenuousness of the probe made Mercier smile.

"No? So maybe they don't. But I heard von Sosnowski was here in Warsaw, a broken man, his hair gone white in prison, drinking, living in penury in a room somewhere."

Mercier, about to respond, was distracted by a loud guffaw from a nearby guest and looked over Malka's shoulder to discover the man at Anna Szarbek's apartment, Maxim, in conversation with a gentleman wearing a monocle and an official sash. At Maxim's side, Anna Szarbek, dressed pretty much as she'd been for the night at the Europejski, looking up at Maxim, acknowledging his joke with a smile. A rather tolerant smile, Mercier thought; or was it, perhaps, a *forced* smile?

The Rozens followed his eyes. "Friends of yours?" Viktor said.

"No, not really."

"That's Maxim Mostov," Viktor said, "the Russian émigré. He writes for one of the local newspapers." A shadow crossed his face. "So sad, how some people abandon us, some of the brightest." He shook his head in sorrow.

"How does he come to be here?" Mercier said.

"Oh, he knows everybody, goes everywhere," Viktor said. "People love to see their names in the newspapers."

"He writes gossip?"

"No, dear colonel, not quite. Feuilletons, observations on the passing scene, an elevated form of gossip, perhaps. In the Soviet Union, before he emigrated, he did much the same thing, I believe."

"So why leave?" Malka said. "He was a well-known journalist, in Moscow."

"Not everybody wants to build socialism, my love," Viktor said, half joking. Turning to Mercier, he said, "He was replaced, they're all replaced, those who abandon us. It isn't an easy life, where we come from: chaotic, dreadful in winter, at times disappointing — why not admit it? But, colonel, better than what we had before. Do you see it that way?"

"More or less," Mercier said. "Every country has its difficult side."

"So true, that's so true," Malka Rozen said, touching Mercier's arm. "And we all must help each other, otherwise . . ."

"Oh, I suppose we can go it alone," Viktor said, "if we have to, but friends are always welcome. That's just human nature."

"Very welcome," Malka said. "It's in the Russian soul to appreciate friendship."

That's enough of that. Mercier finished his vodka. "I believe I may have a little more of this," he said, preparing his escape.

Viktor nodded. *Yes, yes, run away.* "Call us sometime, dear colonel. A home-cooked dinner makes for a nice change, in the diplomatic merry-go-round." He moved closer to Mercier and lowered his voice. "We know what the world thinks of us, colonel, but, every now and then, when trouble comes knocking at the door, we're good people to know. Yes?"

Mercier smiled, and bowed his head to indicate that he understood.

In the Buick, headed back to the embassy, Jourdain seemed distracted, not his usual self. "Did you have the vodka," Mercier said, "or the champagne?"

"Champagne. But I just held the glass in my hand. You?"

"The vodka. Maybe a little more than I should've."

"I saw you conspiring with the Rozens.

Did they make advances? Try to recruit you?"

"Yes, as always."

"They're incorrigible," Jourdain said fondly. "I expect they have a monthly quota, like everyone else in that accursed country. That's the way Moscow thinks — x number of solicitations equals y number of recruits. I know bachelors who swear by it."

"I don't think I'll change sides, Armand, not just yet."

"Were they after anything in particular?"

"They asked about von Sosnowski. Supposedly traded by the Germans and now back in Warsaw."

"That's good to know about, if it's true. The German propaganda put his story about as lurid nonsense, sex and espionage, but that's not the whole story. Sosnowski used the darkroom in the cellar of the Polish embassy to develop negatives of photographs of *Wehrmacht* documents. Then one day another Polish agent, this one secretly working for the Germans, went to hang up *his* negatives — phony product — and discovered the real thing: elements of the German battle plans for France and Poland. Not comprehensive — memoranda, first drafts, sketches. One of Sosnowski's girlfriends was in charge of burning the wastepaper at the end of the day, but she photographed it for Sosnowski. The gorgeous Benita von something. She was beheaded, eventually, and so was her friend. Barbaric, the hooded executioner with the axe, but I suppose not much worse than the guillotine. One of the other women disappeared, probably right into the SD. As for Sosnowski, the Poles might well have traded to get him back."

"French battle plan?" Mercier said. "Did we see that?"

"I don't know; that was in 1934, before I was posted here, but we might have. Still, three years old. General Staff plans change all the time. It wouldn't be worth much now, certainly not worth annoying the Poles."

They rode in silence for a time, then Mercier said, "Is anything wrong, Armand?"

Jourdain looked at Mercier, not pleased that whatever it was showed. "I've lost one of my people," he said.

"Bad luck," Mercier said.

"Can't be helped, it does happen, but it's always a shock. He went to work one morning, then, pfft, gone."

"In Germany?"

"Here." Jourdain flicked his eyes toward Marek's back — he was trusted, but not *that* trusted.

"Anything I can do, you'll let me know."

135

"I'll have to write a dispatch. Paris will be irritated — how much I'm not sure, but they won't like it."

"Well, that makes two of us."

"Your little foray in the west? Shooting at German border guards?"

"Bruner was incensed."

Jourdain laughed. "Nothing quite so safe and warm as an office in Paris."

"Yes, a lovely fall afternoon, a window looking out on the Champ-de-Mars. '*Merde*, look what Mercier's done!'" He smiled and spread his hands; life was hopeless. "To hell with them, Armand."

Jourdain's face showed agreement. "I just feel bad about it. He was a decent fellow, the real reptiles always seem to survive."

14 November, 8:22 A.M. In Glogau, in the SD office above the toy shop on Heimerstrasse, one of the secretaries in Major Voss's office answered the telephone, then passed the call immediately to Voss.

"Yes?"

The voice identified itself as an SS sergeant stationed at the passport *kontrol* at the Glogau railway station. "We have made a possible identification, sir, of your person of interest."

"Better than the one last week? This is

136

turning into a comedy."

"We hope so, Herr Sturmbannführer. The subject's passport is issued to one Edvard Uhl, U — H — L. He left on the eight-fourteen express to Warsaw, and he fits the description provided by your office."

"So did the last three, sergeant."

"We regret the errors, Herr Sturmbannführer."

"Very well, let's hope you're right, this time."

Voss hung up. He shouted to one of his lieutenants; the man came running into his office. "We have *another* one — half the men in Germany have bulbous noses. The name this time is Edvard Uhl, find out immediately who he is, but first get somebody on the eight-fourteen express to Warsaw."

The lieutenant looked at his watch, panic in his eyes.

Idiot. In the mock-gentle voice a frustrated parent might use on a stupid child, Voss said, "Send a wireless telegraph message to Zoller, in Leszno, and tell him to get on the train. The Poles take their time checking passports; they won't be leaving Leszno for thirty minutes. And make very sure, lieutenant, that genius Zoller takes with him the description we've issued. Would you do that for me, lieutenant? I would so, appreciate, it, if, you . . . *would!*" Voss resumed his normal growl. "And as for information on this man" — Voss looked at his watch — "you have twenty minutes."

The lieutenant, palms sweating, ran out of the office. *"Bar-gumf,"* he said, under his breath, the German version of a frog's croak.

He was back in eighteen minutes, having bullied clerks —Voss could hear him shouting on the phone — in government bureaux from Glogau to Berlin. The major looked up from a railway timetable spread across his desk.

"Herr Edvard Uhl is a resident of Breslau," the lieutenant said. "I have the address. He is employed by Adler Ironworks in the same city, where he is the senior engineer on a tank design project for the Krupp company. According to his employer, he is this morning at the office of a subcontractor in Gleiwitz."

"And the photograph?"

"On the way, Herr Sturmbannführer, by motorcycle courier from Breslau."

"Get that woman in here, immediately. Anything else?"

"Herr Uhl has received an exit visa, to visit South Africa. For himself only, not his family."

Voss nodded, and rubbed his hands. "A

scenic country, lieutenant. But he'll never see it."

15 November, 5:45 A.M. Standing amid a silent crowd of factory workers, Mercier rode the trolley to Praga for his meeting with the engineer Uhl. It was snowing, not the massive snowfall of the Polish winter, but a taste of the future — big, lazy flakes drifting through the gray light, the street white in some places, wet and shiny in others. Would Uhl show up for the meeting? Maybe not. He'd wobbled badly, the last time out. So, probably not. Mercier put it to himself as a bet and decided he'd bet *no*. And then? Then nothing. Uhl would never be betrayed to the Germans, not by him, not by anyone. Because if Uhl was compromised, all he'd given them would be compromised as well, not that the Germans could do much about it. Change the tank design? The other possibility, that Uhl might have been arrested, was, to Mercier's thinking, unlikely. He'd sent the promised postal card — Hans was enjoying his visit to Warsaw, which meant all was well in Germany.

Mercier stepped off the trolley car at the third stop in Praga, walked past the burnt-sugar smell of the candy factory, and down the narrow alley to the nameless bar. Particularly nameless that morning; the lone drinkers lost in their shot glasses, the bartender bored with the morning paper, one office worker in a shabby suit, untasted coffee going cold in his cup. And, bet lost, Edvard Uhl, sitting at a table in the far corner.

After they'd greeted one another, Mercier said, "And the train ride yesterday, Herr Uhl, how was it? Packed with Gestapo men?"

"All was normal," Uhl said. "From Gleiwitz to Glogau, only a few passengers. Then, on the express to Warsaw, a crowd, but nothing out of the ordinary, just the usual people looking into the compartment to see if there were any seats."

Mercier nodded: *there, that's better.* "So now, to work, Herr Uhl."

Uhl had brought the formula for the case-hardened steel to be used for the new tank bodies, as Mercier had requested. "It's in here," Uhl said, gesturing toward his newspaper. "I had to copy it by hand, the roneo machine was in use all morning." Otherwise, not much new in Breslau: design work on the *Ausf B* version of the *Panzerkampfwagen 1* continued, none of the specifications had changed, the final engineering blueprints would soon be completed.

"Our next meeting will be the fourteenth

of December," Mercier said, feeling for the envelope of zloty in the pocket of his battered overcoat. "I will look forward to copies of the blueprints."

"The fourteenth?" Uhl said.

Here we go again.

"Not the fourteenth, I'm afraid," Uhl said. "I cannot come to Warsaw until the night of the seventeenth."

"Why not the fourteenth?"

"I must go to Schramberg, on business."

"Schramberg?"

"In the Black Forest. There are three of us going, from the ironworks, all engineers. We are to observe tank exercises; then we will be asked for opinions and recommendations. There will be a dinner that night, at the inn in Schramberg, with *Wehrmacht* officials, technical people, and we leave the following morning, the fifteenth. So, you see I cannot come to Warsaw until the night of the seventeenth, and we can meet the following morning."

"Where is there terrain for tanks, Herr Uhl, in the Black Forest?" To Mercier, it sounded like a *story* — this little sneak of a man was up to something. What?

"I don't know where, exactly, but I was told the maneuvers will take place in the forest."

"Tanks don't go in forests, Herr Uhl. There are *trees* in the forest, tanks can't get through."

"Yes, so I thought. Perhaps they wish to have us suggest modifications that might make it possible. The fact is, I don't know what they're doing, but, in any case, I've been ordered to attend, so I must."

Surely you must. "You'll write us a report, Herr Uhl, about the exercises. Be thorough, please: formations, speeds, angles of ascent and descent, how long it takes to go a certain distance. And, also, the names of the *Wehrmacht* officials. Do you need to make a note to yourself?"

Uhl shook his head. "I know what you want."

"Then we'll meet again on the morning of the eighteenth."

Uhl agreed, though Mercier sensed a growing reluctance, as though the day would come, soon enough, when these meetings would end. He slid the envelope into his newspaper and received the steel formula in return. Uhl signed the receipt, then left the bar.

Mercier lit a Mewa, his mind working on what Uhl had told him. Just precisely what forest were the Germans thinking about? The mountains on the border with Czecho-

142

slovakia, the Sudetenland region? There was no forest on the frontier between Germany and Denmark, as far as he knew. And the Polish steppe had virtually been made for tank formations. Where else? The forests between Germany and France? Under the artillery of the Maginot Line forts? Suicide. Austria? Hitler might attack Austria, but it would be a political, not a military, invasion.

That left what? That left the Ardennes, in Belgium, north of the Maginot Line. No. For a thousand reasons, a very remote possibility. But, he thought, *somewhere.*

Mercier finished his coffee, bad as it was. The bar felt oppressive; he disliked waiting for Uhl to leave the area and kept glancing at his watch. Finally, twenty minutes — well, almost. The doctrine on agent meetings said *last to arrive, first to leave,* but Mercier did it his own way, and, to date, nothing had gone wrong.

Out in the street, he hurried through the floating snowflakes, heading toward the tram stop. He was anxious to return to the apartment, to change out of his disguise, this old coat and hat, and be off to the embassy, where he could look at his maps. He peered ahead, to make sure he didn't catch up to Uhl, though anyone dawdling in this weather seemed unlikely, and Uhl had to get his train back to Breslau. Did he use the same tram stop? Mercier couldn't decide; the alley lay almost midway between two stops. As he neared the corner where he took the trolley, he heard its bell ringing behind him and broke into as much of a run as he could manage. In the event, the motorman saw him loping along and waited, and Mercier thanked him as he climbed aboard.

He started to move through the standing crowd toward the rear platform, then stopped dead. Uhl! At the center of the car. Well, they would just have to ignore each other. Evidently, Uhl had gone to the other stop, and the trolley was running late. Mercier found room on the opposite side of the aisle and stared out the grimy window, then chanced one fast look at Uhl. What was this? He wasn't alone. Holding the back of a wicker seat with one hand, briefcase under his arm, he was engaged in animated conversation with — who? An angel. That was the word that sprang into his head. Because she stood on Uhl's left and was turned toward him, Mercier could see her face, could see that she was very young, barely twenty, and, even in a city of striking blond women, extraordinary — innocent as a child, the rabbit-fur collar of her coat turned up, her long flaxen hair set off by a knit cap, sky blue, with a tassel. Standing close to Uhl, face upturned, she was rapt, transfixed by what he was saying, laughing, gloved hand over her mouth, then giving her hair a seductive shake. Had this just begun? On the trolley? Mercier guessed not — it had started at the tram stop. Again she laughed, leaning toward Uhl, almost, but not quite, touching him. Was she a prostitute? No sign of that, to Mercier's eyes. Or, if she was, an extremely rare version of the breed, not the sort who would pick up a man at a tram stop at six-thirty on a snowy morning.

Immediately, Mercier sensed that something was wrong. He forced himself to look away, at a row of brick factories sliding past the window, until the trolley slowed for the next stop. Then he stole another glance. If they got off together, what would he do?

But they stayed on the tram. Which rolled over the bridge that crossed the Vistula, the snow swirling in the wind above the dark river. Now it was her turn to talk, her face concentrated, wanting the man she'd met, older, experienced, to take her seriously. Was she speaking Polish? Did Uhl speak the language? Breslau had forever been a disputed city — Wroclaw, as far as the Poles were concerned — and it was possible that Uhl spoke some Polish. A woman standing next to Mercier — he could smell the damp wool of her coat — caught him staring and gave him a look: *mind your own business.* He turned back to the window. The trolley was now approaching his stop, in central Warsaw, and, as the motorman pulled on the cord that rang the bell, Mercier glanced up the aisle and saw that Uhl and the blond girl were moving toward the rear platform.

Mercier left by the front door, circled the tram — thus shielded from Uhl and the girl — headed quickly for the shops across the street, and chose one with a set-back entry. *Like some sly private detective,* he thought, *lurking in a doorway.* A fancy perfume shop, as it happened, great clouds of scent rolling out each time the door opened. When the trolley pulled away, he spotted the blue cap in the crowd waiting to transfer to another line. Where the hell were they going? Not to the Europejski. A taxi drove up to the front of the shop, a pair of women in the back, and Mercier arrived in time to hold the door as they emerged. "Oh, why thank you," the first one said. Mercier mumbled "You're welcome" and slid into the seat.

"Sir?" the driver said. He was in his twenties, with a well-oiled pompadour.

"Don't go anywhere, not just yet," Mercier said. "Some friends of mine are waiting for a trolley; we'll just follow along behind."

"Friends?" A wise-guy grin, *who are you kidding?*

"Yes, it's a surprise."

The driver snickered. Mercier peeled twenty zloty off the wad in his pocket — for agent meetings, one carried plenty of money. The driver thanked him, and they waited together, the ill-tuned engine coughing away in neutral.

Waited for ten very long minutes. At last, a trolley arrived and the blue cap climbed aboard, followed by Uhl. "That's the one we want," Mercier said.

As the driver put the taxi in gear and fell in behind the tram, he said, "It's the number four line. Up to Muranow."

Not bad at this, the driver, he'd evidently done it before, pulling over well to the rear of the trolley each time it stopped. The tram tracks curved into Nalewki, the main street of the Jewish quarter: kosher butchers, pushcarts piled with old clothes or pots and pans, men in caftans and fur hats, hurrying along through the snow. Mercier could see that the crowd of passengers inside the trolley had thinned out — had Uhl and the girl somehow gotten away? No, the next stop was

Gesia, Goose street, and they appeared on the rear platform as the trolley slowed. Mercier put his head down.

"That them?"

"Yes."

"Jesus, look at her."

Mercier handed over more zloty and climbed out. He found himself in front of an open stall on the cobblestones, a chicken-seller, scrawny birds hung by their heads from hooks, and a smell that almost made his eyes tear. To Mercier, it now seemed that the girl was leading the way, her arm looped in Uhl's, walking quickly. Mercier hung back, close to the buildings, ready to step into a doorway if one of them turned around. Gesia was an old street — three-story buildings, some wood, others gray stone darkened by time and coal smoke — where every shop called out to potential customers: a clock hung out over the sidewalk advertised a watchmaker; a painted sign showed a pair of eyes wearing spectacles; M. PERLMUTTER — FINE GLOVES.

HOTEL ORLA.

Now Mercier knew where they were going. He dropped back well behind them as they crossed the street, past a crowd of schoolboys with curly sideburns and yarmulkes, past a horse-drawn coal wagon, the driver, wearing a long leather apron, shoveling coal down a chute that led into the hotel's cellar. The Orla — eagle — had the look of hourly rates and no questions asked; as Warsaw slang put it, *a Paris hotel.* Mercier stationed himself where he could see the entry, using the doorway of a shop with stacks of old books piled high in the window, some with Hebrew writing on their spines. After a time, the proprietor of the shop came to his door and had a look at Mercier, then nodded to himself, a faint look of disgust on his face — so here's another one, the watchers of the Hotel Orla.

It was now after nine in the morning, and Uhl, having to return to the Europejski for his valise, would miss the express to Breslau. Well, there was always another train, and Uhl, who had fallen to the charms of the Countess Sczelenska, now took advantage of a new opportunity, but that was the way of the world — Uhl's world, at any rate. An opportunity much too good to be true, Mercier thought, but maybe he was seeing the same phantoms that had spooked the engineer on his last trip to Warsaw.

The Orla was busy — a couple hurried out of the hotel, and, a minute later, another. An officious little fellow, all business, came

striding down Gesia, looked left and right —
feeling guilty, monsieur? — then went inside.
A luxurious black Opel, a German car with
Polish license plates, drew up in front of the
hotel and waited there, engine idling.
Mercier shifted his stance, stared at the
books in the window, watched the morning
shoppers go by, the women's heads covered
with shawls, string bags in hand.

Then, suddenly, the blond girl came out of
the hotel.

What now? She was very pale, and grim-
faced, as she looked around, then walked, almost ran, to a taxi parked a little way down
the street. The snow made it hard to see, but
Mercier thought there might be a silhouette
in the rear window. He couldn't be sure, because the girl was still closing the door when
the taxi took off and sped away down the
street.

Mercier tensed; now he had to go in there
and find Uhl. He was halfway across the
street when a fat man with a red face came
out of the Orla, struggling with the weight of
a parcel wrapped in a bed coverlet and flung
over his shoulder. A step at a time, he moved
toward the Opel. The driver, a sinister little
weasel of a man with tinted glasses, jumped
out and ran around the car to open the
trunk.

For an instant, Mercier didn't know what he was looking at, and then he did. He ran the last few steps and planted himself in front of the man with the parcel. "Put it down." He said it in German.

And so he was answered. "Get out of my way." The weight on the man's shoulder made him take a step to the side.

The weasel came from behind the car and, with a hand like a claw, took Mercier roughly by the elbow. "Better get out of here, my friend, this doesn't concern you."

The man with the parcel tried to brush past him, but Mercier moved to block him. From the corner of his eye, he could see that a few people had stopped to see what was going on. Suddenly enraged, the red-faced man swung his free hand at Mercier and hit him under the eye. Not very hard. Mercier was knocked backward, recovered, and punched the man in the mouth. From behind, the weasel hit him with a blackjack.

Mercier's legs collapsed and he fell to his knees. But the blackjack had been a mistake. Mercier heard a loud clang — the coalman had dropped his shovel — and now, like an avenging giant, face black with coal dust, he grabbed the red-faced man by the back of the collar. When he growled something in Polish, the weasel ran away, jumped into the car, and gunned the engine. The red-faced man broke free, tried to keep his balance, lost it, and, as he fell, the parcel slid off his shoulder and landed on the sidewalk with a soft thump. The red-faced man, now scarlet, rose to a sitting position and reached inside his jacket, but a shout from the car stopped him, and he scrambled to his feet as the coalman walked toward him. Then the passenger-side door flew open, the red-faced man got in and, with a look toward Mercier of pure and absolute hatred, slammed the door as, tires squealing, the Opel drove away.

Now the man that Mercier had seen striding down Gesia came sprinting out of the Orla, shrieked at the departing car, and chased after it. The Opel jerked to a stop, the pursuer got in the back and the car sped off, trunk lid flapping as the wheels bounced over the cobblestones.

Mercier tried to get to his feet, somebody helped him, and the coalman handed him his hat. Fearing the worst, he knelt over the parcel, discovered a strong chemical smell, and saw that the coverlet, yellow daisies on a red field, had been tied shut with two lengths of cord. He worked at the first knot as the crowd closed in around him. Somebody said, "Get a scissors." Finally, Mercier managed to undo the first knot, then the coalman, impatient, reached down and broke the second cord with his hands. As Mercier unfolded the coverlet, the chemical smell grew stronger. *Chloroform,* he thought. Something like that.

Uhl was dead. Eyes closed, mouth slack, snowflakes falling on his face. A voice in the crowd said, "Finished," and several people hurried away. Mercier put his fingers on Uhl's neck and probed for a pulse. Nothing. A woman knelt beside him and said, "Excuse me, please," gently removing Mercier's fingers and replacing them with her own. "No," she said. "It's faint, but it's there. Better get the ambulance."

"Brazen," Jourdain said. "Unbelievable. In broad daylight." They were in the chancery, in Jourdain's office; photographs of diplomats shaking hands lined the walls. "Does it hurt?"

"Yes."

"You're dripping on your collar."

Mercier held a towel filled with ice to the back of his head, which ached so badly it made him squint. "I don't care," he said.

It was Jourdain who had, after a telephone call, retrieved him from the police station, where they didn't care if he said he was the French military attaché: they had reports to fill out, he would be there for a while. Uhl was in the hospital, with a policeman standing in the hall outside his door.

Mercier sat back in the chair, closed his eyes, and pressed the towel to the alarming lump on the back of his head. "Goddamn that little bastard," he said.

There were two sharp raps on the door, which swung open to reveal the ambassador: tall, white-haired, and angry. Mercier began to rise, but the ambassador waved him back down. "Colonel Mercier," he said. Then, "Are you injured?"

"No, sir, not really, just sore."

That out of the way, the ambassador said, "Can we expect more of this, colonel? Gun battles? Brawling in the street? Yes, I know why, and you had to intervene, but still . . ."

"I apologize, sir," Mercier said. "Circumstance."

The ambassador nodded, as though that explanation meant something. "Mmm. Sorry I won't be there when you tell them that in Paris. Because you'll surely be — ah, *summoned*."

Mercier took a breath, then said nothing.

"You'll take care of that — that situation — in the hospital?"

"This afternoon, sir."

"Jourdain will help you; you don't look all

154

that well, to me."

"Count on it, sir," Jourdain said. "And please don't be concerned."

"No, you're right, I shouldn't be concerned," the ambassador said, meaning very much the opposite. "And I so look forward to the evening papers. Photographs, colonel? Will we have to look at it?"

"No, sir. The police were faster than the journalists."

The ambassador sighed. "The press attaché will do the best he can, and I've already made a few telephone calls." Stepping back into the hall, he said, "And colonel? Let it rest there. Please? I don't want to lose you."

Mercier nodded, not ungrateful, and said, "Yes, sir."

As the ambassador prepared to close the door, he met Mercier's eyes and his face changed: subtly, but enough so that Mercier understood that he was perhaps more than a little proud of his military attaché.

At dusk, back in the apartment, Mercier sent Wlada out for the evening papers and saw that the affair had been nicely smoothed over. An altercation at the Hotel Orla, an attempted abduction, foiled by a passerby. One Hermann Schmitt had been drugged by unknown assailants, political motives were suspected, the police were investigating.

Wlada, having left Mercier to his reading, now returned to the study, Mercier's battered old hat held firmly in both hands. "Colonel, I can do nothing with this, it's *ruined*," she said, extending the hat so that he could see what she meant. On the brim, the black print of the coalman's thumb.

"Please don't worry so, Wlada," Mercier said gently. "It's not ruined. Not at all."

28 November. The eight-fifteen LOT flight, Warsaw to Paris, was only a third full, and Mercier sat alone toward the rear of the airplane. Out the window, the fields of Poland were white with snow, and the plane bumped and jerked as it fought through the winds and climbed into the blue sky above the clouds.

Bruner and his superiors had, as predicted by the ambassador, recalled him to Paris for consultations, so he could look forward to a few disagreeable meetings and at least the possibility that he would be transferred from his assignment in Warsaw. On the other hand, he'd been guilty of fighting Germans, and the Poles would not be pleased if Paris pulled him back to the General Staff for doing that.

On the afternoon following the attempted abduction, he'd visited Uhl in the hospital, where he'd come to realize that the engineer was, whatever else he may have been, a lucky man. How he'd been discovered Mercier didn't know, though he had spent a long time taking Uhl through the details of his home and office life. The luck came into play because Uhl had been issued a visa for travel to South Africa. Yes, he'd planned to run away — from Breslau, from "André," from work and family. With his countess, or alone if necessary. The SD or the Gestapo, Mercier believed, had learned of the visa and, fearing his imminent flight, had determined they'd better snatch Uhl while they could still get their hands on him. Otherwise, they would simply have allowed him to return to Germany, watched him there, and arrested him at their leisure.

Somebody, most likely the officer in charge of the case, had panicked and ordered an almost spur-of-the-moment abduction by German operatives in Poland. Which had almost succeeded, then come to grief, but, even so, better than having a suspected spy vanish into thin air. Now Uhl was Mercier's problem — what to do with him? In the short term, Mercier and Jourdain had to assume the hospital was being watched and so, after three days there, Uhl left the building on a stretcher, covered by a sheet, which was slid into the back of a hearse. Then, at the funeral home, out the back door and into a rented room on the outskirts of the city. "Now," Jourdain had said, "we just have to keep him away from the ladies."

"I suspect he's learned his lesson," Mercier answered. "He'll never again meet a seductive woman without wondering."

For the long term, the problem was harder, and Mercier and Jourdain spent hours on possible solutions. Mercier was surprised to discover how much he cared, but, like all the best military officers, he felt a great depth of responsibility for those under his command, and injury to one of them, no matter his opinion of that individual, affected him far more than the civilian world would ever understand.

Given: Uhl could never go back to Germany. And he couldn't go to South Africa either; German agents would be waiting for him. Also given: the *Deuxième Bureau* of the General Staff wasn't going to provide a lifetime of support for their former spy — Uhl would have to work. Under a new identity, his life history rewritten in an office at *2, bis,* in Paris. Work where? Martinique and French Guyana were no more than brief candidates, Canada was the logical choice — Quebec, where the French General Staff had friends who could help them out, and make sure that Uhl lived a quiet, and very private, life. This project was being worked on in Paris, and Mercier expected to hear about it when he reached the city. *Ordered to go to Paris,* he thought, smiling to himself. *How life is hard!* He'd written to his cousin Albertine, so his rooms in the vast Mercier de Boutillon apartment in the Seventh Arrondissement would be made up and waiting for him. The steady drone of the engines made him sleepy; he stared out at Cloudland below him, a kingdom of children's books, and dozed off.

When he woke, they were flying over Germany: crisp little towns, then crisp little farm fields. Beneath him, the snow thinned out, then stopped, leaving the woodlands dark and bare as winter came. From his briefcase he took a popular new book, currently a bestseller in Germany, called *Achtung — Panzer!* by Colonel Heinz Guderian, commander of Germany's 2nd Panzer Division. With a French/German dictionary on his lap, Mercier went to work.

We live in a world that is ringing with the clangor of weapons. Mankind is arming on all sides, and it will go ill with a state that is unable or unwilling to rely on its own strength. Some nations are fortunate enough to be favored by nature. Their borders are strong, affording them complete or partial protection against hostile invasion, through chains of mountains or wide expanses of sea. By way of contrast, the existence of other nations is inherently insecure. Their living space is small and in all likelihood ringed by borders that are inherently open, and lie under constant threat from an accumulation of neighbors who combine an unstable temperament with armed superiority.

Well, surely he's read de Gaulle's book — and produced a similar opening paragraph. Mercier turned pages — skimmed through a history of British and French tank attacks in the latter half of the Great War — then came upon Guderian's description of the situation in the first months of 1937.

At the beginning of 1937 the French possessed . . . more than 4,500 tanks, which means that the number of tanks exceeds by a wide margin the number of artillery pieces, even in the peacetime army. No other country shows such a disproportion *between armour and artillery. Figures like these give us food for thought!*

True, Mercier thought, the numbers were known, but what to do with these machines? Ah, that was the dessert of the food for thought.

Toward the end of the book, Mercier found the tactical conclusions: the successful use of tanks depended on *surprise, deployment en masse,* and *suitable terrain.* These were, Mercier knew, precisely de Gaulle's conclusions, in his book and in successive monographs, urging the formation of tank units which he called *Brigades du Choc. Shock formations* — to break the stalemate of a static trench war. Tanks should fight together, *in numbers,* not be scattered to support companies of infantry. As for *terrain,* Mercier would have to read fully, but Guderian seemed to concentrate mostly on the subject of national road systems to bring tanks to the front, and avoidance of ground broken by shellholes — natural tank traps — or churned to liquid mud by preparatory artillery barrages. These, in the Great War, sometimes went on for days, as massed field guns fired as many as five million shells.

And forests? Not specifically mentioned, though perhaps more lay buried in the text.

And, Mercier thought, now that Uhl was lost, he would have to find some other way to observe the planned *Wehrmacht* maneuvers at Schramberg.

At five-thirty, leaving a taxi in the rue Saint-Simon, Mercier felt the Parisian mystique take hold of his heart: a sudden nameless ecstasy in the damp air — air scented by black tobacco and fried potatoes and charged with the restless melancholy of the city at the end of its day. Oh, this was home all right, he knew it in his soul — not the autumn mists of the Drôme, not his pointers running free in a field, but home nonetheless, which some part of him never left.

Here, in the depths of the Seventh Arrondissement, the residents were rich, quiet, and cold, stewards of the inner chamber. A walled city, its walls hiding formal gardens and silent monasteries, Napoleonic barracks and foreign embassies. One saw the residents only now and again: retired army officers in dark suits, women of the nobility, perfect in afternoon Chanel.

Halfway up the narrow street: 23, rue Saint-Simon. Mercier rang the bell by the familiar door — built for the height of a carriage — and the concierge, who'd known him for twenty years, let him in. He crossed the interior courtyard, ignored by the twittering sparrows, his steps on the stone block loud in the thick silence of the building, and climbed to the second floor, unlocked the door, and entered the apartment: bought in the middle of the nineteenth century by his great-grandfather, only the plumbing updated, the rest as it had always been — leaded glass windows in small panes, vast, gloomy carpets, massive armoires and chests. Not elegant, the furnishings, but sturdy. The Merciers lived on country estates, and the women of the family had always treated *the Paris apartment* as a tiresome necessity — people of their class always had to go to Paris for one reason or another, and the alternative was *hotels,* and *restaurants.* Unthinkable. Thus they'd been economical in the purchase of slipcoverings and draperies, everything dark, not to show use and meant to last. The fabrics were protected by closed shutters and heavy drapes — the sun was not allowed in here.

Mercier dropped his briefcase and valise in the bedroom and found a note from his cousin Albertine on the night table.

Dearest Jean-François,
Welcome. I am out for the afternoon but I shall return at six-thirty, and we can

go out for dinner, if you like, or I can cook something if you're too tired. Looking forward to seeing you,

Albertine.

In Mercier's past, Cousin Albertine occupied a very special niche. She was the youngest daughter of his father's favorite brother, later to die in the war, and they'd grown up as neighbors — his uncle's property a few miles away from their own — so together often: at Christmas and Easter, in summer when they were home from their respective boarding schools. Surely she'd always been the odd one out of the Mercier clan: tall, awkward, pale, serious, and curiously redheaded — auburn, really — with freckles scattered across her forehead. Where, the family wondered, had she come from? All the other Merciers were dark, like Jean-François, so, it was theorized, some ancient gene had surfaced in his cousin and made her different. The other possibility was never considered — or, rather, never spoken aloud. . . .

One Saturday morning at the end of summer, when Mercier was fourteen and Albertine sixteen, Uncle Gérard and his family had come to visit. The adults and the other children had gone off somewhere — to a livestock auction in a distant village, as Mercier remembered it — and he and Albertine were left alone in the house. The servants downstairs were preparing midday dinner; they would be twelve at table, for various other family members would be joining them.

In his room, Mercier was dressing for dinner, in underpants and his best shirt, in front of a wall mirror, working at tying his tie. First the bottom part came out absurdly short, then too long. On his third attempt, the door opened and, in the mirror, Cousin Albertine appeared. She watched him for a moment, then, with a strange look on her face, at once shy and determined, came up behind him. "Can I try it?" she said.

"I can do it," he said.

"I want to try," she said. "To see if I can."

"How do you know about ties?"

"I watch my brothers do it."

"Oh."

This was intended to mean, *oh, I see,* but came out as more of an *oh!,* because, as Albertine reached around him, her heavy breasts, in a thin summer dress, rested lightly against his back.

"Now," she said, "we cross it around and loop it through."

In the mirror, Albertine's face was dreamy,

165

her eyes half closed, mouth slightly open. Also in the mirror, the front of his underpants highly distended. For a few seconds, they stood like statues, then she whispered, "I want to see it," hooked her thumbs in the waistband of his underpants, and pulled them down.

"Alber-*tine!*"

"What?"

She reached out and closed her hand around it, her skin warm and damp. He leaned back against her, then moved away. "We're not supposed —"

"Oh foo," she said. So much for family morals. "You like it," she said firmly, and ran her finger along the underside, back and forth. "Don't you?"

He could only nod.

She pressed against him, above and below, and he reached back, hands on her bottom, and pulled her closer. She now stroked him with index finger and thumb: *where had she learned to do this?* He was very excited and, a few seconds later, came the inevitable conclusion, accompanied, from deep within him, by a sound somewhere between a sigh and a gasp.

"There," she said softly, taking her hand away.

"Well, that's what happens."

"I *know* that."

He started to move away from her, but she wrapped her arms around his shoulders and held him tight. Close to his ear, she whispered, "Now it's my turn."

"What?" His heart quaked.

She raised her dress, revealing white cotton underdrawers, and bunched it around her waist, then took his hand and placed it between her legs. He'd never touched a girl there and had no idea what was expected of him, but immediately found out, as she pressed his hand against herself and began to move it. In the mirror, he could see her face: eyes closed, lower lip held delicately between her teeth. With his free hand, he again reached around her, where, in slow rhythm, her bottom tensed, relaxed, and tensed again. After what seemed to him like a long time — he began to wonder what he was doing wrong — she exhaled hard, her breath audible, and held on to him as though she might fall down. Astonishing! It had never occurred to him that this happened to a girl; his friends at school had a completely different version of things.

He pulled up his underpants, then sat down hard on the edge of his bed. Albertine resettled her dress, then came and sat beside him, brushing her long hair off her face.

"Did you like it, Jean-François?"

"Yes, of course."

"Both things?"

"Yes, both."

She kissed him, a dry kiss on the cheek. "I think you're sweet," she said and, for a moment, rested her head on his shoulder.

This was not the only time, for the Mercier cousins; it happened once more before they went north to their schools. The following week, the cook baked grand brioches, as big as cakes, and his mother asked him to take two of them over to Uncle Gérard's. Mercier, already a cavalry officer in his daydreams, climbed on his bicycle and pedaled like a fury over the tiny dirt lanes that wound through the hills to his uncle's house. Once there, amid the usual disorder, he set the brioches down on the table in the kitchen, then waited while his aunt wrote a thank-you note. Albertine appeared, as he was retrieving his bicycle from the steps that led to the terrace, and told her mother she would ride with him part of the way back home. Halfway there, they walked their bicycles away from the lane and found a grove of cork oaks, and, this time, Albertine suggested that they take off all their clothes.

Mercier hesitated, uncertain of what lay

ahead. "I don't want you to have a baby," he said.

She laughed, brushing her hair aside. "I'm not going to do *that*. Cousins mustn't do *that,* but we can play. Playing is always allowed."

What rules she was following he did not know, but in the days after their first encounter, before he went to sleep and when he woke in the morning, he had ravished his gawky cousin in every way his imagination offered and was now more than ready for anything she might think up. And so, her skin white in the hot sun, Albertine posed prettily for him and then, at their leisure on a summer's day, as the cicadas whirred away in the high grass, they played twice.

True to her word, Albertine returned to the apartment at six-thirty. Her hair was darker now, styled short, falling just to her jawline. She wore a quiet tweed suit with big buttons, skirt well below the knee, and a fancy silk scarf from one of the fashion houses, wound around her neck and tucked into the vee of her suit jacket. With pearl earrings and fine leather gloves, she was very much an aristocrat of the Seventh. As in all their meetings over the years, he could find the Albertine he'd known that summer; she was, as he put it to himself, *still in there;* he could find her if he tried.

She made them drinks, vermouth with lemon, and showed him the latest additions to her collection — onyx cameos and intaglios on small wooden stands, filling the shelves of two glass-fronted bookcases. Some of the new ones were ancient, Greek and Roman, others from tsarist Russia and the Austro-Hungarian empire. "They are exceptional," he said, taking time to study them, appreciating what she'd achieved. Then they walked out to the boulevard and over to a busy brasserie on the rue Saint-Dominique. A compromise: she didn't want to cook, it was too early to go to a proper restaurant, and neither of them cared that much. So they ordered *omelettes* and *frites* and a bottle of Saint-Estèphe.

"It is so good to see you, Jean-François," she said, taking the first sip of her wine. "Is life going well? I expect you miss Anne-marie."

"Every day."

"And do you see anyone?"

I wish I could, he thought, Anna Szarbek's image smiling up at him on a nightclub dance floor. "No," he said. "I would like to, but it isn't easy, meeting somebody — who's available."

"Oh you will, dear," she said, looking at him fondly. "People do find each other, somehow."

"Let's hope so. And you?" Years earlier, there had been a fiancé, then another, but, after that, silence.

"Oh, I've settled into my life," she said. "How are the girls?"

"Thriving, but passionately busy. Béatrice is in Cairo, her sister, Gabrielle, in Copenhagen — I haven't seen them for a long time. At Christmas, perhaps. I might see if Gabrielle will come down to the house in Boutillon. That is, if I can get there myself."

"And Warsaw? Is that a good place to be, for you?"

He nodded. "I certainly see enough of it — hotels, restaurants, cocktail parties, receptions."

"The glamorous life!"

His tart smile told Albertine all she needed to know about that.

"Always difficult, a new job. But I assume you're good at it," she said.

"It has its ups and downs — as you say, a new job."

"You don't like it?"

"No, but I'm a soldier. I do what they tell me."

"What *is* that? Are you a spymaster?"

171

"Nothing so dramatic. Mostly I am a liaison between the French and Polish General Staffs. Everybody has to know what everybody else is up to."

The *omelettes* — *aux fines herbes* — arrived, with mounds of *frites,* crisp and golden and powerfully aromatic. Albertine, suddenly maternal, salted both their portions. "Still, you must learn secrets."

"Bad manners, Albertine, when the host country is an old friend."

"Yes, of course, that makes sense," she said, thinking it over. "Maybe German secrets."

"Well, if they come swimming by in the stream, I net them."

"Evil bastards, Jean-François, they've got their whole country in prison. I have friends who are Jews, a couple, fled from Frankfurt with the clothes on their backs. Surely great threats to the government: cellists, both of them. Did you know that, by German law, persons of more than twenty-five percent non-Aryan blood are forbidden to play Beethoven, Mozart, Bach, or any other Aryan composer? Can you imagine? I know I shouldn't pry, but if you get a chance to put a boot up their backsides I trust you'll give it an extra shove for me."

"I'll remember that," he said. "You never

know what might happen." He poured more wine for both of them. "And you, Albertine? What goes on with you?"

She shrugged. "I work hard at what I do — charities, boards of directors, and so forth, wherever they need people they don't have to pay. Oh, speaking of boards, some awful woman, Madame de Michaux is her name . . . had dinner with you in Warsaw? She was eager to tell me about it. Very taken with you, she was."

"Yes, I'd forgotten her name. The dinner was a banquet, at the Europejski."

"Perhaps, since you're in Paris, you'll go and see her."

"Albertine, don't be wicked."

She smiled. *I can be, as you well know.* "Here's one bit of news. I'm going to Aleppo, in December."

"Any special reason?"

"I might buy something for the collection, we'll see. I'm going with a friend of mine, she's a professor of archaeology at the Sorbonne, so that will give me entrée to the local collectors — and the tomb robbers." She paused, then said, "Have you a secret mission for me, as long as I'm there?"

"I'm not concerned with Syria, dear. And best not to say such things."

"Oh foo," she said. "I wasn't born yester-day."

He laughed and said, "Albertine, you are incorrigible."

Albertine's eyes wandered, then fixed on a nearby table. Mercier ate some *frites,* then looked over to see what interested her. A very handsome man was having dinner with his daughter, maybe twelve, who was chattering away while she worked at eating a plate of escargots. She was quite adept, using the shell-holding tool with one hand, probing for the snail morsel with a special fork, yet more than keeping up her end of the conversation. The father listened earnestly. "Yes? . . . Really? . . . That must have been interesting."

Albertine leaned toward Mercier and said, "Are you watching this?"

"What's going on?"

"Can't you see?"

"No, what is it?"

"He's teaching her how to have dinner with a man."

Mercier took another look. "Yes, I do see, now that you mention it."

Albertine was amused, and pleased with what she'd discovered. "How I love this *quartier,*" she said. "And, come to think of it, this country. I mean, where else?"

■ ■ ■ ■

Back at the apartment, Albertine made sure
that Mercier had everything he needed, then
went off to her room, down the hall. He tried
to read Guderian, but it had been a long day,
they'd finished the Saint-Estèphe, and German military theory wasn't the best bedside
companion. He thought about the following
morning: Bruner, the others. Would he de-
fend himself? Or just sit there and listen?
The latter, an easy decision, the best way to
keep his job. His pursuit of the *Wehrmacht*'s
intentions — the abandoned tank trap, a
careful reading of Guderian's book — had
changed the chemistry of his assignment in
Warsaw. This, along with the abduction of
his agent Uhl, had turned a desk job into
something very much like a fight, so to walk
away now would be to walk away from a
fight. He had never done that, and he never
would.

It was quiet outside, in the hidden rue
Saint-Simon, quiet in the building, and quiet
in the apartment; private, cloistered. Warm
enough, with the radiators going, the room
mostly in shadow, with only a small lamp on
the night table lighting his bed. From down
the hall, he heard the faint sound of music —
Albertine apparently had a radio in her room

— a swing orchestra playing a dance tune, then a woman vocalist, singing a song he recognized: "Night and Day." Was Albertine reading? Or lying in the darkness, listening to her radio? Not, he thought, that he would ever find out. Not that he would walk down the hall and knock at her door. Not that she wanted him to do that. Nor would she — walk down the hall and open his door. Not that he wanted her to, not really. Not that much, anyhow.

29 November. In his best uniform, shoes polished to a high gloss, Mercier walked up the rue de Grenelle, past the walled Soviet embassy, then along avenue des Invalides to the avenue de Tourville. The chill gray morning, typical for the city this time of year, did nothing to soften the official buildings, the heart of military Paris. Saluted by the sentry, he entered *2, bis,* climbed the stairs to Bruner's office, and at ten hundred hours sharp, as ordered, he knocked at the door.

Bruner took his time, and after he got around to calling, "Come in," his greeting was subdued — polite and cold. "How was your flight, colonel?"

"It was uneventful, sir. On time."

"When I served in Warsaw, I always found LOT to be dependable." Bruner took a sheet of paper from his drawer and placed it before him, squaring it up with his fingertips. He had, Mercier sensed, flourished with his promotion to full colonel and his new position. Short and tubby, with a soft face and a dapper little mustache, he virtually glowed with vanity, and its evil twin, the infinite capacity for vengeance when insulted. "So then," he said. "Our lost spy in Germany."

"Yes, colonel."

"How did this happen?"

"I don't know."

"You'll have to find out, won't you."

"He thought he was under surveillance on the previous trip. Somehow the Gestapo, or a counterespionage unit of the SD, uncovered him. I've questioned him at length, and he's been forthcoming, but he doesn't have the answer."

"And what do you propose to do about it? It's a serious loss, a view on German armaments, which imply tactics, and that is information crucial to our own planning. We're in the midst of a political conflict these days, the politicians don't want to spend money on tanks and planes — we still have serious unemployment — but Hitler has no such problem. He spends what he likes."

"I am aware of this, colonel."

"Perhaps this position, in Warsaw, is not to

your taste, Colonel Mercier. Would you like me to arrange a new assignment?"

"No, colonel. It is my preference to remain in Poland."

Bruner returned to their lost spy, then spent some time on the shooting incident in Silesia, and around again. He was like a terrier — once he took hold, he wouldn't let go. But, at last, with a final threat or two, Mercier was dismissed. "There will be more meetings, Colonel Mercier, so please be good enough to stay in contact with my adjutant for the next two days. You are also scheduled to see General de Beauvilliers. Call his office for the details."

Oh no. Not de Beauvilliers. Now, Mercier thought, he really would be sent off to some fever-ridden island.

When he left Bruner's office, he badly wanted coffee. There'd been no sign of Albertine when he got up, and he hadn't bothered to make it for himself, so he descended to the officers' mess in the basement and found an empty table. There were three officers at the next table, including a major, a fellow military attaché he recognized from his training class the previous spring. They acknowledged each other; then, as Mercier ordered coffee from a mess steward, the major resumed telling a story, which the

178

other two were clearly enjoying.

"So they took me to the far end of the palace," the major said, "to a glorious room: divans, you know, and gauze curtains."

"Perhaps you were in the harem."

"Perhaps. But there were no women about. Just the sultan, the chief eunuch, the head of the army — the sultan's younger brother — and me. For a time, we made small talk: the progress of the new railroad, their war with one of the mountain tribes. Then a servant — turban, dagger tucked in sash, those slippers with the toes turned up — entered with a brass tray. Which held four little pipes, made of silver, filigreed silver, very old and beautiful, and a silver bowl holding four brown — well, lumps, the size of small pebbles."

"Ah," said one of the other officers. "Opium."

"No, hashish. As the honored guest, I was served first. Which meant the servant put a brown lump in the bowl of a pipe and held a taper over it until I managed to get the damn thing to light."

"You couldn't decline?"

"I could've, but you can't be rude to sultans. That might have been the end of French concessions in the sultanate."

"How was it?"

179

"Harsh. Quite harsh — I had to stop myself from coughing. Then the sultan lit up, followed by the general and the eunuch. The smoke is very fragrant, sweet; not like anything else. When we were done, the servant took the pipes away. And *then* we began to negotiate. Imagine! I'd memorized a list of objectives — what we wanted, what we could offer in return —"

"And so you offered them Marseille."

"They didn't ask for it, but just as well they didn't."

"And you felt . . . ?"

"Light-headed. And peaceful. With a great desire to smile, an overwhelming desire."

"And did you? Smile?"

"Not quite. I managed to force the corners of my mouth to stay where they were. Meanwhile, the eunuch was watching me carefully, and the general began to talk about Schneider-Creusot cannon, seventy-fives. Then, right in the middle of it, the sultan cut him off and began to tell a story, the silliest story, really, about his visit to France before the war, some hotel in Nice, and shoes left outside the rooms at night to be shined by the porter, and his cousin switching them around — two right shoes here, two lefts down the hall. Doesn't sound so funny, now, but if you'd been there. . . ."

■ ■ ■ ■

Mercier finished his coffee and left the building. The major's story — an attaché *stupifié* with hashish in some desert kingdom — had been, in its way, instructive. Droll, rather than violent, but nonetheless, like his own experience, a misadventure of foreign service. Perhaps the major too had been *recalled for consultations.* Well, Mercier thought, he'd survived; endured that pompous ass Bruner without losing his temper, the parting shot no more than an order to replace Uhl, at least to the extent of having the Schramberg maneuvers observed. But that was more than reasonable — he would have done that without a trip to Paris. What lay ahead of him now was a session with the *Service des Renseignements* — the clandestine service of the *Deuxième Bureau* — which would not be a scolding, simply an interview. And a meeting with General de Beauvilliers, which *was* worth worrying about, but just then Mercier didn't feel like worrying. On the walk home he took the rue Saint-Dominique, a commercial street, busy in the late morning, where he saw a bunch of red gladioli in a florist's shop and bought them for the apartment.

181

■ ■ ■ ■

30 November. Sturmbannführer August Voss rode the express back from Berlin to Glogau. There was only one other passenger in the first-class compartment and Voss gazed out the window but saw nothing, so much was his mind occupied with anger. He'd gone up to the central command office on Wilhelmstrasse for the normal monthly meeting with his superior, but the meeting had not been at all normal. His superior, Obersturmbannführer Gluck, a bright young lawyer from Berlin in his previous life, had criticized him for the Edvard Uhl affair. No compliments for unveiling a spy, only disapproval for that absurd folly at the hotel in Warsaw. Gluck wasn't sarcastic or loud, not the type to slam his fist on the desk — he was too high and mighty for that. No, he *regretted* the incident, *wondered* if it wasn't just a bit *precipitous* to snatch this man in the middle of a foreign city, and *unfortunate* that the abduction had failed. This was Gluck's typical manner: quietly rueful, seemingly not all that perturbed. But then, when you left the office, he had your dossier brought out and destroyed you. And what came next was a new assignment — where you'd be tucked away in some cemetery of a

182

bureau where they gathered up failures and kept them busy with meaningless paper.

The deed, for all Voss knew, might already have been done. But, he vowed to himself, the story wouldn't end there. Zoller, his operative in Leszno who'd followed Uhl up to Warsaw, had been transferred to the Balkans — the Zagreb station, let him deal with the Croats and the Serbs — and Voss had made sure that everyone in his office knew it. But, much more important, the jackass who'd intervened outside the Hotel Orla would be dealt with next.

Voss had worked at that, hard, in the days following the aborted kidnapping. Who was he? The Warsaw operatives knew what he looked like, and Voss had hauled the leader, a Polish fascist, down to Glogau and given him the tongue-lashing of his life. *"Find him, or else!"* Voss didn't care how. And the man had done the job in less than a week. His chief thug, once a professional wrestler in Chicago, had kept watch on the main Warsaw hospital and, lo and behold, there he was. Visiting in the morning, leaving an hour later, and followed back to the French embassy. He wore an officer's uniform, but the operative had gotten a good look at him at the Hotel Orla and thought he was the same man.

In Glogau, Voss had not reported this discovery in a dispatch, sensing he might need it at the meeting in Berlin. And, he thought at first, he'd been right. When Gluck's criticism finally wound down, he'd said, "Well, at least we've identified the man who interfered," then paused, anticipating words of praise.

They weren't spoken, only a polite "Yes?"

"A Frenchman, working at the embassy. An army officer."

"Military attaché?"

"Perhaps, we can't be sure. But we'll find out, once we've got our hands on him."

"Your *hands* on him, Sturmbannführer Voss? A military attaché? In diplomatic service at an embassy?" Gluck had stared at him, his blue lawyer's eyes as cold as ice. "You don't mean that seriously, do you?"

"But . . ."

"Of course you don't. You are irritated by failure, naturally, who wouldn't be, but an attack on a serving military attaché?" Gluck closed his eyes and gave his head a delicate shake: *this must be a nightmare, where I'm forced to work with fools.* "Do we, Sturmbannführer Voss, need to discuss this further?"

"No, sir. Of course not. I perfectly understand."

In the compartment on the Berlin/Glogau

train, Voss's fury rose as he recollected the conversation — how he'd *crawled!* The other passenger glanced over at him and rattled his newspaper. Had he spoken aloud? Perhaps he had, but no matter. What mattered was that this Frenchman would pay for sticking his nose where it didn't belong. The Polish operative had described him as "handsome, aloof, aristocratic." Yes, exactly, just the sort of Frenchman one could truly loathe. *Well, Pierre, you will answer for what you did to me.* It couldn't be done officially, but there were always *alternatives;* one simply had to *take the initiative.* In his interior monologue, Voss mocked his superior. That didn't cure him, nothing would cure him, but he felt better.

"Where?" In the apartment, Albertine turned toward Mercier, the bottle of vermouth suspended over a glass.

"The Brasserie Heininger. For lunch, tomorrow."

"Down at Bastille? That place? For lunch with a general?"

"Yes."

"Good heavens," she said.

1 December. Papa Heininger, proprietor of the brasserie just off the Place de Bastille, unconsciously straightened his posture when

185

he saw the two officers waiting to be shown to their table. He edged the maître d' aside with his hand and said, "Good afternoon, messieurs."

The older one, at least a general from his uniform and insignia, said, "Yes. The reservation is in the name 'de Beauvilliers.'" He turned to the other officer, who walked with a stick, and said, "We're upstairs, where it's quiet."

Perhaps it would be, Mercier thought, but it wasn't here. The Heininger was famously excessive: white marble staircase, red plush banquettes, pudgy cupids painted on the walls between the gold-framed mirrors, golden passementeries on the drapery. The waiters, many wearing muttonchop whiskers, ran back and forth, balancing giant silver trays crammed with pink langoustines and knobby black oysters, and the lunchtime crowd was noisy and merry; in clouds of cigarette smoke and perfume they laughed, talked above the din, called out for more champagne.

When they'd climbed the staircase, Papa Heininger showed them to a table in the far corner, only to discover a silver-haired gentleman and a much younger brunette side by side on the banquette, whispering tenderly with their heads together. They were also notably well-dressed — but not for long. Heininger was aghast and started to speak, but the gentleman at the table turned a fierce eye on him and he stopped dead. "There's been a mistake," he said, and began an elaborate apology. The general cut him off. "Just anywhere will do," he said, his voice midway between a sigh and a command.

They were then taken back downstairs, to table fourteen, which bore a RÉSERVÉ sign on a silver stand. Papa Heininger, with a dramatic flourish, whipped it away and said, "Our most-requested table. And please allow me to have a bottle of champagne brought over, with my compliments."

"As you wish," the general said. Then, to Mercier, as he slid onto the banquette, "The infamous table fourteen." He nodded his head toward the mirror on the wall, which had a small hole with crackled edges in its lower corner.

"That can't be what it looks like."

"In fact it is. A bullet hole." From de Beauvilliers, a tolerant smile. In his sixties, he had the face of a sad hound, long and mournful, with the red-rimmed eyes of the insomniac and a shaggy gray mustache. He was famously the intellectual of the *Conseil Supérieur de la Guerre,* the high committee of military strategy, and was said to be one of the most powerful men in France, though precisely what he did, and how he did it, remained almost entirely in shadow. "A few months ago," he continued, "June, I think it was, they had a Bulgarian headwaiter here who played at émigré politics and got himself assassinated while hiding in a stall in the ladies' WC. The gang also shot up the dining room, and all the mirrors had to be replaced. All but this one, kept as a memorial. Makes for a good story, anyhow. Personally, I come here for the *choucroute* — I've seen enough bullet holes in my life."

The champagne arrived in a silver bucket, and both men ordered the *choucroute*. "You may put an extra frankfurter on mine," de Beauvilliers said. The waiter twisted out the champagne cork and poured two glasses. When he'd hurried off, de Beauvilliers said, "I would've preferred beer, but life has a way of thwarting simple pleasures." He tasted the champagne and had a look at the label. "Not so bad," he said. "Did Bruner give you hell?"

"He did."

"Don't worry about him, he has his place, in the scheme of things, but he's kept on a short leash. I want you in Warsaw, colonel."

"Thank you," Mercier said. "There's work to be done there."

"I know. Too bad about the Poles, but they've got to be made to understand we aren't coming to help them, no matter what the treaties say. We might be able to, if de Gaulle and his allies — like Reynaud — had their way, but they won't get it. French military doctrine is in the hands of Marshal Pétain, de Gaulle's enemy, and he won't let go."

"Defense. And more defense. The Maginot Line."

"Precisely. De Gaulle's up at Metz, commanding the Five-oh-seventh Tank Regiment. But there won't be many more, no armoured divisions, not until nineteen-forty, if then."

"May I ask why?" Mercier said.

"It's what I ask myself," de Beauvilliers said. "What some of us have been asking since Hitler marched into the Rhineland in 'thirty-six. But the answer isn't complicated. Pétain, and *his* allies, are committed to the theory of Methodical Battle. Hitler to be appeased — to gain time, to cement our alliance with Great Britain — then a battle of attrition. The British navy blockades, the Germans starve, and we launch a counteroffensive in two to three years. It worked in nineteen-eighteen, after the Americans showed up."

"It won't work again, general. Hitler is committed to armoured regiments. He was there, in nineteen-eighteen, he saw what happened."

"He did. And he knows that if the Germans don't win in six months, they don't win period. But France feels it can't compete: political constraints, lack of money, a shaky procurement system, not enough men, not enough training areas. Gamelin, the chief of staff, has nothing but excuses."

"The Germans are building tanks," Mercier said. "I was watching them, until I lost an agent. And they're planning maneuvers in Schramberg — in the Black Forest. They are, I believe, thinking hard about the Ardennes Forest, in Belgium, where the Maginot Line ends."

"We know. Of course we know. And we've conducted war games based on a tank thrust through the Ardennes. But what matters in war games is the conclusion, the lesson drawn."

"Can you tell me what that was, general?"

De Beauvilliers took a moment to consider his answer. "We are, in France, obsessed by the idea of *great men* — nobody else would build the Panthéon. So Marshal Pétain, the hero of Verdun, much honored, idolized, even, has persuaded himself that he is omniscient. In a recent pamphlet, he wrote, 'The Ardennes forest is impenetrable; and if the Germans were imprudent enough to get entangled in it, we should seize them as they came out!' "

"That's nonsense, sir," Mercier said. "Forgive my brevity, general, but that's what it is."

"I believe I used the same word, colonel. And worse. But now, what can we do about it?"

"*Les choucroutes!*" The waiter served them — for each a mound of sauerkraut, pork cutlet, thick, lean slices of bacon, and a frankfurter — two for the general. A small pot of fiery mustard was set between them. "A perfect dish for a discussion of Germany," de Beauvilliers said to Mercier. Then, to the waiter, "Bring me a glass of your best pilsener."

"One should have what one wants," Mercier said.

"At lunch, anyhow, one should. Tell me what's going on in Poland."

As the general attacked his first frankfurter, Mercier said, "You know I lost an agent — almost lost him to the Germans, but we have him hidden away in Warsaw for the moment. Otherwise it's quiet. The Poles are doing their best to buy weapons, but it's a slow process; the Depression still cripples their economy. But they remain confident. After all, they won their war with the Russians, and resolved their border disputes in Silesia and Lithuania, and they haven't forgotten any of it. They're still fighting the Ukrainian nationalists in the east, who are secretly armed by the Germans, but they're not going to give away territory."

"Confidence isn't always the best thing."

"No, and Pilsudski's death hurt them. After he died, the government swung to the right, and there's a strong fascist presence in the universities — actions against the Jews — but the fascists remain a minority. I should add that I'm not expert here. Mostly I concentrate on the army, not the politics."

De Beauvilliers nodded that he understood, then said, "One bit of gossip that came my way is the retrieval of von Sosnowski, traded for a German spy."

"It came my way as well."

"Really? From where?"

"Russians. Intelligence types from the Warsaw embassy. At a cocktail party."

"You'll want to go carefully, there." De Beauvilliers paused, a forkful of sauerkraut in midair, then a fond smile was followed by, "Jurik von Sosnowski, the Chevalier von Nalecz, yes; now *there* was a good spy." He ate the sauerkraut and said, "He had a long reach, did Jurik. Right into Section I.N. Six — *Intelligenz Nachforschung*, intelligence research — of the German General Staff, Guderian's office. And brought out the plan of attack, with tank regiments, for the invasion of Poland. But, in the end, the Poles suspected that the Germans knew what he was doing and were feeding him false information."

"That seems odd, to me," Mercier said. "It implies that the true plan was something else. But what could that have been? Artillery bombardment of the border fortifications and a slow advance? I would doubt that, myself."

"He may have gotten his hands on the invasion plans for us as well, but nobody ever told us he did. Anyhow, he was active for a few years, and arrested in 'thirty-four, so it's likely the details have all been reworked."

"Yes, likely they have."

"Only one way to find out, of course," de Beauvilliers said. A certain expression — rueful amusement, perhaps — flickered over his face for an instant, then vanished. "Invasion plans," he said. "Many gems in this murky business, colonel, all sorts of rubies and emeralds, always worth stealing if you can. Ahh, but invasion plans, now you have diamonds. And they only come from one mine, the same I.N. Six that Sosnowski penetrated with his German girlfriends. But, alas, that probably can't be done again."

"Probably not."

"Still, if by circumstance, the right person, the right moment . . ."

"In that case, it could be tried."

"Surely it could. Well worth it, I'd think. But I doubt seduction is the answer, not anymore, not with the Gestapo and the SD. And old von Sosnowski was one of a kind, wasn't he — a hundred women a year, that was the rumor. Wouldn't work again, I'd say, reprise isn't the answer. No, this time it would have to be money."

"Quite a lot of money," Mercier said.

From de Beauvilliers, a rather gloomy nod of agreement. However, all was not lost. As he leaned toward Mercier, his voice was quiet but firm. "Of course, we do have a lot of money."

That said, he returned to his lunch. Mercier drank some champagne, then, suddenly, and for no reason he could think of, he was very conscious of the life around him, the Parisian chatter and laughter that filled the smoky air of the restaurant. A strange awareness; not enjoyment, more apprehension. *Like the dogs,* he thought. Sometimes, at rest, they would raise their heads, alert to something distant, then, after a moment, lie back down again, always with a kind of sigh. What would happen to these people, he wondered, if war came here?

3 December, Warsaw. Now the winter snow began to fall. At night, it melted into golden droplets on the Ujazdowska gas lamps and, by morning, turned the street white and silent. Out in the countryside, the first paw prints of wolves were seen near the villages.

Mercier's mail grew fat with Christmas cards; the Vyborgs sent a manger with infant and sheep, similarly the Spanish naval attaché. From Prince Kaz and Princess Toni — postmarked Venice — a yule tree dusted with bits of silver, and a *Hope to see you in the spring,* in girls' academy handwriting below the printed greeting. From Albertine a warm holiday letter, not so different from the one he'd sent her. By now she would be in Aleppo, he imagined, and found himself remembering the darkened hall that led to her room and the faint music he'd heard.

From the Rozens, a Chanukah card with a menorah, and another from Dr. Goldszteyn, his sometime partner in the foursomes at the Milanowek Tennis Club. Inside the card was a letter, on a sheet of cream-colored stationery.

Dear Colonel Mercier,
We wish you a Merry Christmas and a Happy New Year. Sadly, I must take this occasion to say goodby. My family and I will soon be in Cincinnahti, joining my brother who emigrated a few years ago. This will be a better situation for us, I believe. For your kindness and thoughtful consideration I thank you, and wish you happiness of the season. Sincerely yours,
Judah Goldszteyn

Mercier read it more than once, thought about answering the letter, then realized, a sadder thing than the letter itself, that there was nothing to be said. He was not able to throw the letter away, so put it in a drawer.

The mail also included invitations, fancy ones — the Warsaw printers thrived this time of year — to more official gatherings than Mercier could ever hope to attend, and a few private parties. *RSVP*. He declined most, and accepted a few. A handwritten note from Madame Dupin, the deputy director of protocol at the embassy, invited him to a *vernissage* "for one of Poland's finest young painters, Marc Shublin." The *vernissage* —

"varnishing," it meant, thus the completion of an oil painting — was an old Paris tradition, the first showing of an artist's new work, typically at his studio.

Mercier had added the note to his *no* pile, but Madame Dupin, bright and forceful as always, had shown up at his office a day later. "Oh really, you must come," she'd said. "Congenial people, you'll have a good time. Marc's so popular, we're having it at an abandoned greenhouse on Hortensya street. Please, Jean-François, say yes, the young man's worth your evening, my friend Anna is invited, and everything else this year will be so boring. Please?"

"Of course, Marie, I'll be there."

On the afternoon of the eleventh, in suit and tie, Mercier took a trolley to the outskirts of the city to meet a man called Verchak. This was a favor done for him by Colonel Vyborg, thus an offer that could not be turned down, though Mercier doubted it would be productive. Verchak had served with the Dabrowsky battalion in the Spanish civil war and, wounded in the fighting, had been allowed — "because of his family," Vyborg had said — to return to Poland. Most of the battalion had been made up of Polish miners, from the Lille region of France, almost all of them members of the communist labor union, who'd fought as part of the XIth International Brigade, prominent in the defense of Madrid. Emigré communists knew better than to try to re-enter Poland, so Verchak was a valuable rarity, according to Vyborg.

The two-room apartment in a workers' district was scrupulously clean — cleanliness being the Polish antidote to poverty — and smelled of medicine. Mercier was taken to the second room, bare of decoration except for a small cedar tree set on a bench and hung with beautiful wooden Christmas ornaments, where he was shown to the good chair, while Verchak sat on a handmade plank chair across from him. Pana Verchak served tea, offered sugar, which Mercier knew not to accept, then left the room.

A broken man, Mercier thought — no wound was physically apparent, but Verchak was old and slumped well beyond his years. His Polish was slow and precise, for which Mercier was grateful, and someone, Vyborg no doubt, had urged him to be forthcoming. Mercier said only that he was Vyborg's friend and wished to hear of Verchak's experience of the war in Spain.

Verchak accepted this and began a recitation, clearly having told his story more than once. "In the first week of November, it was cold, and rained every day; we took the village of Boadilla, near the Corunna road, that led from Madrid to Las Rozas. The Nationalists wanted to cut that road and lay siege to the city and, after some hours, while we prepared defensive positions, they attacked us. They surrounded the village."

"What sort of attack was it?"

Verchak looked out the window for a moment, lost in his memory, then turned back to Mercier. "We couldn't stop it, sir," he said. "First the planes bombed us, then came tanks, then two waves of infantry, then more tanks. But we held on for a long time, though half of our men were killed."

"You fired at the tanks."

"With machine guns, but it meant little. One of them we set on fire, with a field gun, and we shot the crew as they came out of the hatch. One or two others got stuck in a ravine, and we put hand grenades under the engine in the back. But there were too many of them."

"How many?"

Verchak slowly shook his head. "Too many to count. We were next to the Thaelmann Battalion, German communists, mostly, and they said it was called 'Lightning war.' "

"In Polish, they said that?"

"No, sir. In German."

"So then, *Blitzkrieg?*"

"It might've been that. I don't remember."

"It was their word? The Germans in the Thaelmann Battalion?"

"I think they said they'd heard it from the German advisors who fought with the Nationalists."

"How did they come to hear it, Pan Verchak? From a prisoner?"

"They might've, sir, they didn't say. Perhaps they listened to the Germans talking on their radios. They were very clever people."

"Did the planes return?"

"Not that day, but the following morning, as we moved back toward Madrid. We were out of ammunition. They sent us blank cartridges, the officers in Madrid."

"Why would they do such a thing?"

"For courage, people said, so we wouldn't retreat."

"Did the men in the tanks talk to the planes, Pani?"

"I wouldn't know, sir. But I do know it can be done."

"Really? Why do you say that?"

"I saw it with my own eyes, later, when we fought at the Jarama river. The tanks were on *our* side there, big Russian tanks, and I saw a tank commander, halfway out of the open hatch, using a radio and watching the Russian war planes in the sky. He shouted at them — I was only a few feet away — when the bombs began to fall on our own trenches. Then, after he shouted, the bombing stopped. Not soon enough, sir, some of the comrades were killed, but it did stop. Of course, he shouldn't have been out of the tank, for the Moors shot him." Verchak stopped for a moment, as though he could see the tank commander. "It was a terrible war, sir," he said.

Verchak's wife returned to the room soon thereafter, a signal, Mercier thought, that her husband could not continue much longer. When Mercier rose to leave, he slid a thousand zloty into a piece of folded paper from his notepad and put it under the Christmas tree. The Verchaks looked at each other — should they accept such a gift? — and Pana Verchak started to speak. But Mercier told her it was an old French tradition, in this season, that entering a home with a Christmas tree, a gift must be left beneath it. "I have to follow my traditions," he said, and, as he'd well known, they would not argue with that.

11 December. Ominous weather, as night fell, the air ice cold and completely still. At

eight-thirty, Mercier strolled over to the old greenhouse on Hortensya street, a facility long disused, that had once served the parks and gardens of the city. It was, Mercier thought, typical of Madame Dupin to adopt some artist in the city where she worked; she was forever *doing* things, involving herself in an endless series of projects and pastimes. Shublin was at the door of the greenhouse, Madame Dupin at his side. He was young, with a roughneck's good looks, and very intense. What other pleasure, beyond the satisfaction of patronage, he might have provided for Madame Dupin was open to question — as, in fact, was her erotic life, a subject of some speculation in the diplomatic community. That night she was effusive and excited, taking Mercier's hand in both of hers and near joyful that he'd actually shown up. Clearly, she'd feared he wouldn't.

Shublin and his friends had gone to great lengths to turn the old greenhouse into an artist's studio. The artist's props — skulls, statuettes of deformed people and imaginary beasts, easels bearing newspaper découpages, a dressmaker's mannikin on a wire cage — had been imported for the evening, and his largest canvas hung from an iron beam on ropes, flanked by a pair of skeletons, their names on cardboard squares tied beneath their chins. Mercier immediately liked the painting, as well as the others propped against the cloudy old glass walls: fire. Fire in its every aspect — orange flames roaring into azure skies, black smoke pouring from a brilliant yellow flash, fire, and more fire.

Mercier, his costume for a bohemian soirée a bulky sweater and corduroy trousers beneath a long overcoat, with a black wool scarf looped insouciantly — he hoped — about his neck, was introduced here and there. For a time, he spoke with a professor of art history and brought up the subject of Polish war paintings, for him a particular treasure he'd discovered in Warsaw — huge battlefield scenes laden with cavalry and cannon, exquisitely detailed and compelling. But the professor didn't much care for them, and, discovering that Mercier was French, went on and on about Matisse. Mercier spoke also with Shublin's girlfriend, who was very up-to-date on European politics — perhaps the last thing in the world he wanted to talk about. But she was smart and amusing, and Mercier discovered he was, as promised, actually having a good time. The wine and vodka were plentiful, and platters of hors d'oeuvres had been brought in from a good restaurant, generously provided by Madame

Dupin. With secret embassy funds? Lord, he hoped not.

It was nine-fifteen when Anna Szarbek appeared. The same Anna Szarbek; dark-blond hair, swept across her forehead and pinned in back, deep green eyes, wary and restless, the slight downward curve of her nose and heavy lips suggesting sensuality. Suggesting it to him, certainly. His heart rose to look at her, he wanted to rush her through the night in a taxi, off to his bedroom, there to relieve her of coat, boots, sweater, skirt, and all the rest, there to see what he'd barely touched the night they danced together. And then . . . Well, his imagination was in perfect order, and therein her desire, in their first moment together, was the equal of his, and his desire was making him almost dizzy. But not so much that he didn't search the room for Maxim, who was nowhere to be seen, and Mercier, elated beyond reason, felt a great smile appear on his face. His search of the room did reveal Madame Dupin, turned partly away from a conversing group, a sharp, inquisitive eye directly on him. Was this why she'd wanted him here? Was she *matchmaking?* Could that be true? Back and forth he went.

Trapped, meanwhile, by the most boring man on earth — "But, you understand, the laws of the city expressly forbid them to build a wall there! Myself I find it almost impossible to believe" — Mercier kept saying "Mm," and "Mm," his eyes wandering rudely over the man's shoulder. Anna was easy to spot — her sweater was a deep red, with a design in tiny pearls below a raised collar — as she navigated through the crowded greenhouse. Stopped to have a look at the skeletons, peered nearsightedly at the cardboard nameplates, responded with a wry smile, and moved on.

"We could go to court, serve them right, having to hire some expensive lawyer. . . ."

"Mm. Mm."

Now she saw him. She had been looking for him. His heart leapt. "Forgive me, I think I'll have another glass of wine."

"You don't have a glass of wine."

"Then I'll go and get one."

Mercier worked his way toward her, and they exchanged conspiratorial smiles — *oh what a crowd* — at the difficulty of his progress. At last they stood together and shook hands, her skin cold from the night outside. "Very nice to see you again," he said.

"I think I saw you at the foreign office cocktail party," she said. Her voice was slightly husky — he'd forgotten that, as well as the faint accent.

"You did. I saw you too, but I couldn't get over to say hello."

"You seemed busy," she said.

"An official reception. I had to be there. But this is much nicer."

"A Marie Dupin affair, they're always good parties. Poor Maxim had to interview a politician, so I almost didn't come, but, I thought, why not? And I'd promised."

"Something to drink?"

"Yes, good, I can use it. The cold tonight is awful, even for Warsaw."

They made their way to the bar in the far corner. "Two vodkas, please," Mercier said. Then, to Anna, "Is that all right with you? Insulation against the weather."

"Yes, thanks. I knew it would be freezing in here, I mean, it's *glass*."

"They have kerosene heaters."

Anna wasn't impressed. "Poor plants."

"Not anymore. What do you think of the paintings?"

"A little frightening — they're not cozy fires."

"War fires, you think?"

"Violent, anyhow. At least they don't show what's burning. Houses, or ships."

"Maybe you're meant to imagine them."

She nodded, *yes, could be,* searched in her

bag, found a cigarette and a lighter, and handed the lighter to Mercier. He lit her cigarette and said, "I'll go find you an ashtray, if you like."

"Let's go together, I don't know a soul in here."

As they began to move toward the hors d'oeuvres table, a heavy gust of wind hit the greenhouse, then the sound of hail, loud against the glass roof. It stopped almost immediately. "I don't know anybody either," Mercier said. "You're supposed to introduce yourself around, at these affairs."

"Not me. You have to be the bright and cheerful sort to do that. I'm not. Are you?"

"No."

"I didn't think so."

"I depend on introductions, then I can socialize. Otherwise —"

"It's the dreadful corner. And the hopeful smile."

They circled around the professor, now with an older woman wearing a cloche hat and still raving on about Matisse. Then Madame Dupin materialized in front of them. "Hello you two, I see you found each other."

"We did," Anna said. "You've got a good crowd."

"Marc is pleased, anyhow I think he is; he

doesn't talk, I *was* afraid of the weather, but, as you see . . ."

"We're in search of an ashtray," Mercier said.

"Over by the food. Try the smoked sturgeon while you're there, it's from the chef at the Bristol." Again the wind moaned. "Oh my," Madame Dupin said. A brief shower of hail rattled furiously against the greenhouse. "*Listen* to it, perhaps we'll have to stay all night." She scowled up at the heavens, the embattled hostess, then said, "I'm off, my dears. Please try and circulate."

When she'd gone, Anna said, "Maybe we should."

Mercier shrugged. "Why?"

She grinned. "Such a scoundrel," she said, and gave him a playful push on the shoulder.

"Oh yes, that's me," he said, meaning very much the opposite, but wishing it were so.

At the food table they found an ashtray, then tried the sturgeon, the smoked trout, and salmon roe with chopped egg on toast. Anna ate with zeal, once making a small sound of satisfaction when one of the hors d'oeuvres was especially good. Next, back to the bar for another vodka, and they clinked glasses before they drank. Outside, the storm began to beat wildly against the glass.

"Maybe we'll have to stay all night," Mercier said.

"Please!" she said. "You'll get me in trouble."

"Well, at least let me see you home."

"Thank you," she said. "That I would like."

Twenty minutes later, they said good night to Shublin and Madame Dupin and left the greenhouse. Mercier looked around for a taxi, but the street was deserted. "Which way is home?" he said.

She pointed and said, "Up there. It's a block off Marszalkowska, where we can take a trolley car, or we're much more likely to find a taxi."

They set off, heading west, then north, against the wind, which howled and moaned in the narrow street, sent a sheet of newspaper flying past, and made it difficult to walk. It wasn't so bad at first, but soon enough striding boldly into the storm changed to walking sideways, hunched over, eyes half shut, the hail stinging their faces. "Damn!" she said. "This is worse than I thought."

Mercier kept searching for a taxi, but there wasn't a headlight to be seen anywhere.

"I'm going to have to hang on to you," she said. "Do you mind?"

"Not at all."

She held his arm with both her own, tight against her body, and hid her face behind his shoulder. Moving slowly, they made their way to Marszalkowska avenue, the Broadway of Warsaw. "How much further?" Mercier said. He sensed she wasn't doing well.

"Twenty minutes, on a nice day."

She was trembling, he could feel it, and, when he turned to look at her, there were frost crystals in her eyelashes. "Maybe we'd better get inside somewhere," he said. The cold was brutal, her sweater thin, and her winter coat more stylish than warm.

"Allright. Where?"

"I don't know. The next place we see." Up and down the avenue, the Marszalkowska cafés and restaurants were shuttered and dark. In the distance, a man made slow progress, holding his hat on his head, and the streetlamps, coated with ice, glowed dimly on the whitened pavement, with not a tire track to be seen.

"My father used to talk about these storms," she said. "They blow down from Siberia, a gift to Poland from Russia." Her teeth chattered, and she held him tighter.

Mercier had begun to consider doorways, maybe even trying the door of one of the cars parked on the avenue, when he saw, up ahead somewhere, light shining on the sidewalk. "Whatever that is," he said, "that's where we're going."

He felt her nod, urgently: *yes, anything.*

The light came from a movie theatre, from a ticket booth set back beneath a small marquee. The old lady in the booth wore one shawl over her head and another around her shoulders. As Mercier paid, she said, "You shouldn't be out in this, my children."

In the theatre, the audience, unaware of the storm outside, was laughing and having a good time. Mercier found seats and rubbed his frozen hands.

"That was awful," Anna said. "Really. Awful."

"Maybe it will die down," Mercier said. "At least we'll be warm for a while."

On the screen, a diminutive soldier with a Hitler mustache was saluting an officer, a vigorous salute yet somehow wrong — a parody of a salute. A close-up of the officer's face showed a man at the end of his patience. He spoke angrily; the soldier tried again. Worse. He was the classic recruit who, believing he has assumed a military posture, only manages to mock the prescribed form. Mercier leaned over and whispered, "Do you know what we're watching?"

211

" '*Dodek na froncie,*' Dodek Goes to War. That's Adolf Dymsza."

"I know that name."

"The Polish Charlie Chaplin."

"Have you seen it?"

"No, actually I haven't." After a moment, with a laugh in her voice, she said, "Were you concerned?"

"Of course," he said.

"You can be very droll, colonel."

"Jean-François."

"Very well. Jean-François."

From behind them: "*Shhhh!*"

"Sorry."

Mercier tried; but the film was more romantic comedy than farce, and the hiss and crackle of the sound track was particularly loud, so he missed much of the dialogue, and that's what was making the audience laugh. At one point, Anna also laughed, and Mercier whispered, "What did he say?"

In order not to annoy the man behind them, she whispered by his ear. "In French, it's 'That's odd, my dog said the same thing.'" But then, she didn't turn away, she waited, and, when he turned toward her, her eyes closed and they kissed — tenderly, her lips dry, moving softly against his. After a few long seconds, she sat back in her seat, but her shoulder rested against his, and there it stayed.

Forty minutes later, the film ended and they had to leave the theatre. The storm had not abated. They walked quickly, her hands in the pockets of her coat; neither one of them wanted to be the first to speak. Then, as the silence grew heavy, Mercier saw a horse cab. He waved and shouted, the driver stopped, and Mercier took Anna's hand and helped her into the carriage. This might have been an opportunity sent down by the gods of romance, but it wasn't to be. Anna was quiet, and thoughtful. Mercier tried to start a light conversation, but she, politely enough, made it clear that talking was not what she wanted to do, so he sat in silence as the intrepid horse, its blanket covered with melting hail, clopped along the avenue until Anna directed the coachman to turn into the street that Mercier remembered from the night he'd taken her to the Europejski.

He helped her out of the carriage as he asked the driver to wait — he would take the cab back home — then the two of them stood facing each other. Before he could say anything, she put her hand flat against his chest and held it there — a gesture that silenced him, yet somehow, and he felt it strongly, meant also attraction — desire mixed with regret. He could see in her face that she was troubled: about what had happened in the movie theatre, about what had happened all evening. "Good night," she said, "Jean-François."

"May I see you again?"

"I don't know. Maybe better if we don't."

"Then, good night."

"Yes, good night."

In Paris, during Mercier's meeting with the people at the *Deuxième Bureau,* the *Wehrmacht*'s planned tank maneuvers at Schramberg had been discussed at length. And so, on the tenth of December, four German agents of the *Service des Renseignements* had been sent into the town: an elderly gentleman and his wife, who were to celebrate their wedding anniversary by walking the low hills of the Black Forest; a salesman of kitchenwares from Stuttgart, calling on the local shops; and a representative of UFA, the Berlin film production company, in search of locations for a new version of the Grimm brothers' fairy tales.

Not a bad choice for a fairy tale, the older part of Schramberg: winding streets, half-timbered cottages with sloping rooves, shop signs in Gothic lettering. Adorable, really. And the townspeople were eager to talk, to praise their charming Schramberg, understanding perfectly the benefits to be had from film crews, who famously threw money about like straw. The best kind of business: they came, they annoyed everyone, but then they went away and left their money behind.

So the local dignitaries, the mayor, the councilmen, went on and on, describing the *gemütlich* delights of the town. Though this was, please understand, not the best moment to visit. The *Wehrmacht* was coming, everybody knew it, one of the roads that wound up into the hills had been closed off, all the rooms at the inn had been reserved, and a few supply trucks were already there, with more to arrive at any moment. Oh well. Still, the good gentleman could see for himself how picturesque the forest was, and, if the area up on the Rabenhügel, Raven Hill, was torn up by the army's machines, there were plenty of other places just as scenic. More scenic! And would the company be hiring local people to perform in the film? In a crowd, perhaps? Or even, say, as a mayor? Naturally they would, said the UFA man, it was always done that way. What about those two hefty fellows, seated by the window in the Schwarzwald coffeehouse, having their second breakfast? Oh no, *they* weren't local!

They had just arrived, they were here to make sure that, that — um — that everything went well. Wink.

For the anniversary couple, in loden-green outfits and matching alpine hats — a vigorous yodel could not be far in the future — the same story, as they produced their touring map for the lady who'd rented them a room. No, no, not there, that was forbidden, until after the fourteenth. You cannot go east of the town, to the Rabenhügel, but to the south — ah, there it was even lovelier, the magnificent pines, the tiny red birds that stayed the winter; south, much better, and would they care to have her make a picnic to take along? They would? *Ach, wunderbar!* She would see to it right away.

And so for the salesman, in his Panhard automobile with sample pots and pans in the backseat, headed over to the town of Wald-mossingen. Halted at a sawhorse barrier manned by three soldiers, he was told that this road was closed, he would have to go back to Schramberg, and then down to Hardt and circle around. Of course he knew the way, and only took this road for the scenery. Was this permanent, this road-closing? No, sir, only for a few days. "Heil Hitler!"

"Heil Hitler!"

13 December. Mercier took the early LOT flight to Zurich, then the train to Basel and a taxi to the French consulate. Climbing the stairs to the consul's office, he was his darkest self, tense and brooding and in no mood for polite conversation, a pre-combat condition he knew all too well. But the consul, a Mediterranean Frenchman with a goatee, was just what the doctor ordered. "So, colonel, a stroll in the German woods?"

Maybe the best approach, Mercier thought, irony in the face of danger. And it would be dangerous. The *Wehrmacht* wouldn't care much for a foreign military attaché observing maneuvers — there to discover strengths and weaknesses, what certain tanks could do in the forest and what they couldn't. Because, if it came to war, such intelligence would lead to casualties, and could be the difference between victory and defeat.

The people at *2, bis,* in receipt of reports from their German agents, had acted quickly, sending to Warsaw maps of the Schramberg district: the roads, the walking paths in the forest, the hill known as the Rabenhügel, and two nearby hills with a view of the site to be used for maneuvers. A coded wireless message from the General

Staff Meteorological Service predicted a nighttime temperature of 28 degrees Fahrenheit, reaching 35 degrees by noon, and a possible light dusting of snow on the morning of the fourteenth. Mercier had his own field glasses, and the rest of his equipment, as promised in Paris, had been brought down to Basel by courier; a suitcase stood behind the consul's office door.

The consul hefted it up onto a table, handed Mercier the key, and watched with interest as the contents were brought out: a Swiss army greatcoat — its insignia long ago removed — a peaked wool hat with earflaps, a blanket roll, a knapsack. When Mercier unwrapped a Pathé Baby, the 9.5-millimeter movie camera, the consul said, "Thought of everything, haven't they."

With the camera, a typed sheet of instructions. Simple enough: one cranked the handle; the action was operated by a spring. One roll of film was in the camera, ten more could be found in the knapsack; directions for reloading followed, with a diagram.

"What about distance?" the consul said.

"I would assume the lens has been refitted. Otherwise, they'll have the march of the tiny toys. But even so, it can be enlarged at the laboratory. At least I think it can."

"So, just aim and press the button?"

Mercier pointed the camera at the consul, who waved and smiled, then went to a closet and produced a six-foot walking staff fashioned from a tree branch. "I won't tell you what we went through to obtain this, but Paris insisted that you have it."

"War wound."

"Then it will help. But please, colonel, try not to lose it," the consul said. "Now, you'll be leaving at dusk, your driver will arrive in an hour. If you'd like to rest until then, we've set aside a room for you. Care for something to eat?"

"No, thank you."

The consul nodded. "It was always that way for me, in *la dernière.*" The phrase was common among people who'd been there, it meant *the last one.* He opened a drawer in his desk, produced a Swiss passport, and handed it to Mercier. Albert Ducasse, from Lausanne, thus a French-speaking Swiss. The photograph, applied at *2, bis,* was a duplicate of the one in his dossier in Paris. The consul cleared his throat and said, "They've instructed me to ask you to leave your French passport with this office."

Whose idea was that, Bruner's? Out of uniform, on foreign ground, in covert surveillance, he was, by the rules, a spy. But out of uniform, with a false identity — that made him a *real* spy.

"Of course," the consul said, "if you are caught, in that situation, you could be shot. Technically speaking, that is."

"Yes, I know," Mercier said. And gave the consul his passport.

In the early dusk of winter, Mercier climbed into an Opel with German plates. The young driver called himself Stefan and said he was from an émigré family that had settled in Besançon. "In 'thirty-three," he added. "The minute Hitler took power, my father got the suitcases down. He was a socialist politician, and he knew what was coming. Then, after we settled in France, the people you work for showed up right away, and they've kept me busy ever since."

They crossed into Germany easily enough, Stefan using a German passport, and drove north on the road to Tübingen that passed through Schramberg. "About an hour and half," Stefan said. "I'll take you into the town and out on the forest road, where I'll pick you up tomorrow night, so mark the spot carefully."

"Before the roadblock."

"Well before. It's one-point-six miles from the Schramberg town hall."

"And then, tomorrow night . . ."

"At nineteen-oh-five hours. Stay in the woods until then, I'll be there on the minute. Is it only a one-day maneuver?"

"Likely more, but they want me out by tomorrow night."

"A good idea," Stefan said. "Don't be greedy, that's what I always say. And you'll want to watch out for the foresters."

"Don't worry, I'll keep my head down."

"They're always in the woods, cutting, pruning." After a moment he said, "It's a strange nation, when you think about it. Fussy. Rules for everything — the branches of each tree must only just touch the neighboring branches, and so on."

"How do you come to know that?"

"*Everybody* knows that. In Germany."

They drove on, through pretty Schwabisch villages. Every one of them had its *Christbaum,* a tall evergreen in the center of town, with candles lit as darkness fell, and a star on top. There were also candles in every window, and red-berried holly wreaths hung on the doors. By the side of the road, at the entry to each village, stood a sign attacking the Jews. This was, Mercier thought, a kind of competition, for none of the signs were the same. *Juden dirfen nicht bleiben* — "Jews must not stay here" — was followed by *Wer die Juden unterstuzt fordert den Kommuniss-*

221

mus, "Who helps the Jews helps communism," then the dramatic "This flat-footed stranger, with kinky hair and hooked nose, he shall not our land enjoy, he must leave, he must leave."

"Perhaps an amateur poet, that one," Stefan said.

"One publishes where one can," Mercier said.

"Bastards," Stefan said. "I grew up in the middle of it. Hard to believe, at first. Then it didn't go away, it grew." He shifted into second gear, the Opel climbing a grade where forest closed in on the darkening road. He had been rambling along in rough-hewn émigré French, now he switched to native German and said, quietly, *"Ihr sollt in der Hölle schmoren!"* Burn in hell.

Twenty minutes later, they reached the town of Schramberg. A few *Wehrmacht* officers wandered along the winding streets, pausing to look in the shop windows, out for a pre-dinner walk to stir the appetite. In honor of the army's visit, swastika flags lined the square in front of the ancient town hall, their deep red a handsome contrast to the green *Christbaum,* its candles flickering in the evening breeze. Stefan turned right on the street just past the town hall, took a good look at the odometer, and then, as the street turned into a narrow paved road and the town fell away behind them, switched off the headlights. "They don't need to know we're coming," he said, peering into the gathering darkness, squinting at the odometer. Finally he slowed and let the car roll to a stop. "At the center of this curve," he said. "See the rock? That's our mark."

As Mercier reached into the backseat for his walking staff, Stefan opened the glove compartment and handed him a thick bar of chocolate. "Take this along," he said. "You might want it."

Mercier thanked him and, making sure no headlights were visible, stepped out of the car and started to cross the road. Stefan rolled the window down and, his voice close to a whisper, said, "Good hunting. Remember, nineteen-oh-five hours, by the rock." In two moves he reversed the car and drove back toward Schramberg.

Pure night. Mercier thought of it that way. Faint stars, wisps of cloud, and not a sound to be heard. He reached into his pocket and found his pencil sketch of the *Deuxième Bureau's* map. He had to climb the hill above the road, turn east, and walk a distance just short of two miles, descending the first hill, climbing a second, and descending again, to a point just below the crest, where there would be, presumably, a view of the tank maneuvers. For the moment he was warm enough, though he could feel the first bite of the night-borne chill. Wool hat, surplus greatcoat, walking staff, and knapsack — the Swiss hiker, if anyone were to see him, but it was planned that nobody would. And, he thought, with a camera in his knapsack, they'd better not. He entered the forest and started to climb, his footsteps almost silent on the pine-needle litter on the forest floor.

His knee ached soon enough, and he was grateful for the long staff. When he heard the whine of an approaching car, he moved behind a tree, then watched the headlights as they swept along the road, sped around the curve, and disappeared. That would be, he thought, the changing of the guard at the roadblock. Ten minutes later, the car returned, headed back to Schramberg, and Mercier resumed his climb.

The forest never thickened, it was as Stefan had described, a woodland treated as a kind of garden, every tree identified and carefully nurtured. Even fallen tree branches were removed, perhaps taken away by the poor, for use as firewood. Suddenly some animal, sensing his presence, went running off across the hillside. Mercier never saw it;

a wild boar, perhaps, or a deer. Too bad he didn't have his dogs with him, they would have smelled it long before it broke cover, frozen into motionless statues, each with left foreleg raised, tail straight, nose pointed toward the game: *that's dinner, right over there.* Then, when the rifle shot didn't follow, they would look at him, waiting for a release from point.

How he missed them! Well, he'd see them when he went home for Christmas. If he managed to get there. And, even if he did, his daughter Gabrielle probably wouldn't join him. She'd often meant to, but then her busy life intervened. And Annemarie wouldn't be there. Not ever again. So it would be just him and the dogs, and Fernand and Lisette, who lived in the house and maintained the property — it belonged more to them now than to him. *And they're getting older,* he thought, hired by his grandfather, a long time ago. What, he wondered, would they make of Anna Szarbek? Well, that he'd never know. *Stop and rest.* He put a hand on a pine tree, forcing himself to stand still until his breathing returned to normal. Whatever drove him, nameless spirit, had been forcing him uphill at full speed.

Did he truly need to be on this hillside? Any trusted agent could have operated the camera, but the people at 2, *bis* were determined he should himself stand in for his lost spy, and he'd shown them every enthusiasm. Still, it was — oh, not exactly dangerous, France wasn't at war with Germany, but potentially an embarrassing failure, more a threat to his career than his life.

Again he walked. Confronted by a ravine, with a frozen streamlet at the bottom, he slid down one side and then, a bad moment, had to claw his way up the opposing slope. An hour later he was midway down the second hillside, the trees on the facing hill silver in the light of the rising moon. He had a look with his field glasses, searching for an advance unit, but saw nothing. So he unrolled his blanket and sat on it, back braced against an oak tree, ate some chocolate, and settled in to wait for dawn.

Slow hours. Sometimes he dozed, the cold woke him, then he dozed again, finally waking with a start, face numb, hands so stiff they didn't quite work. He struggled to his feet, rubbing his hands as he walked back and forth, trying to get warm. His watch said 4:22 but there was, a week before the winter solstice, no sign of dawn. In the black sky above him, the stars were sharp points of light, the air cold and clean and faintly scented by the forest. Then, in the distance, he heard the faint rumble of engines.

He concentrated on the sound and discovered it was not coming from the direction of Schramberg, west of him, but from the north. Of course! The *Wehrmacht* hadn't bothered to set up a tank park on the outskirts of town — a long, complicated business involving commissary, medical units, and fuel tankers — they were coming from an army base, likely somewhere near the city of Tübingen.

He rolled up his blanket and climbed until he found a thick forest shrub, branches bare for the winter but still good cover. The sound rose steadily, reaching finally an enormous crescendo: the roar of huge unmuffled engines and the loud clatter of rolling treads. A tank column, stretched far down the road. How many? Thirty tanks in a formation was common; he had to guess there were at least that many. The earth beneath Mercier trembled as the first lights of the column appeared on the road, and the air filled with the raw smell of gasoline. Two staff cars appeared at the foot of the Rabenhügel, then a tank, and two more, the rest of the column obscured from view by the curve of the hill.

An officer climbed out of the leading staff car, signaled with his hand, and, moments later, Mercier heard the stuttering whine of motorcycles and saw moving lights among the trees. He tracked them with his field glasses, the riders gray forms, working up the shallow grade, skidding on the pine-needle carpet, steadying themselves with a foot on the ground as they wove through the trees. Suddenly, his peripheral vision caught the motion of a silhouette, uphill from his position and moving fast, which he managed to catch a glimpse of just before it vanished: a small bear, whimpering with panic as it ran, low to the ground, in flight from the invasion of its forest. When he again looked at the road, a few officers and tank commanders had gathered by one of the staff cars, smoking and talking, playing a flashlight on a map spread out on the car's hood.

Army time. Nothing much going on. Waiting. Twenty minutes later, a pair of Mercedes automobiles came up the road from the direction of Schramberg, a civilian in an overcoat got out, gave a *Heil* salute to what Mercier took to be the senior officer, and received one, a rather casual version of the raised arm, in return. The officer pointed, the civilian got back in his car, and it drove away. Perhaps the engineers, Mercier guessed, there to observe the maneuvers.

At eight o'clock sharp, the rising sun casting shadows on the hills, the tanks made their first attempt at climbing the Rabenhügel.

Mercier, working quickly, reached into his knapsack and brought out the camera, made sure that the handle was fully wound, pointed it at the climbing tanks, and pressed the button. In the wall of engine noise he could barely hear it. Also, some other sound distracted him; he puzzled for a moment, and that almost did for him. A drone, only just audible above the engine thunder, somewhere above him. *Merde,* that was an airplane! He dove to the earth, slid beneath the branches of the shrub, and rolled onto his back.

Circling lazily in the morning sky, a Fieseler Storch reconnaissance plane, small and slow, looking like a fugitive from the 1914 air war, but lethal. Had they seen him? Was the radio alert to a staff car below already sent? He covered his face with the gray-green sleeve of his greatcoat and lay perfectly still. The plane's circuit took it north, then, coming back toward him, it descended, now less than a hundred feet above the hilltop. At its slowest speed, it skimmed over his head; then, thirty seconds later, the drone faded away to the west. But Mercier stayed beneath his shrub, as the plane returned once more, now gaining altitude. For fifteen minutes it circled the site of the maneuvers, then disappeared.

By the time Mercier was back to his cover position behind the shrub, the tanks were spread out across the hill, a few hundred feet above the road, but the exercise was not going well. He could see at least six of them, the light model Uhl had been working on. Down by the road, one of the tanks had failed immediately; the crew had the rear hatch cover off and were kneeling on the deck in order to work on the engine. A second had climbed thirty feet, then stopped, blue exhaust streaming from its vent as the commander crawled between the treads to check on ground clearance. A third had tried to mow down a pine, had broken it off, then got hung up on the stump and thrown a tread. The other three had reached the crest of the hill and were now out of sight. But Mercier could see that all was not well for one tank at least, because, in the distance to the north, a column of black smoke rose slowly above the forest.

They worked at it all morning, and for most of the afternoon. Now and again, the Fieseler Storch returned for thirty minutes, and Mercier had to hide beneath the shrub. Then, late in the afternoon, the weak December sun low in the sky, they tried something new. From the north, a blue Opel sedan drove up and parked next to the staff cars. This was, clearly, somebody's personal car: a few years old, its paint job faded and dusty, a dent on the door panel. The driver, a young *Wehrmacht* officer — a lieutenant; Mercier could see the insignia with his field glasses — talked to the senior officers for a time, then took a length of iron pipe, long enough so that its end stuck out the rolled-down rear window, from the car. While the others watched, hands clasped behind their backs in a classic officer pose, he knelt by the front of the Opel and wired the pipe to the bumper. Mercier adjusted the field glasses and focused on the lieutenant's face as he chatted away while he worked at twisting the ends of the wire until it was secure. *Oh well, likely it won't work, but you never know. . . .* For a moment, Mercier wasn't sure what he was looking at, but then, when the lieutenant produced a measuring tape, he understood perfectly: the pipe was the width of a light tank. The lieutenant slid behind the wheel and drove cautiously up the hill. More than once he misjudged distance, one end of the pipe banging into a tree, and had to reverse the Opel and try a different path. But the idea was simple and effective.

If you contemplated a tank attack through a forest, all you needed was a car and a length of pipe. If the pipe on the car fit through the trees, so would a tank.

In the town of Schramberg, the anniversary couple was enjoying the fourth day of their vacation. On the morning of the fourteenth, after a copious breakfast, as the lady who'd rented them a room waved from the doorway, they set off for their daily walk in the Black Forest. Such a sweet couple, in their loden-green walking shorts, high stockings, and alpine hats. They headed south out of town, as their kind hostess had recommended, but then turned north, using a compass to make sure they weren't going around in circles. After an hour's walk, they took a radio receiver from a knapsack and ran its aerial up a tree, fixing it in place with a piece of string. No result, so they kept walking. On the fourth attempt, it worked. Holding a pair of headphones to his ear, the elderly gentleman smiled with satisfaction: a babble of voices — commands, curses, *yes, sirs* and *no, sir*s, the radio traffic of a tank formation moving over difficult terrain. The anniversary couple were now within range of shortwave tank radios, about five miles. They connected a wire recorder to the receiver and settled in for the day. Likely the people they worked with would make sense of it; certainly the couple hoped they would.

Not worked *for,* the way they thought about it, but worked *with.* They had refused payment, their spying was an act of conscience. Sincere Christians, German Lutherans, they had watched with horror as the Nazis violated every precept sacred to them. But then, what to do about it? They could not leave Germany, for a list of commonplace domestic reasons, so they had traveled up to Paris, a year earlier, taken a room at an inexpensive hotel, written a note to the General Staff headquarters, and settled in to wait. It took a week, then two men appeared at the hotel, and the couple offered their services. No, they didn't care to be paid. They had prayed together for hours, they explained, down on their knees, trying to make this decision, but now it was made. The people who led Germany were evil, and they were obliged, by their faith, to act against them. "Very well," said one of the men. "Give us your address in Germany. We'll see about who you are and then, in time, someone will get in touch with you."

Three months later, someone did.

■ ■ ■ ■

THE BLACK FRONT

■ ■ ■ ■

22 December, 1937. The Schorfheide. Fifty miles northeast of Berlin, a region known for its deserted countryside, its marshland and forest, deep lakes, bountiful game, and splendid hunting lodges. Notably Hermann Göring's Karinhall, where, some months earlier, at one of the field marshal's infamous parties, he had appeared wearing a leather jerkin, grasping a spear, and leading a pair of bison on a chain. The bison had been induced to mate, while the guests fell to awed whispers, and the story was told everywhere.

For Sturmbannführer August Voss, that evening, a party not to be missed, held at a Berlin banker's hunting lodge not far from Karinhall. "I think he bought them," said Voss's friend Meino, referring to the wolf pelts, bearskins, and stag antlers that decorated the pine walls. The two men stood before a crackling fire in a fieldstone fireplace, drinking champagne, following a dinner of wild boar and potatoes in cream.

"Look at him," Voss said. "I doubt he hunts anything."

The banker, in eager conversation with an SS colonel, was a fat little elf who rubbed his hands and laughed no matter what anybody said. He looked like a man who'd never been outdoors, much less hunting.

"Maybe he hunts women," said Willi, third in the trio of SS pals.

"Or boys, more likely," Meino said.

Voss reached inside his black tunic, brought out a cigar, and lit it. "Care for one?" he said to his friends.

Meino declined. Willi produced one of his own and said, "I'll have this."

They'd met years earlier: Meino built like a gross cherub, with big belly and behind, and balding Willi, with a fake dueling scar, made by a kitchen knife, on his cheek, and a newly installed *von* in front of his name. He now worked in the administration office of the SD in Berlin, while Meino was second-in-command of the Regensburg headquarters. They'd joined the SS in the late twenties, together fought communist dockworkers in Hamburg, together beaten up their share of Jews, got drunk together, threw up together, were staunch friends and brothers-in-arms — that would never change.

"Where are the wives?" Willi said.

"In the parlor, gossiping," Voss said.

Willi frowned. "No good will come of that," he said.

"What about this Frenchman?" Meino said, returning to an earlier part of the conversation.

"He's the military attaché in Warsaw," Voss said. "Made me look like a fool. Then Gluck hauled me up to Berlin and roasted my ass."

"Gluck?" Willi said.

"Obersturmbannführer, my boss."

"Oh, *that* prick," Willi said, expelling a long plume of cigar smoke.

"Lawyer prick," Meino said. "No?"

"Yes, before he discovered the party. *Opportunist.*" Voss spat the word. "I said something about getting even, but that made him even madder."

"So what? You can't let it end there," Willi said.

"Willi's right," Meino said. "I hate these French fairies — they think they own the world."

"This one needs to be taught a lesson," Voss said.

"That's right, Augi," Meino said. "You can't let him get away with it."

Voss thought for a moment. "Maybe we ought to pay him a visit, up in Warsaw. The three of us. Bring some friends along."

"Jah," Willi said. "Mucki Drimmer." Then he laughed.

"Where's old Mucki, these days?" Meino said.

"Dachau," Willi said. "Just under the commandant. I once saw him tear a telephone book in half."

"Isn't that a trick?" Voss said.

"Drimmer does tricks, all right. But not with telephone books. Tricks with a pair of pliers, and handcuffs, that's Mucki's style."

Voss laughed, then looked at his empty glass. "Back to the bar, for me."

Willi gave Voss an affectionate smack on the shoulder, people nearby turned around at the sound of it. "Cheer up, Augi, we'll put this right. Too long since I've been in Warsaw."

Then they went off to the bar.

23 December. Mercier's flight to Paris on the twenty-second had been delayed, and they'd landed at Le Bourget in darkness. He'd stayed at the apartment, cold and silent with Albertine off in Aleppo, decided he couldn't face dinner in a restaurant, so went to bed hungry, and feeling very much alone. He was glad to be out of there, at six the following morning, taking the express to Lyon,

240

then changing to the local for the trip down to Montélimar. And there stood Fernand, in his Sunday suit, by the battered old farm truck, smiling as Mercier walked toward him.

The truck, not much bigger than a car, had been a Renault back in the twenties but had become, over time, a collection of replacement parts cannibalized from every sort of machine. A handsome green, long ago, it had faded to the color of a gray cloud, the seat a horse blanket atop crushed springs, the two dials on the dashboard frozen in middle age, the gearshift sounding like a madman with a hammer. The engine managed a steady twenty miles an hour on a flat grade, but hills were an adventure meant only for the brave. It took them over two hours to reach Boutillon and then, twenty minutes later, at the end of a long allée of ancient lime trees, the house.

Still there, his heart rose at the sight of it. Not fallen into ruin, not quite, but surely dilapidated, the shutters askew, the earlier stonework laid bare in patches. Even so, a grand presence — foreign visitors wanted to call it a château, but it was just an old stone country house. Nevertheless, home. *Home.* Lisette stood before the door, alerted by the dogs, who'd heard the truck coming from a great distance down the road, as had most of the neighborhood. The dogs came galloping up the drive, barking like crazy, then ran alongside until the truck rolled to a halt, the ignition was turned off, and, a few beats later, the engine stopped.

They were excited to have him back, Achille and Céleste, a reserved excitement in the manner of the Braque Ariégeois: a muted whine or two, a lick on the cheek as he knelt and tousled their lovely floppy ears. Master greeted, they immediately wanted to go to field, anxious to work for him, their highest form of affection. "Not yet, sweethearts. Later on. Later." For now, Lisette made him an omelet, which he ate at the zinc-topped table in the kitchen; there was fresh bread from the Boutillon bakery and a glass of wine from a bottle with no label. As Lisette cleared his plate, Fernand brought him a telegram that had arrived that morning: HOME THE 27TH. gabrielle. "Madame Gabrielle will arrive on Friday," he said.

"I will make up her old room," Lisette said simply. But Mercier could tell that she was very nearly as excited as he was.

It was getting late in the afternoon, so he changed into his country clothes, smelling of months in a damp armoire, and took the dogs for a run. They pointed on birds, were released, then flushed a hare, which zigzagged away and just barely managed to get down a hole. Balked, they stood there, heads canted in puzzlement — *why does this happen?* — then turned to him, awaiting an answer, but even he, master of all, could do nothing. He stood by them, gazing over the pale winter field toward the mountains in the east. Then he walked for a long time, as dusk came on, at least some of the way across his property, once a run of wheat fields but now, since the 1920s, given over to the commercial growth of lavender.

Lavender had always grown wild in the Drôme, but the agronomists had learned how to grow it as a crop, and the perfume companies in Grasse paid well for whatever he could deliver. At harvest time, the air was heavy with the scent, as a few trucks, but mostly horse-drawn carts, piled high with purplish branches, moved slowly along the narrow roads. Enough money to live on, back when, but not now; life as a penurious country gentleman awaited him if he resigned his commission. The property-line lawsuit brought by his eastern neighbor had dragged on for years; bills from a lawyer in Montélimar arrived semiannually. Fernand and Lisette were paid for their service, wood and kerosene had to be bought in winter, straw and hay provided for Ambrose, the plow horse now living alone in a stable with eight stalls — a sad thing for a family with generations of cavalry officers — and Ambrose wasn't getting any younger. Gasoline for the truck, field help at harvest time, and taxes — *oh, the taxes* — it all added up.

Full dusk now, in typical winter weather for the south, the chill, moist air sharpened by a steady wind from the east. Foreign visitors called it the *mistral,* but that was the northwesterly and went on for days, famously making people crazy — an old law excused crimes committed from madness brought on by the incessant moaning of the *mistral* wind. He didn't want to go back to the house, not yet, he would turn for home at the end of the field, by a cluster of gnarled olive trees and a few cypress, tall and narrow. This land, like so much of the French countryside, was a painting, but Mercier felt his heart touched with melancholy and realized, not for the first time, that beautiful places were hard on lonely people.

"Achille! Céleste! Let's go, dogs, time for dinner."

They came loping across the field, tongues out now because they were tired, and headed for home.

■ ■ ■ ■

He stayed up late that night, reading in bed, wearing a sweater over his pajama top in order to stay warm. The kerosene heater had been turned on as darkness fell, and, when he went up to his room, found that Lisette had preceded him with a lidded copper pan on a long handle, filled with embers from the fireplace, and warmed the sheets, but the stone house breathed winter into every room, and you had to sleep with your nose beneath the covers.

The journals he'd brought with him from Warsaw should have put him to sleep, but they had the opposite effect. With smoke drifting up from a cigarette in the ashtray on the night table, he worked his way through an article in a journal called *Deutsche Wehr* — *German War* — one of several publications issued by the German General Staff. The writer made no secret of what Germany had in mind for the future: an army of three hundred divisions, sufficient fuel for ten thousand tanks and the same number of aircraft, and a prediction that medium and heavy tanks would be built to join the lighter models already in production. If the *Deuxième Bureau* had been clever enough or lucky enough to steal such information, it would have caused a riptide of reaction — meetings held and papers written as French military doctrine was re-examined in light of German intentions, yet here it was, for all the world to see. Did they read this journal in Paris? And, if they did, did they believe it? Or did they think that because it wasn't kept secret, it couldn't be true? *Woe to us if they do,* Mercier thought, and took a drag on his cigarette.

Turning to the *Militärwissenschaftliche Rundschau,* the military science review, he found an article by the chief of staff of the German Armoured Corps that discussed an attack in the north, a massive tank thrust through the Ardennes into Belgium and down into France, the same route they'd followed in the 1914 war and more or less what he'd witnessed at the Schramberg tank maneuvers. He'd sent the film off to Paris, with a detailed report of his observation, including the coordinated operations of air and ground forces. He couldn't say: *this is important;* he could only do his best to be descriptive, technical, and precise. What then? A note to General de Beauvilliers? No, not appropriate, simply: *listen to me.* And, really, why should they?

The German articles had, he thought, a

companion piece, which he'd read earlier that year, a book by the French general Chauvineau called *L'Invasion est-elle encore possible?* Is invasion still possible? With a foreword by none other than Marshal Pétain. Back in Warsaw, in a file cabinet, was a hand copy of Pétain's words, which Mercier had thought worth saving:

If the entire theatre of operations is obstructed, there is no means on earth that can break the insurmountable barrier formed on the ground by automatic arms associated with barbed-wire entanglements.

And, same drawer, same folder, General Chauvineau himself:

By placing two million men with the proper number of machine guns and pillboxes along the 250-mile stretch through which the German armies must pass to enter France, we shall be able to hold them up for three years.

Thus the answer to the question *Invasion, is it still possible?* — was *No.*

Two-ten in the morning: he turned the light out and pulled the covers up to his eyes.

Outside, the steady wind rattled his window and sighed at the corner of the house.

Christmas Eve. Fernand and Lisette had gone off to Grignan in the truck to spend Christmas Day with their son and daughter-in-law and grandchildren, so Mercier had the house to himself. Then, at seven in the evening, his Uncle Hércule, who lived on a Mercier property some ten miles south of his own, picked him up in the family Citroën, shiny and new, and took him home for the Christmas celebration. His father's only surviving brother, and easily his least favorite, Hércule was a thin, fretful man who'd become wealthy by speculating in South American railroad stocks, turned violently political, and now absorbed himself in writing right-wing pamphlets and letters to newspapers, often on the subject of Bolshevik designs to corrupt public waterworks. Still, holidays were holidays, and assorted Merciers must be gathered under one roof, attend midnight mass, then sit down together to *réveillon,* the traditional Christmas meal of black and white sausages and goose stuffed with chestnuts.

A long, long evening for Mercier. Fourteen people in the parlor, various aunts, cousins, nieces, and nephews, his uncle raving about the government, his widowed aunt, Albertine's mother, undertaking recollections of Mercier and Annemarie's years together, with mournful looks in his direction, two nephews in a tense conversation — one couldn't actually argue on Christmas Eve — about some silly American movie; another aunt had been to Greece and found it "filthy." Mercier was asked about Warsaw and did the best he could, but it was a relief when they left, in an assortment of automobiles, at eleven-fifteen, headed for the church in the village of Boutillon.

At the door of the church, Mercier knelt and crossed himself, then the family dutifully spent a few minutes in front of the Mercier family crypt, a flat marble slab with an inscription carved in the wall above it.

ICI REPOSENT LES DÉPOUILLES
MORTELLES
De Messires:
François Mercier de Boutillon Décédé à
Montélimar Le 29 Juin 1847
Mad^e La Chevalier Sa Femme née de
Mauronville Décédé à Boutillon
le 21 Février 1853
Albert Mercier de Boutillon Décédé à
Boutillon Le 8 Août 1868
Seigneurs de Boutillon et Autres Places

Transférées en ce Lieu Le 15 Août 1868
Sous les Auspices de Mr Combert Maire
et de Mr Grenier Curé de Boutillon
Au frais de Général Édouard
Mercier de Boutillon
Légion D'Honneur Domicilié à Boutillon

The crypt had been installed by Mercier's nineteenth-century ancestor Édouard, who'd paid for it — duly noted in stone, along with his decoration and the names of the mayor and the priest — moved a few mortal remains there in 1868, and then himself died in battle at the city of Metz, during the 1870 war with Prussia. And that was, Mercier thought, the problem with a family crypt, his family anyhow — the male ancestors fell in foreign fields and there, in vast cemeteries or graves for the unknown, they remained.

For Mercier, it was the ceremony of the mass that eased his soul: the sweetish smoke trailing from the censer, the ringing of the bell, the Latin incantations of the priest. In Warsaw, he attended early mass, at a small church near the apartment, once or twice a month, confessing to his vocational sins — duplicity, for example — in the oblique forms provided by Catholic protocol. He'd grown up an untroubled believer, but the war had put an end to that. What God could permit such misery and slaughter? But, in time, he had found consolation in a God beyond understanding and prayed for those he'd lost, for those he loved, and for an end to evil in the world.

As the service reached its conclusion, Mercier found himself suddenly aware of the congregation, the crowded rows of men and women, their heads raised toward the priest at the altar. And then, once again, he felt, as he had during his lunch at the Brasserie Heininger with General de Beauvilliers, a certain dark apprehension, a sense of vulnerability. This was midnight mass, not the manic gaiety of a Parisian lunch, but it was the same shadow. Was it, he wondered, brought on by the General Staff journals he'd been reading? If you took them seriously, they doomed these people to another war. But, he thought, he mustn't let his imagination run away with him. Conflict between nations was eternal, inevitable, and this one, between France and Germany, might burn itself out in the endless warfare of politics: in the struggle between radicals and conservatives, in the brutal economics of armament, in the carnival of treaties and alliances.

Mercier looked at his watch; it was Christmas. Soon enough the new year, 1938, and perhaps, he thought, a better year than this.

27 December. Mercier arrived early at the Montélimar railway station, anxiously watched the windows as the carriages rolled to a halt, then waved as Gabrielle stepped down onto the platform. How lovely she was, not her mother's looks, more a touch of his, the determined, pale Mercier forehead, dark hair, gray-green eyes. He was relieved to see that she was alone, not that he didn't like his son-in-law, a correspondent for the Havas news agency in Denmark, he did — but now he would have her all to himself.

As the truck rumbled toward Boutillon, she told him that she'd stayed overnight at the apartment, having taken the express from Copenhagen, through Germany, to the Gare du Nord. A trip ruined by what she called "that hideous Nazi theatre," SS men and their dogs, swastikas draped everywhere. "One grows weary of it," she said. "In the newspapers, on the radio, everywhere."

"A national illness," he said. "We'll have to wait it out."

"I'm afraid of them, the way they are now."

"You and half the world, my love."

"Perhaps we should have done something

about it. Paul certainly thinks so."

They came upon a flock of goats in the road, driven along by a young girl with a switch. Mercier stopped the truck as the girl herded the goats to one side. As he drove slowly past, she held the lead goat by the scruff of the neck. "Looking backward, yes," he said, as the truck gained speed, "but all we can do now is wait. And prepare for war."

"And you're in charge of that," she said.

Mercier laughed. "I'm in charge of a desk."

"Still," she said, "the Germans on the train were pleasant enough."

"No doubt. That's the worst part — they pretend not to notice. It's all that '*Still, sprach durch die Blume.*' "

"Which means?"

" 'Hush, speak through a flower.' Don't say anything about the government unless you praise it."

Gabrielle made a sound of disgust.

Enough of that, Mercier thought. "Can you stay through the new year?"

"Alas, I can't. I travel the last day of December; I'll see the new year in at the apartment. But I don't care, Papa, I wanted to see you, and I have vacation for the holidays."

Lisette had roasted a capon for dinner and Mercier found a Château Latour in the cellar, a 1923, which turned out — one never knew — to be perfect. They took the last of it into the parlor, where Mercier built an oakwood fire, using grapevine prunings for kindling. The dogs sat patiently, watching him as he worked, then lay on their sides in front of the fireplace and went to sleep.

"I've been wondering," Gabrielle said.

"Yes?"

"Are you seeing anyone, in Warsaw?"

"No, dear. Not really."

"You should, you know. It's not good for you to be alone."

"It's not so easy, Gabrielle, after a certain age."

"I would imagine, but still . . . you've surely met *somebody,* that you liked."

"I have, but she's taken."

"Married?"

"No, not yet."

"Well then, perhaps you should pursue her."

"Oh, I have, in a way."

Gabrielle looked dubious. "Really? Because, you know, if you had — well, many women would find you hard to resist."

"Mmm. I suspect you are biased, Gabrielle, love, but you're kind to say that."

"I'm not being kind, Papa. It's true."

"So then," he said. He took a sip of wine, then rose and added a log to the fire. "Any new paintings? At the national museum?" Gabrielle was the curator for western Europe, outside Scandinavia.

She shook her head at the change of subject and made a *what a difficult man* face. "Oh, all right, I'll leave you alone," she said. Then, "As for new paintings, there's too much to buy, that's my sad news. We're approached constantly by dealers who represent Jews. So, it's a buyer's market. You wouldn't believe what's become available."

Gabrielle went on. A wealthy Viennese, forced to sell his kitchenware company, had managed to smuggle a wonderful Flemish master, a de Hooch, into Copenhagen, and now . . .

Mercier was attentive — the time with his daughter was not to be wasted — but, deep within, he was very angry. *It doesn't go away.* You twisted and turned, spoke of this or that, but then there it was, waiting for you.

In time, they talked about Béatrice, his older daughter in Cairo. "How she loves it!" Gabrielle said. "You'll see, I brought along some of her letters. Her students are eager to learn, and Maurice works at the archaeological sites, the tombs, the buried villages. It would be perfect, she says, but she only

hopes they can stay there. Because of the political situation, in Egypt. . . ."

Gabrielle left on the thirty-first. Mercier had
to spend the New Year celebration *chez*
Uncle Hércule. Keeping to tradition, the
collected Mercier de Boutillons went out
into the garden at midnight, in drizzling
rain, to bang pots and pans in honor of the
new year. Then, on the third of January, he
took the train back to Paris and returned to
Warsaw the following day, to find the city
white and frozen.

On the fifth, his first day at the embassy, he
found two cables awaiting him. The first,
from Colonel Bruner, was very terse, little
more than an acknowledgment of his report
on the *Wehrmacht* tank maneuvers at
Schramberg, with faint praise to be read between the lines. The second cable, from
General de Beauvilliers, was rather more
generous, particularly on the subject of two
of the bureau's agents who had recorded
radio traffic during the exercise. The general
cited, specifically, one instance — "Q-24, a
ravine up ahead of you, about six hundred
feet" — where the pilot of the Fieseler
Storch worked by radio with the tanks
below. The French General Staff had little
interest in this concept — air-to-ground

communication — though de Beauvilliers believed it would be crucial in future warfare. "The marshal" — he meant Pétain — "and his clique think only of naval blockade and static defense."

Mercier was flattered to be so taken into the general's confidence, but, as he reached the end of the cable, found that such flattery would have its price.

Of course you will recall our interest in the *Wehrmacht* General Staff, specifically the section I.N. 6, and, should an opportunity present itself, we expect you will take full advantage of it, by any means necessary, in order to advance our knowledge of their thinking.

But, what if an opportunity did not present itself? Clearly, the general assumed he would know what to do about that.

At the intelligence meeting on the seventh, Jourdain began with his usual summary of recent political developments. And there was, as usual, no good news. Late in December, King Carol of Roumania had appointed the fascist poet Octavian Goga to head the government as virtual dictator. Anti-Semitic measures began immediately, and the

Czechs had reinforced border units at Sighet, where refugees were trying to get out of the country.

In Vienna, the trial of twenty-seven Austrian Nazis, accused of antigovernment activities, was now under way. German diplomats had tried to stop it, which led to a speech by the Austrian chancellor Schuschnigg, saying in effect that Austria wished to retain its independence as a nation. "He is holding firm," Jourdain said. "But we'll see how long that lasts." In Spain, Republican forces had taken the city of Teruel, but fascist forces were expected to counterattack, as soon as frontline units could be resupplied. In the USSR, the purges continued; longtime Bolsheviks arrested, interrogated, and shot. There was to be a new public trial, of Bukharin, Rykov, and Yagoda, the former head of the NKVD. "I expect they'll admit to their guilt, on the witness stand," Jourdain said dryly, and added that their own Jean-Paul Sartre had recommended suppression of public statements about the trial, since that might discourage the French proletariat. "Certainly discourages the Russians," the naval attaché said.

"And next, you'll recall Hitler's statement in December that Germany would never rejoin the League of Nations. However, Germany and Poland *have* reaffirmed their commitment to protect the rights of Poles and Germans living in each other's countries. Meanwhile, the League will be holding a conference in Belgrade, on the twentieth of this month, on the protection of ethnic minority rights in all European states, and on the progress of legal claims. It's an important conference — no laughing, gentlemen — the ambassador is invited, the chargé d'affaires will attend."

So, Mercier thought, *legal claims.* That meant the lawyers would be there, and *that* meant Anna Szarbek would be there.

Did he dare? The memory of Gabrielle, urging him on to pursuit, said he should. When the meeting ended, he had a look at his calendar — the twentieth fell on a Saturday, the League people would have a weekend in Belgrade, then begin talking on Monday. He walked from the chancery over to the public part of the embassy and climbed to the third floor, where the ambassador had installed a water cooler, just outside Madame Dupin's office. Mercier always took a cup of water when he happened to find himself there, not caring so very much for water, but liking, despite his forty-six years, the bubble that

259

floated to the top and made a noise.

He liked also, that morning, the fact that Madame Dupin never closed her door; her office was open to the world. "Jean-François? Come and say hello!"

First, in the gravest and most observed of French traditions: *what did you do on the holidays?* She'd been to Switzerland, she said, at a ski lodge. Cheese fondue! Villagers in costume! Folk dancing! *And,* Mercier thought, his attentive smile firmly in place, *God knows what else.* When his turn came, he dutifully reported on his visit to Boutillon.

And then, attacked.

"I'm told there's a League of Nations conference in Belgrade, in two weeks."

Madame Dupin shuffled through some papers, then said, "Yes, there is, a conference on legal rights, and ethnic minorities. Of interest to you?" She seemed skeptical.

"Perhaps. I understand the chargé is going."

This time she rummaged in her OUT box. Along with her duties as deputy director of protocol, Madame Dupin also managed embassy travel arrangements. "Here he is. Taking the night express on Friday — it only runs twice a week." She looked up, slightly puzzled at his question, then not. "Oh, of course! *Now* I see, Jean-François! You are, well, more than interested, aren't you." Her eyes glittered with conspiracy.

"I'd suppose your friend Anna will be there," he said, smiling.

"I presume she will be, as a League lawyer. Perhaps I should ask her."

"No, please don't. I just thought . . ."

"Shall I book your ticket?"

"I'll do it. The embassy shouldn't pay."

"Such an honorable fellow, our Jean-François." Her sly grin meant: *you devil!*

9 January. Slowly, the social wheels of diplomatic Warsaw began to grind once more. A cocktail party at the Dutch embassy, at six, to meet the new commercial attaché, Mynheer de Vries. Mercier pinned on his medals and trudged downstairs, where Marek and the Biook awaited him. They crept along the icy streets, high banks of shoveled snow on either side, a rather dispirited Mercier smoking his Mewa in the backseat. He'd booked a first-class room on the night express to Belgrade, expensive enough, and likely pointless. Anna Szarbek had made a decision that evening in the carriage, and now he was going to make a great fool of himself. Why had he allowed Gabrielle to provoke him into this? There were other women in Warsaw, among the restless wives of the diplo-

matic community, and the social set that fished in the same waters. *Merde,* he thought. *I'm too old for this.*

The cocktail party wasn't as grim as he'd feared. He avoided the Dutch gin, held a glass of champagne in his hand, and sampled the smoked salmon and pickled herring. Touring the room, he looked for Anna Szarbek, but she wasn't there, nor was Maxim. He did find Colonel Vyborg, standing alone, and he and the Polish intelligence officer exchanged news of their holidays. When Mercier mentioned his discoveries about German tank formations in the *Wehrmacht* journals, Vyborg just frowned and shook his head. "A bad dream," he said. "They write books and articles about what they intend to do, but nobody seems to notice, or care."

Then Mercier spent a few minutes with Julien Travas, the Pathé News manager, who had a luscious girl by his side. "A full house tonight," Mercier said. "All the usual characters, including us."

Travas shrugged. "They seem to ask me, I seem to go, and so they ask me again — they must have bodies to fill the room. And Kamila here has never been to one of these things. Enjoying it, dear?"

"I think it is very interesting," Kamila said.

"Mynheer de Vries has met Greta Garbo."

"And thinks you look just like her. Am I right?" Travas said.

"Well, yes, he *did* say that. Exactly that."

"Colonel Mercier is a war hero," Travas said.

"Oh yes? You must tell me your story, colonel."

"Someday," Mercier said. "At the next party."

Oh no! Here came the Rozens, everybody's favorite Russian spies, the sweet old couple bearing down on him like feeding sharks. "I think you're in demand," Travas said, steering his prize away. *"À bientôt,"* he said with a grin.

"So here you are!" Malka Rozen said, patting his cheek. "I *told* Viktor you'd be here, didn't I, Viktor."

Viktor Rozen looked up at her from his permanent stoop and said, "You did. It's true. Here he is."

"Now see here, my French comrade," Malka said. "Don't you like us? The most delicious dinner awaits you at our apartment, and you must eat sooner or later, no? You can't live on canapés."

"I've been very busy, Madame Rozen. The holidays —"

"Naturally," Viktor said. "But now it's January, the long freeze, time to visit friends, have a drink, a nice chicken — is that so bad?"

"Not at all," Mercier said, charmed in spite of himself. "Tell me," he said, "how are things back in the motherland?" *That ought to do it.* A shadow crossed Viktor's well-lined face. Was he actually, Mercier wondered, going to *say* something?

"The trials —"

"The trials of *winter*." Malka cut him off, and gave him a look.

"That's it," Viktor said. "Always difficult, our winter, but we seem to survive."

"Did you go home for the holidays?" Mercier said.

"No." Viktor's voice was excessively sharp. "I mean no, it's such a long train ride. To Moscow. Maybe in the spring, we'll go back."

Malka changed the subject. "You know what I think, Viktor? I think that Colonel Mercier won't come to dinner unless he gets an invitation. A written invitation."

"You're right," Viktor said. "That's what we should do. Send him a letter."

"You needn't do that," a puzzled Mercier said. "Of course I am so very busy, this time of year —"

"But it will make a difference," Malka said.

"I'm sure it will."

Mercier looked around the room. Had Anna Szarbek arrived? No, but Colonel de Vezenyi, the Hungarian military attaché, caught his eye and waved him over, so Mercier excused himself. And, oddly, the Rozens seemed happy enough to let him go.

For the next half hour, he circulated, visiting briefly with the usual people, saying nothing important, hearing nothing interesting, then thanked his hosts, told Mynheer de Vries they'd see each other soon, and gratefully headed out the door into a cold, clear evening.

The gleaming diplomatic cars stood in a long line outside the embassy; he found the Buick, and Marek held the door for him. As he slid into the back, he saw an edge of yellow paper on the floor, tucked beneath the driver's seat. As Marek pulled out of line and drove down the street, Mercier bent over and retrieved the paper — a square envelope. "Marek?" he said.

"Yes, colonel?"

"Did you stay in the car, while I was inside?"

"No, sir. I joined some friends, other drivers, and we sat in one of the cars and had a smoke."

Mercier turned the envelope over, then

back. It was cheaply made, of rough paper, not a kind he remembered seeing. The flap was sealed, and there was no writing to be seen. "Is this yours?" Mercier said.

Marek turned halfway around, glanced at the envelope, and said, "No, colonel."

"Did you lock the doors, Marek? When you joined your friends?"

"*Always,* colonel. I don't fail to do that, not ever."

Carefully, Mercier inserted an index finger beneath the flap and opened the envelope. The paper inside had been torn from a schoolchild's copybook, grayish paper with blue lines. The writing was block-printed, with a pencil, in French. There was no salutation.

We are in great difficulty, recalled home, and we cannot go there, because we will be arrested, and executed. Please help us leave this city and go somewhere safe. If you agree, visit the main post office on Warecki square, at 5:30 tomorrow. You won't see us, but we will know you agree. Then we will contact you again.

Please help us

Mercier read it once more, then said, "Change of plans, Marek."

"Not going home?"

"No. To the embassy."

The ambassador's residence was in the embassy, and he appeared at the chancery, in velvet smoking jacket over formal shirt and trousers, almost immediately after Mercier telephoned. Jourdain took longer, arriving by taxi a few minutes later. When he entered Mercier's office, the letter sat alone on a black-topped table. "Have a look," Mercier said.

Jourdain read the letter and said, "Well, well, a defection. And I thought it was going to be a boring winter. Cleverly managed, isn't it, not a clue to be found, unless you know which country's shooting people when they go home. Who wrote it, Jean-François, any theories?"

"The Rozens," Mercier said.

"You're sure?"

"Yes. They told me to expect it, at the Dutch cocktail party."

"I'm not surprised," Jourdain said. "Stalin's killing all the Old Bolsheviks now, cleaning house, installing his Georgian pals."

"How important are they?" the ambassador asked, reading over the letter once again.

"They're believed to be GRU officers," Jourdain said. "Soviet military intelligence.

We don't know their ranks, but I'd suspect they're senior, just below the military attaché."

"Not NKVD?" the ambassador said.

"No, not the real thugs. Of course they could be anything. Viktor Rozen could be a minor official, and Malka simply his wife."

"I would doubt that," Mercier said. "They work together — the invitation to dinner turns into a request for information, something very minor, then they'll try to give you money."

"Well, now *they'll* take the money," the ambassador said. "Or at least safety, their lives. And the information comes next. Not a provocation, colonel, is it?"

"I don't think so, sir."

"Devious people, the Russians," the ambassador said. "They see life as chess, draw you into some sort of clandestine rat maze, then shut the trap."

"I believe it's a legitimate offer to change sides," Mercier said. "Viktor Rozen seemed, ah, at least worried, maybe desperate. His wife's the strong one."

"Maybe she outranks him," the ambassador said. "That's not unknown. As for what's next, we — I mean you, colonel — cable Paris. Tonight. I'll want to see the text before it goes to the code clerk."

"Tonight?" Jourdain said. "Couldn't we . . . explore the possibilities?"

The ambassador's smile was all too knowing. "Your instincts are perfect, Jourdain, but if we dawdle, the bureau in Paris will want to know why. Still, colonel, don't say more than you have to, just follow the form."

"They'll be out here, sir," Jourdain said. "All over us."

"Maybe. Can't be helped."

"So, five-thirty tomorrow," Mercier said. "A visit to the post office."

"One can never have enough stamps," the ambassador said. "As for me, I'm off to the Biddles' dinner party, you two work out the details."

Jourdain and Mercier talked for a long time — what did they want, what could they get, what was the price of salvation, this week?

10 January. In civilian clothing, but well dressed for the occasion, Mercier strolled around Warecki square in a light snow. Then, precisely at five-thirty, he entered the busy post office, stood on line, and bought a sheet of stamps. Very pretty, they were, the two-groszy issue, blue and gold, with a handsomely engraved portrait of Chopin.

■ ■ ■ ■

14 January. At the Spanish embassy, an evening of flamenco. The ambassador represented the Republican, the legal, government of Spain, but it was known that there was a Nationalist, a fascist, ambassador in Warsaw, waiting to present his credentials. Franco's forces had now cut the country in two parts, holding the larger area, so it was, the diplomatic community believed, just a matter of time.

Mercier arrived at the Spanish embassy precisely at nine and found a seat at the end of a row toward the back. Not quite the usual crowd, he saw, the audience determined by political alliance, so neither the German nor the Italian diplomats were to be seen. But no problem filling the room, because half the Soviet embassy was evidently passionate for Spanish dance. Mercier did find Maxim — that was logical, because an evening of flamenco, *political* flamenco, was just the thing for Maxim's clever column in the newspaper — who'd saved the seat next to him with his folded overcoat. Then, as the lights dimmed and the Spanish ambassador took the stage, a familiar silhouette hurried down the aisle and took the saved seat. What went on in Mercier surprised him — only a glimpse of her silhouette. But enough. The Spanish ambassador was speaking, though Mercier never heard a word of it, until the end: ". . . the old and honored heritage of our nation, tonight gravely wounded and in peril, but which, like the passionate art we bring you this evening, will endure." Thunderous applause.

Mercier liked the flamenco well enough — the fierce guitar, the hammering rhythms of the dance — but his heart was elsewhere. And as the troupe returned for a second encore, he walked quickly up the aisle and out the door into the room where the reception would be held. On a long table covered with a red cloth, bottles of wine and plates of bread and cheese. He stood to one side and waited as the audience filed out.

Maxim was delighted to see him. He strode over, swung his hand back, then forward, grasping Mercier's extended hand as though he meant to crush it. "Here's the general! Say, how goes the war?" Standing slightly behind him, Anna raised her eyes, looked at Mercier, then lowered them.

"It's going well enough," Mercier said.

"Glad to hear it, glad to hear it, general, keep up the good work." With a proprietary hand on Anna's arm, he headed for the wine.

An intense crowd, that night. As Mercier

made his way across the room, the conversation was loud, excited, fervent. Opinion on the war in Spain was savagely divided — the battle for an ancient nation had become a battle for the heart of Europe. At last, by the door to the lobby, he spotted the Rozens, being lectured by a comic-opera official, a minister of some state, in tailcoat, pince-nez, and Vandyke beard. As Mercier approached, Viktor said something to the official and began to lead him away, the man making slashing motions with his hand as he talked.

Malka Rozen wasted no time. "It must be soon," she said, her voice an undertone, her false smile broad and beaming.

"Are you being watched?" Mercier said. "Here? Tonight?"

"I can't say. They're very good at it, when they don't want you to know."

"Our answer is yes — we're going to help you get out of Poland."

"Thank God."

"But you will have to help us, in return. You will come bearing gifts, as they say."

"What do you want?" The determination beneath the warm exterior was like steel.

"Photographs, that's best. Or hand copies. Of documents relating first to France — operations in Poland that involve French interests — and then to Germany."

"Why do you think we have anything like that? Our work is against Poland, not France, or Germany."

"Madame Rozen," Mercier said. He meant: *please don't play games with me.*

"And if we can't get anything you want? Then we die?"

"You work for people, madame, and I work for people. Maybe they're not so different, the people we work for."

"I hope they are," she said.

"Are you saying you won't try?"

"No, no. *No.* We'll try. But we don't have long. We were directed to return to Moscow last week. We told them we had important meetings in Warsaw, so our return was postponed — two weeks from today. After that, the knock on the door at midnight, and finished. For twenty years of secret work, for twenty years of faith and obedience, nine grams." The weight of a revolver bullet, Soviet slang for execution.

"We'll meet again, in four days," Mercier said. "There's a talk being given at the Polish Economic Ministry, 'The Outlook for 1938.' Surely you won't want to miss that. But, in an emergency, you can signal us. At the central post office, you'll find a Warsaw telephone directory in the public booth, the one by the window. On page twenty-seven, underline the first name in the left-hand column. Do this at nine in the morning or three in the afternoon, and we'll pick you up at the café on the other side of Warecki square, thirty minutes later."

"Page twenty-seven? Left-hand column?"

"That's correct. But I expect to see you on the eighteenth. And I expect you'll have something for us by then. At least a beginning."

She thought a moment, then said, "So, all-right, we'll look through the files." Her mood had changed: to resignation, and something like disappointment. Yes, she knew all too well what his job entailed, but she'd sensed in him some basic decency she'd hoped might play to their advantage and so had approached him and not the British — the other logical choice. But now, she discovered, he was like all the rest, and would play by the rules. When he didn't answer immediately, she said, "Maybe there's something."

"You'll do what you have to do, Madame Rozen. You know what's at stake."

Viktor returned, having shed the talkative official. "Playing nicely, children?"

Her look, sour and grim, told him what he needed to know.

Mercier nodded a formal goodby, walked away, and out the door.

■ ■ ■ ■

On the eighteenth, Mercier was among the first to arrive at "The Outlook for 1938," but the Rozens never appeared. He tried, sitting on a hard wooden chair, to keep his imagination in check, but it didn't work. As the economic minister droned on — "With the reopening of the Slawska mine, Silesian coal production . . ."—he could see them, as in a movie, opening the door at midnight, led to a waiting car, driven up to Danzig, then put under guard on a Soviet ship bound for Leningrad. Then the Lubyanka prison, the brutal interrogation, and the nine grams in the back of the neck. Mercier knew also that not all Stalin's victims got that far; the lucky ones died early, from rough treatment, or purely from fright. He hoped he was wrong — there had been no signal, and there were all sorts of explanations for the Rozens' absence — but feared he was right.

With Jourdain supervising the watch on the post office, Mercier left the embassy on the afternoon of the nineteenth. At home, he packed carefully, then dressed even more carefully, choosing a shirt on the fourth try — a soft one, thick and gray, with a maroon tie, and a subdued tweed sport jacket. Then he considered the supposedly "woodsy" cologne he'd bought the previous day, but decided against it. He was determined — strange, how desire worked — to be as much his usual self as he could be. And he guessed, given burly Maxim, that Anna Szarbek wasn't the type who liked men who wore scent. What *did* she like? What did she like about *him*?

Such obsession was better than brooding about the Rozens. There had been a flood of cables from Paris: someone in the bureau wanted double agents, the great prize of their profession, who would reveal what the Russians knew, and tell the Russians what the French wanted them to believe. The classic game of spies. But there was no time for that, and Mercier and Jourdain wound up *defending* them, like lions with a kill. The Rozens would give up their agent networks, Polish and possibly German, when they were interrogated in Paris, and would, before they were taken out of the country, steal from the Soviet embassy whatever they could. That is, Mercier thought, *if* they were still free. Or *if* they were still alive. Because there were occasions when these affairs ended very quickly.

Marek drove him to the Warszawa-Wiedenski station at 4:45 P.M., early for the 5:15 departure. His plan was to watch Anna Szarbek arrive — making sure that Maxim had not come to see her off — then "discover" her as they waited to board the train. At first, he was excited. From a vantage point by a luggage cart piled with trunks, he watched the platform; the locomotive, venting white steam with a loud hiss, and the smell of trains, scorched iron and coal smoke, suggesting journey, adventure. But then, as the hands of the platform clock moved to 5:10, excitement was replaced by anxiety. Where *was* she? When the conductor stationed himself by the steps to the first-class *wagon-lit,* Mercier realized he had to get on the train. Was he to travel by himself? In white letters on a blue enameled panel by the door, the train's route was announced:

Warszawa - Krakow - Brno
Bratislava - Budapest - Beograd

Beograd — the Serbo-Croatian name for Belgrade — was some seventeen hours away. Hours to be spent alone, apparently, in the splendor of his expensive compartment. Had she somehow managed to board the train without his seeing her? Perhaps she'd never even planned to attend the conference. But there was nothing to be done about it, and on the chance he simply hadn't noticed her arrival, he climbed the steps and a waiting porter showed him to his compartment. Splendid it certainly was. All dark-green plush and mahogany paneling, the shade of the reading lamp made of green frosted glass in the shape of a tulip, a vase in a copper bracket holding three white lilies. When night fell, the porter would open out the long seat and make the bed.

He raised the window and looked out on the platform, where a few passengers were running for the train as the conductor shooed them along, but not the one he was looking for. Then the whistle sounded, the train jerked forward, and a very chastened Mercier slammed the window shut and fell back on the seat. As the train left the city and gathered speed, the porter appeared, asking if he preferred the first or second seating in the dining car.

"Which seating has Pana Szarbek chosen?"

The porter peered at his list, down, up, and down again. "The lady is not listed, Pan," he said.

"Then, the second."

After the porter moved on, Mercier walked along the broad corridor, glancing at the occupants of each compartment, finding an assortment of passengers, reading, talking, already dozing, but not the one he was seeking. He reached the end of the car and entered the next — also a first-class sleeper — but saw only the embassy chargé d'affaires, thankfully absorbed in a newspaper as Mercier hurried past.

He returned to his own compartment, soon tired of the January countryside, lowered the tasseled silk shade, and, with a sigh, took a novel out of his valise, *The Red and the Black,* Stendhal, which he'd found in the library at the apartment, a book he hadn't read in years. It was, according to one of his instructors at Saint-Cyr, a political novel, very nearly a spy novel, one of the first ever written. But Mercier had not chosen the book for that reason — rather, it was akin to the tweed jacket, an adjunct of his traveling costume, and meant for Anna Szarbek's eyes. He had always an instinct for something improving, demanding, but by page fourteen he gave up and brought out what he really wanted to read, a Simenon *roman policier, The Bar on the Seine,* which he'd found in the French section of a Warsaw bookstore.

At eight-thirty, the train making steady progress across the dark fields, the porter rang his triangle, two chimes, signaling that the second seating would now be served. As

Mercier followed his fellow travelers to the door at the end of the corridor, the conductor collected his passport — a courtesy to first-class passengers that kept their sleep from being disturbed as they crossed borders through the night and, in addition, a courtesy often exploited by secret agents.

The dining car, each table lit by candles, was even more romantic than his compartment — well-dressed couples and foursomes gathered over white tablecloths, conversation low and intimate, the rhythmic beat of wheels on rails perfecting a luxuriant atmosphere of suspended time. Seated at a table for one, Mercier immediately noticed a handsome woman at the adjacent table, also alone, in black velvet jacket, her face lean and imperious beneath ash-blond hair going gray. The waiter arrived immediately and addressed her as *Baronin,* the German form of baroness, and, after he'd taken her order, she and Mercier exchanged an appreciative glance of recognition: *here we both are, how interesting.* When the waiter reappeared, he brought an apple on a plate — nowhere to be found on the menu — which she ate slowly, with knife and fork, her every motion precise and graceful and, somehow, suggestive. Meanwhile, Mercier abjured the cream of asparagus soup and toyed with a trout fillet in wine sauce. Too forlorn to eat, he sent the fish away and ordered a brandy. And so did the baroness.

A few minutes after nine o'clock, Cracow. As the locomotive idled in the station, the baroness finished her brandy, rose from the table, smiled at Mercier, and made for the door to the first-class *wagon-lit*. Well, he was done with his brandy as well, waited until she'd left the dining car, then headed in the same direction. Walking down the corridor, he saw that she was just entering her compartment, Compartment *C*, and her door closed gently as he passed.

Back in his own compartment, he found that the bed had been made up, the Polish National Railways blanket turned down at a crisp angle. He stretched out on top of it, raised the shade, and turned off the reading lamp. Outside, southern Poland in moonlight. They were going west now, a few miles above the border, the train rattling along at high speed. The little station at Oswiecim flew past, followed by Strumien, as they neared Karvina, where they would enter Czechoslovakia. Mercier was hard on himself. No more wild fantasies, he thought, that would never see the light of reality. Restless and unhappy, he realized he could not sleep in this condition, and decided to go for as much of a walk as the train would allow. He went out into the corridor, where, to the right, lay only a few compartments, from *H* to *A,* including *C,* and turned left.

Past the other first-class *wagons-lits,* a succession of second-class carriages, where the passengers sat on faded leather seats. Very smoky here, some travelers already asleep, others, lost in their thoughts, gazing into the darkness beyond the windows. He walked the length of the carriage, and was halfway down the next, when he saw a woman in a long gray coat, severely cut. She wore soft leather boots and a black beret, set slantwise on dark-blond hair pinned up in back. Engaged in conversation with a young woman in the seat by the window, she was facing away from the aisle. As Mercier paused by the seat, the young woman looked up at him. "Hello," he said. "Anna?"

She turned, startled to see him there, and said, "Oh." For a moment, she froze, eyes wide with surprise, lips apart. Finally she said, in Polish, "Ursula, this is Colonel Mercier."

The young woman acknowledged him with a formal nod and said, "Pleased to meet you, colonel."

"Ursula used to work at our office in Danzig," Anna said. "We met at the station in Cracow."

Mercier looked at his watch. "One can have a drink in the dining car now, the second seating has ended. Would you and your friend care to join me?"

"Ursula?" Anna said. "Want to come for a drink?"

Ursula thought it over, but her sense of the situation was sharp enough. "I don't think so. Why don't you go?"

"Are you sure?"

"Oh . . ."

"Don't be shy, you'll enjoy it! Ursula?"

"Thank you, but you go ahead, Pana Szarbek. Maybe later, I might join you."

As they walked toward the forward part of the train, Mercier said, "Do you have a suitcase?"

"I dropped it off — my compartment's up here somewhere — then I went back to visit with Ursula."

"Your own compartment?"

"A double. I've got the upper berth."

They reached the dining car and were shown to a table by a window. When they were settled, Anna said, "This is a surprise. Are you going to the conference?"

"Well, I could. The subject is certainly interesting."

Her eyes searched his, uncertain.

The waiter appeared, and Mercier said, "What would you like? A cocktail?"

"Maybe I would. Yes, why not."

"It's a long night ahead, might as well do what you like."

"Then I'll have a gin fizz."

"For me a brandy," Mercier said to the waiter.

Anna looked around, then said, "Very luxurious. You always seem to be in nice places."

Mercier nodded. "I'm fortunate, I think. My fellow officers are either in barracks or stuck on an island somewhere, taking malaria pills."

"You *are* fortunate."

"Well, not always, but sometimes. It depends."

She was again uncertain, hesitated, then said, "What interests you, colonel, about the conference?"

He went on about it for a time — national minorities, political tensions — until their drinks arrived. She took a sip of the gin fizz, then a second. "Good," she said. "They know how to make these."

"You can have another, if you like."

She grinned and said, "Don't tempt me."

"No? I shouldn't?"

"You were saying, about the conference."

"I really don't care about the conference, Anna."

"Perhaps you have — ah, a *professional* reason, to go there."

"I don't."

"Then . . . ?"

"I'm on this train because I found out about the conference, and guessed, hoped, that you would be on this train."

She hunted around in her handbag and found her cigarette case — Bacchus and the naked nymphs — put a cigarette between her lips, and leaned forward as he lit it. "So," she said, "an adventure on a train."

"No," he said. "More."

She looked out the window, then said, voice husky, her faint accent stronger, "There's no need to say such things, colonel." When she turned back toward him it was clear that she didn't at all mind the idea of an adventure.

"But it isn't just something to say." He paused, then added, "And, by the way, it's Jean-François. I think we agreed on that."

Suddenly, she was amused. "If I had a pocket mirror . . ."

He didn't understand.

"Well, you look quite a bit like a colonel, at the moment," she said. "Jean-François."

The tension broke. His face relaxed, and he put his hand on the table, palm up. After a pause, she took it, then inhaled on her cigarette and blew the smoke out like a sigh of resignation. "Oh Lord," she said. "I'd bid all of this goodby, you know, after the night of the storm." She waited a little, then said, "I suppose you've taken a fancy room, all to yourself."

"I have."

"And there we shall go."

"Yes. Now?"

"I'd like that second gin you suggested, if you don't mind."

"Why would I? I'll have another brandy."

She squeezed his hand.

He beckoned to the waiter.

They carried their drinks back to his compartment. "My, my," she said. "Lilies." He helped her off with her coat, inhaling her perfume, and hung it on a hook as she put her beret on the luggage shelf. The compartment was almost entirely filled by the bed, so she sat across the far end, her back against the panel by the window. She took her boots off, revealing black stockings, wiggled her toes, and sighed with relief.

Unlacing his shoes, Mercier said, "A long day?"

"Dreadful. All sorts of people to see in Cracow."

The train slowed, then entered a small station and, with a hiss of steam, came to a halt.

"What's this?" she said. "Not Brno, not yet."

"Kravina. Border control. Did you give your passport to the conductor?"

"Yes. When I got on."

Mercier took his jacket off and folded it on the luggage rack above him, put his tie on top of it, and settled at the head of the bed, back against the pillows, legs stretched diagonally down the blanket. A group of Polish and Czech customs officers came walking along the platform, heading for the second-class carriages. One of them glanced in the window.

"Did Marie Dupin tell you about the conference?"

"I heard about it; then I asked her."

"This was her idea all along, I suspect. Putting us together."

"She likes to take part in her friends' lives."

"True. She does."

She took the last sip of her drink and put the glass on the shelf below the window. Then she laced her fingers behind her head, closed her eyes, and moved around to get comfortable, sliding forward so that the hem of her skirt slid well above her knees. In the station, someone called out in Czech and a woman laughed.

"A nap?" he said, teasing her.

Very slowly, she shook her head. "Just thinking."

A porter, pushing a baggage cart that squeaked as it rolled, trudged past the window. Anna opened her eyes, turned to see what was going on, then closed them again. "Ahh, Kravina."

The locomotive vented steam, a passenger went past in the corridor, a suitcase bumping against the wall, and the train started forward, very slowly, the pillars of the station creeping past the window. Anna extended her leg and put her foot on top of his. Warm and soft, that foot. The train gained a little speed, crossing the town, past snow-covered streets and lamplit squares. A faint smile on her face now, she reached beneath her skirt, left and right, undid her garters, and rolled her stockings down, not far, just enough so that he could see the tops. Mercier turned off the reading lamp, then crawled over to her, and, telling himself not to be awkward, finished the job — his hands sliding over her legs, white and smooth, as the stockings came down. She opened her eyes, met his, and spread her arms. It was very quiet in the compartment, only the beat of the train, but, when he embraced her, she made a certain sound, deep, like *ohh,* in a way that meant *at last.* Then they kissed for a while, the tender kind, touch and part — until she raised her arms so he could take her sweater off. Small breasts in a lacy black bra. For a day at the Cracow office?

Madame Dupin, you told.

He kissed her breasts, the lace of the bra against his lips, and they wrestled out of their clothes until she wore only panties — again black and lacy — and he took the waistband in his fingers. They paused, shared a look of exquisite complicity, and she raised her hips.

Somewhere between Kravina and Brno, he woke, cold, the covers down, the speeding train hammering along the track between low hills. She slept on her stomach, curved bottom pale in the light made by the moon shining on snow. As he ran his fingers up and back, he watched her come awake, her mouth opened slightly, then widened as her eyebrows lifted — the delicately wicked face of anticipation.

At Brno station, the sleep of exhaustion.

But after Bratislava, as the train roared through a tunnel, he woke again, to find her making love to him, very excited, her hand between his legs, while her lower part, moist and insistent, straddled his thigh. "Easy . . . easy," she whispered.

Coming into Budapest, in the first trace of dawn, only a fond embrace. But very fond.

They went to the dining car for breakfast. The same waiter, discreet as he could be, yet somehow he made them aware that he knew exactly how they'd spent the night, and that he was a man who believed in love. "Do you eat breakfast?" she said.

"No, usually coffee and a cigarette. But I didn't eat yesterday, so" — he searched the brief menu — "I'll have the Vienna roll, whatever that might be."

"A sexual act?"

"Perhaps, we'll see. Not much privacy in here so it's probably cake."

It was, walnuts and apricot filling in butter-laden pastry. "Lord!" he said. "Try a little bite, anyhow." He fed her.

"What's next? Belgrade?"

"In two hours. Should we talk about Warsaw?"

"Maybe a few words."

"I'm in love with you, Anna. I want you with me."

"I will have to make things final, with Maxim."

"I know."

For a moment, she was lost in thought. Then touched his knee, beneath the table. "It's just the prospect of working it all out, saying things, leaving."

He nodded that he understood.

"I think I would have left him anyhow. But, are you sure? That you want to do this?"

"Yes. You?"

"Very sure. Since the storm. No, a day or two later. Anyhow, we can talk all this out in Belgrade."

"Not for long. I have to go back tomorrow: Sunday."

"*What?* No rights of national minorities?"

"Which hotel are you staying at?"

A long trip back to Warsaw. After a night together at the Serbski Kralj — King of Serbia — hotel, she'd accompanied him, late Sunday afternoon, to the railway station. In his compartment, he'd lowered the window, and she'd stood on the platform, hands in the pockets of her long coat, and they'd gazed at each other as the train pulled away, until he could see her no longer. Then he'd stared out at the winter dusk for a while, reliving various moments of the time they'd shared. But, finally, it was Simenon — all too soon finished — and, inevitably, Stendhal — far more compelling than he'd remembered — followed by the trout, this time consumed, and, back in his compartment, deep and dreamless sleep.

Paradise, really, compared to what Monday held in store. He'd gone directly to the embassy from the station, and into a meeting with Jourdain and the other military attachés. The usual grim business. He stayed on afterward, to speak privately with Jourdain.

"There's been no signal from the Rozens," Jourdain said. "We've had our Poles in and out of the post office."

"They missed the meeting on the eighteenth," Mercier said.

Jourdain looked up from his papers. "Has something happened?"

"Perhaps. We'll just have to wait and see."

Jourdain made a small sound of frustration. "We spend our lives waiting," he said.

"On a different subject, I've had a change in my — ah, personal life. Somebody I like. What would happen if she were to join me, in the apartment?"

Jourdain thought for a moment, then said, "I wouldn't, if it were me. They can't really tell you what to do, in your private life, but I suspect they think of the apartment as a kind of semi-official residence. *Somebody* will write a memorandum, you can count on that, and, after everything that's gone on the last few weeks, I'm afraid there might be a storm. The ambassador likes you, but I wouldn't want to ask him, if I were you, for protection in this area. Forgive me, Jean-François, but it's better if I tell you what I really think."

"I knew. More or less. Just thought I'd ask."

"Anyhow, congratulations. Who is she?"

"Anna Szarbek."

"The League lawyer?"

"Yes."

"Hmm. Lucky man," Jourdain said.

Back in his office, a clerk delivered mail from the diplomatic pouch. Wading through drivel of every degree — a change in the form for filing certain reports, a new chargé d'affaires appointed in Riga — he came upon a yellow manila envelope. Inside — attached to a note from Colonel Bruner — a white envelope addressed to "André," his work name in the Edvard Uhl operation, holding a letter, handwritten, in German:

6 January, 1938

Dear André,

I write from Paris, and I am informed that this letter will reach you in Warsaw. I leave soon, for a new life in Canada, a new job, with a small company, and a new place to live, a small town near the city of Quebec. So, I have already started to learn to speak French. Now, I do not regret what I did. As I look toward Germany and see what goes on there, perhaps it was for the best.

I am writing on the subject of the Countess Sczelenska. I know now that she was not a countess, and her name was not Sczelenska. This doesn't matter to me. I still have dear memories of our love affair. I don't care how it came to happen — my feelings for her are undiminished. I miss her. I like to think she might have some feeling for me, as well. At least I can hope.

Would you say farewell for me? Tell her of my affection for her? And that, should this unhappy Europe some day find itself in better times, perhaps, on that day, we might meet again. I would be eternally grateful if you would say these things to her on my behalf.

A flowery German closing was followed by Uhl's signature.

The note from Colonel Bruner stated that the letter was being sent on to him because it was now felt that the bureau might, in certain circumstances, have further use for Uhl, and they wanted to keep him happy. Of course Mercier would not reveal to Hana Musser, who'd played the role of Sczelenska, where Uhl was, or what he was doing, but it might not be the worst thing to let her know of the letter's existence and Uhl's sentiments. "Just in case, in future, we need to induce him to undertake new work on our behalf."

Mercier had maintained Hana Musser's small stipend; he might require her services, and, also, he liked her — though he would never tell Bruner that. He wrote out a brief dispatch: acknowledged receipt of the letter and agreed to let Hana Musser know of Uhl's safety, his affectionate farewell, and his hope to, some day, see her again.

25 January. Mercier's regular meeting with Colonel Vyborg was scheduled for that morning, but there would be no *ponczki* — or so it seemed — since Vyborg had shifted the meeting from their usual café to his office at General Staff headquarters, in the

Tenth Pavilion of the Warsaw Citadel: a vast fortress, containing the Savka Barracks, built under the nineteenth-century Russian occupation and located north of the central city, facing the Vistula. Vyborg's office was down a long hallway from the room where, famously, Marshal Pilsudski had been held prisoner, in 1900, by the Russian secret police.

Mercier arrived promptly at eleven, to discover that Vyborg had ordered the café to deliver a dozen *ponczki*s to his office, where they'd been laid out on a plate from the regimental china service. There was coffee in a silver urn, and the cups and saucers were also from the regimental china. Sugar, cream, linen napkins — what sort of news, Mercier wondered, awaited him? On the wall above Vyborg's desk, a beautifully drawn map, in colored pencil, of an estate called Perenska, with some of the surrounding countryside included. Mercier walked over to the map to have a better look at it.

"My country home," Vyborg explained. "The map was drawn by Captain de Milja, in our Geographical Section."

"It is very handsome," Mercier said.

"I'm pleased you find it so."

They settled at a table by the window,

looking out at the river. Vyborg poured coffee, Mercier attacked a *ponczki,* and they chatted for a time, this and that. Mercier knew that Vyborg might soon be made aware of Soviet networks spying on Poland — if the Rozens were still alive — but he could say nothing. This information would go from the *Deuxième Bureau* to the head of Oddzial II, Polish military intelligence, the *Dwojka* — protocol, always protocol. And, since a separate section handled the USSR, the information would not damage Vyborg personally. The discovery of spies was a double-edged sword — congratulations on finding out, why didn't you know earlier.

When they were done with gossip, Mercier said, "Any special reason to meet in your office?"

"There is, I'm afraid. Something not for a café." In Vyborg's voice, a slight discomfort.

So then, bad news. Mercier lit a Mewa and waited.

"We have reason to believe," Vyborg said, "that certain people are interested in you."

"Which people, Anton?"

"A woman of Ukrainian origin, who works at a travel agency on Marszalkowska, was observed, on three occasions, watching the building where you live. And seen both near your embassy and on your street, a German

297

of Polish nationality, a nasty-looking character called Winckelmann. He was using a fancy Opel, black, the 1937 Admiral model" — Vyborg looked down at an open dossier — "Polish license plate six, nine-four-nine. For what looked a lot like surveillance. This Winckelmann is known to work, from time to time, as a driver for SD officers at the German embassy."

"A nasty-looking character, you say. A small fellow, with a pinched face? Who might remind one — diminutive but fierce — of a weasel?"

Vyborg was delighted. "A weasel! Yes, exactly. Evidently you've seen him."

"The day of the Uhl abduction. Also, the same car. Did you say *you've* seen him?"

"Not in person." Vyborg produced, from the dossier, a photograph, which he handed to Mercier.

Taken from a window above Ujazdowska avenue with a long-range lens, the slightly blurred image of a man behind the wheel of a parked automobile, eyes staring up and to the right, apparently watching the street in the rearview mirror.

"The weasel?"

Mercier nodded, then looked up at Vyborg and said, "Your agents were in a building on my street? And near the embassy? You aren't going to tell me this is a coincidence, are you?"

Vyborg said, "No, I'm not," quietly, an admission made with only faint reluctance. "You mustn't be angry, Jean-François. The *Dwojka* cares for its French friends and makes sure, every once in a while, that all goes well with them. It's done by the counterintelligence people — not my department — and, as you might suppose, the same sort of thing goes on in Paris, with *our* attachés."

Vyborg wasn't wrong, Mercier suspected, but, even so, he didn't like it. He took a sip of his coffee.

"None of us are saints, my friend; we all watch each other, sooner or later. Have another *ponczki.*" Vyborg lifted the platter and extended it toward Mercier.

As Mercier chewed, he watched a barge on the river, working upstream.

"And, I would say, in this case the practice works to your benefit. Any idea what's going on?"

Mercier thought it over. "I don't know. Perhaps the fact that I spoiled their abduction —"

"Very unlikely. People in this business know that once these little wars begin, it's very hard to stop them. A silent treaty — we keep our hands off each other. I don't mean recruitment, that never ends. They might probe to see if you were gambling, or doing whatever it might be that could be used for blackmail, but, as far as I know, you lead a rather respectable life. And if they *were* recruiting, it wouldn't look like this."

Mercier shrugged. "Uhl wasn't all that important. At least, we never thought he was. A view into German tank production; surely they're running similar operations in France."

"Of course they are. Anyhow, as the host country, we have some responsibility for your well-being — I hope you won't hold it against us."

"No, Anton, I understand."

Vyborg made a certain gesture, palms brushing across each other, washing his hands of an unpleasant task. "So now you know," he said with finality. "May I have my photograph back?"

The following days were not easy. Mercier waited for Anna to call, as they'd agreed in Belgrade, and for the Rozens, who did not signal. They lived in a room near the Soviet embassy, but to go anywhere near there would, he knew, be more than foolish. When he told Jourdain about his meeting with Vyborg, the second secretary wasn't sure what the surveillance might mean; all Mercier could do was stay alert and report the incident to Paris. Technically, a complaint could be made to the German embassy, through diplomatic channels, but all they would hear back was polite denial, innocent as dew. And, as a potential enemy, Germany had to be treated with restraint — one learned more from smiles than frowns. So Mercier returned to work, now much too aware of people and automobiles, and trusting the telephone even less than usual — a wisp of static on the line implying more than it ever had before. By the twenty-ninth, a cold front froze the city, temperatures below zero, the nights dead still under brilliant stars, and Mercier's life froze with it.

But, not so bad, that life. The evening of the twenty-ninth found him stretched out on the chaise longue in the study, finishing *The Red and the Black,* a swing band on the radio, a fire in the fireplace, a brandy at his side. The cook had left earlier. Wlada had finished washing up and gone to her room. Mercier turned a page, and somebody pounded on the street door. He looked up, and heard it again, this time accompanied by a muffled voice. What was this?

He swung his legs off the chaise and put on

his slippers. Now the pounding was louder, and so was the voice — distantly, he thought he could make out the sound of his name. He went to the window, cranked it open, the cold air hitting him like a fist, and leaned out. Whoever was hammering on the door was in the alcove and couldn't be seen, but the voice was clear as a bell. "Mercier! Please! Let me in! Please!" A woman, shouting in German. And he recognized the voice: Malka Rozen.

Mercier ran for the door. Wlada was already there, in her bathrobe, trembling, looking at him desperately. "Calm down, Wlada," he said, rushing out the door and down the stairs. From above, one of the upstairs tenants was peering anxiously over the banister. "Colonel?" he said. "Is everything . . . ?"

"Sorry," Mercier shouted back. "I'll see about it."

From above, an irritated grunt followed by the slamming of a door.

"Oh God," Malka Rozen said as he let her in. "He's hurt."

"Come upstairs." As they climbed, Mercier held her elbow, steadying her. She wore an old coat and a shawl over her head.

"You must find Viktor," she said, her voice edged with panic.

As they reached the apartment, Mercier said, "What happened?"

"It's them. They know."

"Merde."

"What?"

"Doesn't matter." He led her inside, past Wlada, who held her hand over her mouth. Malka turned and grabbed Mercier by the wrists. "He's in the park, a little park, up at the top of Ujazdowska."

"Why?"

"He fell, on the ice, and hurt his ankle; he couldn't walk. So he told me to go on ahead."

"The park. Three Crosses Square? In front of a church?"

"Yes. A church."

"Wlada," as Mercier hurried back toward the study, he lost a slipper, "take Pana Rozen into your room and lock the door."

"Yes, sir," she said. Then, to Malka Rozen, "Please, Pana, come with me." Her voice was shrill with panic.

Mercier kicked off the other slipper, whipped the drawer of his desk open and took out the 9-millimeter Browning, checked to see if it was loaded, and put it in the waistband of his trousers. Then he pulled on his shoes and squirmed into his overcoat. Checking to make sure he had his keys, he called out to Wlada, "Don't let anybody in here, Wlada. Wait for me to come back." He had at least one Soviet spy, and he meant to keep her.

The night was brutal. Mercier shivered and tried to run, but his knee didn't like the weather any better than he did, so he limped along as quickly as he could. She hadn't meant Lazienka park, had she? That was at the *other* end of Ujazdowska. No, she'd said *church*. Saint Alexander's. *Please God, let her be accurate.* Mercier took the Browning from his waistband and moved it to the pocket of his overcoat. *The first thug I see — that's it.* He gripped the butt tightly and swore as the cold worked through his clothing. Curse the stupid war wound — why couldn't he go faster? A man attempting to walk a shivering dog took one look at the expression on Mercier's face and pulled the dog away, back toward his building.

By the time he saw the cross and dome atop Saint Alexander's, Mercier was out of breath. The tiny park was enclosed by a line of evergreen shrubs and an iron railing. *Vault over.* He damned the stupidity of his inner voice and hobbled along the fence, looking for the gate. Once past the shrubs, he saw a man seated on a bench, hands in pockets, head almost touching his knees. Gone? It was not unknown. Dawn in Warsaw would sometimes reveal bodies, glazed with ice, dead where they'd sat down to rest, or passed out drunk, on a freezing night.

Mercier found the gate and rushed to the bench. *Yes, Viktor Rozen.* Eyes closed, mouth open. Mercier said, "Wake up, Viktor, we must get you away from here," and tugged at Rozen's shoulder. There was something wrong with him. Mercier said, "Are you ill? Wounded?" Rozen didn't respond, Mercier gripped him under the arms and raised him to his feet. Rozen revived, swaying as Mercier held him upright, then, with Mercier bearing most of his weight, took a small step, then another.

Out past the shrubs, the engine of a car. A car going very slowly. Mercier hung on to Rozen with one hand, drew the Browning from his pocket with the other, and waited for a Russian to appear. But the car went past.

"Let's go inside, where it's warm," Mercier said, voice gentle.

Rozen took a step, then another, and began walking, with a moan every time his foot hit the ground. *Sprained ankle.* "Not too far now," Mercier said. "Keep walking, we'll be there soon." Viktor didn't answer; he seemed distant, vague, not completely conscious of where he was. Had he been drinking? No, something else.

Rozen staggered along. Mercier staggered with him, past the iron palings and elegant buildings of the avenue. Suddenly, Viktor began to sing, under his breath. Mercier swore. This was very bad, he'd seen it on winter battlefields; soldiers who talked nonsense and did odd things — taking their boots off in the snow — and died an hour later. "Viktor?"

Rozen giggled.

Mercier shook him hard.

"Stop! Why do you hurt me?"

"We have to hurry."

"Oh."

Rozen actually managed to move faster, supporting his weight on Mercier's shoulder. Then, as Mercier searched for a house number, to see how close they were, a man emerged from the shadow of a doorway, walked quickly out to the avenue, then stopped dead, a few feet in front of them. Short hair, thick body, a pug face. Mercier moved to put himself between Rozen and the man, took the Browning out of his pocket and held it away from his side. The man stared at him, face without expression, and stayed where he was. When he opened his mouth — to speak? To call out to his fellow agents? — Mercier aimed the gun at his heart, finger tight against the trigger. The man blinked, and his face turned angry, very angry; he wasn't afraid of guns, he wasn't afraid of Mercier. But then he turned, slowly, all insolence, and walked across the avenue, his footsteps loud in the night silence.

When they were again under way, Mercier said, "Who was he, Viktor?"

"Some fellow."

"Someone after you?"

"I wouldn't know."

Mercier was exhausted by the time he got Rozen up the stairs. He fumbled for his keys, opened the door, shoved Rozen inside, leaned him against the wall, and pulled the door shut behind them. At which moment Malka emerged from Wlada's room, pushed past him, and cried out, "Viktor!"

"He's suffering from exposure," Mercier said. Then he called out to Wlada, who peered, wide-eyed, from the safety of her room. "Go run a bath, Wlada, hot water, as hot as you can get it."

"Yes, sir."

Wlada ran ahead of them into the bathroom. Malka and Mercier held Viktor up between them. He was singing again, a children's song. "What's wrong with him?" Malka said, horrified.

"It's the cold."

When they reached the bathroom off Mercier's bedroom, Wlada was already on her knees, finger under a stream of steaming water. "Get his clothes off," Mercier said. As Malka began to unknot Viktor's tie, Wlada fled.

"She is very nervous, your maid."

"She'll survive. Tell me what happened."

"Someone at the embassy, a friend, a friend from the old days, suddenly wouldn't talk to me. But it was in his eyes — he'd been questioned, I could *feel* it. So I knew. Then, tonight, we stayed late, but there were people in the file room, security people, and all I could do was look at one of my own operations, where I'm permitted to look, and then I went and got Viktor, and we left. As we walked down the street to our building, we saw one of their cars, so we went into a little grocery store, where we always shop, and left by the back door. Nothing new to us, conspirative work. . . ."

"Were you able to take anything from the embassy? From the files?"

"Yes, it's hidden in our room. But they'll find it soon enough."

"What sort of —" In the study, the whirring ring of the telephone.

"Go ahead, colonel," Malka said. "I'll get him into the tub."

In the study, Mercier stared at the telephone for a moment, looked at his watch, ten-thirty, then picked up the receiver and, voice tentative, said, "Hello?"

"Hello, Jean-François, it's me." She paused, then said, "Anna."

"Are you allright?"

"Is it too late to call? You sound . . . distracted."

"No, some excitement here, but nothing to worry about." *There's a naked Russian spy in my bathtub, otherwise . . .*

"Well, it's done. I came back on Thursday, and I've found a place to live. A room and a little kitchen, over on Sienna street. Seventeen Sienna street. Not much, but all I could afford."

"Don't worry about money, Anna."

"Perhaps I shouldn't have called, you sound — maybe not a good time to talk?" In her voice, suspicion: *who are you with?*

"I'll explain later, it's only work, but, ah, very unexpected."

"I see. It wasn't so good with Maxim. A lot of shouting, but I suppose I knew that would happen."

"I can't blame him. He's losing a lot. A lot."

"Yes?"

"Yes. Can I telephone you at work? Tomorrow morning?"

"You still have the number?"

"Anna!"

"Very well, then. Tomorrow."

"I can't come over there right now. I want to, you don't know how much, but I have to take care of this — situation."

Her voice softened. "I can imagine."

He laughed. "When I tell you, you'll realize there's no way you could have imagined. Anyhow, you're my love, and I'll call you, see you, tomorrow."

"Good night, Jean-François."

"Tomorrow?"

"Yes. Good night."

Mercier returned to the bathroom. The door was closed. "Do you need anything?" he said, his voice rising above the running water.

"No," Malka said. "He's taking a bath."

Mercier went back to the study, looked in his address book, and dialed Jourdain's number at home. The phone rang for a long time before it was answered. Finally, Jourdain's voice. "Yes?"

"Armand, it's Jean-François. Sorry to call

you so late."

"I don't mind."

"The meeting with the ambassador — is it still at eight-thirty?"

"It is, in my office."

"There was some talk of moving it to nine-thirty."

"No, eight-thirty, bright and early."

"Very well, I'll see you then. Sorry if I disturbed you."

"Don't be concerned. Good night, Jean-François."

There was no meeting. The telephone call was a signal — operations could now begin to take two Russian spies out of Poland.

1:45 A.M. Outside, the silence of a winter night, so cold that frost flowers whitened the windows of the study. Viktor Rozen, now apparently recovered, sat near the fire, wearing Mercier's bathrobe, his heaviest sweater, and two pairs of his socks. He warmed his hands around a glass of hot tea laced with brandy, sipping it Russian-style, through a cube of sugar held between his teeth. Malka sat by his side, smoking one cigarette after another.

"There wasn't much to do with France," Viktor said. "Our agents in Polish factories reported on armaments produced under French license, and we tried to reach your diplomats. . . ." Both Rozens gave Mercier a glance. *And you see how that turned out.*

"Our own operations worked against the Poles," Malka said. "A major on the General Staff, a director of the telephone company, maids at the hotels, a few factory workers. And significant penetration of the socialist parties — Moscow Center is obsessed with this, so that's where we spent money."

"What were the maids doing?" Mercier asked.

"Going through briefcases. Foreign diplomats, businessmen, anyone important. Including the Renault delegation from Paris, back in October. One of them kept a diary, foolish man, a, how shall I say, a very *frank* diary. His conquests."

"Did you use it? Against him?"

"Who knows, what Moscow does. We just sent the photographs of the pages."

"Well, try to remember the name — you'll go through all that in Paris," Mercier said.

"When do we leave?" Viktor said.

"Tomorrow," Mercier said. "That is, today."

"They'll be watching everywhere," Viktor said. "You'd better be armed."

"Don't worry, we're prepared for, eventualities."

"I hope so," Malka said.

They sat for a time and watched the fire, logs glowing red, a firefall of sparks. Viktor said, "Mostly, we did what everyone does — war plans, arms production, political personalities, border defenses." He shrugged. "I doubt it's very much different from what you do, colonel."

Mercier nodded — that was likely true. "Any German networks?"

"Quite a number of them," Malka said. "But we didn't handle them. That was the preserve of the elite."

"Not you?"

She smiled. "Once upon a time, a few years ago, but the Jews in the service aren't so favored, these days. They no longer trust us, the Old Bolsheviks — look what they were going to do to Viktor and me. Don't tell the world, but Stalin's just as bad as Hitler."

"Why not tell the world?"

"Because they won't believe it, dear colonel." She threw the end of her cigarette into the fire and lit a new one.

"So, no German information."

"Gossip," Viktor said. "In an embassy, you hear things."

"Such as?"

"Surely the Poles already know. Camp Rummelsburg, in Pomerania, where they train spies to work in Poland. It opened in 'thirty-six, they're thought to have run about three thousand people through there. And, of course, the Polish branches of I.G. Farben and Siemens-Schuckert are used as espionage centers. But, as for names and dates, this never came our way. Maybe if we'd had some time with the files . . ."

"Any gossip about the I.N. Six?"

"I.N. Six?" Viktor said.

"Guderian's office," Malka said. "In the Bendlerstrasse." The address of the German General Staff.

"Oh," Viktor said. He pondered a moment, then shook his head.

"What do I remember about I.N. Six?" Malka said. "Was that CHAIKA? Kovak's operation?"

"No, no, it wasn't Kovak, it was Morozov."

"He's right," Malka said. "It was Morozov."

"What's CHAIKA?" Mercier said.

"A codename. Means the bird, very common water bird, makes a squawk? In all the harbors, everywhere."

Mercier came up with *seagull,* but didn't know the German. "I'll look it up," Mercier said. "What does it have to do with I.N. Six?"

"A GRU officer called Morozov had this operation a few years ago," Malka said.

"Someone who worked in the I.N. Six office, codename CHAIKA, had concealed a political affiliation, from the early thirties. He'd been a member of the Black Front, Adolf Hitler's opponents in the Nazi party, the left wing. You remember, colonel, the Strasser brothers?"

"I do. Gregor was murdered in 'thirty-four, the Night of the Long Knives. But his brother Otto survived."

"He did, went underground, and continued his opposition."

Mercier knew at least the basic elements of the story. The Nazi party, soon after its birth, had split on ideological lines; some of the original members were committed to the socialist agenda — it was, after all, the National Socialist Party, *Nazi* the German slang derived from the first word — and proposed sharing German wealth and land with the working class. But the wealthy supporters of the party, Baron Krupp, Fritz von Thyssen, and others, wanted no part of that and Hitler, desperate for money, sided with them, ordered the murders, in 1934, of some of his opponents, and forced the others to pledge support to the right-wing side of the ideology. Otto Strasser, Mercier knew, was still in opposition, operating from Czechoslovakia.

"Anyhow," Malka continued, "Morozov determined to put pressure on this CHAIKA, to force him to become a Soviet agent."

"What happened?"

"Morozov was purged. But this operation never really got under way, because . . ." She stopped, unable to remember the reason.

"Because of the name!" Viktor was delighted with his memory. "Morozov had the name — Kroll? something like that — from a German informant who'd been a member of the Black Front and was now hiding in Poland, but the problem was that the Black Front used false names — after all, they were being hunted by the Gestapo. So the name Kroll, or whatever it was, was meaningless, there was nobody in the I.N. Six with that name."

"Not Kroll," Malka said.

"I think it *was.*"

"No, it wasn't."

"What then?"

"Köhler, dear. That was it."

Viktor smiled fondly and said to Mercier, "Isn't she something?"

30 January, 6:35 A.M. Fully dressed, his Browning automatic on top of his folded overcoat, Mercier telephoned Marek, his

wife answered, and the driver was called to the phone. "Good morning," he said.

"I must go to the embassy, Marek."

"Yes?" Marek's voice was cautious, Mercier almost always walked the few blocks to the embassy.

"To prepare for a meeting," Mercier said.

"When shall I come for you?"

"As soon as possible."

"Ten minutes," Marek said, and hung up.

By 6:50, they were under way, the Rozens in the backseat, Mercier sitting beside Marek. Mercier had left the building first, walked up and down the street, then returned for the Rozens. Marek on one side, Mercier on the other, they ran for the idling Buick.

"We're going to Praga," Mercier said. "Do you have a weapon?"

Marek patted the side pocket of his bulky coat.

"Don't hesitate," Mercier said.

"Who are we expecting?"

"Russians. NKVD Russians."

"Will be a pleasure."

They crossed the Vistula, now a sheet of gray ice, wound through the factory district, down a side street, and into the loading yard of a vacant foundry, the smell of scorched brass strong on a windless morning. Jourdain was waiting by his car, slapping his gloved hands against each other to keep the blood moving. "Nice day for a ride in the country," he said to Mercier, his words accompanied by puffs of white steam. Then, to the Rozens, "Good morning, I'm here to help you." Formally, they shook hands.

"Where's Gustav?" Mercier said.

"He should be along in a minute; he's been trailing your car since you crossed the river."

A motorcycle pulled into the yard, skidding to a stop on the cinders. The rider's face was shielded by a wool scarf, worn just below his goggles. He nodded hello and revved his engine by way of greeting.

"No point waiting, Jean-François. Gustav leads the way, you follow, I'll be right behind you."

As they drove away from the factory, Malka Rozen said, "Where are we going?"

"Konstancin," Mercier said.

They drove fast through the early morning streets of Praga, past factory smokestacks, the black smoke hanging still in the frozen air, crossed back into Warsaw, turned southeast, and followed the river, the motorcycle slowing, then accelerating, as Gustav watched for idling cars, or trucks moving to block the way. Speed was something of an art, Mercier realized — the traffic policemen gave them a look, but did nothing. Gradually, the city fell away and they moved swiftly along a country road, through the village of Konstancin — elaborate houses and well-groomed gardens — and out the other side.

Mercier saw that Marek was intent on the rearview mirror, shifting his eyes every few seconds. "What's back there, Marek?"

"A big car; he's been with us since the outskirts of the city."

"What kind of car?"

"It has a hood ornament — perhaps the English car, called Bentley?"

Rozen — Russians and Poles understood each other's languages — said, "Nothing to worry about."

"You're sure?"

"Too rich for us."

Not if it's been stolen.

But a few minutes later, Marek said, "Now he turns off," and Mercier relaxed. It was quiet in the car. Up ahead, Gustav leaned over as they sped around the curves, and then he signaled, pointed down a dirt road, and swung into it. They slowed, bouncing over frozen ruts and potholes, turned hard at a sharp corner, and jolted to a stop. Parked in the road: an ancient relic of a truck, its bed holding rows of milk cans. Gustav reached inside his leather coat and produced a cannon of an automatic pistol, a box magazine set forward of the trigger guard. As the motorcycle sped around the truck on the driver's side, Mercier twisted around to see that the Rozens were staring at each other, and Malka had taken Viktor's hands in hers. "Get on the floor," Mercier said, turned back, drew his own weapon, and opened the door a crack. From the right-hand side of the truck, a path ran up a hillside and disappeared. A dairy farm up there? Maybe. Maybe not.

Gustav came skidding to a stop by the driver's window of the Buick. He said, his words muffled by the scarf, "Nobody in there. What do you want to do?"

"Wait." Mercier left the Buick and, keeping his eyes on the hillside, walked backward to Jourdain's car. "No driver," he said.

"They'd have been on us by now," Jourdain said.

"I think so too."

Mercier walked back past the Buick and, as he did, Marek got out of the car and started to follow him, but Mercier motioned for him to stay with the Rozens. Reaching the truck, he yanked the front door open and looked inside. On the seat, a newspaper and half a sandwich in a piece of brown paper.

Planting one foot on the running board, he hauled himself up and slid behind the wheel, searched the dashboard, flipped the starter switch, and gave the engine some gas. When it coughed, Mercier pulled out the choke and it rumbled to life. He shifted into first gear and raised the clutch, driving forward a few yards, then turning the wheel hard. The truck went bumping into a pasture. Mercier looked back, made sure he'd left room for the cars to get by, then turned off the engine.

As Mercier walked back toward the Buick, a man pushing a handcart loaded with milk cans appeared on the crest of the hill, dropped the handles, and came running, shouting and waving a clenched fist.

Mercier was then next to the motorcycle and Gustav waggled his huge pistol and said, "Shall I calm him down?"

"Don't bother."

"He is quite upset."

"So would you be."

Jourdain was leaning against the hood of the Buick. He raised an eyebrow, his expression ironic and amused. *"Vive la France,"* he said.

A mile down the dirt road, a hand-painted sign said *Konstancin Flying Club*. Since the 1918 rebirth of the country, flying had become immensely popular, and private clubs dotted the countryside surrounding the wealthier villages. Not much to look at: a few old planes parked in a field of dead weeds, a limp wind sock on a pole, and a tin-roofed shack. Watching the treeline, Mercier and Jourdain hurried the Rozens inside. One of the embassy guards was waiting for them, stoking a potbelly stove with a poker.

"All quiet?" Jourdain said.

"All quiet," the guard answered. "Too cold to fly."

"Any idea when they'll be here?" Mercier said to Jourdain.

"I was at the embassy around midnight, sent the signal, and got a confirmation. So, they're on the way."

The Rozens sat on lawn chairs, Malka found a tin ashtray from a Warsaw café and lit a cigarette. Viktor sighed and looked mournful. The desperation of flight had given way to the reality of the future, Mercier thought. The Rozens would never again go home. "Tell me, colonel," Viktor said, "where do you think we might live?"

"I don't know," Mercier said. "In a city, somewhere. It will be worked out later."

"They won't stop looking for us," Malka said.

"You'll have to keep that in mind," Jourdain said. "Wherever you go."

"We will," Viktor said. "Forever."

"Still, a better fate than what lay in store for you," Mercier said.

Viktor nodded: *yes, but not all that much better.*

When Mercier heard a drone in the distance, he checked his watch — just after eleven — went outside, and saw a plane descending on the northern horizon. He watched it for a time, then returned to the shack. Malka Rozen was looking out the window. "Stay inside until we're sure," Mercier said. Gustav, dozing in a kitchen chair, awoke and joined Malka at the window. Mercier went back out, Jourdain followed him. A trimotor Bréguet circled the field, then landed, bouncing across the uneven ground, coming to rest close to the shack.

Mercier shivered in the cold. The door of the plane opened and a man in a flying overall hopped out, then offered a hand to someone behind him, but the hand was not taken. A moment later, Colonel Bruner appeared in the doorway, dressed in full uniform and standing at attention, as though he expected to be photographed. Mercier swore under his breath.

"Ah, the hero arrives," Jourdain said.

"Well, they belong to him now — he's bringing the prize home to Paris, to be the envy of all eyes."

The three men greeted each other, Bruner his most formal self, drawn up to his full height, such as it was, and ruddy-cheeked with excitement. "So," he said, "where are my spies?"

"They're inside," Mercier said.

They went into the shack, and Bruner was introduced to the Rozens; he was silent, his hands clasped behind his back, his greeting a bare nod. "You can put their luggage on the plane," he said to Mercier.

"We have nothing," Viktor said.

This, for some reason, Bruner found irritating. "Oh? Well, let's hurry along, shall we?"

They filed out the door and walked to the airplane. A co-pilot appeared at the entry and helped Viktor climb up, then it was Malka Rozen's turn. Looking back at Mercier, she said, "Thank you, colonel," took a deep breath, and wiped her eyes. "It's the cold air," she explained, as the co-pilot helped her aboard.

"Very well, then," Bruner said, triumphant, savoring his success. He entered the plane and was followed by the pilot, who closed the door behind them. The Bréguet made a tight turn, taxied down the field, lifted at last, cleared the trees, and headed west, soon a black dot in the sky, its drone fading, then gone.

Back at the embassy, in the midst of writing a dispatch describing the exfiltration of the Rozens, Mercier telephoned Anna Szarbek and invited her for dinner at his apartment. He completed the dispatch, took it down to the code clerk, then went back to Ujaz-dowska avenue. The coming evening called for planning and logistics: a shopping list for the cook, Wlada to spend the night at her sister's house.

At 8:20, a proper twenty minutes late, Anna Szarbek arrived in a taxi — she'd declined Mercier's offer to pick her up — and knocked at the street door. Mercier rushed to let her in, and they embraced — tentatively, a faint apprehension on both sides. But then, following her up the staircase, the sway and shift within her soft skirt so intoxicated him that, by the time he reached the landing, he was more than prepared to skip the preliminaries altogether. Nonetheless, after a tour of the apartment, he started the fire, lit the candles, and poured champagne. On the sofa, she looped her arm through his and rested her head on his shoulder. "I hope you weren't disturbed," she said, "that I called so late, last night."

"Not at all."

"You sounded — absorbed."

"Too much excitement. Some of my work showed up here, two people, and had to be dealt with. A — how to say — a fugitive situation."

"They came to your *apartment?*"

"They weren't invited, my love. They needed refuge, and they knew where I lived, so . . ."

"Did you have the police?"

"No, thank God. I managed without them."

"You are actually brave, aren't you?"

"Not if I can help it."

"Oh, I don't think you can help it, Jean-François, I think it's in your blood, from what you said in Belgrade."

At the hotel in Belgrade, they had told their growing-up stories and exchanged family histories, Mercier's reaching back to the Crusades. "All those warrior ancestors," she said. She took his hand, studied the signet ring, and said, "It's this." She slipped it off, put it on her finger, then spread her hand to admire it. "Now you may address me as *countess.*"

"I'm not anything like a count, countess,

just a lowly *chevalier,* a knight in service to the king."

"Still, a noble." She put the ring back on his finger. "The only one I've ever known."

"Ever?" This was more than unlikely.

"I mean, as I know you." She took off her boots, tucked her feet up beneath her, and slid her hand between the buttons of his shirt. "I'm just a Polish girl from Paris."

"Oh poor you," he said. "Poor lawyer."

"Good in school, love. With hardheaded parents — parents with no sons. So, somebody had to do something." They were silent for a time, and he became aware of her hair, silky against his skin, and her fragrance. "I find it warm in here," she said, undoing a button on his shirt, then another. "Don't you?"

The cook, perfectly aware of what was planned for the evening, had done her best — a roasted chicken and boiled carrots left in a warm oven — and later that night, Anna in Mercier's shirt, he in the bathrobe, they ate — it was a sin to waste food — what they could.

3 February. All courtesy, the noble Mercier had telephoned Anna and invited her to his next obligation, a dinner party given by the Portuguese consul. "I appreciate your asking

me," she'd said, "but I suspect you are reluctant and, honestly, so am I." This was, and they both knew it, the social reality of diplomatic Warsaw. Some courageous souls insisted on bringing their "fiancées" to balls and dinner parties, and nobody ever said a word about it, but . . . Mercier was frankly relieved, and, on the evening of the third, he was accompanied to the consulate by Madame Dupin.

In the library, joining the men for cigars after dinner, Mercier found himself in the company of one Dr. Lapp, believed, by a certain level of local society, to be the senior *Abwehr* — German military intelligence — man in Warsaw. Officially, he worked as the commercial representative of a Frankfurt pharmaceutical company, but nobody had ever known him to sell a pill. Very much an old-fashioned gentleman, Dr. Lapp — the honorific referred to a university degree; he was not a medical doctor — of slight stature, in middle age, and bearing some resemblance to the sad-faced comedian Buster Keaton. And, like the comedian, he was often to be seen in a natty bow tie, though tonight he wore traditional dinner-party uniform. They had met before, on various occasions, but had never actually spoken at length. "Life going well, for you?"

he said to Mercier.

"Not too badly. Yourself?"

"One mustn't complain. Were you in Paris, for the holidays?"

"I was, then I went down to the south."

"I envy you that, colonel."

"The south?"

"Paris. A magnificent city. Would that be your preference, if your career took you there?"

"I like Warsaw well enough, but I wouldn't mind. And for you, Dr. Lapp, would you prefer Berlin?"

"I only wish I could."

"Really? Why is that?"

"Frankly, I find the situation in the capital not much to my taste."

This was flagrant, and Mercier showed the edge of surprise. "You don't care for the present regime?"

"Mostly I don't. I am a loyal German, of course, and surely a patriot, but that can mean many things."

"I suppose it can. You are, perhaps, a traditionalist?"

"And why not? The culture of old Europe, civility, stability, was not such a bad thing for Germany. But it's all gone now, and the people who are in power these days will presently have us at war, and you know what that meant in 1918."

"Not so much better for us. We called it victory, and marched through the streets in 1918, but *victory* is a curious word for what happened in France."

Dr. Lapp nodded, and said, "Yes, I know. Where were you, on that day?"

"In fact I was a prisoner of war at Ingolstadt, Fort Nine."

"Our most illustrious prison, at any rate. For our most eminent prisoners — the Russian Colonel Tukhachevsky, now sadly executed by his government; your Captain de Gaulle, lately a colonel; France's most prominent airman, Roland Garros; and plenty of others. So you were, at least, in good company. How many escape attempts, colonel?"

"Four. All of which failed."

"Of course I would have done the same thing. Honor demands it."

"And where were you, on the day of the armistice?"

"At my desk, faithful to the last, at the naval General Staff office in Kiel. My section concerned itself with the submarine service." Dr. Lapp paused, then said, "Tell me, are you still in touch with Colonel de Gaulle?"

Mercier hesitated, unsure where Dr. Lapp

was leading him, but more than conscious of being led. Toward some variety of treason, he sensed. But to France? Or Germany? Finally, he could think of nothing to say but the truth; it would have to do. "From time to time, a letter," he said. "We are more colleagues than friends."

"And do you subscribe to his theories of warfare? I've read his book."

"I've read it as well, and I believe it should be taken seriously. I suspect, the next time around, it will not be trenches and wire."

From Dr. Lapp, a gracious smile: *success.* What success was that? "I agree," he said. "But better, far better, if there is no next time around. I wonder if, sometime, we could speak in a more private setting?"

To this, Mercier had to say *yes.*

"Some people I know may not be so much the enemies of France as you would think. Do I need to elaborate?"

"No, Dr. Lapp. I believe I perfectly understand you."

Without speaking, Dr. Lapp acknowledged this understanding. Did he bow? Did his heels come together? Not overtly, yet something in his demeanor implied such gestures without the actual performance.

Mercier left the library, collected Madame Dupin, and hurried her out to the car. "Did

331

something happen?" she said.

"It did." Before Marek could pull away from the curb, Mercier took a pad from his pocket and feverishly made notes, trying to reproduce the conversation with Dr. Lapp.

"Something good, I hope."

"Maybe," Mercier said. "It won't be up to me."

The following morning, he was in Jourdain's office as the second secretary was hanging up his coat. When they were settled at the table, Mercier read from his notes. "Astonishing," Jourdain said. "It sounds like he wants to open some sort of secret channel between us and the *Abwehr.*"

"Shall I report the contact?"

Jourdain drummed his fingers on his desk. "You're taking a chance either way. If you report immediately, they may say *no.* But, if you don't do it now, eventually you will, and then they'll have a tantrum."

"Why on earth would they say *no?*"

"Caution. Fear of provocation, false information, trickery. Or some variety of internal politics."

"That would be foolish, Armand."

"Yes, wouldn't it though. Because I suspect this contact was carefully planned and could lead to important information. First of all, what was Dr. Lapp even doing there? Surely he wasn't invited as a stray German businessman. No, he was invited as an *Abwehr* officer. So, he asked the consul — or someone above him asked someone above the consul — to arrange for both of you to attend the dinner. Don't forget that Salazar, the Portuguese dictator, is an ally of Germany. May I see the notes?" Mercier handed the pad to Jourdain, who turned a page and said, "Yes, here it is. He manages the conversation in such a way that he makes a seemingly spontaneous reference to the submarine service in Kiel. And that means he's referring to Admiral Canaris, head of the *Abwehr* and captain of a submarine in the Great War. Better, if he truly served in Kiel, he is likely a friend of Canaris — a friend for twenty years. So, he is more than reliable."

"And Canaris is, potentially, disloyal?"

"Maybe. One hears things, wisps, straws in the wind, but who knows. What is certain is that the *Abwehr* loathes the SD: Hitler, the Nazis, the whole nasty business. It's as much social as it is political, the *Abwehr* see themselves as gentlemen, while the Nazis are simply gangsters. And the *Abwehr,* as part of the General Staff of the *Wehrmacht,* does not want to go to war."

"Why me, Armand?"

"Why not you? This all came about because your spy lost his nerve on a train. And then word got around that it was a French officer who fought off an SD abduction up on Gesia street. So Dr. Lapp wonders, *Who is this Colonel Mercier?* Looks up your *Abwehr* file, sees that you served with de Gaulle, sees that you're progressive and not part of the old Pétain crowd. Then he goes back to his boss and says, 'Let's approach Mercier, we think he can be trusted.'"

"Trusted?"

"His balls are in your hand, Jean-François — he has to assume you won't squeeze."

"Why would I?"

"Exactly. They have you figured out."

"I mean, what could I make them tell me? I was up half the night, thinking about what happened, and I finally realized that the information I most want, from the Guderian bureau, the I.N. Six, is the one thing I'll never get, not from the Bendlerstrasse — they won't betray their own."

"Correct."

"He certainly knew my history, prison camp and so forth. Recited the names of my fellow prisoners."

"Of course he knew. He spent a lot of time, preparing for his *chance meeting,* which is plain old good intelligence work. Really, it's too bad about the Nazis — if Dr. Lapp and his friends ever took power, Germany would be a very useful ally." Jourdain extended his index finger and pointed east, toward Russia.

"Is there any chance of that?"

"None. Blood will flow, then we'll see."

A Shadow of War

11 March, 1938. In Warsaw, one lately heard the expression *przedwiosnie;* an ancient term for this time of year, it meant "prior to spring." The streets were white with snow, but sometimes, early in the morning or toward evening, there was a certain gentle breeze in the air — the season wasn't turning yet, but it would. The softening of winter was not so different in Saint-Germain-en-Laye, an aristocratic village at the edge of Paris where, in centuries past, the French had stored royal fugitives from across the Channel, in expectation of the ascent of Catholic monarchy to the English throne. They'd given that up, more or less, by March of 1938, and now used one of the former exile mansions to hide the two Russian spies from Warsaw.

Separately and together, the Rozens had been interrogated. First the handwritten autobiography, then the questions, and the answers, and the new questions suggested by the answers. The Rozens told them everything, revealed a treasure trove of secrets going back to 1917, when, young and idealistic, they'd given themselves to the Russian revolution that would change the world. Which it certainly had — producing counterrevolutionary fascist regimes in Hungary, Italy, Roumania, Bulgaria, Spain, Portugal, and Germany. Fine work, Comrade Lenin!

And so, in cities across the continent, quite a number of individuals sipped their coffee on the morning of the eleventh, blissfully unaware that their names and indiscretions were filling the pages of *Deuxième Bureau* files and that this information would presently, in some cases anyhow, be forwarded to the security service of whatever nation they called home. Therefore, again in some cases, tomorrow would *not* be a better day.

For instance, the émigré Maxim Mostov, a literary journalist in Warsaw. At dawn, as the *przedwiosnie* breeze brushed tenderly against his bedroom window, he slept peacefully with a proprietary arm thrown over his new mistress, a sexy Polish girl who worked as a clerk at the Warsaw telephone exchange. Sexy and *young,* this one — the loss of his previous girlfriend had bruised his self-esteem, so here in bed with him was some exceptionally succulent compensation.

The four men from the *Dwojka* certainly thought so, giving one another a meaningful glance or two as she struggled into a bathrobe. Leaving the bedroom door open — please, no jumping out the window, not this morning — they permitted the couple to get dressed, then escorted Maxim back to the Citadel. And if he'd been frightened by the knock on the door and the appearance of the security service, the march through the chill stone hallways of the Citadel did nothing to soothe his nerves. Nor did the two men across the table, military officers who wore eyeglasses; for Maxim, an intimidating combination.

He had, of course, done nothing wrong.

Malka and Viktor Rozen had been — well, not really friends, more like *acquaintances*. That was the proper word. And did he know that they were officers of the Soviet spy service? Well, people *said* they were, and he'd suspected that people might be right — but such rumors often went around, in a city like Warsaw. And what had he told them? No more than gossip, the very things he wrote about, quite publicly, in his feuilletons.

So then, had he accepted money?

Maybe once or twice, small loans when he

found himself in difficult circumstances.

And had the loans been paid back?

Some of them, he thought, as best he could remember, possibly not others; his life was chaotic, money came and went, he was always busy, going about, finding stories, writing them, this and that and the other thing.

And did he have family in the USSR?

He did, one surviving parent, two sisters, uncles and aunts.

Perhaps the Rozens mentioned them, now and again.

In fact they had. Asked after their health, in the normal way of people from the same country.

Did they say, for example, that they were *worried* about them — their health, their jobs?

No, not that he could remember. Maybe once, a long time ago.

At that point, the two officers paused. One of them left the room and returned with a third, this one rather formidable, tall and thin-lipped, with pale brush-cut hair, who wore the boots of a cavalry officer and was, from their deference toward him, senior to the interrogators. He stood to one side of Maxim, hands clasped behind his back.

"We will continue," the lead interrogator said. "We want to ask you about your friends. People you know in the city. Later, we'll ask you for a list, but for the moment we want to know if they helped you."

"Helped me?"

"Told you things. Gossip, as you called it, about, for example, diplomats, or anyone serving in the Polish government — the kind of people you met at social events."

"I suppose so. Of course they did — when you talk to your friends, they always tell you things: where they've been, who they've seen. It's common human discourse. You have to talk about something besides the weather."

"And did you pass any of this information on to the Rozens?"

"I might have. There's so much. . . . I can't think of anything specific, not anything . . . secret, not that I can recall."

"Very well. Take, for example, your former friend Pana Szarbek, who I believe you intended to marry. She is employed by the League of Nations, did she tell you things about her work? Things about, say, contacts in foreign governments?"

Here Maxim paused. Evidently, the subject of his former fiancée was a painful one — he'd been hurt, was now likely angry about her leaving him for another. Which was, for Maxim, as for much of the world, quite normal, as it was also normal to feel that those who have hurt you should themselves be hurt in return, unless you were the sort of person who didn't care for the idea of spite.

"Well?" the interrogator said. "Do you understand the question?"

"Yes."

"And so?"

"I don't remember her doing that. She didn't often speak about her work, not in specific terms. If she had a troublesome case she might say it was difficult, or frustrating, but she never spoke of officials. They — for example, tax authorities — were simply part of her job."

The interrogator looked past Maxim, at the tall officer standing to his left, then said, "Now, what contacts did you have with employees of the Polish government?"

In Warsaw, the endgame of the Rozen confessions went on for more than a week. Senior officers of a major on the Polish General Staff confronted him when he arrived for work — they were, at least technically, responsible for what he'd done, so the wretched job fell to them. They spent an hour with him, then placed a revolver on his desk, left the office, and closed the door. Fifteen minutes later he reappeared, weeping, and trying to *explain*. They sent him back inside and, soon enough, were rewarded with the sound of a shot. The hotel maids were visited at home — one didn't want to go stirring up the guests — where the scenes varied: some tears, some defiance, some absolute silence, and one case where a young woman slipped out a back door and was never seen again. As for the rest, from factory workers to a company director, they were arrested, questioned, tried in secrecy, and sent to prison. Not all of them; some were actually not guilty — the Rozens, confessing for their lives, had been somewhat overzealous in the naming of informants. As for Maxim Mostov, he was, after lengthy discussions within the senior *Dwojka* administration, deported. Driven to the Russian frontier and put on a train.

21 March. The vernal equinox arrived with a slow, steady rain. The grimy snow of winter began to wash away, and though Warsovians ruined their shoes and cursed the slush, they felt their spirits soar within them. Similarly, Colonel Mercier, who admitted to himself, the evening of the twenty-first, that he was as happy as he'd ever been. The apartment Anna Szarbek had found on Sienna street

was not unlike an artist's studio. One large room — with adjoining kitchen and bath — on the top floor, with grand windows slanted toward the sky. "Have you ever wanted to be a painter?" he said.

"Never."

"Does this studio not inspire you?"

"Not to paint, it doesn't."

He saw her point. It had become their preference to make this place home to their love affair. Not that the Ujazdowska apartment wasn't elegant and impressive, it was, but a private loft better suited their private hours. Sometimes they ate at the small restaurants of the quarter, but mostly they lived on cheese and ham — now and then Anna managed to produce an omelet — drank wine or vodka, smoked, talked, made love, and had some cheese and ham.

Mercier's vocational existence had, thank heaven, returned to normalcy. He had reported the contact with Dr. Lapp to *2, bis,* and the response had been . . . silence. "They're frozen solid," Jourdain had theorized. "Either that, or they're fighting over the bone." This was all well and good, Mercier thought, but somewhere down the road there would be a telephone call or a letter and he would have to bid or fold his cards — he couldn't pass. But if *2, bis* wasn't in a hurry, neither was he.

Anna stood at the window, watching the raindrops slide down the glass, her mood pensive. "I did hear something disquieting," she said. "I ran into the janitor's wife at the market — the janitor who works where I used to live — and she said that Maxim had been taken away by some sort of civilian police, returned, with an escort, to pack whatever he could, and left. He told her he was being sent back to Russia."

"I'm sorry to hear it," Mercier said.

"It can't be true, I tell myself, that you had anything to do with this."

Mercier was startled, but didn't show it. It took only a few seconds for him to work out the sequence of events, beginning with the Rozens' defection. "I have no need to do such things," he said.

"No, it's not like you," she said slowly, as much to herself as to him.

"It sounds as though he's been deported. Maybe he was selling information — to the wrong people, as it turned out."

"Maxim? A spy? That's what you're saying, isn't it?"

"It wouldn't be the first time. Foreign journalists will sometimes take money, from, as I said, the wrong people."

She left the window and sat in an easy

chair. "I suppose he might have done something like that. He never had enough money, felt he'd never reached his proper place in the world. He was desperate to be important — loved, respected — and he wasn't."

"What I can tell you is, if he's been deported, he's lucky not to be in prison."

Anna nodded. "Still, I feel sorry for him," she said. Then, looking back at the window, "Will this stop soon, do you think? I wanted to go for a walk."

"We can take the umbrella."

"It's not very big."

"It will do." Mercier stood. "I think we left it by the door."

The vernal equinox came to Glogau as well, but there, in the SD office above the toy shop, it rained bad news. That morning, Sturmbannführer August Voss received a formal letter from his superior in Berlin. In the next room, the lieutenants heard a prodigious oath and, faces tense, looked up from their work and stared at each other. *What now?* On the other side of the wall, Frogface Voss tore the letter into strips, then had to piece them back together to make sure his eyes had not deceived him. They hadn't. The axe had fallen; he was being transferred to Schweinfurt. *Schweinfurt!* What was in

Schweinfurt? Nothing. A ballbearing factory. Such an office would handle internal matters only. A visitor from Holland? Follow him! A complaint about the government, overheard in a tavern? Haul the traitor in! Filthy, silly, local nonsense — Gestapo country, the SD little more than a spectator. And, to drain his cup of humiliation down to the last miserable dreg, his chief lieutenant was to be promoted and would supervise the Glogau office. *The reorganization to be completed in thirty days from this date.*

So, now that French bastard had really done it. With trembling hand, he snatched up the telephone receiver and called Major Meinhard Peister, his friend Meino, in Regensburg.

27 March. Meino and Willi and Voss rode the train up to Warsaw. They'd wanted to drive in Willi's new Mercedes, but the Polish roads in March could be more than an adventure, so they took a first-class compartment on the morning express. They weren't alone, a young couple had the seats by the window, but something about the three men made them uncomfortable, so they got their valises down and went looking for somewhere else to sit. "That's better," Willi said, with a wink, once they were gone.

"We'll need a car, up there," Meino said. He'd put on weight, now more than ever the gross cherub.

"It's all arranged," Voss said. "They'll pick us up at the station."

From his briefcase, Meino produced a bottle of schnapps. "Something for the trip." He pulled the cork, took a sip, and passed the bottle to Willi, who said *"Prost"* before he drank. Then he said, "What do you have in mind, Augi?"

"Give him something to remember," Voss said. He nodded up at his valise.

"What's in there?"

"You'll see."

"Been a long time since we did this," Meino said.

"A few years," Willi said. "But I haven't forgotten how."

"Remember that giant pig, up in Hamburg?" Voss said.

"Tried to run away? That one?"

"Who?" Meino said.

"The communist — the schoolteacher."

"Screamed for his mama," Willi said.

Meino laughed. "That one."

"We'll want to get him alone somewhere," Willi said.

"Don't worry about that," Voss said, taking a turn with the schnapps. "My people up there have been watching him. It may take a day or two, but he'll be alone sooner or later. Or he'll be with his doxy."

"Nothing like an audience," Willi said.

"Better," Voss said. "For what I have in mind."

In Warsaw, they were picked up by Winckelmann, driving the Opel Admiral, and taken to a commercial hotel south of the station. "Likely he's home for the night," Winckelmann said. "But we'll see about tomorrow."

"I can't stay here forever," Willi said.

"He's at the embassy a lot of the time, but he goes out to meetings. That would be the best, if you want to get him alone."

"That's what we want," Voss said.

"See you in the morning," Winckelmann said. "Eight-thirty."

They went out that evening, to a nightclub up on Jasna street called the Caucasian Cave that Winckelmann had suggested — one of the so-called "padded nightclubs," walls covered with heavy fabric to keep the riotous noise inside. The club was in a cellar, with a doorman who wore the big fur hat common to the Caucasus. They ate lamb on skewers, an old Jew played the violin, and a few of the girls got up to dance — girls in heavy makeup, gold earrings, and low-cut peasant blouses. One of them sat on Willi's knees and tickled his chin with a feather. "Care to go outside?" Willi said, in German. "To the alley?"

"The alley! You must be kidding me," she said. "You boys come over from Germany?"

"That's right."

"Don't see many, in here."

"We go where we want."

"I guess you do. Staying at a hotel? I might come up and visit you."

"Not tonight."

"With your wife, Fritz?"

"Not me."

"Well, I'm not an alley girl," she said, hopping off. She walked away, flipping the back of her skirt up to reveal her thighs. "See you later," she said, over her shoulder, "unless you find a cat."

"Quite a mouth, on that one," Meino said.

"Maybe we'll come back here," Willi said, "with twenty divisions. Then she'll sing a different tune."

They ordered another round of vodkas, told stories, and roared with laughter. This was the life! But as the evening wore on, the clientele changed, and Jews in sharp suits, with slicked-down hair, began to appear, well known in the club, greeted heartily. They looked sideways at the three Germans, and one of them whispered with the girl who'd sat on Willi's knees.

Voss sniffed the air and said, "It's starting not to smell so good in here."

"Time to move on," Meino said.

They tried one more place, the Hairych, on Nalewki street, but there they overheard the gangster types talking about them in Yiddish, so they went back to the hotel, drank for a time, and went to their rooms. The next morning they drove around with Winckelmann, got a glimpse of the Frenchman, walking to work, then spent the rest of the day in the car, bored and irritated. They stayed at the hotel on the twenty-eighth, waiting for a telephone call from Winckelmann, but it never came. Willi began to complain, he'd taken time off from work, but he couldn't hang around Warsaw forever. "Maybe we'll just go see him tonight," he said. "At his apartment."

But Voss didn't like that idea, and neither did Meino.

A cold, mean little drizzle on the morning of the twenty-ninth, the worst weather possible for Mercier's aching knee, and a dreary day in store. He had correspondence to answer, dispatches to write, a meeting in the morning, another in the afternoon, and then, at five, he had to go out to Wola, the factory district at the western edge of the city, to the Ursus Tractor Company on Zelazna street, which manufactured automobiles and armoured vehicles. There would be a tour of the plant; then he was to meet with the managing director in his office. Walking to work, leaning on his stick, Mercier grumbled to himself, "Fine day to visit a factory." The dispatches took forever — information had to be looked up — and, at the meetings, he could barely force himself to concentrate. It was just the kind of day when one didn't care about anything.

At twenty minutes to five, Marek picked him up outside the embassy and set off for Wola. It wasn't all that far, but the drive seemed to take forever. Finally they reached the Wola district, deserted at this hour, the night shifts at the factories already at work. Set well back from Zelazna street, across a railroad track, the Ursus plant: vast buildings of soot-colored brick, beneath a low gray sky at twilight. Marek stopped the car and said, "When shall I pick you up?"

Mercier calculated. "Come back at seven. I know this will take at least two hours."

"I can stay, colonel, if you like."

"No, don't bother. See you at seven."

With a sigh in his heart, Mercier walked

across the tracks, then down a brick walkway to the administration building. A senior manager was waiting for him and took him off to the production sheds. Pure industrial hell. Giant machinery, banging away to wake the dead, rattling chains, showers of sparks, and the manager shouting over the din: here the armoured cars are assembled; they weigh this much; the clearance is this high. Mercier peered at the engines while the workers, in grease-stained overalls, smiled and nodded. He dutifully made notes and was eventually shown a completed vehicle, where he sat in the turret, cranked the handle and, lo and behold, the thing swiveled. Slowly, but it worked. Still, he knew what could happen to these cars — blown over on their sides, pouring smoke and flame — if they ever went to war. He'd seen it.

They walked for what felt like miles, then he was taken to see the managing director. An amiable gentleman, in a handsome suit, anxious to impress the French visitor. Again the weight, the speed, the thickness of plate, the firing rate of the gun. Coffee was served, with a plate of dry cookies. Skillfully, Mercier played the role of honored guest, but his thoughts were elsewhere. Lately, he liked to imagine Anna Szarbek, down at his house in the Drôme, dogs in front of the fireplace, everything he cared for, gathered up together, safe at night.

The director accompanied him to the front door; he left the building and took a few steps along the brick walkway. Now where was Marek? Across the tracks, Zelazna street was empty and dark, lit only by a single lamp at a distant intersection. He looked at his watch, 6:48, and thought about going back inside; the drizzle would have him soaking wet if he stood there until the Buick appeared. Then three men came around the corner of the building, and the one in the middle raised a hand and said, in German, "Good evening, colonel, we want a word with you."

What was this?

The one in the middle suddenly moved faster, and Mercier could see something in his hand. For a moment, it didn't make sense, not at a factory, this time of night, for it looked like a riding crop, the leather loop at the end circling the man's wrist. He ran the last few steps toward Mercier, his face contorted with rage, and swung the riding crop, which lashed Mercier across the cheek and knocked his hat off. Mercier stepped backward and raised his hands, taking the next blow on his palms. For a second, no feeling; then it burned like fire.

"Get his hands," the man said.

The other two advanced, Mercier swung at them with his stick, which hit the one on the right — the one with a big belly — across the forehead. Mercier had swung as hard as he could, using both hands, and he thought the stick might break, but ebony was a hard wood; the impact produced only a thud, and the man sat down on the brick walkway and held his head. Meanwhile the tall one, with a dueling scar on his cheek, had grabbed Mercier's arm and hung on to it as his friend swung again, a downstroke that landed on Mercier's shoulder. Mercier kicked at the man with the riding crop, lost his balance, and fell on his back, the tall one landing on top of him. The man was panting, his breath foul and reeking of alcohol. As Mercier tried to push him off, he growled, "Stay still, you French bastard."

"Fuck you," Mercier said, and tried to hit him with his forearm.

The man with the riding crop, cursing wildly, stumbled around Mercier, trying to find an angle for another blow. Then, from the direction of Zelazna street, a gunshot, and he stopped dead, riding crop frozen at the top of its swing. The tall one rolled off Mercier and struggled to his feet. "Time to go," he said. The two of them went to help their friend — he groaned as they stood him upright — and, moving quickly, trotted around the corner of the building and disappeared. Mercier's instinct to pursue them was immediately suppressed.

Looking toward the direction of the shot he saw a broad shape running across the railway tracks — Marek — who arrived a moment later, extended a hand to Mercier, and said, "Where did they go?"

"Was that your shot?" Mercier retrieved his stick and hat.

"It was. When I parked on Zelazna there was another car there, and a little man jumped out and aimed a pistol at me. Said something like *Halt!*"

"And?"

"I took the Radom from my coat and shot him." *What else?* Out in the darkness, the sound of a powerful engine, accelerating as the driver shifted up through the gears, then fading into the distance. Marek said, "Do you need help, colonel?"

Mercier shook his head, one finger cautiously touching the burning welt on his cheek. "What happened next?" he said.

Marek shrugged. "You know. He fell down."

Slowly, they walked across the tracks toward the Buick, Mercier's knee aching with every step. "Who were they?" Marek said.

"No idea," Mercier said. "They spoke German."

"Then why . . . ?"

Mercier couldn't answer.

They climbed into the car and Marek drove up Zelazna, then took the first right into a long street, dark and empty, wet pavement shining in the headlights. Peering through the cleared space made by the windshield wipers, Mercier saw what looked like a mound of discarded clothing, half on the sidewalk, half in the street. Marek nudged the brake and, when the mound became a man, stopped the car and they both got out. The factory wall that met the sidewalk had windows covered with wire mesh and, from somewhere inside, came the slow, rhythmic drumming of a machine. For a moment, they stared down at the body, its face wedged into the gutter, then Marek slid his foot beneath the man's waist and turned him over. "That's him," he said. A flowered tie lay over to one side, and there was a small red hole in the pocket of the shirt. "What did they do? Throw him out of the car?"

"Looks like it."

"Afraid of being stopped, I guess. With a body in the trunk."

The face was blank, eyes open. Like the others, he wasn't anybody Mercier had ever seen. Marek bent over and patted the man's pockets, found a wallet, and handed it to Mercier. Inside, a Polish identity card with the name Winckelmann — a name he'd heard from Vyborg — and a photograph of the man he'd come to think of as *the weasel*. He looked down at Winckelmann's face and realized that in death he'd become a different self.

"What now, colonel? The police?"

"No. Just put the wallet back."

"So, nothing we know about," Marek said, clearly relieved.

"Nothing we know about."

Mercier was supposed to be at Anna's at seven-thirty, and when he came through the door she was startled, then turned his chin to look at the welt.

"I was attacked," he said, before she could ask. "One of them hit me."

"Attacked? Who attacked you?"

"I don't know who they were."

"What did they hit you with? Come into the light."

She was very agitated, touching his cheek with her fingers and anxious to care for him. "You sit there. I'll get a cold cloth." Mercier

360

doubted it would help but knew better than to say so. She ran cold water on a clean dish towel, then pressed it to his face. "Hold that there," she said. "What makes such a horrid mark?"

"A riding crop."

"No! Who would do such a thing?"

How much to tell her? "They were Germans, and I suspect it was revenge of some sort, but please, Anna, don't ask anything about that part of it."

"Your work," she said, angry and disgusted.

Mercier nodded.

"They could have killed you, you know."

"I'll have to think up an explanation. I walked into a door — something like that."

"A drunkard's explanation, my dear."

"Hmm. Very well, then it was a drunk who hit me."

"Dreadful. Will you not tell them the truth, at the embassy?"

"I can't," he said. "There would be endless difficulties."

"Then say nothing. An absurd domestic stupidity, too silly to explain."

He thought for a moment, then said, "Of course, what else."

"Does it feel better?"

"Yes. The cold helps."

She rose abruptly, went looking for her purse, and lit a cigarette — she insisted on buying imported Gitanes at the fancy tobacco shop — and almost immediately the studio smelled like a French café. She did not return to her chair, but walked to the windows, then turned and faced him. "What makes you think they won't try something again?" she said, her voice now sharpened to a lawyer's edge. "Or do you believe they were . . . satisfied?"

"Maybe, maybe not. But if I brought this to my superiors as a problem, they might decide to end my assignment here."

"They're not pleased with you?"

"Not especially. Or, rather, not all of them. It's sometimes true that the more you succeed, in an organization, the more enemies you make."

"Always true," she said. She returned to the easy chair and shook her hair back. "Know what?"

"What?"

"I think you like this kind of war."

He shrugged. "*Like* isn't the word, but the job has grown into me. I wanted to quit, a few months ago, but not now. Now there's a particular operation under way. It's important, possibly very important."

She smiled and said, "Is it ever difficult for

you that you can't speak openly of such things?"

"Very difficult," he said. "Especially here, with you."

"Oh well," she said. "I guess it doesn't matter." She busied herself with the compress, putting more cold water on the towel. "Does this make it feel better?"

He said it did, and the conversation turned to their evening together — going out, doing something, a change. A search of the newspaper turned up a French film, and an hour later they went to the movies.

5 April. At last, a response to the contact with Dr. Lapp. But it did not arrive in any of the forms Mercier had anticipated. Not cabled dispatch, not letter by pouch, and not, thank heaven, Bruner's appearance in Warsaw, which Mercier had feared. No, it came by mail, a personal letter to his apartment, in lovely blue script. Undated, with no heading. A secret communication? Yes, in a way it was.

My dear colonel,

Kindly forgive the delay in answering your communication, but it inspired a most disheartening turmoil in these parts — your rural connection will have given you the opportunity to observe chickens in a barnyard beset by a playful dog.

In any event, it will be my pleasure to continue discussions with the individual in question, and much the best to do so in this city, where we can meet quietly, privately, and in comfort. A telephone call to Auteil 7407 — a local call, naturally — will initiate a meeting the same day, and no mention of names will be required. This method of contact is exclusive to the individual in question.

Please be good enough to destroy this letter, which finds you, I trust, in good health and good spirits.

With my most sincere good wishes,
Aristide R. J. de Beauvilliers

10 April. And then, in time, a second communication. Had Dr. Lapp foreseen the frenzy that his offer would produce within the French General Staff? Mercier suspected he had. Mercier suspected that Dr. Lapp was one of those senior officers in the shadow world with a sophisticated sense of human behavior — not a visionary, a cynic — and a man who understood that, at the end of the day, the *Abwehr,* the *Deuxième Bureau,* and all the rest of them worked pretty much the

same way. This time the communication came in the form of a note that arrived in a sealed envelope delivered by a private courier. It said simply that it would be good to see Mercier again and suggested the following day, at 5:15 in the afternoon, at the Gorovsky Bookstore, 28, Marszalkowska. And signed, *Dr. L.*

For the event — and Mercier informed no one, in the spirit of de Beauvilliers's letter, where he was going or why — he wore his best suit and a freshly laundered shirt, with somber tie — and made sure to enter the store at precisely 5:15. At this hour, there were only two or three customers, and he found Dr. Lapp, now in his traditional bow tie, in the back. When he looked up and saw Mercier, he said, "Do you know this book?" He held it up, *Rosja — Polska, 1815–1830,* and said, "Szymon Askenazy, one of their great historians. There are actually quite a few."

"Do you read comfortably in Polish, Dr. Lapp?"

"I do, though I must keep a dictionary at hand."

Mercier found this combination — Buster Keaton reading esoteric Polish history — modestly amusing. Dr. Lapp closed the book and put it back in its place on the shelf. "I believe the office will be more comfortable," he said.

"The manager won't mind?"

Dr. Lapp's smile was impish. "We own the store, colonel. And it does very nicely."

The office had drifted, over the years, to a state of comfortable decay — peeling paint, water stains on the ceiling, furniture worn out years ago — with stacks of books on the desk, in bookcases, on the floor, everywhere. A private world, calm and lost, the view through the cloudy window a courtyard where a wooden bench encircled a giant elm. Only the telephone, an antique from the twenties, told the visitor that he was not in the previous century. On the walls, posters for art exhibitions and concerts — the French were avid for culture, whether they liked it, understood it, paid for it, or not, but the Poles beat them hands down. Dr. Lapp sat in the desk chair, its wheels squeaking as he drew himself up to the desk. "Any luck, colonel?"

"Yes, though they took their time answering my dispatch."

"I rather thought they might."

"But very good luck, I believe. I've had a communication from a man called de Beauvilliers, General de Beauvilliers."

Dr. Lapp allowed Mercier to see that he

was impressed, and said, "Indeed."

"You know who he is?"

"I do. The perfect choice."

"He suggests that you meet with him in Paris. Would that be satisfactory?"

"It would."

"I've brought along a telephone number he sent; he will see you the day you call. And you needn't mention your name, the number is for your exclusive use." Mercier placed a slip of paper on the desk.

"Very thoughtful of him. You couldn't have made a better choice."

"It wasn't up to me, Dr. Lapp, this was General de Beauvilliers's personal decision."

"Even better," Dr. Lapp said. "A General Staff is always a field of divergent opinions — ours is no different — but among these officers there are always two or three who have an intuitive understanding of what the future might hold."

"One wouldn't have to be all that intuitive to understand Herr Hitler's intentions."

"You would think so, wouldn't you, but you'd be wrong. Do you know the Latin proverb *Mundus vult decipi, ergo decepiatur*? Herr Hitler's favorite saying: *The world wants to be deceived, therefore let it be deceived.* And he isn't wrong. Newspapers on the continent explain every day why there won't be war. And I assure you there will be, unless the right people determine to stop it."

"I can only hope this meeting is a step in that direction," Mercier said.

"We shall see."

For a moment, Mercier paused. Here was an opportunity — take it, or not? He had from the Rozens a name, Köhler, an affiliation, the Black Front, and a target, the I.N. 6 bureau of the German General Staff. And, if Dr. Lapp couldn't help him take a step forward, then no one could. "I wonder, Dr. Lapp," he said slowly, "if I might ask you a favor."

"One may always ask, colonel. Are you asking at General de Beauvilliers's behest?"

Mercier paused, then said, "No, it's nothing he suggested, for this conversation, but I don't believe he'd mind, if he knew."

"You've been honorable, colonel, which I appreciate. You haven't . . . taken advantage . . . of a situation that could put me in real danger. So then, what sort of favor do you require?"

"I've become interested, in the course of my work here, in the Black Front, Hitler's most determined enemies in Germany."

Delicately, Dr. Lapp cleared his throat. "I do know who you mean, colonel, and regret that they haven't been more effective. But I suggest you go carefully with this crowd, those who remain with us — most of them are in the ground, or wherever the Gestapo put them. Very extreme, these people. Captain Röhm, before he was murdered in 'thirty-four, recommended that the conservative industrialists be hanged. Dear me."

"I will be careful, Dr. Lapp; I would greatly prefer to remain aboveground. But I cannot move forward on a certain project until I obtain information that only a senior Black Front member might possess."

Dr. Lapp leaned toward him and folded his hands on the desk. "Now," he said, "I must ask you if this project involves *German* interests, or is it particular to the interests of the Nazi party, the present regime? And, please, colonel, an honest answer."

This last was, Mercier understood, a veiled threat. "To the best of my knowledge, the interests of the Nazi party."

Dr. Lapp nodded, then looked at Mercier in a way that meant *I hope you know what you're doing.* "Have you pen and paper?"

Mercier produced a small pad and a fountain pen.

"The man who might help you is hiding in Czechoslovakia, in the town the Poles call Cieszyn and the Czechs Tesin — much-disputed territory, as you'll know. Presently he uses the name Julius Halbach, because he is hunted by the SD and the Gestapo. As a member of the Black Front, under yet another alias, he served directly under Otto Strasser and was active in the clandestine radio operation that broadcast propaganda into Germany. Last year, the head of that operation was murdered by SD operatives at an inn near the German border, but Otto Strasser and Halbach escaped.

"Halbach is a man in his mid-fifties, and his story is typical. At one time he was a professor of ancient languages — Old Norse, Gothic, and so forth — at the university in Tübingen. In the late twenties, there was some sort of scandal, and he was forced to resign, his life ruined. Typical, as I said; the Nazi party was built on ruined lives — a failed career, the bitterness that feeds on injustice, redemption promised by a radical political movement.

"Now comes the difficult part, which is that you may speak with him, and you might wish to offer him money, but you may not threaten him. And that is because *we* talk to him, through the good offices of an extraordinary woman, the kindest old soul in the world, a piano teacher in Tesin. I doubt he knows that he's talking to us, but he is forthcoming — so don't bruise him, agreed?"

"Agreed."

"Currently, he is employed as a teacher at a private academy in Tesin and rents a room in a house at six, Opava street. And, I should add, I don't know what your plans are but I would not, if I were you, postpone this contact too long. He remains active in the Black Front underground, writing anti-Nazi pamphlets that are smuggled into German Silesia, and, because this infuriates the security services, he is not long for this world."

Mercier put away his pad and pen. "Thank you," he said.

"I hope it will help."

"Surely it will. And, Dr. Lapp, should you require further assistance, you know where to find me. Otherwise, we'll meet at diplomatic events in the city."

"No doubt we shall. With all the formality of sworn enemies." Dr. Lapp was amused and showed it, the Keaton prune face breaking into a sunny smile.

Mercier stood, and they shook hands. "I wish all my enemies . . ." he said, not bothering to finish the thought.

"Indeed."

Mercier was in his office early the following morning, laboring away at what he now called, for his personal use only, *Operation*

Halbach. This was not easy, but the excitement of the chase drove him on, hour after hour, until midday, when a luncheon at the Hotel Bristol intervened, followed by a long meeting, and cocktails with the Roumanians at six. Then, to make up for lost time, he took the dossier off to Sienna street, where he sat at the kitchen table while Anna stroked his hair and looked over his shoulder. "Ahh, funny little numbers."

"It's hard to work, at work."

"I know too well," she said.

"Only an hour."

She blew gently on the hair at the back of his neck. "Take your time, my dear, I like conscientious men."

He didn't answer, took a roneo of a Tesin town map, and ran a finger down Opava street.

Anna went off to bathe, returned in a towel, lay back on the bed — the towel chastely arrayed across her middle — retrieved her book, and turned on the radio. "It appears we're in for the night."

"I fear we are."

"When you tire of it, come and say hello."

Later, she crawled under the covers and fell asleep, and at midnight he joined her. But she was restless, lay awake in the darkness, then got out of bed and prowled around the room. "Can't sleep?" he said, rising on one elbow.

"Not right now."

He lay back down, watched her white shape in the darkness as she paced about, and finally said, "Are you looking for something?"

"No, no. I'll come back to bed in a minute."

By late morning of the following day, 13 April, he'd finished his plans for the operation and sent a dispatch off to de Beauvilliers, marked for the general's eyes only. This was no business for *2, bis* — not directly from him, it wasn't. De Beauvilliers would have them provide what was required, but he would not ask, he would simply order, and the internal politics of the bureau would be successfully tamed.

The response took some time, and it was 17 April when the general's courier showed up at Mercier's office in the chancery. A young man in civilian clothes, he introduced himself as an army captain. "I came over on the train," he said, "and I'm going back on the morning express, so best look through this now, and you'll have to sign for it." He removed a few files from a small valise and pried up the false bottom. "German border control, Polish border control, I hope I don't have to do this again."

Mercier did as the captain suggested, licking his thumb as he counted hundred-reichsmark notes.

"It's all there," the captain said. "And there's a verbal message from General de Beauvilliers. 'Please be careful, do try *very* hard not to get caught. And best to avoid a visit to the casino.'"

"Assure him I'll be careful," Mercier said. He signed the receipt.

The captain said, "The valise is for your use, naturally," wished Mercier *Bon courage* and good luck, and went off to a hotel.

19 April. Tesin, Czechoslovakia — Cieszyn to the Poles — the former Duchy of Teschen, held over the years by this prince or that empire, changing sides with European wars and royal marriages as the centuries slid past. Just another small town, the usual statue and fountain in the central square, but grim and poor as one left the center and traveled out toward the edge, in the direction of the coal mines. On Hradny street, rows of narrow houses, women on their knees out on the stoops, with buckets and rags, trying to scrub away the Silesian grime. After Hradny, Opava, where the signs above the shops

turned from Czech to Polish, and a tiny bar stood across the street and down the block from number 6. Four stools, two tables, a miniature Polish flag by the cash register.

Mercier had made his way to Tesin on a series of local trains, sitting in second-class carriages, then taken a room in the hotel by the railway station. And stayed out of sight, keeping to his room, emerging only twice — once to buy a cheap briefcase, then, an hour later, setting out for the long walk to Opava street. He was being as cautious as he could be, for this was no normal operation. A normal operation would have included a supporting cast: cars and drivers, a couple with a child, old men with newspapers under their arms. And of this drama he would have been the star, summoned from his dressing room only when the moment came to take center stage and deliver the grand soliloquy. But not this time. This time he had to do the work by himself.

He ordered a beer. The man behind the bar brought him a pilsener, then lingered a moment, taking a good long look at him. *And who the hell are you?* It was that kind of neighborhood. But the beer was very good. He turned on the stool and stared out the window, the melancholy stranger. Out past two well-attended strips of flypaper, the house on Opava street. Where a child now climbed the steps, home from school, swinging a blue lunchbox as she disappeared through the door. Next, a woman came out with a net bag, and returned fifteen minutes later with her marketing. Mercier had a second beer. The barman said, "Warm day, we're having."

Mercier nodded and lit a Czech cigarette from a packet he'd bought at the railway station. It was after five when a man, dressed in worker's blue jacket and trousers, entered the house across the street. Mercier looked at his watch: where was Halbach? Two young women came through the door, joked with the barman, then took one of the tables and began to conspire, heads together, voices low. Mercier now realized he could hear music. In a room above the bar, someone was playing a violin — playing it well enough, not the awful squeaks of the novice, but working at the song, slower, then faster. A song Mercier knew, called "September in the Rain"; he'd heard it on Anna's radio at Sienna street. Was this, he wondered, a classical violinist, forced to play in a nightclub? A man with a small dog came into the bar, then two old ladies in flower-print dresses. And then, suddenly, Mercier was again overtaken by a certain apprehension, a shadow of war. What would become of these people?

Busier now, out on Opava street — work was over for the day — time to chat with neighbors, time to walk the dog. Mercier ordered his third beer, set a few coins down on the counter, and looked back out the window in time to see Julius Halbach enter 6, Opava street. Anyhow, a man who looked like a teacher, in his mid-fifties, tall, wearing an old suit, expensive a long time ago, and carrying a bulging briefcase. Mercier glanced at his watch: 5:22. *I hope you're Halbach,* he thought, as the man plodded wearily up the steps and disappeared through the door. Too much to ask for a photograph, he'd decided, before his meeting with Dr. Lapp. That would have been dangerously close to an act of treason, whereas, a genial conversation in a bookstore, while conferring on another matter . . .

Mercier stayed where he was, now numb and slightly dizzy from an afternoon of beer drinking, for another thirty minutes, then gave up. The family was home, their lodger was home, in for the night. Tomorrow would be the day, 20 April, 1938, at approximately 5:22 in the afternoon. Tomorrow, Herr Halbach was in for the shock of his life.

■ ■ ■ ■

Mercier stopped at the café across from the railway station, had a sausage and a plate of leeks with vinegar, bought a newspaper — Tesin's Polish daily — and returned to the hotel. Was the room as he'd left it? Yes, but for the maid, who had moved his valise in order to mop the floor. Opening the valise, he was relieved to find his few things undisturbed, though the important baggage stayed with him, in the briefcase.

It was quiet in Tesin, a warmish evening of early spring. When Mercier pulled the shade down, a streetlamp threw a shadow of tree branches on the yellowed paper. He turned on the light, a bulb dangling from the ceiling, and worked at the newspaper — what he wouldn't give for a *Paris Soir*! Still, he could manage, once he got going. Henlein, the leader of the Sudetenland German minority in Czechoslovakia, had given a speech in Karlsbad, making eight demands on the government. Basically, he called for the Czechs to allow German-speaking areas to have their own foreign policy, in line with "the ideology of Germans": a demand that surely came directly from Adolf Hitler, a demand that could never be met. The fire under the pot was being stoked, soon it would boil.

Then, on the same page, news that the *Anschluss,* joining Austria to Germany, had been approved in a plebiscite by Austrian voters. A triumph — nearly all the Austrians had voted, ninety-nine to one in favor. Now there was a victory that deserved the word *rousing!* Just below that, a correspondent reporting from the Spanish civil war; the city of Vinaroz had been taken by Franco's forces, isolating the government-held city of Castile from Catalonia. Another victory for fascist Europe. Mercier turned the page. A grisly murder, a body found in a trunk. And the soccer team had lost again. Followed by a page of obituaries. Mercier threw the newspaper on the floor.

He lay there, smoked, stared at the ceiling. He had no desire to read, and sleep was a long way off. On the other side of the wall, a man and a woman in the adjacent room began to argue, in a language Mercier couldn't identify. They kept it quiet, secretive, almost a whisper, but the voices were charged with anger, or desperation, and neither one would give in. When it didn't stop, he got up, went to the window, and raised the shade. Across the square, the outdoor *terrasse* of the café was busy — a warm night, spring in the air, the usual couples with drinks, a few customers alone at tables, eating a late dinner. Then the barman walked over to a large radio set on a shelf and began fiddling with the dials. Mercier couldn't hear anything, but most of the patrons rose from their tables and gathered in front of the radio. He rolled the shade back down, undid the straps on his briefcase, and made sure of its contents.

20 April. Mercier strolled up Opava street at 5:10 P.M., but Halbach was nowhere to be seen. Keeping the house in sight he walked to the corner, then started back the other way. He felt much too noticeable, so turned into a cross street where he discovered a tram stop. Was this how Halbach returned from work? He waited for ten minutes, then walked back out onto Opava, and there he was, almost at the house. Mercier moved as quickly as he could and caught up to him just as he reached the door. "Herr Halbach?"

Frightened, Halbach spun around and faced him, ready to fight or run. "What is it? What do you want?"

"May I speak with you a moment?"

"Why? Is it about the bill?"

"No, sir, not that at all."

Halbach calmed down. Mercier was clearly alone; the secret police came always in pairs, and late at night. "Then what? Who are you?"

"Is there somewhere we can speak? Privately? I have important things to tell you."

"You're not German."

"No, I'm from Basel — a French Swiss."

"Swiss?" Now he was puzzled.

"Can we go inside?"

"Yes, all right. What's this about?"

"Inside? Please?"

Downstairs, the family was at dinner. Mercier could smell garlic. Halbach called out "Good evening," in Polish, then climbed the stairs and opened a door just off the landing. "In here," he said. "Just leave the door open."

"Of course," Mercier said.

A small room, meagerly furnished and painted a hideous green. On one wall, a clothes tree held a shirt and a pair of trousers; on the other, a narrow cot covered by a blanket, and a nightstand with four books on top. At the foot of the cot, a single rickety chair completed the furnishings. The window looked out on the plaster wall of the adjacent building, so the room lay in permanent twilight. Halbach put his briefcase down and sat on the edge of the cot, while Mercier took the chair. When he was settled, Halbach opened the drawer in the nightstand, then gave him a meaningful look, saying, "Just keep your hands where I can see them."

Mercier complied immediately, resting his hands atop the briefcase held on his knees. Was there a pistol in the drawer? Likely there was. "I understand," he said. "I understand completely."

For a moment, Halbach stared at him. He was, Mercier thought, perhaps the homeliest man he'd ever seen: a long narrow face, with pitted skin, and small protruding ears emphasized by a Prussian haircut — gray hair cut close on the sides and one inch high on top. His Hitler-style mustache was also gray, his neck a thin stem — circled by a collar a size too large — his restless eyes suspicious and mean. "Well?" he said. "Who are you?"

"My name is Lombard. I represent a chemical company in Basel. My card."

Mercier drew a packet of cards from his pocket and handed one of them to Halbach, who said, "Solvex-Duroche?"

"Solvents for the metals industry."

Halbach studied the card, then put it on the nightstand. "What would you want with me?" Suspicion was slowly giving way to curiosity. "I'm a teacher."

"But not always. Or, rather, that is your vocation. It is your political history that brings me here."

Halbach's hand moved toward the drawer, Mercier feared he was about to be shot. "Please, no violence," he said softly. "I'm here to make an offer, nothing more than that, and if you're not interested I'll go away and that will be the end of it."

"You said politics . . . meaning?"

"Your resistance to the present government in Berlin."

"You know who I am," Halbach said, an accusation.

"Yes, I do know that."

"So, you're no chemical salesman, Herr Lombard, are you."

"Actually, I am, but that's no part of our business today."

"Then who sent you?"

"That I can't tell you. Suffice to say, powerful people, but not your enemies."

Halbach waited for more, then said, "How did you find me?"

"As I said, powerful people. Who know things. And, I feel I should point out, it wasn't all that difficult to find you."

"In other words, spies."

"Yes."

"Not the first I've encountered, Herr *Lombard*. And no doubt working for the Swiss government."

"Oh, we never say such things out loud,

Herr Halbach. And, in the end, it doesn't matter."

"To me it does." He had suffered for his politics, he wasn't about to compromise his ideals.

"Then let me say this much — a neutral government is not a disinterested government, and, as I said before, in this instance on *your* side."

Now Halbach was intrigued — he'd spent enough time with Mercier to sense he needn't be afraid of him, and felt the first flush of pride that "powerful people" were interested in him. Which, of course, they should be, despite his present misery.

Now Mercier advanced. "Tell me, Herr Halbach, this life you live now, as a fugitive, how long do you expect it to last?"

"For as long as it does."

"Months?"

"Certainly."

"Years?"

"Perhaps." A shadow settled on Halbach's face. He knew it couldn't be years.

"You read the newspapers, you're aware of Hitler's intentions in Czechoslovakia — what's going on in the Sudetenland."

"Casus belli." Halbach flipped the tactic away with his hand, his voice rich with contempt.

"True, a reason for war, and perfectly transparent to those who understand what's going on. Still, Hitler may well send his armies here. What then? Where will you go?"

"To a cellar somewhere."

"For months? Or days?"

Halbach would not give him the satisfaction of an answer, but the answer hung unspoken in the air.

"You asked why I was here, Herr Halbach. I'm here to offer you sanctuary."

"Sanctuary," Halbach said. The word had its effect.

"That's correct. The people I represent want you to continue your resistance, but you cannot do so in Czechoslovakia. The Gestapo will find you, today or tomorrow, and the result for you will be very unpleasant. Very, very unpleasant. With the best of luck, it's only a matter of time."

"What is this sanctuary?"

"Money, and a new nationality."

"How much money?"

"Five hundred thousand Swiss francs."

"That's a fortune!"

Mercier's brief nod meant, *of course it is, but not for us.*

"Five hundred thousand, you said?"

"I did. And a Swiss passport. The passport

of a Swiss citizen, not the papers of a foreign resident."

"For nothing more than writing a few pamphlets?"

"No, there is more."

Silence in the little room — quiet enough to hear the family eating dinner below them. Halbach lowered his voice. "And what would that be, Herr Lombard?"

"A visit to an old friend, a request — a request accompanied by the same offer I've made to you, so you will not go empty-handed, a few days' work on his part, a successful result, and then, for both of you, new lives. Wealthy lives. Safe lives."

Now Halbach saw the trick. "All this you offer would be in the future, naturally, and conditional. Just around the corner, just up the road."

"No, sir, it doesn't work like that. Simply agree, and I will hand you a hundred and fifty thousand Swiss francs."

"Now? This minute?" Halbach stared at the briefcase.

"Yes."

"How do you know I won't accept the money and disappear?"

"Because then you will have stolen it, Herr Halbach. Stolen it from us." Again, silence. Mercier waited, the soul of patience; he could almost see Halbach's mind working, back and forth. Finally Mercier said, "What will it be, sir, shall I be on my way?"

Halbach's voice was barely audible. "No," he said.

"Then we are in agreement?"

Halbach nodded. He'd begun to grasp the very sudden turn his life had taken, and he didn't like it, his expression sour and resigned, but, really, what choice did he have?

"Please understand," Mercier said, his hands now holding the sides of the briefcase, ready to hand it over, "that your actions will be directed against the Hitler regime, not against the German people, not against your homeland. We know you would never agree to harm your country, misguided though it might be."

Halbach didn't answer, but Mercier sensed that he'd accepted the distinction — this wasn't treason, this was resistance. From the foot of the stairs, a woman's voice. "Herr Halbach? Will you be having your dinner?"

"Not tonight, thank you," Halbach called out.

Mercier handed him the briefcase. It was heavy and full: thirty packets, bound with rubber bands, of fifty hundred-franc notes. Halbach unbuckled the straps and opened the flap, took out one packet, counted twenty, riffled the rest, and put it back. When he looked up at Mercier his face had changed; the reality of the banknotes had struck home.

"And three hundred and fifty thousand more, Herr Halbach, when the work is completed."

"In cash?"

"There's a better way, a bank transfer, but I'll explain that in time."

Halbach again looked in the briefcase. No, he wasn't dreaming. "What do I have to *do,* for all this? Kill somebody?"

"A train ride to Berlin. A conversation."

Halbach stared, opened his mouth, finally said, "But . . ."

Mercier was sympathetic. "I know. I know, it's risky, but not foolish. With a Swiss passport, hiding in a small hotel, you'll be reasonably safe. And I'll be there with you. Of course, danger is always part of this business. For me to come here today is dangerous, but here I am."

"I'm a wanted criminal, in Germany."

"You won't be in Berlin for more than a week, and, except for arrival and departure, you will be visible for only one evening. We want you to contact a man who used the alias 'Köhler,' an old comrade of yours, from the Black Front, now serving in a section of the General Staff, and make the same offer to him that I've made to you."

Mercier had worked this sentence out and memorized it. The question he didn't want to ask was: *Do you know Köhler?* Because a simple "Who?" would have ended the operation.

"Hans Köhler," Halbach said, his voice touched with nostalgia. After a moment, working it out, he said, "Of course. Now I see what you're after."

Casually, Mercier said, "I expect he serves under his true name."

"Yes, Elter. Johannes Elter. He is a sergeant in the *Wehrmacht*. Luckily for him, Strasser ordered that every man in the Front use a *nom de guerre*."

Not so lucky. It had left Köhler vulnerable to just the sort of approach that Halbach was going to make. But, Mercier thought, there was plenty of time for that, now was not the moment.

"When will this meeting take place?" Halbach asked. He rebuckled the briefcase and placed it on the floor beside him.

"Soon. Political events are moving quickly; we don't want to get caught up in them. We leave tomorrow."

"Tomorrow! My classes, at the school —"

"Class is canceled. The Herr Professor

is indisposed."

"I have a friend in Tesin, Herr Lombard, a friend that's made a great difference to me, the way I've had to live here. I would like to say goodby."

Mercier's voice was as gentle as he could manage. "I am sorry, Herr Halbach, but that won't be possible. If she's been a confidante, she'll understand, and a postal card from you, in Switzerland, will let her know you've reached safety." He rose and offered his hand — Halbach's palm was cold and damp. "Enough for tonight," Mercier said. "We'll meet tomorrow, ten-fifteen at the railway station. Try to get some rest, if you can, it will be a busy day."

"Tomorrow? We go into Germany?"

"Oh no, not at all. We go to Prague, then back east and into Poland. An easy crossing."

21 April. Sturmbannführer Voss's friend Willi — fake dueling scar on his cheek, *von* now leading his surname — was well-liked at 103 Wilhelmstrasse, the SD's central office in Berlin. Properly submissive to his superiors, genial to his underlings, quite a good fellow, and sure to rise, when the time was right. And when would that be, exactly? War would do it, but Hitler was such a little tease

when it came to war, showing his drawers one day, then giggling and running away the next. Austria he had — the plebiscite on the *Anschluss* had been a stroke of genius. Czechoslovakia he would have, though that would require force of arms; the Czechs were a stubborn, stiff-necked crowd, blind to their best interests, and they rather liked having their own nation. And those arms were still in production; all across Germany, the factory lights burned until dawn. Would it be this year? Probably not, maybe the following spring. More likely 1940. And some very sage gentlemen were saying 1941.

But war was only one way, there had to be others. For instance, a triumph. Some daring operation run against the French or the English. Willi, however, did not run operations, he worked in the SD administration. Certainly important, if you knew how these things worked, though not the sort of position that produced a stunning success. Still, there had to be *some* way, for a smart chap like Willi to find a path to the top.

For example, a visit to the urinals in the bathroom on the third floor. Obersturmbannführer Gluck, August Voss's superior, the former Berlin lawyer, regularly answered the call of nature around eleven in the morning, so Willi had observed. And so, that morning, he too heard the call. Gluck, when Willi arrived, was just buttoning his fly. Willi said good morning and addressed the porcelain wall. Gluck washed his hands, dried them, and began to comb his hair. When Willi was done, he stood at the sink next to Gluck and said, "Fine speech, the Führer gave last night."

Gluck's nod was brusque. He set the comb carefully on his part, then drew it across his head.

"You are Sturmbannführer Voss's superior, are you not, sir?" Willi said.

"I am. What of it?"

"Oh, nothing. I was just wondering . . . if something's gone wrong with him."

"What would be wrong?"

"I'm not sure. Do you have a moment, sometime, when we could talk?"

"Now is a good time. Why not come along to my office?"

Gluck had a most pleasant office, quite large, with a view out over the Wilhelmstrasse, the government neighborhood of the city. Down below, *Grosser Mercedes* limousines with swastika flags above the headlights, generals strolling with admirals, motorcycle couriers rushing off with crucial dossiers, a military beehive. Gluck sat formally at his desk. He had, Willi could see by the photograph next to the telephone, a very attractive wife and two handsome sons, both in SS uniform. Gluck waited patiently, then said, "Something I should hear about?"

"I believe you should." Willi was just a bit hesitant, not happy about what needed to be said. "He's an old friend, Voss is, from the early days of the party. And, I always thought, the best sort of officer. Keen, you know. Quite the terrier."

"And?"

"A few weeks ago he invited me and another friend to go up to Warsaw. A change of scene, see the night life, bother the girls. Just a holiday away from family life, a chance to be naughty. When you work hard, it can be just the thing."

"I suppose it can." *Though not for someone like me.*

"So there we were, having a good time. But then he drags us off to some factory district. Where we wait around, while I'm trying to figure out what's going on. He'd been drinking, more than usual I'd say, and you couldn't reason with him; better to just go along. Then he sees some fellow in a French uniform come out of a factory — apparently he was waiting for him, because he runs off and, and *attacks* him. Pulls a riding crop from under his coat and beats him on the face."

Gluck kept his composure. Pressed his lips together and seemed thoughtful, but that was all. "He did mention something about this, I don't recall when it was. He'd lost a suspect, which is surely regrettable, but not the end of the world. However, Voss took it badly, personally, saw it as — how to say — a vendetta."

"I couldn't believe my eyes, when it happened. Then, after we returned home, I wondered if he didn't perhaps have some difficulty in his private life, something that could be resolved, informally, with your help."

"I know of no such problem. And it wouldn't matter if I did."

"No, of course not. I wasn't going to say anything but I did worry about it, and then, when I chanced to see you this morning, I thought I'd better mention it. Before anything *else* happens."

"You were right to do so, Sturmbann-führer. Did he tell you what he had in mind, before you went to Warsaw?"

"He didn't. We were just going to have a good time, as I said."

"And you were how many?"

"Three."

"You don't name your other friend, but I guess I can understand that."

"I will if you order me to, sir."

"No, let it be."

"I don't like to be the bearer of bad news."

"For the good of the service, you had to be. And much better that I know about it, because, if he blows up again, and it becomes known, *I'm* the one who will suffer."

"Will you confront him, sir?"

"I don't plan to, at the moment."

"Because, if you do, I would respectfully ask you not to say how you came to learn what he did. We have friends throughout the service, and I don't trust Voss to keep silent."

"You needn't worry about that, and I would ask the same of you. This is one of those incidents that is best managed quietly."

"You can depend on me, sir, to keep it that way."

Gluck slouched sideways in his chair, an official burdened with one more problem on a day when there would be many more. He met Willi's eyes and said, "I appreciate what you've done; I'm sure it wasn't easy for you. And, if some day you need a friend, let me know. I'm not an ungrateful man."

"Thank you, sir."

"Of course it is the end for your friend Voss, sad to say, at least in this organization. He will be returned to duty in the SS; trust them to find something more suited to his . . . his particular character."

"I am sorry to hear that, but perhaps it's for the best. This kind of behavior can't be tolerated."

"Not by me, it can't."

A growing silence, end of conversation. Willi stood and considered a *Heil Hitler,* but sensed that Gluck was one of those officers indifferent to such gestures, so squared his shoulders, came to attention, and saluted with his voice. "Herr Obersturmbann-führer."

"You are dismissed, Herr Sturmbann-führer," Gluck said. "I will need to use the telephone."

21 April, 10:15 A.M. Tesin railway station. Halbach was prompt to the moment, the remnants of his fugitive life in a cheap suit-case, briefcase clamped beneath his arm. Then the two of them, the French aristocrat and the Nazi professor, boarded the 10:32 train to Prague. It would not be a long trip, just over an hour, but time Mercier meant to use, if he could find a vacant compartment. This was, with a tip to the conductor, avail-

able, and, as the train got under way, Halbach wondered aloud why they were going to Prague.

"In Prague there is a certain photographic studio, run by a discreet gentleman, who will take your passport picture. The service is expensive, but the photograph will be properly affixed to your new passport. It is a service much in demand, lately."

"I've known such people," Halbach said.

"Also in Prague, a private bank — a very private bank — called Rosenzweig, principally a Jewish bank. Does that offend you, Herr Halbach?"

"Not at all, I don't care about the Jews. Hitler's a fanatic on the subject, and, time was, we thought that might be the end of him, but to date he has his way with them."

"The Rosenzweig Bank will accept your Swiss francs, no questions asked, and transmit them to a numbered account at a bank in Zurich." Mercier reached into his pocket and withdrew a slip of paper on which he'd copied, very carefully, the number sent to him by de Beauvilliers. "You'll want to keep that safe, and I would memorize it as well, because this is an anonymous account. Similar arrangements have been made for your friend Elter."

"When will I have the passport?"

Mercier handed it over. "A new life," he said.

"As Herr Braun, I see."

"A common name."

"My fifth or sixth. It will serve."

"Do you have a family, Herr Halbach?"

"I did. A wife and child."

"They can travel with you, on this passport."

"No, that's finished, that part of my life. After the murders of 'thirty-four I had to go underground, so I sent them away. For safety's sake I no longer know where they are, nor do they know where I am. Whatever might happen to me, I could not bear the idea that they would share my fate."

"And Sergeant Elter?"

"He does have a family: a wife, three children."

"You knew him well?"

"Well enough. When you work secretly, there is endless time to kill, waiting for this, waiting for that, so people talk. He's a common enough fellow, Pomeranian by birth, a steady family man. Perhaps his single distinction is a commitment to politics — he loved the party, it was a second home to him. It meant, to Elter, the raising up of a defeated nation, the return of pride, the end of poverty. Poverty is a dreadful business, Herr

Lombard, a bitter thing, and particularly hard on those who've known better times. Every day, a small humiliation. It is, to the French, *la misère*, the misery, and that's the proper word. Elter was an idealist, as was I, but it did not destroy him. He escaped, because he never held a high position in the Front. And he was never betrayed."

"Still, he could be, no?"

"I suppose it's possible. Under interrogation a fellow member might say his true name, but there are not many left who know it, I'm one of the last."

"You may have to remind him of that, Herr Halbach."

Perhaps Halbach believed he would be asking a favor of his former comrade, but now the price of Swiss francs had been quoted. "Tell me about him," Mercier said.

"In his forties, precise, finicky. Bald, with a monk's fringe, eyeglasses, not at all remarkable, the office clerk. Much absorbed in hobbies, as I recall, stamp and coin collections, model trains, that sort of thing."

"Perhaps a dog? He walks at night?"

"He had a bird. A little green thing — he would whistle to make it sing."

"You last saw him when?"

"A year ago, he came to Czechoslovakia to report to Otto — they'd discovered a spy in the organization. Two of our people almost arrested by the Gestapo. They shot through the door, the Gestapo shot back, and taunted them as they died."

"How did he know that?"

"A neighbor."

"Was Elter in the war?"

"Not in combat. He was a supply clerk, in the rear echelon. And a clerk he remains at the General Staff office, in charge of buying paper and pencils, typewriter ribbons, paper clips, and what have you, and keeping track of it all. They may be Germany's great warriors, on the Bendlerstrasse, but, if they want a pencil, they must ask little Elter."

"Does he gamble, perhaps? Visit prostitutes?"

"Gamble? Never, he pinches every pfennig. As for prostitutes, maybe now and then, when things are difficult at home."

"Herr Halbach, here is an important question: do you believe he will cooperate with you, as an old friend, seeking his help?"

Halbach took his time, finally saying, "There must be a better reason, I fear."

"Then we will provide one," Mercier said.

The photography studio was in a quiet residential district, a small shop, dark inside, with a little bell that jingled merrily when the door was opened. Inside, painted canvas flats with a hole for the jocular customer's head, allowing him to be photographed as a golfer, a clown, or a racing car driver. Halbach's photo was added to the passport in an office at the back of the shop, where a radio at low volume played a Mozart symphony. It was a well-used passport, with several entry and exit stamps, that gave the bearer's profession as "sales representative" and so completed Halbach's cover identity. Mercier was relieved to see that the photographer worked with infinite care, consulting a notebook that specified the proper form for every sort of document used by the the nations of the continent. When the job was done, the man addressed Halbach as *Herr Braun* and wished him good luck.

Next, a men's clothing store where Halbach was outfitted, the sort of suit, hat, and raincoat appropriate for a representative of the fine old Solvex-Duroche company. He now looked prosperous, but he was still Julius Halbach, not only homely but distinctive. Mercier fretted over this but could do nothing. False beard? Wig? Tinted spectacles? No, theatrical disguises would make Halbach look like a spy, surely the last thing Mercier wanted.

The people at the bank, a large room on

the fourth floor of a commercial building, were genteel and all business — this was simply the transmission of currency, and Mercier suspected it went on all day long. They did not ask to see a passport, simply wrote out a receipt, having deducted their commission from the amount to be wired. As Mercier and Halbach descended in the elevator, Mercier handed over a hundred reichsmark, to use as pocket money, and told Halbach to rip up the receipt and, when opportunity provided a trash can, to throw it away. After lunch, they took the train back to Tesin, then crossed easily into Poland. There followed another train ride, to Katowice, where they stayed at the railway hotel.

On the morning of 23 April, a taxi took them to the outskirts of the city, where, at a garage that was little more than an old shed, Mercier bought a car. Not new, but well cared for, a 1935 Renault Celtaquatre, a two-door saloon model. Not too bad from the front — a fancy grille — but the bulbous passenger compartment ruined the look of the thing. "Very practical," the garageman said, "and the engine is perfect." Mercier drove around the corner and removed the last two items from beneath the false bottom of his valise: a Swiss license plate and the accompanying registration. After changing plates — he had to work at the rusty screws with a coin — they drove into Germany.

They stopped only briefly at the German border *kontrol,* two Swiss salesmen traveling on business, but Halbach stiffened as the guard had a look at his passport. "So now we spend an afternoon looking at the scenery," Mercier said, as the striped crossarm was lowered behind them. But Halbach was not to be distracted, he sat rigid in the passenger seat, and Mercier could hear him breathing.

A good road, heading north to Berlin; all the roads in Germany were good now, a military necessity for a country with enemies east and west. Mercier drove at normal speed; it would take some six hours to reach Berlin, and he did not want to arrive in daylight. Halbach maintained his brooding silence, lost in his own world. Earlier, with a new life ahead of him and one last mission to be accomplished, he'd been expansive and relaxed, but now came the reality of Germany, and it had reached him. For Mercier, it was not so different from the drive to Schramberg — town after town with signs forbidding Jews, swastika flags, uniformed men on every street. The symbols of power, raw power, the state transcendent. Halbach ought to be used to it, he thought — he was, after all, a member of the Nazi party, a left Nazi but a Nazi nonetheless — but now it meant danger, and the possibility, the *likelihood,* that his new life would be destroyed before it had barely begun. Once again, he would lose everything.

A typical April day for Central Europe, changeable and windy. The skies darkened, raindrops appeared on the windshield, the wipers squeaked as they rubbed across the glass. From Gleiwitz they traveled north to Breslau, a three-hour drive. As they crossed the Oder, the sun broke through the clouds and sparkled on the dark current. On to Glogau, where Mercier stopped at a café, bought liverwurst sandwiches and bottles of lemonade, and they had lunch in the car. When they stopped for gas in Krossen, the teenager who worked the pump stared at Halbach, who turned away and pretended to look for something in the glove compartment. At dusk: Frankfurt. Mercier's knee began to throb — too long in one position — but Halbach, it turned out, had never learned to drive. Mercier got out and walked around the car, which helped not at all. In the center of Frankfurt, a policeman directing traffic glowered at them and waved angrily: *move!* Halbach swore under his breath. A coal delivery truck broke down in front of them, the driver signaling for them to go around, and Mercier almost hit a car coming the other way. He was sweating by the time they reached the western edge of the city. Then, finally, at 7:30, the eastern suburbs of Berlin.

"Where do we stay?" Halbach said. "The Adlon?"

Berlin's best, and just the sort of place where Halbach might encounter somebody from his past. Dangerous, so de Beauvilliers, or his trusted ally at 2, *bis,* had specified Der Singvogel, the Hotel Bluebird, out in the slum district of Marianfelde. Mercier had never been in Berlin. Halbach had visited a few times, but the Tübingen professor of Old Norse was useless when it came to directions. They stopped, asked for help, got lost, but finally found their way to Ostender Strasse, parked the car, and, baggage in hand, entered the Singvogel.

"My God," Halbach said. "It's a brothel."

It was. To one side of the reception desk, a blond Valkyrie with rouged cheeks, wrapped tight in the streetwalker's version of an evening gown, was flirting with two SS sergeants, splendid in their black uniforms and death's-head insignia. One of them whispered in her ear and she punched him in the shoulder and they both had a merry laugh.

The other SS man took a long look at Mercier and Halbach. Drunk, he swayed back and forth, steadying himself with a meaty hand on the counter. He turned to the woman behind the desk and said, "Such fancy gents, Traudl. Better see what they want."

Traudl was big and flabby, with immense upper arms that trembled when she moved and chopped-off hair dyed jet black. "Staying the night, boys?"

"That's right," Mercier said. "Maybe a few days."

The SS men whooped. "That's the thing!" the drunken one said. "Get your prick good and red!" He caught Halbach staring at him and said, "What's wrong with you?"

"Nothing."

"The girls are in the bar," Traudl said, before this went any further. "When you're in the mood."

"Watch out for the skinny one," the Valkyrie said. "I know that type."

Traudl looked at the keys on the board behind her. "I give you thirty-one and thirty-seven . . ."

"Maybe they want to share," the SS man said, his voice suggestive.

". . . five reichsmark a night, pay now and I'll show you upstairs."

Mercier paid for three nights and Traudl led them to the staircase. She more skated than walked, her carpet slippers sliding over the scuffed linoleum floor.

The rooms were cubicles, partitions ending a foot below the ceiling, with chicken wire nailed over the open space. "Toilet down there," Traudl said. "Enjoy yourselves, don't be shy." She gave Halbach a big wink and pinched his cheek. "We're all friends here."

Mercier had worked in worse places — by candlelight in muddy trenches — but the Singvogel was well up the list. It was the SS men, Mercier suspected, who led the songfest in the bar below, starting with the Horst Wessel song, the classic Nazi anthem, and moving on to the SS favorite, the tender "If Your Mother Is Still Alive. . . ." Only a prelude. As the night wore on, the bordello opera was to lack none of its most memorable moments: the breaking glass, the roaring laughter, the female screams — of mock horror and, once, the real thing, God only knew why — as well as the beloved duet for grunts and bedsprings, and the artful cries of the diva's finale.

Still, they had to work. It helped that Halbach knew where Elter lived, in a tenement in the Kreuzberg district. It was also time, at last, to tell Halbach what he needed from the I.N. 6 office. "But only two contacts, between you and Elter," he said. "Of course we must be especially careful the second time, when documents will be delivered. If you are betrayed, that's when it will happen." Downstairs, the shouts and crashing furniture of a good fight.

"That will bring the police," Halbach said.

"Not here. They'll take care of it."

They listened for the high-low siren, but it never came. "Remember this," Mercier said. "It is Hitler and his clique who want to take the country into war, but there could be nothing worse for Germany. Remind Elter of that. His work on our behalf will provide information that can impede their plans, which would be the highest possible service to the German people. If war comes here, they are the ones who will suffer."

"Yes, the moral argument," Halbach said sourly, not at all convinced.

"You know what to do if it doesn't work."

And, to that end, the following afternoon, Mercier and Halbach left the hotel and drove to the central area of the city, where the former bought a camera, and the latter made a telephone call.

24 April, 6:20 P.M. In darkness, but for the lights twinkling on the station platform, the train clattered down the track. A freight train, eight cars long: two flatcars bearing tanks, an oil tanker, a mail car, its lit windows revealing canvas bags and a brakeman smoking a cigar, and finally a caboose. The train sped past the station — the stationmaster held a green flag — slowed for a curve, then accelerated down a long straightaway, through a field with grazing cows. Smoke rose from the stack of the locomotive, which blew its whistle, two mournful cries in the night. Ah, the railway crossing. The bar came down; a produce truck waited on the road. Then a sharp grade, climbing to a bridge that crossed a stream, a descent, and a long curve, which led to another station. The train slowed and rolled to a perfect stop beneath a water tower.

There followed a moment of appreciative applause, and someone turned on the lights. "Well done," said a man with a beard, squatting down to examine the locomotive at eye level. Others agreed. "Quite perfect." "A good run."

Johannes Elter said nothing. Only stared, wide-eyed, at the apparition in the doorway, which searched the room, then waved to him. The weekly meeting of the Kreuzberg Model Railway Club, in the basement of a local church, was one of the few pleasures in his humdrum existence, but now, even here, his past had returned to haunt him. "A former acquaintance," he explained to the man beside him, a stockbroker with an estate in the Charlottenburg district.

Halbach circled the trestle tables, then offered his hand. "Good evening, Johannes. Your wife said I would find you here."

Elter returned the greeting, a smile frozen on his face.

"Can we speak for a moment?" There was no conspiracy in Halbach's voice, but, in a pleasant way, he meant *privately.*

"We can go upstairs," Elter said.

"Don't be too long," the stockbroker said. "We are electing officers tonight."

"I'll be right back," Elter said. Coming directly from work, he wore the uniform of a *Wehrmacht* corporal.

Halbach, heart pounding, followed Elter up the stairs to the vestibule. The church beyond was empty, the altar bare. It had been Lutheran once but now, in line with the dictates of the Nazi regime, was home to a rather secular denomination known as "German Christian." Elter waited until Halbach climbed the last step, then, his voice low and strained, said, "What are you *doing?* Coming here like this."

"Forgive me," Halbach said. "I had to come."

"Has something changed? Are you now free to go anywhere?"

"No, they are after me still."

"You could ruin me, Julius. Don't you know that?" Elter's face was ashen, his hands trembling.

"It was Otto who sent me to see you," Halbach said.

Elter was stunned. "He's alive?"

"He is," Halbach said. "For the time being."

"Where . . . ?"

"I mustn't say, but what's happened is that he's fallen into the hands of foreign agents."

Silence. Finally Elter said, "Then that's it."

"It need not be. But they will turn him over to the Gestapo and, if they do, he'll be forced to tell what he knows. And that *will* be the end, for me, for you, for all of us who are still alive." Halbach let that sink in, then said, "Unless . . ."

Elter's voice broke as he said, "Unless *what?*"

"It depends on you. On you alone."

"What could *I* do?"

411

"They want information, from the office where you work."

"That's espionage! Who are they?"

"They are Swiss, or so they say. And they offer you two things if you comply: a Swiss passport, in a new name, and five hundred thousand Swiss francs. So you must choose, Johannes, between that and the Gestapo cellars."

Elter put a hand on his heart and said, "I don't feel well." Down below, the lights went out and another train began its run, the locomotive tooting its whistle.

Halbach reached out and rested his hand on Elter's arm. "This was inevitable," he said, not unkindly. "If not today, tomorrow."

"My God, Julius, why do you do this to me? I was always a faithful friend."

"Because of that, I do it."

"But I don't have information. I know nothing."

"Trash. That's what they want. Papers thrown away in the wastebaskets."

"It's burned! Every bit of it, by the janitors."

"When?"

"At nine in the evening, when they come in to clean the offices."

"You must do it before nine."

"But there's too much; how would I carry

412

it out of the building?"

"They want only the material from the section that works on plans for war with France: three days of it. Leave the rest for the janitors."

"I thought you said they were Swiss."

Halbach grew impatient. "Oh who knows what these people are up to, they have their own reasons. But the money is real, I know that personally, and so is the passport. Here, have a look." Halbach reached into his jacket and handed Elter the Braun passport.

Elter looked at it, then gave it back. "I don't want to leave Germany, I have a family."

"That's up to you. Your money will be in an account in Zurich. You'll be given the number and the passport on Friday. You'll have to put in a photograph, but they will tell you how to manage that."

Elter looked suddenly weary. "I don't know what to do."

"Do you want to die, Johannes?"

Elter's voice was barely audible. "No."

Halbach waited. Finally, Elter shook his head, slowly, sickened by what life had done to him. "Friday, you said?"

"At the Hotel Excelsior. In the Birdcage Bar. Come in civilian clothing, put the papers in a briefcase. Seven-thirty in the evening. Can you remember?"

"Seven-thirty. The Birdcage Bar."

Halbach looked at his watch. "Walk me out, Johannes."

They left the vestibule and stood for a moment in the doorway of the church. Across the street, Mercier was sitting behind the wheel of the Renault, clearly visible with the driver's window rolled down.

"Is that one of them?" Elter said.

Halbach nodded. "Old friend," he said, "will you still shake hands with me?"

Elter sighed as he took Halbach's hand. "I never imagined . . ." he said.

"I know. None of us did. It's the wisdom of the gods — to keep the future dark."

In the car, Mercier watched the two men in the doorway. The one in uniform turned, and stared into his eyes with a look of pure hatred. Mercier was holding the camera below the window; now he raised it, looked through the viewfinder, and pressed the button.

Mercier wasted no time. His valise and Halbach's suitcase were already in the trunk of the Renault. Now he wound his way out of Kreuzberg and onto the road that ran north to Neustrelitz. Beside him, Halbach leaned his head back on the seat and closed his eyes.

"Not very far, is it?"

"Three hours, no more than that."

"Will he be at the bar?"

"I trust he will. Do you agree?"

"I'm not sure. He'll think about it, try to find a way out. And then . . . well, you'll see, won't you."

A fine spring night. The road was dark and deserted and Mercier drove fast. It was 11:30 when they reached the city of Rostock and, a few minutes later, the port of Warnemünde. At the dock, the ferry — a ferry from a cartoon; its tall stack would pump out puffs of smoke in time to a calliope — was already taking on passengers, headed across the Baltic to the Danish port of Gedser. Just up the street, at the edge of the dock, a customs shed held the border *kontrol,* where two passengers waited at the door, then entered the shed.

"Shall I walk you through the *kontrol?*" Mercier said.

"No, I'll manage."

"There's one last train for Copenhagen tonight, on the other side. Of course, once you're in Denmark, you may do whatever you like."

"I suppose I can. I'd almost forgotten, that sort of life."

"Will you fly to Zurich?"

"Perhaps tomorrow. The funds will be there?"

"We are true to our word," Mercier said. "It's all in the account."

Halbach looked out the window; the two passengers left the customs shed. "And will this," he said, "all this, make any difference, in the long run?"

"It may. Who knows?"

Halbach climbed out of the car, retrieved his suitcase from the trunk, returned to the passenger side, and looked in at Mercier, who leaned over and rolled the window down. "Likely I won't see you again," Halbach said.

"No, likely not."

Halbach nodded, then walked toward the dock. At the door to the customs shed, an older couple, poorly dressed, entered just as he arrived. Then, a moment later, Halbach followed them. Mercier waited, the Renault engine idling. The ferry creaked as it rose and descended on the harbor swell. Mercier checked the time: 11:39. A sailor walked down the gangway and stood by one of the bollards that held the mooring lines. Now it was 11:42. Somebody in the customs shed reached out and closed the door. Had something gone wrong? They couldn't get this close, just to . . . Five minutes, six, then ten.

Should he go to the shed? To do exactly what? Above the door, the breeze toyed with the red and black flag. 11:51. The sailor at the bollard began to unhitch the mooring rope, and the ferry tooted its cartoon horn, once, and again. A few passengers had gathered at the railing, looking back into Germany. Mercier's hands gripped the wheel so hard they ached, and he let go. Now the couple left the shed, the man supporting the woman with an arm around her waist. When the sailor called out to them the man said something to the woman, and they tried to hurry. Mercier closed his eyes and sagged against the seat. *Not now. Please, not now.* The sailor tossed the mooring line onto the deck and strolled over to the other bollard. Two crewmen appeared at the end of the gangway, ready to haul it aboard.

Then Halbach came out of the shed, tall and awkward, running, holding his hat on his head as he ran. At the end of the gangway, he turned and looked at Mercier, then disappeared into the cabin.

Mercier took a hotel room in Rostock; then, early the following morning, drove back to Berlin and, at the northern edge of the city, parked the car. Carefully, he searched the interior and the trunk, found no evidence left behind, and locked the doors. There it would remain. He took a taxi to the Adlon and settled in to let the days pass. He felt much safer now that Halbach was no longer in the country, and he had to work to keep elation at arm's length. Because Elter might not show up at the Birdcage Bar, because the Gestapo might show up instead — if he'd been caught in the act, or if he'd been so foolish as to go to his superiors. Or, really, was that so foolish? Play the contrite victim, tell all, hope for the best.

No, Mercier told himself. That look of murderous hatred had revealed something of Elter's true self — the brute inside the clerk. Mercier had not been displeased by that look, far from it. It meant secret strength, just what Elter would need to do what he had to. Save Otto Strasser? Save Halbach? A joke. Elter would save Elter. And then, struggling along on a corporal's pay, war on the horizon, *welcome to Switzerland.*

The Adlon was busy, only a luxurious double had been available. A warm room, and very comforting, lush fabrics in subdued colors, soft carpet, soft light. Mercier took off his shoes to stretch out on the fancy coverlet, stared at the ceiling, missed Anna Szarbek. The telephone on the desk tempted him sorely, but that was out of the question.

Still, there was something about these lovely rooms, not just flattering — only success brought you to such places — but seductive. Now he wanted her. She liked nice things, nice places. She would march about in her bare skin, showing off her curves. He rose from the bed, went to the telephone, and ordered dinner brought to the room. Better to stay out of sight. *Friday*.

28 April. Hotel Excelsior. A vast beehive of a hotel, buzzing with guests — the swarm concentrated at the reception counter and spread out across the lobby. Mercier waited his turn at the desk, signed the register, and handed over the Lombard passport — this was not the Singvogel. A bellboy took his valise and they rode the elevator to the eighth floor, as the operator, wearing white gloves, called out the floor for each stop. In the room, he tipped the bellboy and, after he'd left, paused before the mirror: anonymous as he could be, in dark blue overcoat, gray scarf, and steel-gray hat. He left the valise in the room and descended to the lobby.

Across from the reception, the Birdcage Bar. Mercier pushed the padded door open, and yes, there it was, as advertised: a gilded cage suspended from the ceiling, its floor covered with oriental pillows for the comfort of the bird presently in captivity, an indolent maiden, very close to nude but for her feathered costume and tight gold cap. At rest when Mercier entered, she now rose, circled the cage, went to her knees, held the bars, and reached out for a passing guest, who circled the outstretched hand with a nervous laugh and rejoined his wife at their table.

Standing at the bar, Mercier surveyed the tables in the room. Elter? Not yet, it was only 7:20. Surveillance? No way to tell, dozens of people, drinking and talking; it could be any of them. Would this contact have been safer under a railway bridge? Maybe, but too late now. Mercier left the bar, and found a chair in the lobby, a potted palm on one side, a marble column on the other. Elter came through the door at 7:28, wearing hat and overcoat and carrying a large briefcase by its leather handle. He peered about him, found the neon sign above the door to the bar, and headed across the lobby. Mercier watched the entry doors — two dowdy women with suitcases, a young couple, a beefy gent holding a newspaper, who walked toward the elevator. Mercier stood up and hurried over to the bar. Elter was just inside, looking around, not sure what to do next — every table was taken. "Herr Elter," Mercier said, "would you please come with me?"

Mercier led him to the elevator and said, "Eight, please." Above the door, a steel semicircle, where an arrow moved over the floor numbers as the car rose. Four. Five. . . . Eight. Mercier got out, Elter followed, and they walked together down a long empty hall. It was very still inside 803, a common hotel room with a print of an old sailing ship above the bed, and almost dark, but for the ambient light of the city outside the window. Mercier left it that way, he could see well enough. "Please put the briefcase on the bed," he said.

Elter stood at the window. Mercier opened the briefcase. Papers, of various sizes, many of them crumpled and straightened out, sketches, memoranda, a study of some sort, several pages long. From the pocket of his jacket he brought out a manila envelope, its flap unsealed. "You'd best have a look at this," he said to Elter.

"Very well," Elter said, his voice quiet and firm.

Mercier opened the envelope and handed Elter a Swiss passport. "There is an address in here, a photography studio in Prague. They will complete the passport for you. Can you go to Prague?"

"Yes. I don't see why not."

"In this envelope is also an account number and the address of a bank in Zurich. The account holds five hundred thousand Swiss francs, you need only submit the number. Is that clear?"

"It is."

"Did you tell anyone about this?"

"I most certainly did not."

"Your wife?"

"No."

"Best keep it that way, until you leave Germany."

"I have no intention of leaving."

"Well, that's up to you." Mercier snapped the briefcase closed and picked up his valise. "It would be best," Mercier said, "if you remain in this room for fifteen minutes."

Elter was studying the bank information, hand-printed on a square of notepaper. "There is one thing I wanted to ask you," he said.

"Yes?" Mercier had taken a step toward the door, now he turned back.

In the darkened room, the two men in hats and overcoats stood, for a moment, in silence, then Elter said, "Will you seek further information? About the I.N. Six section?"

Mercier's mind raced. "We might."

"I've thought about this night and day, since Halbach approached me. And I came to a certain conclusion. Which is, if I can be of service, and you are willing to pay . . ."

It was the last thing Mercier expected to hear, but he recovered quickly. "We have your address, Herr Elter. And we always pay people who help us."

Elter nodded. "Then I'll expect to hear from you."

"Good night, Herr Elter," Mercier said, turning back toward the door. "And be careful."

"Yes, good night," Elter said.

Mercier left the room and descended to the lobby. He checked out, retrieved his passport, found a taxi at the entry to the hotel, and returned to the Adlon.

The briefcase held seventy-three papers, now laid out on the bed in his hotel room. Some of it useless — *Meet with Klaus, 4:30 Thursday* — some of it valuable. A draft for a report on the fuel consumption of Panzer tanks. A hand-drawn sketch of an area within the Ardennes Forest, with arrows showing potential attack routes. A roneo copy of a forest survey map, made by French military cartographers in 1932, according to the legend in the lower corner. This copy bore handwritten symbols and numbers — meaningless to Mercier — which implied that copies of the map were being used as worksheets. A draft for a memorandum on the ground clearances of various tank models, some of the designations unknown to Mercier. Planned? In production? A significant proportion of the documents had originated with a certain *Hauptmann* — captain — Bauer, including a note from Guderian himself, thanking Bauer for his contribution to a discussion of meteorological patterns on France's northeast frontier.

But what particularly interested Mercier was what *wasn't* there; nothing on the subject of the Maginot Line, nothing to do with the defense system built on France's eastern frontier — no forts, no bunkers, no pillboxes. If Germany were to invade France, the attack would come with tanks, through the Belgian forests. That was the position of the I.N. 6, that was the position of the German General Staff, that's what was laid out in seventy-three papers on a bed in the Hotel Adlon.

Was this enough? For the generals in Paris? Well, there was more to be had; they could go back to Corporal Elter. Surely they would. A gift from the gods — the gods of greed — and entirely unanticipated. Nonetheless, a victory.

But if this was victory, it had taken him

somewhere very close to exhaustion. Weary beyond strength, Mercier managed to rid himself of socks, shirt, and trousers, made sure of the lock on the door, turned off the lamp, and lay down on the other bed. He lit a cigarette and stared at the papers. In the morning, he would hide them below the false bottom of his valise, take a taxi to Tempelhof airport, and fly to Le Bourget. A taxi ride to de Beauvilliers's apartment in the Seventh Arrondissement, a report to be written, and then back to Warsaw. A job well done.

Or so he thought. In Warsaw, a hero's welcome on Sienna street — where Anna went shopping and returned with the best Polish ham, rye bread from the Jewish bakery on Nalewki street, and a bottle of Roederer champagne. Then, later on, a black negligee, purchased for the hero's return, which turned her shape into a pale image obscured by shadow — for as long as it stayed on. At the embassy, the following morning, again the hero. They didn't know what he'd been doing, but they knew it was some sort of operation, and they could see he had returned safe and sound and in a good mood. "It went as you wished?" Jourdain said. Mercier said that it had, and Jourdain said, "Good to have you back."

■ ■ ■ ■

Over the next few days, perfectly content with meetings and paperwork, he waited for word from Paris. It came on a Monday, the eighth of May, a telephone call from General de Beauvilliers. A series of oblique pleasantries, "Overall, we are quite impressed here," not much more than that, one had to be cautious with the telephone. And then, finally, "I'd very much like to have a talk with you, I wonder if you could come over here. I believe there's an early flight in the morning." Merely a suggestion, of course.

Mercier hung up and called Anna at the League office. "I'm flying to Paris tomorrow."

A sigh. "Well, I hate to give you up. Is it for long?"

"A few days, perhaps."

"But I'll see you tonight."

"You will, but that's not why I called. Would you like to come along?"

"To Paris?" She said it casually, but there was delight in her voice. "Maybe I could. I'm supposed to be in Danzig on the tenth, but I can try to move it back."

"Do what you can, Anna. There's a LOT flight at eight-thirty. We can stay on the rue

Saint-Simon, at the apartment. What do you think?"

"Paris? In May? I'll just have to make the best of it, won't I?"

9 May. At five-thirty, he met with de Beauvilliers in an office at the Invalides, in the maze of the General Staff headquarters. Gray and Napoleonic as it was, the trees were in new leaf and birds sang away outside the window. "Surely you are the hero of the moment," de Beauvilliers said. "I have to admit, the day we had lunch at the Heininger, I didn't really believe it was possible, but you did it, my boy, you did it to perfection."

"Some luck was involved. And, without Dr. Lapp —"

"Oh yes, I know, I know. Credit goes here and there, but we've broken into the I.N. Six, and we'll go back for more."

"Will you want me to handle the contact with Elter?"

"We'll see. Anyhow I wanted to congratulate you, and I wanted to talk to you before your meeting with Colonel Bruner; he's waiting for you in his office. First of all, you're going to be promoted to full colonel."

"Thank you, general."

"Bruner will tell you again, so you'll have

to pretend to be surprised, but I wanted to be the one to give you the good news. And that isn't all. You will want to think this over, but I'm requesting, officially, that you come here and work for me. It's a small section, very quiet, but you'll find people like yourself. And what we do is meaningful, sensitive, far beyond the usual staff drudgery. Does it appeal to you, colonel, work in the upper atmosphere?"

"It does. Of course it does."

"Good, we'll talk again, maybe tomorrow, but best go see Bruner and have your meeting."

Mercier walked over to 2, *bis,* avenue de Tourville, then waited for fifteen minutes in Bruner's reception before he was admitted to the inner sanctum. The colonel's freshly shaved face glowed pink, and he sat at attention, puffed up to his grandest *hauteur.* "Ah, Mercier, here you are! A great success, our brightest star. Congratulations are certainly in order — bravo! There will be a promotion in it for you, you can depend on that, *colonel.*"

Mercier was dutifully surprised, and grateful.

"Yes, you've surely given us a view into the I.N. Six," Bruner said. "We've had meeting

428

after meeting, and we're still working on the documents. This information will, believe me, be taken into account as we make our own plans."

"That's what I hoped for, colonel."

"And so you should have. Of course, we do have to consider the possibility that we're being misled."

"Misled?"

"Well, it's almost too good to be true, isn't it. And a recruitment as well. No doubt the future material will support what we already have."

"*No* doubt? Why do you say that, colonel?"

"The Germans are clever people, not in any way above misleading an opponent. It's the oldest game in the world: guide your enemy away from your true intentions. Are you unable to look at it from that perspective?"

"I suppose I can, still . . ."

"Now see here, Mercier, nobody's taking anything away from what you've done. You deserve credit for that, and, as a full colonel, you'll have it. But you must accept that we have to take other possibilities into consideration, and that includes an *Abwehr* operation using rogue Nazis, supposedly rogue Nazis, to send us down the wrong path."

Mercier worked hard to conceal his reaction from Bruner, but he failed. "Halbach was the real thing, Colonel Bruner."

"Yes, so your report suggested, but how can you be sure? Was the Halbach you found the real Halbach? Or an *Abwehr* officer playing the role of Halbach? Well, I can't pretend to know that for a certainty — can you?"

"Not for a certainty. Nothing is ever certain, particularly in this work."

"Ah-ha! Now you're on to the game! I'm not saying this is final, but it's one view, and we would be negligent if we didn't take it seriously. No? Not true?"

"Yes, sir," Mercier said, now eager to be anywhere but Bruner's office. "I understand."

"I'm glad of that. We know you have ability, colonel, you are an excellent officer, that's been proven. Surely wasted on an attaché assignment in that Warsaw rats' nest. General de Beauvilliers has asked for your transfer, and you can pretty much count on our agreement. Does that please you? Colonel?"

Mercier nodded, not trusting himself to speak.

"Well then, I won't keep you. I expect you'd like to go out and celebrate."

Mercier walked home through a rich spring

afternoon, a Parisian spring, that mocked him in every way. Amid chestnut blossoms fallen on the sidewalk, the outdoor tables of a café were at full throb with city life — the lovers, with their hands on each other; conversing businessmen, afloat on a sea of genial commerce; the newspaper readers, solemn, intent on the politics of the day and a favored journalist's acid comments; and the women, lovely in their spring outfits, alone with an aperitif, and perhaps, perhaps, available. A wondrous theatre, Mercier thought, each and every spring, now, next year, forever.

As he walked, his soldier's heart steadied him. Bruner and his cronies, all the way up to Pétain and *his* cronies, had denied him, would not have their version of military doctrine spoiled by what he'd learned — there would be no German tanks, no attack through the forests. The current thinking could not be wrong, because they could not be wrong.

Had they betrayed France? Or just betrayed Mercier? He would, in time, find a way to accept their decision and in the future, working for de Beauvilliers, he would certainly press on, trying to prove that his discovery had been true. That's what an officer did, forever, down through the ages. If an attack failed, you gathered your remaining troops and attacked again. And again, until they killed you or you took their position. He knew no other way. Yes, he was angry, and stung. No, it didn't matter. He could only remain true to himself, there was no other possibility.

And the people on these lovely old streets? The crowd at the café? Would they be forced to live with a lost war? He hoped not, oh how deeply he hoped not, he'd seen the defeated, the occupied, the lost — that could not come here, not to this city, not to this café.

Then he sped up, walking faster now. Now he wanted to be back with people who cared for him, his private nation.

Back on the rue Saint-Simon, as Mercier let himself in the door, he heard a raucous laugh from the parlor. Then Albertine's voice. "Is that you, Jean-François?"

Mercier walked down the hall to the parlor.

"Welcome back, love," Anna said. "We've been having the best time." Clearly they were. On a glass-topped bar cart, a half bottle of gin stood next to a seltzer bottle, alongside a squeezed-out lemon and a sugar bowl.

"We've taught ourselves to make gin fizzes,

right here at home," Albertine said. Both she and Anna were flushed, the latter sitting sideways in an easy chair, her legs draped over the arm.

"The conqueror has returned," Anna said. "Covered in laurels."

Mercier collapsed in the corner of the sofa, took his officer's hat by its stiff brim and sailed it across the room, where it landed on a brocaded loveseat. "They fired me," he said. "The bastards."

"What?" Anna said.

"We'd best make a new batch," Albertine said, rising unsteadily and making her way to the drinks cart.

"I gave them treasure," Mercier said. "They threw it on the dung pile."

"Oh, *those* people," Albertine said. "I'm sorry if they've treated you badly, but you ought not to be so shocked."

"What happened?" Anna said, twisting around in order to sit properly.

"I found a way to acquire important information. They, the officers of the General Staff, have chosen not to believe it."

"Half of them are in the *Action Française*," Albertine said, naming the high-brow French fascist organization. She worked a cut lemon around a glass corer, then poured the juice into a highball glass. "They want

France to be allied with Germany, the only enemy they think about is Russia."

"Who knows what they want," Mercier said. "They tossed me a promotion and they're transferring me back to Paris."

"And that's so bad?" Albertine said.

"My highly placed ally likely went to war, but he didn't win. Now he's rescued me, I'm going to work for him. I guess that's a promotion as well."

"Nothing quite like winning and losing at once," Albertine said, adding sugar to the glass. "You'll feel better in a moment, dear."

"You're leaving Warsaw?" Anna said.

"Yes. I don't suppose you'd care to come along, would you?"

"Am I *de trop?*" Albertine said.

"No, no. Stay where you are," Mercier said. "Could you do that, Anna? Move to Paris?"

"If you want me to. I'd have to resign from the League."

"They hire lawyers in Paris," Albertine said. "Even woman lawyers."

"Well, we don't have to decide all this tonight," Mercier said. "But I'm not going to have us living in two places."

"Ah, good for you," Albertine said. Then, to Anna, "He's the best cousin, dear, is he not? And he might do for a husband."

"Albertine," Mercier said. "We'll talk about it in the morning. For now, where's my gin fizz?"

"Just ready," Albertine said. She brought Mercier his drink and settled down at the other end of the sofa. Then she raised her glass. "Anyhow, *salut,* and *vive la France,*" she said. "It's the good side, and I do mean the three of us, who will win in the end."

They didn't.

Twenty-four months later, with Guderian in command, a massive German tank attack through the Ardennes Forest breached the French defenses, and — on 22 June, 1940 — France capitulated. The former Colonel Charles de Gaulle, by then promoted to general, left France and led the resistance from London. After many adventures, Colonel Mercier de Boutillon and his wife, Anna, also made their way to London, where Mercier went to work for de Gaulle, and Anna for the Sixth Bureau, the intelligence service of the Polish resistance army.

And on 25 June, 1940, Marshal Philippe Pétain accepted the leadership of the Vichy government.

ABOUT THE AUTHOR

Alan Furst is widely recognized as the master of the historical spy novel. Now translated into seventeen languages, he is the author of *Night Soldiers, Dark Star, The Polish Officer, The World at Night, Red Gold, Kingdom of Shadows, Blood of Victory, Dark Voyage,* and *The Foreign Correspondent.* Born in New York, he now lives in Paris and on Long Island. Visit the author's website at www.alanfurst.net.